CABIN ON

PINTO CREEK

By

A J Hawke

Mountain Quest Publishing
ISBN: 978-0-9834505-1-1

Edition: March 2011

Table of Contents

CHAPTER ONE

Elisha Evans gripped his mid section as the pain of hunger ripped through his core. Letting his bay gelding, Jasper, amble along the faint trail, he searched through the forest for signs of small game. Three days without anything to eat except some pine nuts left him trembling with weakness. Where was that ranch? Back down the trail, he had been told of it. The J Bar C ranch belonging to Sam Weathers couldn't be many more miles ahead. At least Jasper had found plenty to eat along the trail as the spring grass showed itself after the melting of the snow.

A sound from the forest caused him to turn where he saw a cow with a young calf through the trees. Quickly he drew his rifle from his scabbard and put it to his shoulder. Sighing he lowered the rifle. The cow wore a brand. Not yet, he wouldn't kill another man's beef. Not yet. Gathering the reins Elisha encouraged Jasper on up the trail, toward the peak of the ridge. Cresting the height, he saw it.

Elisha Evans slumped in his saddle as he looked down the slope at the ranch house ahead. Jasper stopped and stood head down, not even bothering to nibble on the grass. Days of riding had extracted a heavy toll on the horse. Elisha fared even worse.

About to meet folks he needed to impress if he hoped to get a job, Elisha glanced down at his faded overshirt, once blue but now a slate gray with frayed edges along the collar and cuffs. More hope than thread held his clothes together. His boots, scuffed and worn down, showed more wear than his old saddle and saddlebags. He sighed and rubbed his lower back as he sat straight in the saddle.

Taking off his hat, Elisha wiped his face with his bandana. The beauty of this northern part of Colorado Territory was something to behold. Beyond the nearby hills, a distant range of snow-capped mountains stood like sentinels. Compared to where he had come from, he'd have no problem getting used to this.

A slow ten-day ride to the south, Elisha had spent a long, cold winter on a ranch spread out across dry scrubland. With the first signs of spring, Elisha drew his pay—what little there was of it after paying for the bay gelding—and rode out.

He patted Jasper's neck. "Just a way more and you can rest. Sure hope they welcome strangers. Here I am, twenty-five my birthday this month, and I'm looking out over another man's ranch looking for work." Gathering the reins, Elisha sighed and gently kicked the horse in the flanks. "Might as well face it, Jasper, you didn't pick no winner."

Elisha desperately wanted a job on this ranch, as he had nowhere else to go. He picked this place partly because he was broke and partly because of the land's beauty. Right now, hope was all he had.

He nudged Jasper forward, down the trail toward the main ranch buildings. A large log ranch house with a covered porch running the length of the structure's front sat off to the right. Curls of smoke rose from two chimneys. To the left a bunkhouse had several smaller buildings scattered around it. Behind the main house, a log corral held several horses with a big barn that boasted its prominence. Elisha feasted his eyes on a solid and prosperous ranch. He longed to have a spread like this someday, but he had no more to show for the last ten years than when he left the home place at fifteen years old.

His stomach grumbled. He drew a deep breath, savoring the aroma that hung in the air. Roast beef. He hoped they'd offer a meal and bed for the night as was the custom. He rode easy as Jasper ambled into the yard between the bunkhouse and the ranch house.

A lanky man of medium height approached with a big grin. "Howdy. Welcome to the J Bar C. I'm Fred Lewis, the foreman here." The man took off his hat and ran his fingers through hair as red as a fiery sunset. "Of course, most of the boys call me Red."

Elisha dismounted then offered his hand. "Elisha Evans. Any chance I could impose for a meal and rest over the night?"

"Sure. We're always glad to have folks come by. Put your horse in the corral, find a spot in the bunkhouse, and wash up for supper." Red turned toward three ranch hands, slumped down on a bench with their hats shoved back. "Hey, Josh, come show Elisha where to put his stuff."

A lean, sandy-haired cowhand got up from the bench and ambled over. "In case you couldn't figure it out, I'm the youngest rider here. Of course, I do more work than the rest of these drovers." A wide grin spread across his boyish face. "Come with me." He led him to the corral where he watched Elisha unsaddle the horse.

Elisha turned his horse loose in the corral. A pipe coming down the slope behind the corral fed into the watering trough. Elisha nodded. Yes, he was definitely going to have a spread like this someday and he'd do anything he could to get one. He wasn't about to spend the rest of his life as a busted-up cowhand.

He picked up his saddlebags and pack. "So, you get to greet and help the visitors."

"Here, I got your saddle." Josh tossed it onto his shoulder as if it were a five-pound sack of Arbuckle coffee.

"Thanks, partner." He'd been on the trail since daylight. The pain in Elisha's back was near intolerable and his knee felt near to giving way on him. But knowing the other cowhands watched, he tried to walk alongside Josh without limping. After dropping his things next to an empty bunk, Josh showed him where to clean up for supper.

Elisha washed the dust from his face and neck. He tried to comb his hair with his fingers, but it refused to lie flat and his dark curls still hung across his forehead, strayed over his ears and down his neck.

Josh sat on a nearby bench. "Mr. Weathers might be hiring more riders for the summer, if you're interested."

Elisha was definitely interested. "Who does the hiring, Mr. Weathers or Red?"

"Oh, Mr. Weathers does all his own hiring. He's a real hands-on boss with everything but branding. He leaves that to us." Josh's grin spread across an open face.

Elisha followed Josh through a side door at the west end of the house, then into a large kitchen with a long table set for supper.

Red, already in the kitchen, pulled Elisha aside as the cowhands pushed past and sat at the table with much scraping of chairs on the wood floor. "Let me introduce Sam Weathers, the owner." They stepped toward the ranch owner. "Sam, this here's Elisha Evans, the cowhand I told you about. He's stopping for the night with us."

Sam Weathers, a large, solid man who looked to be in his early fifties had a full head of gray hair. He extended his calloused hand to Elisha. His sun-worn face, lined from years of riding, told of the life he'd led. Elisha liked his look.

"Welcome to the J Bar C. Glad you could stop by." His bass voice dominated the room. "Go shove one of those fellows over and sit for supper."

"Thanks, Mr. Weathers, don't mind if I do. Appreciate your hospitality."

"Well, you know how it is. With places so far apart and news hard to get, anyone riding by is more than welcome."

Elisha gave a nod, then turned toward the table where Josh had saved a spot for him.

The aromas of roast beef, biscuits, coffee, and something cinnamon mingled together, and Elisha couldn't wait to dig in, he was that starved.

Mr. Weathers took his seat at the head of the table, everyone bowed their heads, and Elisha followed suit.

"Lord, we thank you for the bounty we have before us," Mr. Weathers prayed, "We thank you for the work we have to do and that none are sick or hurt. We thank you for bringing us a visitor to liven up the day. Forgive us when we do wrong and help us do right. We pray in the name of Jesus Christ. Amen."

Mr. Weathers reached for the bowl of mashed potatoes. "Let's eat up, boys."

At once, dishes clattered as the hungry men piled their plates, then passed the bowls and platters of potatoes, gravy, corn, and beans around the table. Elisha figured these men worked long, hard days like most cowhands, so when it came to eating, they didn't spread it out with a lot of talk.

This suited Elisha, as he ate his first real meal in months. He didn't want to seem too greedy, so he paced himself with Josh. When the young rider took his fifth biscuit, Elisha stopped eating. He couldn't keep up with the young man.

Elisha glanced at the head of the table. Maybe they could use another hand. Mr. Weathers had to know he was riding the grub line and needed a job bad.

After the meal, Mr. Weathers pushed back from the table. "Elisha, follow me and let's talk a bit."

"Yes sir." As he entered the front room, Elisha quickly scanned it. Clearly a man's room, filled with heavy homemade furniture, braided rugs, and bare windows. A large desk stood close to the huge fireplace at the far end of the room. Two overstuffed chairs faced the fireplace. Most impressive were the shelves filled with books on the walls behind the desk. One day he would have a home like this.

Mr. Weathers waved toward one of the chairs in front of the desk then took his own behind it.

"Tell me something about yourself, Elisha. You have the look of a seasoned hand." His friendly tone belied his rugged look.

Elisha decided to be blunt honest and hope it worked for him. "I grew up on an east Texas farm. At fifteen, I rode west and joined up with Tom Haden on his ranch. When he took a herd up the trail from Fort Richardson to Abilene, Kansas, I went with him. I got me a little nest egg together and started my own place out in the Buffalo Gap area, but drought and prairie fire did me in and I lost everything." He leaned forward in his chair, his elbows resting on his knees.

Mr. Weathers listened without comment, his gaze intent on Elisha.

"I worked on different ranches in Texas, and Colorado." Elisha shifted in the chair to ease his back. "Then last summer, I got busted up pretty bad when my horse fell on me. I managed to find a place through the winter, but it wasn't much. I'd heard about this country up here—these mountains—and wanted to see it, so I started out about ten days ago. I hoped to get on with y'all, at least for the summer."

Elisha sat back in his chair and wiped the sweat off his forehead with his sleeve. Must be the heat from the fireplace was too hot, or if he was honest with himself, fear that he wouldn't get a job—maybe both.

Mr. Weathers nodded as if he'd heard the story before. Rubbing the back of his neck, Mr. Weathers studied Elisha's face. "What kind of shape are you in after your fall last year?"

Elisha stared down at his rough, work-hardened hands. How should he answer? In truth, he wasn't sure what he could do. He looked up at the man across the desk from him. "I'll be honest with you, Mr. Weathers, I got banged up pretty bad—broken ribs, a broke leg, and a knot on my head. That all seems to be healed pretty good, although my leg is still not as strong as it was. It's coming back, but it's slow." Elisha took a deep breath. "The worst part is my back. I'm hopeful it'll straighten itself out, and to be upfront with you, I can't do a full day of roping and branding yet." Elisha quietly waited. He'd said his bit, and spoken frankly. He couldn't do more.

"I appreciate your honesty. Some boys would've come in here and tried to bluff their way by promising what they couldn't deliver, and that would've made me mad."

Elisha nodded. He'd made the right decision by speaking the truth.

Mr. Weathers shifted in his chair. "How do you feel about working off by yourself for weeks on end? Have you worked much as a line rider?"

"Some of my best jobs have been when I got out on the range by myself. I like to get on a horse and ride all day with nothing but sky in front of me. I also like to get hold of a book and read. Don't get me wrong. I like people good enough, but I can get tired of them too."

Mr. Weathers's big, booming laugh filled the room. "I know what you mean, son. Some people just got too many words in them." He sat in silence for a moment. "I may have a job for you, but it's not the best. It's up north in the hills—mountains really—a full day's ride. There's a cabin up there, and a good spring. The job would be to ride the line and keep my cattle moved back toward the ranch." He stopped and rubbed his chin, as if thinking before he continued.

"I wouldn't want you coming back down to the ranch but once a month to get supplies. I'll pay you twenty dollars a month and all your grub."

The job was exactly what he needed, a place where he could pace himself. "I'd be right proud to work for you." Elisha sat up straight in his chair. He worked to conceal his excitement so as not to look like a greenhorn. "I can't promise you an honest day's work yet. I don't want to take the job without you knowing that." Elisha hated to say it, but now it was out on the table.

"I understand, but if you can take the solitude, and keep my cows from wandering into the next territory, that would be enough. So, do we have a deal?"

"We do." Elisha stood and shook hands with Mr. Weathers.

"Let's talk about that area and what you'll need to take up there from the ranch stores."

Elisha sat back into the comfortable chair. A flare of pain shot through his lower back. After a long day of riding, sitting usually caused his back to stiffen, but he didn't want to ruin it now that he had the job. Elisha bit his tongue. Maybe he could hide the pain.

Mr. Weathers seemed unaware of Elisha's struggle. "I don't know what's still up at the cabin. It's been empty for about four months now. We'll send you up with plenty of supplies." Mr. Weathers leaned back in his chair and scratched his head. "Josh can help load the wagon tomorrow. Then, the next day you can go on up there. I'll draw you a map before you leave. In the last week, I've had the hands cleaning tree limbs and boulders out of the wagon trail. Any questions?"

First, the hearty meal and a warm place to bunk for the night, now a job with a place to live for the next few months. Elisha could barely take it all in. He let his shoulders relax a little from the relief of it. "Not at the moment. By tomorrow I may have several." All he wanted was to find his bunk and lay down.

"Well, then I'll let you get on to the bunkhouse." Mr. Weathers got up and walked Elisha to the front door. "Glad to have you with the J Bar C, Elisha. I'll see you in the morning."

"Good night, and thanks again for the job." Elisha swallowed. "I won't let you down."

~ ~ ~

Elisha woke in the dark. Where was he? He lay still until he remembered. The J Bar C Ranch. The grayness outside the window told him it was almost dawn. He dressed and pulled on his boots. He stifled a laugh of relief. He had a job.

He stepped out of the bunkhouse in the still beginnings of the day. The cold air hit his face and helped him wake up. The soft cooing of doves in the trees at the back of the ranch house reminded him of his childhood home and the early morning sounds of long ago. His favorite time of day always came before anyone else stirred from sleep.

He found a bucket of hot water waiting beside the basin on the shelf at the back of the bunkhouse, a sign that someone was thinking about the hands. He wondered who would be up and about so early. Elisha poured some of the water into the basin, washed, and shaved. He had thrown the water out of the basin onto the grass when an older cowhand rounded the corner of the bunkhouse.

"Morning, I'm Abe, short for Abraham Jones." Standing shorter than Elisha, Abe had a thick neck and broad shoulders. His receding hairline gave his face a look of intelligence. Not a handsome face, but friendly. He was dressed in worsted brown pants and a cotton gray shirt, with sturdy boots and a Stetson hat with a wide brim. Although nothing fancy, Abe's clothes were much better than anything Elisha wore.

He stepped back to let Abe have room at the basin, and tipped his hat. "Elisha Evans."

"Heard the boss had taken you on. It's a good spread. Hope you like it." Abe poured fresh water into the basin. "Nate and Smithy always makes sure we have hot water to wash up with." He began scrubbing his face.

Elisha went back into the bunkhouse to put away his shaving gear. Despite the pain in his back, he felt better this morning. When he stepped out of the bunkhouse, he shivered. Good thing he'd donned his jacket, his only protection against the crisp air.

In the corral, his bay, Jasper munched on hay. Elisha found a pitchfork in the barn and in a few minutes had shoveled the muck out of the corral. He didn't want to do too much the first day, and decided he would leave the barn to someone without an injured back.

Boot heels struck the ground behind him. He turned to see Abe approaching.

"On mornings like this we head on in to the kitchen and get coffee." Abe rubbed his hands together against the morning chill.

Elisha followed Abe into the warm kitchen where two older men set bowls and platters of food on the table. The smell of fresh brewed coffee was like a perfume.

"This is Elisha, the new hand." Abe waved toward the two older men. "You met Nate and Smithy last night." Picking up a blue enamel cup, he threw it to Elisha. "Fill it up."

Elisha caught the cup in one hand and reached for the big pot of hot coffee at the end of the table. The coffee smelled strong enough to help him last the day.

"Go ahead and sit, Elisha," Nate said. "Dig in." He stepped outside then rang the iron triangle next to the door.

Nate and Smithy looked similar enough to be brothers. Nate was taller and leaner. Both men looked to be in their sixties and had gray hair. Their friendly faces wrinkled and weathered, spoke of days spent on the range. They were dressed the same way as the riders but each had on a long, white bib-apron made of heavy cotton. Elisha guessed that they hadn't started out as cooks but with age, they had settled down on the J Bar C in a job they could physically handle. Over the years, he'd seen a lot of cowhands end up that way. He didn't plan to be one of them.

As he and Abe loaded up their plates with fried ham, gravy, fried potatoes, biscuits, butter, jam, and syrup, Mr. Weathers and the others came in and did the same. Elisha had a big bite of biscuit stuffed into his month.

Mr. Weathers tapped the side of his cup with his knife. "Morning boys, let's pray."

The others were prepared for the prayer.

Elisha swallowed the biscuit, but kept the other half ready for when the prayer was over.

"Lord, we thank you for the night's rest, and we thank you for the new day of work. Thank you for the bounty of this table and bless the hands that prepared it. Keep all who work here safe today. We offer this prayer in the name of Jesus, the Christ. Amen."

Elisha had never had a boss who prayed so much around the ranch hands, but it somehow reassured him that this was a good place to work. Not ever having prayed much himself, he didn't mind hearing it from his new boss. He finished his breakfast and was about to get up when Mr. Weathers tapped on his cup again.

"All right, boys. First, welcome Elisha Evans, our new hand," Mr. Weathers nodded at Elisha.

He felt his cheeks go hot as he responded to the nods and grins from the men.

"Josh, get what gear Elisha needs to stay up at the cabin north of Pinto Creek. Tomorrow you ride up there with him. Spend a couple days there and help him get settled."

Mr. Weathers handed Elisha a list of supplies. He paused for another sip of coffee. "Now, here's what I want the rest of you to do today."

Elisha didn't listen, but rather looked over the list that Mr. Weathers had written out for him. The only things he didn't see were a couple of lanterns, some extra oil, a hammer, and nails.

By the time Elisha and Josh had packed most of the supplies into a small wagon, the sun shone directly above them. Fighting the rising pain in his back, Elisha was glad for the noon break. He beat his hat against his leg as he walked toward the ranch house. Why couldn't he work a full day without hurting? Maybe by the end of the summer he would be in better shape.

Only Abe, Josh, Mr. Weathers, Red, and Elisha showed up for dinner, since most of the hands were out for the day rounding up the herd.

This time Elisha waited for the prayer. Then he spooned a liberal amount of mashed potatoes onto his plate and then passed the bowl on to Josh. He took a good-sized steak from the platter Red passed to him. While waiting for the bowl of gravy to make its way around the table, he took two biscuits and broke them open ready to drown in the gravy. By the time all the bowls and platters had made it round the table, Elisha contentedly attacked the full plate of food.

Josh told Red and Mr. Weathers what they had loaded.

"What about some warmer clothes for Elisha?" Mr. Weathers sat down his fork.

Josh scratched his head. "I didn't think of that."

"And be sure you get him some boots if we have his size. That work up there can wear them out." Mr. Weathers poured another cup of coffee.

Would the work really be that rough? Or had Mr. Weathers taken notice of the poor state of Elisha's own boots? He couldn't decide whether he should be embarrassed or appreciative.

As they left the kitchen, Red said, "Let's take a look at what you have packed, and make sure you haven't overlooked anything."

Josh led the way to the wagon.

"We need to add a couple of rifles and a hundred rounds of ammunition, just in case," Red said.

What did Red think he would be using all that ammunition on? Was there something they weren't telling him?

"Mr. Weathers wants to know when you'll return for supplies. That way, if you don't come back by that date, we'll know to go looking for you,"

Elisha grinned. "I don't rightly know what day of the month this is, so unless you give me some sort of calendar, we may have a problem."

"Know what you mean," Red laughed. "When you're working cattle, days seem to run into each other. I'll ask Mr. Weathers if he has an extra calendar."

Josh led the way to the barn and opened up a smaller storeroom. He pulled clothes off the shelves including a pair of new boots. He handed the boots and a pair of heavy wool socks to Elisha. "Try these on for size."

Elisha pulled his old pair off and exposed his holey socks. The boots were a perfect fit. He grinned like a kid with a Christmas gift. "Thanks."

After supper, Mr. Weathers asked Red and Elisha to meet him in the front room. He spread a piece of tanned hide out on his desk. "This is a map of the ranch, but it's from our memories, and neither Red, nor I've been up there often. You can add to it as you get other landmarks. I want you to consider the ridge to the north as the boundary of my ranch, but I'd like the cattle pushed at least five miles south of the ridge."

"Also, keep an eye out for wolves, bobcats, and bears." Red leaned over the map. "It should be easy after you get the cattle back across the creek, but what with the winter drift, there may be a bunch of cattle up under the ridge."

Mr. Weathers tapped the map. "Keep any cows you find drifting south."

"Ask Josh about the country up there," Red said. "He knows it as well as anyone."

"We'll see you and Josh off in the morning."

Elisha headed back to the bunkhouse with the map and a hand-written calendar. The only light in the bunkhouse was the glow from the fire in the stove. After he was in his bunk, he thought about the day. He shifted on the bunk, trying to ease his aching back. Determined to do a good job, he just hoped he was up to the work.

CHAPTER TWO

In the early morning light, Elisha tied his horse to the tailgate of the wagon and climbed onto the seat. Josh mounted and had two horses on lead ropes.

Mr. Weathers came out of the house with a gunnysack. "Nate and Smithy thought you boys might like to take some cooked food along." He handed the sack up to Elisha and then stepped back. "Take your time going up there, but if you can, try to get there by dark. I'll expect you back here in thirty days to pick up supplies." Mr. Weathers slapped the rump of the horse nearest to him.

The sun had barely peeked over the horizon when Elisha flicked the reins, and they moved onto the wagon trail heading north out of the ranch yard. He looked up the trail, almost lightheaded with the hope of better days to come. He sat straighter on the wagon seat, sure he could do the job.

A slight breeze blew in his face as he drove the wagon and took in the signs of spring. Pure enjoyment! He had a job deep in the hills toward the high mountains. He'd have a roof over his head and plenty of food. What more could he ask? Elisha hadn't felt it in such a long time, but this morning there was no mistaking—his weary bones fairly sighed with contentment.

As they left the low foothills north of the ranch, the trail led through a forest that grew denser as they made their way through. They climbed steadily up the trail and over the hills that gradually rose into the higher mountains.

When they came to a creek, they stopped to rest. Elisha, stiff and sore, climbed down from the wagon. He pulled out the gunnysack Mr. Weathers had given him, walked over to some trees with a deep bed of moss under them, and dropped to the ground. Hot pain seared through his lower back. He clenched his jaw to brace for the spasm to pass. They still had a ways to go. He had to make it.

"There's some good looking sandwiches here, plus doughnuts and pie, and I don't know what all," he said, trying to divert his attention off his aching back.

Josh plopped down on the ground. "My breakfast has gone and left me. I've been thinking about eating for an hour now." He took a sandwich of fresh, homemade bread with a thick slab of roast beef and bit into it with gusto.

Elisha hoped they could make it before dark. "How far do you think we've come?"

Josh stopped chewing. "This creek was always what I considered halfway. Bear in mind, the next half is steep and twisty. We won't make as good a time."

Fallen branches and rocks on the trail had slowed them down a couple of times already. Elisha swallowed the last of his sandwich. "I hope the trail is clear."

Josh shot a glance at Elisha, then looked away, clearing his throat.

"You got something to say?" Elisha stretched out his legs on the fresh spring grass and crossed his arms.

"Well, yeah. It probably ain't none of my business, but just how bad is your back?" Josh glanced sideways at Elisha and then looked out over the creek. "Mr. Weathers told me to help you out if need be. You seemed to be doing all right, but when you climbed down from the wagon just now, I could tell you got a problem."

"I thought I hid it."

"Oh, I just happened to notice," Josh spoke too quick, as if not wanting to offend.

"I'll tell you. Right now, it hurts something fierce. If I get rest tonight, it'll feel better. When I do anything extra, like chopping and moving that tree back there on the trail, my muscles catch. Feels like a big fist got hold of me right in the middle of my lower back, and I can't move or breathe. After a while, it sort of releases. It'll keep doing that off and on, and I can't do anything until it lets up. It's been like this since last summer when my horse fell on me." Elisha rubbed his hand over his face.

He got to his feet with only a slight lurch against the tree. "The first thing is get these horses moving and head on up the trail." Picking up the half-filled gunnysack, he walked to the wagon as Josh gathered up the horses. Elisha waited until Josh's back was turned, then pulled himself up on the wagon seat. It was all he could do to keep from groaning as the strain brought on one of the spasms. Catching his breath, he flicked the reins and got the horses moving. The sooner they made it to the cabin, the sooner he could lie down.

The rest of the way to the cabin, Elisha struggled through an agony of pain so severe that he couldn't think, see, or even drive the horses. He gave them their head and let them follow the trail.

A small sliver of sun peeked from behind the hills to the west when they topped a rise, then the whole mountain range opened up before them. Snow-capped peaks turned pink by the setting sun, rose majestically in the distance. Elisha caught his breath as he lost himself in the beauty. For a moment, the pain receded.

The valley lay before them with the cabin nestled up next to a ridge in the distance. Beside the cabin was a small corral with a shed. Off to the east side of the cabin, Elisha could make out a creek running through the trees. It was a beautiful sight made more so by Elisha's desire for the day to be over.

"If we get a move on, we can make it by dark," Josh shouted.

Elisha waved his hand weakly in agreement and flicked the reins to get the horses going.

As if understanding their day's work was almost over, the horses increased their effort with only a little encouragement. They soon pulled up in front of the cabin.

"Let me corral these horses, and then we can look over the cabin." Josh led the three horses into the corral.

Head hanging and pain exploding through his back, Elisha made no move.

Josh ran to the wagon. "Why didn't you tell me? We could've stopped."

Elisha managed a small grin. "Because, when I get down from this wagon seat, I'm not getting back up on it—ever. I may need your help to get down though."

With Josh's assistance, Elisha descended from the wagon. "Let me stand here a minute." Elisha hung onto the side of the wagon. The pain across his lower back reached a new excruciating height. He breathed in and out slowly to relax his muscles. After a moment, he steadied himself and put his whole weight on his feet. Taking a couple of steps, he leaned against the cabin wall. "If you can get the door open, we'll see what this cabin looks like on the inside."

Josh lit a lantern, then ventured into the cabin. The light cast a soft glow in the room. "If you can stand for a few more minutes, I'll bring in bedding and make up a bunk."

"Thanks, that would help."

Josh brought in Elisha's bedroll, and spread it on a bunk. "Go ahead and lie down. I'll get a fire going and unload the food. We'll leave the rest till morning."

Another crescendo of pain crested and left him at the edge of his endurance. Elisha eased down on the bunk and allowed Josh to pull off his boots.

As Josh tugged the blankets over him, Elisha said, "Hate to leave you to do all the work. I'll make it up to you some day."

"You'd do the same for me. Besides, by morning you'll be fine."

Elisha could only hope so. The frown of doubt he saw on Josh's face added to his own.

~ ~ ~

Morning brought an awaking in a strange bunk in a strange room. Elisha eased himself up on his elbow, then looked around. *The cabin on Pinto Creek.* He sat on the edge of the bunk and pulled on his boots. His back ached, but the terrible spasms had subsided. Elisha rubbed his arms in the chilly air and reached for his hat and coat. The fire was almost out. He added logs and watched to make sure they caught.

Josh snored softly in the other bunk.

Glancing around, Elisha took his first real look at the cabin. With a little cleaning, the place could be a nice place to call home. A fireplace dominated the east wall. On the opposite wall, two narrow bunks stood end to end. The north wall held a small two-burner stove. The front door opened from the south wall. In the center cabin, two chairs sat at a small table. A battered tin basin set on a rickety washstand to the left inside the door. He liked the split log floor. Each wall had a small window with real glass in window frames that opened inward on hinges. The windows were large enough to let in air and light, but not large enough for someone to climb through. Located high on the walls, Elisha had to stand to see out them.

Cooking utensils, dishes, and tools lay scattered on the floor. A few old clothes hung on nails by the bunks. Dust covered everything, but it wasn't as bad as Elisha had feared. He glanced around but saw no evidence animals had been inside. The only occupants appeared to be a couple of spiders.

The rafters were high enough Elisha could stand upright without worrying about bumping his head. Examining the rafters, he could see how to build a loft for storage.

Elisha grabbed a bucket and stepped outside. He breathed deeply of the fresh early morning air. Doves cooed softly in the branches of overhead trees. Smiling at the sound, he walked down to the creek and filled the bucket with water. When he returned to the cabin, he pulled open the iron door at the front of the little two-lid stove and built a fire with kindling and moss from a wooden box nearly. The stove had a door in the front end for wood or removing the ashes. Near the back was a small oven. The stove could use a good cleaning, but otherwise seemed serviceable. After getting the coffee started, Elisha laid bacon in the skillet to fry.

He heard a half groan and yawn, and looked over to see Josh stretching.

Elisha poured coffee into the cups. "Rise and shine, breakfast is ready."

"Morning," Josh mumbled as he yawned some more. "How's your back?"

"Better. And I plan to stay off that wagon seat."

Josh climbed out of bed, pulled on his pants and boots, then sat at the table. "Smells good, and we got hot coffee. Not bad." He took a biscuit and soaked it in the bacon grease.

Licking his fingers after he'd finished his meal, Josh asked, "Where do we start?"

Elisha poured himself a second cup of the strong coffee. "I think we best get the horses staked on some grass, so they can graze. Then we get the cabin cleaned up and supplies unpacked."

Josh nodded. "I could do the horses by myself, but the both of us can do it in nothing flat." He wiped his plate clean with the last of his biscuit.

The day went quickly as they worked. Elisha nailed split log shelves on each side of the stove. They put the foodstuff and cooking utensils on them. Elisha liked things orderly. With Josh there to help, he also nailed planks across half the rafters above the room to make a loft for extra storage.

As they unpacked the boxes, Elisha found one full of books that Mr. Weathers evidently put on the wagon. He immediately put up a shelf about three feet above the bunk nearest to the stove. With the books placed on the shelf, he could see himself lying on the bunk in the evening easily reaching for a book. He hadn't had one to read for over a year. Reading was something he enjoyed, but it wasn't often that a boss encouraged him.

Josh stuffed clean straw into the two ticking covers and made up the beds.

Elisha liked the look of straw mattresses compared to the hardwood bunk.

~ ~ ~

By the end of the second day they had the cabin in good shape, the gear put away, and they had dragged several fallen trees close to the cabin ready to chop for firewood.

The next morning Elisha saw Josh off on the trail south back to the ranch house. Then he saddled Jasper and headed northwest into the breaks in the hills to get the lay of the countryside. Soon he found small herds of cattle that had drifted into the ravines and box canyons for protection throughout the winter. Along the way, he saw tracks of cattle, elk, deer, coyotes, and even bear. Elisha could see why Mr. Weathers wanted his cattle drifted back toward the ranch headquarters. Up in these hills they could get lost or fall prey to wild animals.

Elisha established a daily pattern of hard work. He hazed cattle back south of the creek, returned to the cabin with relief and ate, banked the fire, and crawled into his bunk, too tired even to think about reading.

After a couple of weeks, he found his exhaustion lessening and his back spasms diminishing in strength and occurrence. The hard work made him stronger.

After supper one evening, he had enough energy left over to break into a book. He pulled the table with the lantern on it over by his bunk. His eyes searched the book titles before he plucked one from the shelf. The History of the American Revolution. By David Ramsay, M.D., of South Carolina. He lay on his bunk and read until his eyes grew heavy. With a sigh of contentment, he returned the book to the shelf and turned off the lantern.

~ ~ ~

The third week, Elisha discovered a spring north of the cabin running into the stream he'd named Dove Creek because of the early morning cooing of doves. He looked out over the lay of the land. How could he change the channel of the run-off from the spring, and bring the water down to the corral and cabin? Back at headquarters, he'd seen some pipe behind the barn. Next time he returned to the ranch he'd add that to his list.

With the books to keep him company in the evenings, and the mountains and animals during the day, Elisha rarely felt lonely. Still, he looked forward to the trip down the mountain to the ranch, marking off each day on his calendar for a month until the day finally arrived. This time, he'd ride his horse, and trail the wagon and team behind him, to save his back. Shortly after dawn, he rode down the trail tall in the saddle, knowing he'd done a man's work over the last month.

~ ~ ~

Elisha rode into the ranch headquarters in the warmth of a late afternoon, exactly thirty days after he'd taken up his work on Pinto Creek. He looked forward to getting together with the men on the ranch. Maybe the solitude of his work affected him more than he wanted to admit.

Mr. Weathers met him in the yard. "Welcome, you're right on time, although I wouldn't have worried if you hadn't arrived for a couple of days yet."

Elisha grinned as they shook hands. "You said thirty days and that's today." The warm greeting felt good. "Besides, I was hungry for Nate's cooking."

"Well, let's get washed up and eat. We'll talk after supper."

Abe stepped up and took the reins. "Let me take care of the horses for you."

"Thanks, Abe." Hearing footsteps behind him, he turned.

Josh ambled up. "Hey, Elisha, how've you been?"

"Well, I pushed a lot of cattle south and rode a lot of miles."

"I worried about you. Mr. Weathers needed me here working on the branding, or I would've come back up to check on you. I still can't imagine working up there all alone."

"Well, I don't mind my own company. Besides, I have those books to read."

The dinner bell sounded and they headed into the kitchen. Elisha waited for Mr. Weathers to say the blessing and then eat the best meal he'd had in a month.

Nate had cooked a roast in a brown sauce that made perfect gravy to go with the potatoes, black-eyed peas, corn, and biscuits. When Nate and Smithy brought out four dried apple pies, the aroma of the apples and cinnamon set his mouth to watering, even after a full meal.

After supper, Elisha went into the front room with Mr. Weathers and sat facing the big desk to give his report. Mr. Weathers showed interest in the areas Elisha had marked on the map, indicating the places he'd worked. Elisha also showed him the tally he kept of the number of cattle he had started back south of Pinto Creek.

"Elisha, you've done a good job this month. I knew I had cows drifting north of Pinto Creek, but not that many."

Elisha pointed to the map. "I laid out a plan of combing the area to the west. Next, I'll move further north and west and get most of the cows headed south. Then I'll work toward the east. I'm not sure how far you want me to go out from the cabin." Elisha waited as Mr. Weathers examined the map.

"Well, twenty miles in all directions from the cabin would be about four hundred square miles. That should be enough of the ranch for you to look after by yourself." Mr. Weathers paused a moment as if considering. "Although I'm not sure you need to go that far northwest since the hills get steep, and I doubt if many of the cattle will drift that far. Going east over to the bluffs is about twenty miles. Have you seen any sign of Indians?"

Elisha shook his head. "Don't think that I haven't kept an eye out."

"You remember what I said about not trying to be a hero. If any Indians show up and want a cow or two, give it to them. Be careful about giving them anything else like sugar, or they'll be back for more. Never ride out without your rifle and revolver." Mr. Weathers leaned forward. "Now, Elisha, tell me about you. You're still as thin as a fence post, but you actually look healthier than when you first headed up to the cabin."

Elisha scratched the back of his neck. What did he want to say? Hard as he'd worked, it still had been one of the most peaceful times he'd experienced in a long time. "It's been a hard month in some ways, I'll grant you that." Elisha combed his fingers through his hair, now curling over his ears from lack of a haircut. "My back is better, but there have been days that I had to lay up and not ride out." He paused a moment and rested his hands on his clean, well-worn trousers. "I've done pretty good as far as getting the work done. Up to you to decide if I've pulled my weight enough to keep paying me." He felt a sudden tightness in his chest. He hoped Mr. Weathers was satisfied with his work.

Mr. Weathers face broke into a smile. "You've done more in the last month up there than most of the other riders did in a whole summer. I hope you'll want to go back and keep at it."

Elisha exhaled a breath he hadn't even realized he was holding. "I've no problem with that. I'm content with the work."

Mr. Weathers leaned back in his chair. "What about being alone?"

"I haven't worried much about being alone." Elisha gave a small grin. "There's been too much to do, and besides, you sent that box of books. As long as I have a book to read in the evenings, I don't miss people." He lowered his voice. "Not having a family, I've been on my own since I was a youngster. A person can be alone in a bunkhouse full of cowhands. Up at the cabin, knowing I'm coming back once a month, I don't feel it more than any other time."

Mr. Weathers nodded. "I know what you mean. I'm glad you enjoy the books." He waved his hand toward the wall of books. "Feel free to take any of these back with you."

"Thanks, I appreciate that." Elisha was still amazed at a having a boss who encouraged him to read. In a way, sharing books gave him a kinship with the man.

They talked a few more minutes about what Elisha wanted to take back up to the cabin.

"What about this pipe on the list?" Mr. Weathers asked.

Elisha explained his plan to get water to the corral and cabin from the spring to the north.

"Intriguing idea. If you can do it, go ahead. Make any improvements you want up there. By the way, here's a thermometer to take back with you." Mr. Weathers handed him a box wrapped in canvas. "Be careful because it'll break easily." He stood, then walked to the door with Elisha. "Get a good night's sleep. I'll see you in the morning."

Thinking over his talk with his boss, Elisha walked tall as he crossed the yard. From what Mr. Weathers said, Elisha sensed he had confidence in Elisha's ability to get the job done. Maybe this job would last through winter. He could only do his best and see what happened.

The first week after returning from the ranch headquarters, he dug a ditch deep enough to put the pipe below the freeze line and let the water flow into the trough at the corral. He jointed another pipe so the water could flow to the cabin. Then he dug a hole in the middle of a log and piped the water into it. He also made an overflow hole to let the water run beyond the cabin and on down to Dove Creek. The pure, sweet spring water was now close to the cabin for both himself, and the horses. Elisha nodded with satisfaction. No more carrying water up from the creek.

Over the next month, he combed the hills and breaks north of the cabin. Twice he went up and back of the ridge, staying out a couple of nights after going beyond the range he considered the boundary of the J Bar C. He crossed through a region of hills that gradually blended up toward the high peaks. There he found several upper valleys that would hold good-sized herds with plenty of water and grass.

As he sat on his horse looking out over one of the upper valleys, he envisioned this becoming his own place. The area was open range. He wanted to file on the springs, part of the source of the large creek that ran the length of the larger valley. He carefully mapped out the area on a piece of tanned hide.

Thinking about having his own place took him back to the little ranch he had started near Buffalo Gap down in Texas. He had worked so hard with so little. But that was when he had a girl he thought he would marry. But she met a traveling salesman and left town without even a note the week before the wedding. A lightning storm set the prairie on fire and burned his place to the ground. Nothing remained of his dreams, but a few head of cattle. He sold them at a loss, paid what he could on the general store account he owed, and then set out to find a job. That had been four years ago.

Now, he avoided women. Seemed every time he met a girl, at a social or in a town, the first thing he wondered was whether she'd leave if she got a better offer. The hurt had gone deep. He was afraid to trust, yet the loneliness got worse.

~ ~ ~

With such hard labor, his appetite fully returned, and he made good use of the supplies he'd brought back. In addition, he killed a small deer and dried some of the venison, so he could take it out with him on the days he spent away from the cabin. In the Dutch oven Nate gave him, he placed a big venison roast surrounded by wild onions. Adding potatoes made a tasty meal almost equal to Nate's.

Elisha even tried his hand at baking a dried apple pie. Barely able to wait for it to cool, he cut a big wedge and put it on a plate. Sitting on a stump outside with a clear view of the mountains, he cut his fork into the pie. When he tasted the first mouthful, the sweet flavor of apples and cinnamon filled him with uncommon satisfaction.

When he finished enjoying his sweet, he looked around. What to do next? If he had a table and benches in front of the cabin, he'd be able to eat outside in comfort—especially in early mornings and late summer evenings when the warmth inside the cabin stifled him.

A week later, he took an afternoon to build his table and benches. He ate his supper seated at his new table looking out over the distant mountains as the sun set. If he could keep working as hard as he had for the last several months, he saw no reason why he couldn't stay where he was and work for the next year. He hoped Sam Weathers would see it that way, too. With the cowhands he had, Mr. Weathers didn't need another regular rider. Riding the line north of Pinto Creek was the only job available on the J Bar C Ranch.

It would mean spending the winter isolated at the cabin for a few months when the trail would be impassable because of deep snow, but the cabin was snug. If he got enough wood cut, he'd stay warm and dry. He'd want more books, but that didn't seem to be a problem. Mr. Weathers had given him free rein to take any of the books up to the cabin. He didn't relish the months of isolation and was a little afraid of it. But staying at the cabin was better than riding the grub line in the middle of winter.

~ ~ ~

In June, Mr. Weathers sent Abe and Josh up to help Elisha build a barn.

Abe and Josh told him they were impressed with all the work Elisha had done, both inside and outside the cabin.

"Boy, this looks like a real lived-in place now," Josh declared. "Next thing you know, you'll be putting up curtains and bringing in wildflowers for the table."

Elisha laughed. "I don't know about the curtains, but I like the idea of the wildflowers. You can pick some tomorrow."

After getting a fire going in the stove, Elisha soon had a meal on the little table in front of the cabin.

Abe looked to the west, out over the valley and toward the mountains, the sun setting behind them. "This is peaceful," Abe said. "A man could be content here."

Elisha nodded, gazing at the mountains.

Josh didn't say anything.

Before long, one yawn led to another. Elisha wanted to be a good host. "You boys go ahead and use the bunks. I'll sleep here on the floor."

"We're not going to take your bunk." Abe sounded offended.

"Yeah, you old men need your beauty sleep. I'll take the floor," Josh teased and ended the argument by unrolling his bedding and plopping down on the floor.

Other than bodily picking up Josh and throwing him onto one of the bunks, they had no choice. Laughing, Elisha and Abe settled down on the bunks to sleep.

Abe and Elisha were up before daylight. Abe took care of the horses while Elisha cooked breakfast.

When Abe came in to eat, Josh was still asleep on the floor in front of the cold fireplace. With the toe of his boot, he poked Josh in the ribs. "Come on sleepy head, get up."

Josh sat up and yawned. "Why didn't you wake me sooner?"

"You needed your beauty sleep." Abe laughed at the younger man. "Come on, Elisha has grub ready and we got a barn to build."

Elisha directed the two men and with hard work, they completed the barn in two days.

The night after they completed the barn, Elisha woke up groaning in the darkness. When he tried to move, pain made him grit his teeth and clench his fists to stop from crying out. And then, slowly the pain diminished to a dull ache. Elisha gradually relaxed and wiped the sweat from his brow. He lay still, almost afraid to breathe but the spasms abated for a time.

Elisha woke again to the gray light of dawn and rolled over on his side. When the pain didn't return, he put one foot on the floor and then gingerly sat up on the side of his bed. Maybe the hurt's gone for a while. The spasms hadn't come like that for a while. Building the barn had been more than his back muscles could tolerate. He stood, and quietly dressed, put a couple of logs on the sleeping coals in the stove, and made his way to the crock of sourdough so he could make flapjacks.

When one of the men stirred, Elisha asked, "Y'all awake?"

Someone muttered. Then Josh sat up rubbing his eyes.

"I'll make us some breakfast if you boys want to dress and get your gear together. Be sure and tell Mr. Weathers what a good job you did on the barn. I'll get the loft up, build some stalls, and get the doors made, but really ya'll done the hard work."

"You had the work half done by getting the logs ready and notched. We couldn't have begun without that," Abe said.

Josh groaned while he rubbed his back. "I hope that's the last barn we have to build. That's harder work than branding cows."

Abe slapped Josh on the back. "Come on young'un. We can rest as we ride back to the ranch."

Elisha watched them ride down the trail. Abe and Josh were both good men and he enjoyed working with them. However, this northern part of the J Bar C was his responsibility.

Elisha found a small box canyon a half-mile west of the cabin that had a good flowing spring and plenty of grass. He built a barrier across the opening of the canyon and turned the horses loose to graze.

He started his patrol to the east. There were fewer cattle to haze back south of the creek. Beyond the bluffs, the land flattened out and became more arid. He crossed a set of grooves on a trail that had seen a lot of use and realized it was part of the east-west track for wagon trains. It was too far south to be what folks called the Oregon Trail, but it might be the trail used to connect with it by folks coming up through Kansas. No wagons were in sight now.

He circled back to head toward the ranch boundary. The tracks of six unshod horses impressed deep into the soil and paralleled the wagon ruts. Elisha saw his first sign of Indians. He reined his horse and scanned the area carefully. A chill ran up his spine. If he met up with six Utes, he wouldn't stand a chance.

~ ~ ~

In the middle of July, Elisha laid out a solitary meal outside the cabin one evening, and saw a magnificent hawk fly low in the valley.

"Would you look at that!" He looked around and then laughed at himself. There was no one to share the moment with. Ordinarily, solitude didn't bother him, but for some reason this evening, the silence was too loud, and he hungered for the sound of another human voice. "Sure would be nice to have a wife to share my day's work with."

He didn't let his thoughts linger, as there was no sense thinking about what he didn't have. At least he had the visits to the ranch. In the meantime, he'd let the books keep him company. Although, even having the books couldn't quite make up for the lack of having someone special in his life.

CHAPTER THREE

The second week of September, Elisha rode through a stand of aspen trees, whose leaves were a glorious shade of gold. His breath caught at the spectacle. Fall brought out such wonderful colors. After a three-day trip to the eastern bluffs, he returned in the late afternoon. As Elisha drew near to the cabin, he saw smoke rising from his stovepipe.

He reined to a sudden stop. A couple of unfamiliar horses grazed in the corral. He pulled his horse back into the trees on the far side of the creek. After dismounting, Elisha removed his rifle from the scabbard. Wading across the cold creek water, he moved quietly up to the cabin window and stepping onto a stump looked in.

Mr. Weathers and Josh sat at the table, talking.

Elisha crossed the creek, mounted his horse, and then rode up to the cabin.

The two men came out and greeted him.

Josh grinned. "You're not even home to greet your company."

Mr. Weathers took hold of the bridle on Elisha's horse. "We came up to see how things are going,"

Elisha dismounted then took his saddlebags and rifle off his horse. "If I'd known you were coming I'd have gotten back earlier. When did you get here?" He was almost lightheaded with the joy of having company. Maybe the isolation left him more lonesome than he wanted to admit.

Mr. Weathers grinned. "We made ourselves at home and put on the coffee pot."

Josh led the horse toward the corral. "Here, least I can do is put your horse up."

Elisha and Mr. Weathers entered the cabin. As Elisha stowed away his gear, Mr. Weathers sat to finish his cup of coffee.

"Nate packed us a sack of food, so don't worry about supper." Mr. Weathers pointed toward a gunnysack that lay by the stove.

Who'd have thought he'd come home to company? He poured a cup of coffee then took a seat at the table across from Mr. Weathers. "I finished a sweep to the east today. Not many cattle in that direction but I got the few I found hazed back across the creek. More of my time is spent south and west. That's where the cattle drift the most."

"I'd expect that." Mr. Weathers nodded. "The grass is better. In the heat of the summer, the cattle will drift toward the cool of the forest. You look healthy and strong. You seem to be content up here working by yourself."

Elisha felt more at ease with his boss than when he first appeared at the ranch in March. His new confidence made it easier to speak plainly. "I feel good and enjoy my work here."

"Josh and I came up for a couple of reasons. First, I wanted to get away and do some riding into the hills. I haven't ridden up this far since last summer." He glanced around the cabin. "You've really fixed this place up. That barn is exactly what was needed, and I see you've improved the corral."

Elisha couldn't help after such praise but sit a bit taller.

"The other reason I wanted to come up was to talk to you about you staying on through the winter." Mr. Weathers swallowed the last of his coffee. "You've done a good job but this place is isolated. Winter will be a lot harder to deal with than the summer. I want to make sure that if you stay, you're prepared."

Elisha swallowed down his excitement. "This is as good a place to winter as any, even if it's a little away from folks. The winter will be a challenge when the snow comes. But if you're willing to trust me to do it, I'm willing to give it a try."

Mr. Weathers nodded. "Good, then it's settled. Josh and I'll stay until day after tomorrow, and then we'll ride back to the house by the western boundary. I try to ride the entire ranch boundary at least once a year with Josh. Oh, and by the way, I increased your pay to thirty a month."

The raise confirmed a job well done. "Thanks, Mr. Weathers."

Elisha set out the food that Nate had sent. The evening proved enjoyable, as the three men talked of the work of the ranch, both Elisha's part and the crew at the main house.

The next day Elisha showed the two men all the improvements he'd made. He took them to the box canyon he'd found, where he could leave the horses to graze.

Mr. Weathers looked out over the tall grass in the box canyon. "This is a good idea."

When they returned to the cabin, Elisha set the supper out on the table in front of the cabin. A slight breeze circulated the air. It made for a nice change from eating inside.

After he'd eaten Josh said, "You'll mind if I go jump into the creek and cool off?"

"Go ahead. I'm going to sit here and have another cup of coffee." Mr. Weathers said.

Elisha and Mr. Weathers sat, drank coffee, and looked out over the valley and the distant mountains.

Mr. Weathers gazed at the tall mountain peaks to the west. "I always get a little melancholy when I come up here."

Elisha sat quietly, waiting for Mr. Weathers to continue.

"The last hunting trip I made with my son was up through here. I suppose you know I have a son?"

"No. I hadn't heard about your family."

"I married the wrong person for me. Later when the kids started coming, she was the wrong person to be their mother. Of course, at the time I didn't have much choice. I married the only girl within a couple days ride. I later heard a fellow talk about how people sometimes marry because of proximity. Well, that's what I did. My wife was an unhappy person and had strange uncontrollable rages. She would get things into her head that were crazy. No amount of reasoning with her would make a difference."

Elisha sat quietly as Mr. Weathers paused and took a swallow of coffee. "Our son, Joseph, was born, and as far as I knew, he was a normal little boy. However, my wife hated the child. I could never understand why. She made his life a hell on earth, and I mean he was only a little boy."

His voice quivered as he continued. "I did what I could to protect him, but it was never enough. I'd go out with the cattle and stay for days when I didn't have to. It got me away from her, but Joseph couldn't do that."

He closed his eyes and let out a deep sigh. When he opened his eyes again, they were bright with tears that didn't fall. "Then we had our little girl, Christine. She was a lovely child. My wife loved that child all the while growing meaner to our son. I went out with the herd for a couple of days the year the boy turned fourteen. When I came home, he'd been gone almost a week. He'd taken a horse I'd given him for his birthday and left. His mother didn't even go looking for him. Didn't tell me he'd run away, either. A couple months later, my wife and daughter died in a wagon accident. That happened nearly seven years ago.

Mr. Weathers rubbed his forehead and closed his eyes again. "He'd be twenty years old now." When he opened them this time, he fixed a long sad stare on Elisha. "One reason I'll never sell my ranch even though I've had offers, is because if he ever comes back, I want it to be here for him." Mr. Weathers rubbed his eyes. "Must be this place. I don't usually talk about my family. Thanks for listening."

"I appreciate you telling me." The older man had troubles in his life, but managed to keep going. Elisha respected that. Was Mr. Weathers more partial to Josh because it made him think of his son?

Elisha ached for Mr. Weathers. To have lost a daughter to death was tragic, but to have a son somewhere out there and not know if he lived or not was truly heartbreaking.

Come morning Josh and Mr. Weathers saddled up to ride toward the west. "Think about what supplies you'll need through the winter. You won't get but a few more trips to the ranch before the snows."

"I'll do that and I'll see you all in two weeks as scheduled," Elisha promised.

"We enjoyed our visit." Josh waved.

Elisha saluted as they rode down the trail. "You're welcome anytime."

The day after his boss and Josh left, Elisha packed his bedroll and a four days' supply of food and rode to the land he'd recently found over the ridge and foothills, toward the upper valleys. Yes, it was perfect. Here, he'd have a home someday. And a family. New hope burned in his belly as he worked his way back to the cabin.

~ ~ ~

Fall hung on into November with warm days and cool nights, but no early snow. Elisha made three more trips to the ranch headquarters. The last trip during the first week of December Elisha got Smithy, the ranch barber as well as the cook, to cut his hair shorter than usual as this haircut would have to last through the winter. He also packed more warm clothing and blankets plus extra food. Elisha stacked five months of tinned goods, kegs of flour, sugar, cornmeal, and oatmeal, crates of Arbuckle coffee, potatoes, apples, and dried fruit in the loft.

He looked over his supply of books, hoping he had enough for the solitary months ahead. He had spent days and weeks alone in the past, but always with a way to go into town when he wanted. The idea of being isolated for several months with no choice was a little more daunting.

~ ~ ~

After a day of pushing cattle back across the creek, Elisha rode back to the cabin in the first light snow of the season. It was a harbinger of winter to come.

A week later, howling wind woke him from a sound sleep. He rose from his bunk, opened the front door, and looked out into the night. Snow covered the stoop. The temperature had dropped sharply and frigid wind blew through the open doorway. The cold bit him to the bone. He shoved the door closed, then stoked the fire and added a few logs. Shivering, he climbed back into his bedroll and stared out at the semi-darkness. He felt a slight trembling of fear in the pit of his stomach at the five months of coming winter alone.

It snowed on and off hour after hour. By the end of the second day, the snow was a good two feet deep between the barn and the cabin. In places, the wind had blown it into drifts several feet higher. Elisha rigged a rope between the cabin and the barn as a precaution for the next storm. This snow hadn't been what he'd consider a blizzard, but it was a warning of what the winter winds were getting ready to bring.

With morning, the snow stopped falling. Elisha packed a bedroll and extra food and wore a heavy coat over his light one, and rode prepared to spend a night in freezing weather. Being caught in a sudden whiteout could totally disorient a rider within minutes. He kept a careful watch on the clouds, prepared to make a break for the cabin, as he spent the day hazing cattle back south of the creek.

Elisha made it back to the cabin after dark, relieved to be out of the cold north wind. After he made sure Jasper was snug for the night, he shuffled into the cabin, started the fire in the stove with the help of some matches and dried moss, and then did the same thing in the fireplace. The cabin soon felt warm and cozy. Elisha prepared a hot meal to build his strength against the cold.

Elisha's thoughts drifted back to the last winter. The wind had whistled through cracks in the bunkhouse walls at Old Man Spurrier's place, making it perpetually cold and damp. Worse, the entire winter, he never got a full meal. Old Man Spurrier had been mean as a weasel. This little cabin was a palace in comparison. And it sure beat trying to ride the grub line in such weather.

The next morning, he saddled the sorrel mare and rode out to check for cattle to the west. With a strong north wind blowing, he followed the tracks of a few head of cattle drifting back south. Even with his heavy coat, a scarf around his ears and over his hat, along with his fur lined gloves; the cold penetrated like a sharp knife. Shivering, he reassured himself that it was part of the job. Besides, winter hadn't really started yet. He tried to be tough, but he was still cold.

He hunched over, hugging warmth into his hands. When his horse bucked at a deer running across in front of her, it caught him off guard. Thrown from the saddle, he landed hard and felt a burst of pain from his head.

Elisha lay on the ground, with the wind knocked out of him. Sharp pain stabbed into his scalp. Gingerly fingering his head, he located a growing bump. When he finally got to his feet and looked around, the sorrel had disappeared.

Seized by fear of the worsening weather, he tried to figure out how far it was to the cabin. He couldn't think clearly. The sorrel had departed with his bedroll still tied to the saddle. The only protection from the cold of the night and wild creatures—follow the mare's tracks to the cabin.

As he slugged through the snow in boots made for riding, he slipped and landed hard on his hands and knees. With difficulty with spasms gripping his back, he pushed himself back to his feet. A little further, a branch buried in the snow caught his boot and he fell again. Breathing hard, he rolled onto his back. Maybe he should rest awhile. But he couldn't. Not here. Too much danger. Wincing from the pain, he struggled to his feet. The mare's tracks blurred.

Elisha stood by a tree. Why was he out in the cold and the snow? He touched his head and the pain jerked him back to reality. Get to the cabin. He plodded though the snow again.

It would soon be dark and then how could he know which way was home? As he felt a sharp tightening in his chest and difficulty breathing, the outline of the cabin showed in the twilight, Elisha groaned and quickened his steps.

Beside the corral, the sorrel stood, head down, rump pointed toward the cold wind. Elisha couldn't be angry. The horse had done the same thing he had—just tried to get home. As much as he wanted to get inside the warmth of the cabin, he led the horse into the barn and stripped off the bridle and saddle. After feeding and watering the horses, he hurried to the cabin.

He got the fire going in both the fireplace and the stove, but kept his coat and gloves on until he warmed up. How thankful he felt to have made it back with only a couple bruises and a bump on his head. It could have been much worse. Even as he warmed himself by the fire, he shivered as he pictured himself badly injured with no one to help.

He was alone.

CHAPTER FOUR

Toward the middle of December, Elisha woke to a clear day. A glance at his thermometer showed the temperature only a bit below freezing—time to make a quick trip to the eastern boundary. Out in the barn, he decided to take the big black gelding, Shadow, hoping the horse was big enough to handle the snowdrifts better than Jasper or the sorrel mare. Besides, after the mare had thrown him, he was leery of riding her.

It was a beautiful day with a bright blue sky. The snow on the ground sparkled like jewels on a lady's handbag. He'd have no trouble finding the few cattle that drifted north and east of the creek as they left their tracks in the snow. He put in a long hard day in the cold.

As he lay in his bedroll as close to his fire that night, his gaze rested on a twinkling star that hovered low on the horizon. He sat up and stared. It couldn't be a star, not that low. It's probably a campfire. But who would camp in the snow on the edge of the J Bar C range? His chest tightened. Could be Utes.

Elisha, after riding thirty minutes the next morning, saw smoke and what at first, looked like a snowdrift. With great caution, he urged his horse closer. A covered wagon with what appeared to be a broken axle sat in the middle of a snow-covered meadow with a couple of horses tied to the wheels. Elisha reined in his horse and looked around carefully. The covered wagon didn't belong here this time of year. Where had it come from?

The aroma of the fire blended with a smell of coffee, and something cooking in the pot. Then, through the canvas of the wagon covering, the bore of a rifle stuck out aimed at him. He swallowed hard and held up his hands.

He tried to keep the quiver out of his voice. "Howdy. My name's Elisha Evans and I'm a ranch hand with the J Bar C. I don't mean you any harm." He made sure he kept his hands in sight of the rifle holder. "You mind if I get down and help myself to some of your coffee?"

A high-pitched voice answered. "Move slowly. And keep your hands where I can see them."

Elisha dismounted and approached the fire. He poured hot liquid into a cup he found near the fire. After taking a sip of the hot coffee, he saluted the rifle barrel. "Someone makes a mighty fine cup of coffee." Elisha stood easily as he warmed his fingers around the hot cup. "Any chance I could meet whoever made the coffee?"

The canvas parted, and a young boy wrapped in a blanket over his coat appeared. A wool scarf tied his hat on his head. The boy stayed on the seat of the wagon holding the rifle steady on Elisha. Although much of the slender face hid under the scarf, Elisha saw a shimmer possibly from tears. From his size and what face he could see, Elisha put the boy's age at maybe twelve to fourteen.

"Who did you say you are?" A young voice asked.

Elisha's arms were beginning to ache from holding his hands so high in front of him. "Elisha Evans. I work for Mr. Weathers. This here is his range. I ride the line looking for drifting cattle and stay in a cabin over toward the west. I spotted you last night from my camp. I stopped by to see if you all needed any help."

The boy slowly lowered the rifle then climbed down from the wagon. "We thought we could make it out of the mountains and on to the railroad, but the wagon broke down over two weeks ago. Grandfather broke his leg trying to fix it."

Elisha relaxed his weary arms, set the cup down by the fire, and moved toward the wagon. "Is your grandfather in there?"

Tears rolled freely down the boy's cheeks. "Yes, sir. He's real sick."

"All right if I look in on him?"

The boy nodded and stepped aside.

Elisha climbed into the wagon. A gaunt old man with a white beard lay wrapped in blankets with his eyes closed. Elisha leaned over him and listened to his chest. The old man gasped, as if fighting for breath.

Elisha turned to the boy. "How long has he been like this?"

"He's been sort of drifting in and out of sleep for about two days now. I've tried to keep him warm and feed him hot stew, but he keeps getting worse." The boy's eyes looked as wide and unblinking as a frightened deer.

Something in his voice caused Elisha to stare more closely at the boy. "Well, I'll be." This wasn't a boy at all, but a young girl. "What's your name?" he asked softly.

"Susana. Susana Jamison, and that's my grandfather, Henry Jamison."

Elisha wanted to reach out and wipe away the tears, but didn't want to frighten her any more than she was already. He wasn't surprised that he'd taken her for a boy. He still couldn't guess her age.

"Hello, Susana. Where are your folks?"

Her soft voice trembled. "They died in the spring of diphtheria. It's only Grandfather and me."

Elisha carefully pulled back the covers. Rags wrapped crude branch splits tightly around the old man's leg. It didn't look as if the skin had been broken, but he didn't want to unwrap it to check. With the wagon broken down, he could think of only one thing to do—take the old man and girl back to the cabin.

"Listen to me, Miss Jamison. I know you don't know me, but you're going to have to trust me. There's another snowstorm coming and you won't make it through alive. Your grandfather needs to be somewhere warm."

Susana nodded, her expression distressed.

"I'm going to put together a travois, it's like a litter, so we can get your grandfather back to my cabin, but we got to hurry. While I get him ready, you gather what you can carry on a horse. We'll have to leave the rest till later."

She looked wildly about the wagon and put her hand to her throat. "Oh no, we can't leave our things. This is everything we have."

"I know," he said gently. "But we first got to save your grandfather's life."

She swallowed hard as if the lump of fear was almost too big to handle. "I understand," she sighed as if surrendering. "It's just hard."

"I'm here to help you now." Elisha put his hand on her shoulder. "I don't know how you've survived this long out here. But now let's get your grandfather to proper shelter."

He climbed out of the wagon and looked over the two horses standing tied to the wagon. They stood with their tails to the wind, heads hung low. A trace of their ribs poked through their shaggy coats. Elisha hoped the brown mare had enough strength left to drag the travois and that the grey gelding could carry the girl. He'd ride Shadow since neither looked strong enough to carry his weight. Elisha gazed at the sky. Dark clouds rolled in. Time to get moving.

He found two saplings among the trees at the edge of the meadow. Using the small axe he kept with the supplies on his saddle, he trimmed them to construct the travois. With rope he found in the wagon, he quickly put it together, using his own bedroll for a bed. Then he carried the old man—still wrapped in his bedding—out of the wagon and laid him on the travois. The old man didn't rouse except to moan in pain.

Elisha helped Susana pack the rest of their meager food, basic clothing, a Bible, and some family photographs, making sure not to overload the horses. "Susana, get any other blankets and coats you have and put them over your grandfather."

He got Susana settled in the saddle. She had on an old coat too big for her. Probably belonged to her grandfather. After mounting Shadow, he led the way toward the cabin. He caught Susana looking back at the wagon. She wore the same expression he had seen on women's faces at funerals. She turned away from the sight of the abandoned wagon, pulled her coat closer, and leaned into the wind.

The fear she must have in this moment, even of him, tore at Elisha.

It was a long, brutal day. The wind increased and the temperature fell. Elisha allowed only two short stops to rest the horses. At the first stop, he took his wooly chaps off and put them on the shivering girl. The old man looked grayer. They had to get to the cabin soon or they would lose him for sure.

By mid afternoon, it began to snow. With each passing hour, it fell heavier. Elisha tied the three horses together head-to-tail. He couldn't chance losing the girl or the old man in the snow.

Hours later after darkness had fallen, Elisha pulled Shadow up at the door of the cabin.

Susana sat hunched in her saddle with the snow slowly covering her in a mantel of white. It clung to her eyebrows and lashes until it was difficult to see her eyes. Her lips had turned blue and her breath rasped as she tried to breathe the freezing air.

As Elisha stood, beside Susana's horse, he could no longer feel his feet. Heedless of his own condition, he had to care for his visitors. Elisha lifted the girl off the horse and carried her into the cabin where he placed her on one of the bunks. Next, he unhitched the travois, and dragged the old man into the cabin. Elisha didn't know if he had enough strength left to lift the old man onto the bed. His legs trembled with the threat of collapse.

He lit a lantern and fed the banked coals in the fireplace and the cook stove. He needed to warm these people as quickly as possible. Before he could stop to rest, he went back to the horses and led them into the barn, which was warm compared to the cold outside. The three horses already in the barn whinnied their welcome. He quickly unsaddled the horses, pitched some hay for them, and got them each a bucket of water from the trough. It would have been best to give them each a good rubdown, but he had to tend to the old man and young girl first.

Back in the cabin, the girl slept. He covered her with a blanket for the time being, even though her clothes were wet.

The old man was barely breathing and still unconscious. His lips looked bluish and his breathing labored. Not good. Elisha didn't know what to do beside get him warm and try to pour some hot liquid down his throat. He made coffee and put on a pot of water to boil, then dropped in some chunks of beef and cut up some potatoes to make a stew.

Careful to be quiet to keep from waking the girl, Elisha pulled off his wet clothes, put on dry ones and a pair of moccasins. Trembling with exhaustion, he wanted to lie down. But he needed to get some food into all three of them first.

He opened up the gunnysack with the girl's clothes and pulled out a flannel nightgown.

Elisha had to get the girl out of the cold, wet clothes. He took a deep breath and gently shook her. She sat and stared at him with the greenest eyes he had ever seen.

Elisha smiled to put her at ease. "You need to get out of those wet things. Put this on while I get a hot stone wrapped up for your feet." He left her to change and went to the loft to get a couple of wolf furs to wrap around the hot stones. When he returned, her wet things lay in a soggy pile on the floor and Susana had snuggled under the covers.

"Put this at your feet. It'll help you warm up."

Susana reached out one thin arm to take the hot stone wrapped in fur and quickly slipped it under the covers. "Thank you. How is Grandfather?" She turned to study the still form lying on the travois.

"He's asleep. I'll put him on my bunk in a bit. I'm making some beef broth. It'll be ready soon."

"I'm going to lie here if that's all right."

"You rest. When it's ready, I'll let you know."

When he looked over at the girl a few moments later, she was asleep. He pulled the covers up to her chin and watched her a moment. She looked so small, like an exhausted child.

Elisha needed to care for the old man. He carefully lifted the old man off the floor onto the bunk. Large frightened eyes blinked open at him.

"Hello, I'm Elisha. You're safe at my cabin and so is Susana. Rest easy now."

"Hello, young man." The old man's voice was no more than a croak.

"I'm going to feed you some beef broth. You need something warm in you." He turned to the stove, and poured some of the broth off the beef and potatoes he'd been boiling. Stirring until it cooled a bit, he placed a spoonful next to the old man's lips and tipped it into his mouth.

After swallowing a few spoonfuls of the broth, the old man shook his head slightly. "Where are we?"

"You're at the line cabin at the north boundary of the J Bar C. This is Sam Weathers's ranch. I'm the line rider working out of this cabin for the winter."

"Who else is here?" The old man looked around the cabin.

"No one, I work alone."

"How far is it to the ranch house?"

"It's about twenty miles south through the hills and over a mountain pass, but we're snowed in probably for the winter after this storm. If I could, I'd ride to the ranch and get help, but I'm not sure a horse could make it through the hills."

The old man shook his head. "No, don't put yourself in danger. I need to rest up and then I'll be all right."

Elisha nodded. "You and your granddaughter are more than welcome to stay here until you're back on your feet. I got plenty of food and wood to keep us warm."

"Where's my granddaughter?"

Elisha tipped his head toward Susana. "On that bunk all wrapped up in a blanket and sound asleep."

"Thank the Lord for His blessings. And thank you for your kind assistance." The old man sighed and closed his eyes.

Elisha wrapped a hot stone in a fur and put it at the old man's feet. He didn't know what else to do. His belly growled so he put some of beef and potatoes on a plate and ate them with a piece of leftover cornbread. At last, Elisha made up a bedroll on the floor by the fire. It would've been warmer in the loft, but he needed to be close to the fire to feed it through the night.

As he allowed his body to relax, he marveled at how quickly life could change. The old man and girl would be with him until spring, at least four months. He had to offer them shelter, that's what a man did. Yesterday he'd only been concerned with a few cows. Now he had an old man and a young girl to care for in the middle of winter.

CHAPTER FIVE

Susana woke to early morning daylight filtering in through the small windows. She caught her breath as she struggled to raise her head and look around. Nothing about the ceiling looked familiar. A strange man was asleep on the floor by the fireplace and her grandfather was asleep in a bunk. They were the only people in the small one-room cabin. She pushed herself to sit up. All her muscles protested after the terrible ride the day before.

Lying on the split log floor in front of the fireplace was the man. Remembering the bitter cold they had ridden through yesterday, Susana shivered. She rubbed her upper arms to ward off the chill. She stared down at her nightgown and her cheeks burned. Vaguely she remembered the stranger telling her to change out of her wet clothes. What else happened? Where was he and what was he doing while she changed?

Susana wrapped a blanket around her shoulders and rose from her bunk. Tiptoeing over to her grandfather, she smiled down at him. He opened his eyes.

"Good morning, sweetheart." His voice cracked, dry as fall leaves. He looked bad. The ride had been rough for her, but worse on him.

"Morning yourself. How are you feeling?" She knelt beside him so she could hear his whispered response better.

"Not too well, but I'm thankful this stranger got us out of the cold and gave us shelter." He looked over at the man asleep on the floor. "He gave us his bed."

"I hadn't thought about it, but I guess he did. He must be a nice man."

"Yes, I suspect he's a good and kind man. He didn't hesitate to rescue us yesterday." Susana's grandfather shifted in the bed and groaned softly. "Do what you can for him today, honey."

"Are there other people here?" Her eyes roamed over the two bunks and the two chairs pushed up to a small table. The fire in the cook stove burned, adding some warmth, and more heat came from the fireplace. Sparse even if it was one man.

"It doesn't appear to me as if anyone else is here. And if this cowhand lives here permanent, he doesn't have much in the way of earthly goods."

A few dishes and cans of food were stacked on open shelves above a rough, wooden-slab counter while clothes hung from nails driven into the logs of the cabin walls. Stacked neatly in the corner were a saddle, saddlebags, and other equipment. The only indications of luxury were the books on a bookshelf above her grandfather's bunk.

Susana smiled at his observations. "No he's not a rich man," she whispered.

"Right now, his goodness is more important to us." His voice seemed a little stronger.

"How do we know for sure he's good?"

"You watch what he does and you match it with what he says. A man can be good and not a Christian. And if that's what this man is, then that also means he's close to the kingdom. You'll know over time."

"Are we going to be here a long time?" She reached out from underneath her wrappings and took his weathered hand in hers.

"Only God knows what our future will be, child. Don't lose hope that God is always here for us—even in our future."

Susana heard movement behind her and turned around to see the man sitting up with his back partially to her. He had an arm twisted behind him, rubbing the small of his back. Was he in pain? Had he hurt himself helping them yesterday? She noticed how his dark hair curled down over his ears and collar and how his eyebrows arched over his dark eyes. His unlined, tanned face was clean-shaven which was unusual, as most men at least had a moustache. She liked that. Susana felt her cheeks burning for staring at and finding the man handsome.

* * *

Elisha didn't want to eavesdrop, so he turned to face the fire and tried to sit up. One of the almost-forgotten spasms grabbed his back, and he half-sat, trying to breathe until it passed. After having journeyed the long, cold ride home, lifting the girl, then the old man, and sleeping on the floor, agonizing spasms of white pain shot through his back. Once the pain lessened to a bearable level, Elisha moved slowly and carefully to put more logs on the fire. Turning to roll up his bedroll, he caught the girl looking at him.

"Morning, Miss Jamison. How are you?" He smiled at her pretty face and the amazing green eyes.

"Oh, I'm fine." Susana pulled the blanket tightly around her. "Grandfather is also doing better."

"Hello, son. Sorry we took your beds," The old man said in a whisper.

"No problem, sir. It's nice to wake up and have visitors. I don't see many folks up this way." Jamison did look a little better, but the girl looked up at him with a little frown. Although he'd slept in his clothes, she was still in her nightgown, covered only by the blanket. She probably needed some privacy.

Elisha moved quickly to put his bedroll in the loft, then stoked the fire in the stove. He filled the coffee pot with the last of the water in the bucket. Then he put on his boots, coat, and gloves. "I'll get some water, so we can heat it to wash up, and then I got to see to the horses. After that, I'll get us some breakfast going." He'd been doing all the talking. Taking help from a stranger must be uncomfortable for them—about as uncomfortable as having a pretty, young woman sitting on his floor in her nightgown. He looked away from her and left the cabin.

He trudged to the trough behind the cabin. A thin sheet of ice covered the top of the water. Because he'd rigged it so water constantly flowed, it wouldn't freeze as fast as standing water. He filled the bucket and set it inside the cabin, and then closed the door behind him without looking at the girl.

The frigid day, with an overcast sky of heavy gray clouds, held the promise of more snow. Trudging to the barn through the knee-deep snow, he struggled to keep his balance.

He talked to the horses as he mucked out their stalls and put out fresh hay. After giving each horse a bucket of water and a half-bucket of oats, he'd need to turn two out to graze in the box canyon. Mr. Weathers' horses had to come first because he required them to do his work.

Elisha hoped that Susana might have washed and dressed. His stomach rumbled. He could use a hearty breakfast. On his way to the cabin, he gathered up a large armful of wood. Heading around to the cabin door, his arms loaded, he kicked on the door for entry.

The girl opened the door slowly, and then when she saw him with an armload of wood opened it all the way.

He went in and dumped the wood by the fireplace.

"Oh, I should have brought some wood in." She stepped back and folded her hands.

Susana was dressed in a full-skirted brown dress with a high collar and long sleeves. She'd brushed her light brown hair and braided it into a long, single braid that hung down her back, almost to her waist. What did her hair look like when she allowed it to hang freely? The dress didn't emphasize her feminine form, but she seemed older. She looked to be about sixteen.

"No, I carry in the wood." Elisha pulled off his coat and hat, hung them in their usual place on nails by the door. He brushed the snow off his pants. "Let me wash up and I'll get us some breakfast."

"Please, let me fix breakfast. If you'll tell me what you want, I can cook while you wash up." She stood by the stove, squeezing her hands together.

Elisha smiled. "That'd be nice. I'd sure like to eat someone else's cooking for awhile." He pointed out where he kept the salt pork and eggs.

"You have eggs? Where did you get eggs?" Wonderment filled Susana's voice as she held the egg, as if it were a jewel, in her dainty hand.

Elisha laughed. "My boss gets them from town, I suppose, as I've never seen any chickens on the place. The last time I was down at the ranch, the cook insisted I bring up a whole crate. We might as well eat them because they'll start to spoil after awhile. Look around and fix whatever you want."

He lifted the kettle off the stove and poured hot water into the basin. He couldn't remember when he'd shaved with a woman in the room, but his only other choice was to go out to the barn. It was too cold for that, so he took out his mirror, straight razor, and shaved. Maybe Henry Jamison had the right idea having a full beard.

After he'd finished, Elisha threw the water out from the basin into the yard, and came back inside to find that Susana had breakfast on the table. She'd even made gravy to go along with the fried salt pork and eggs and warmed up biscuits he had made the morning before.

Elisha enjoyed eating someone else's cooking.

Mr. Jamison didn't feel up to eating much and nibbled on some biscuit and salt pork as he lay on the bunk.

Elisha didn't usually talk while he ate, and Susana didn't seem to mind.

He finished his breakfast. "I've got to ride out and work. I should be back by dark."

"Do you have to be gone all day?" Susana's eyes widened, and she frowned deeply.

She seemed afraid of his leaving, but didn't want to say it. The look of fear in her eyes was painful to him and he wished he could take it away.

"It's what I do. I'm responsible for keeping the cattle from drifting away from the ranch, and during these winter storms, they'll drift the worst. I have to move them back to the south. It's my job," he told her gently. "You'll be fine here. Keep the fire going and make yourself at home. I've taken care of the horses and I'll bring in more wood before I go. You take care of your grandfather."

Susana nodded. "We'll be all right. It's only that I've been frightened for so many days."

"Let's make sure your rifle is loaded and you can put the bar down on the door. That way you won't have to be frightened. I'll try to be back by dark."

Elisha got her rifle and made sure it was loaded and ready for firing. After leaning the rifle by the door, he put on his coat, hat, and gloves, and then brought in several armloads of split logs. Added to what was already in the cabin, the wood should last until the next morning. He looked over at Mr. Jamison, and saw the older man was asleep.

"Well, I'll head out. Don't worry and get some rest."

He didn't feel right about leaving her, but he had work to do, and Susana and Mr. Jamison would be with him for the unforeseeable future. He didn't know what else to do but take care of them. It was hard for him, but he looked away from her and headed out the door.

Elisha rode east and hazed as many cattle as he could find back south. He'd have gone further and tried to make sure he'd found all of the cattle he'd seen two days earlier, but he wanted to make sure he kept his word to Susana to return to the cabin by dark. He thought of his visitors often through the day, especially Susana. He almost couldn't believe that he would return to the cabin and find them still there. She was sure a pretty, young lady. Those green eyes, one could get lost there. What did she think of an old cowhand out in the middle of nowhere? He shrugged his shoulders to stop his thoughts and concentrated on hazing a bunch of cows back toward the creek.

The deep drifts of snow made it hard going. He dismounted several times and broke a trail to help his horse. The cold penetrated to the bones. He rode most of the day with his gloved hands tucked under his armpits to keep his fingers from freezing.

The sun had disappeared by the time Elisha rode in toward the barn. His stiff fingers fumbled with the buckles on the girth straps on his saddle. He tended to the horses as quickly as he could.

At the door of the cabin, he knocked loudly and called out. He could hear the bar across the door lifted. The door opened and Susana stood in the light.

Elisha stumbled in on what felt like frozen feet. He couldn't stop shivering. He struggled to take off his chaps, coat, and gloves. He pulled a chair close to the fireplace and sat with his feet as close as he could get them to the fire.

Susana handed him a cup of coffee, steam rising from it.

He curled his hands around the cup to warm them before taking a swallow. "Thanks." He fitted his frozen hands around the hot cup. Looking around, he saw the table was set. Fresh cornbread sat on a plate at its center.

A pot of something bubbled on the stove and made his mouth water. He swallowed hard at the thought of a hot meal that he didn't have to prepare.

"You've fixed supper?"

"Yes. Was that all right?"

"Of course it's all right. I'm surprised. I didn't expect you to cook for me."

"I didn't have anything to do except take care of Grandfather, and I thought you would come in cold and hungry." She stood by the stove as if waiting for his approval, more a woman than a girl. "I don't mind. I like to cook. Do you want to eat now, or warm up a bit?"

Elisha took a deep breath. The idea of a young woman having a meal ready for him at the end of a hard day's work was invigorating. "Let's go ahead and eat. I think that'll warm me up as much as anything." Elisha pulled his chair up to the table.

Susana ladled out thick, hot beef and vegetable stew onto a plate and cut a large piece of cornbread for him. She poured herself a cup of coffee and sat down across from him.

He eagerly ate the stew filled with tender pieces of meat. Elisha ate three full plates of the stew with an equal number of helpings of cornbread.

When he was finished, he leaned back with a contented sigh. "That was good. Exactly what a fella needs on a cold, snowy night. I appreciate you having it ready for me." Elisha looked at Susana's grandfather. "How's he doing? Is he sleeping a lot?" The old man appeared more gaunt and shrunken.

"He's slept on and off all day. I've barely been able to get him to eat anything. He wants to drink a little water and then he goes back to sleep. I'm so worried about him." Susana looked over at the old man, her expression soft with a look of love and concern.

"He means a lot to you?" Of course, he means a lot to her! He could have kicked himself, but he wanted her to know he would be her friend in this difficult time. He just wasn't sure how to do it.

"He's all I've got. We don't have much family. They're all back east in Ohio. When I was small, my parents went to California. They didn't go to look for gold, but to open a store and to farm. They did all right and had my little sister and brothers out there." She picked up some of the dishes and took them over to the sideboard, then returned for the pot of stew, which she set on the back of the stove. "Then the diphtheria came and they all died. I don't know why it spared me. Grandfather had been on his way to visit when it happened. I was fifteen and stayed with a neighbor until he got there. He took care of me. You know he's a preacher?"

Elisha shook his head. He didn't know anything about these people, but knowing the old man was a preacher eased his mind about having strangers living with him.

"He took over the farm, but mostly he's a preacher and takes care of people. In the spring, he got sick with his heart. It worried him. He decided that we should start back east to my great aunt Jenny in Ohio. He thought we could make it to the railway in Kansas before winter." She took the last of the dishes to the sideboard, then heated some water to wash the dishes.

"You made that wonderful meal, let me do the dishes." Elisha stood to offer his help.

"No, thank you. You've done so much for us by letting us stay here and eat your food. I'll do it. It won't take long anyway."

Elisha felt a little funny about sitting around, so he added a couple pieces of wood to the fire in the fireplace.

"I didn't want to go back east," Susana said. "But Grandfather is a wise man, and if it's what he thinks is best for me, I'll go."

"A preacher man. I don't know as I've ever met a preacher before."

Susana turned toward him from the dishpan full of dirty dishes. "Have you never been to church?"

"Not since I was a boy in east Texas. My folks used to go when we could get away from the work, but I was a young boy and don't remember much about it. Since then I've not been very religious. I believe in God well enough, it's just that he and I aren't too well acquainted."

"My pa was also a preacher. Everywhere we lived, he'd start a church by inviting folks and talking from the Bible. He got it from Grandfather. I've always been to church." Susana's voice held a comfortable tone as she washed the dishes. "I've listened first to Pa, and then to Grandfather, each reading from the Bible. We always had a time of prayer and Bible reading in the evenings. It's a great comfort."

Her voice was warm and soft, but she seemed to be talking from nervousness. Was she uncomfortable with him? "Would you like for us to read together from the Bible now?" Elisha surprised himself with his question, but since he'd been reading Mr. Weathers' Bible, he liked the thought of sharing it with someone else.

"Would you?" She looked at him from where she washed the dishes. "That would be a comfort."

Elisha got up, reached over to the shelf of books from Mr. Weathers, and pulled out a worn Bible.

"My boss, Sam Weathers, has a lot of books and he loaned me all of these for the winter. This Bible was in the first box he sent up to me, and I been reading it ever since. I don't understand all of it, but it can cause one to think a lot." He settled back into his chair. "What would you like me to read?"

"You choose."

Elisha turned some pages and then stopped. "How about in the Psalms here?"

"That would be good." Susana finished the last of the dishes, then tossed the dirty water outside. She returned to hang the flour-sack towel over the dishpan, and then took a seat across the table from Elisha. She folded her hands in her lap and waited.

Not used to reading aloud, Elisha cleared his throat and began reading the twenty-second Psalm in a strong clear voice. Soon he was lost in the words and they brought comfort to him. He'd read several of the Psalms before he looked up at Susana, but when he did he saw her head bowed and tears sliding down her cheeks.

Elisha didn't know what to say. He waited. He found the reading comforting and interesting, so it puzzled him that she would be crying. He admitted to himself that he didn't know much about young women, nor what they thought.

"Thank you, Mr. Evans." She brought her eyes up to meet his. "That was beautiful. I had no idea you read so well." She said it as though he'd given her a gift.

He cleared his throat again. "You're welcome. And call me Elisha." He returned the Bible to the shelf and added more logs to the fire. He had suspected from the beginning that Henry Jamison and Susana were solid folks, but having a preacher among his guests put them into a special category. He'd always held preachers and teachers in a kind of awe. As a working cowhand, he was an ordinary sort of person, but town people, like preachers and schoolteachers, seemed beyond him.

Elisha had to do something to make better living arrangements with the three of them in the cabin. Susana needed some privacy, but for the moment, he was too tired to figure how to arrange such a thing. Getting his bedroll from the loft, he spread it out in front of the fireplace. He took off his boots and his belt, and then laid down.

"Miss Jamison, please don't hesitate to wake me if you need anything. Keep the lantern going as long as you want. I can sleep through most anything." He closed his eyes, and even though he was lying on the hard floor, it took only moments for him to fall asleep

Elisha woke the next morning and stretched his sore limbs. Sleeping two nights on the floor hadn't been the best thing for his back. He glanced over at the bunks.

Susana sat by her grandfather's bed. Mr. Jamison moaned.

He rolled up his bedroll and put it away. "How is he?" He kept his voice low as he came to stand near her.

She stood and then glanced up at him with a drawn, concerned look. "He's in considerable pain. His breathing is worse. It doesn't seem to be his leg that's hurting—it's his chest. I don't know what to do."

Susana looked so young and small at this moment as he stood next to her. She only came up to his shoulder. She so was vulnerable. He wanted to take away the look of concern on her lovely face and to protect her. But what could he do for her or Mr. Jamison? The old man was fading away right before their eyes.

"All you can do is keep him warm and try to get him to take some broth." Elisha wished he could say something more encouraging. "I got to see to the horses and it may take a couple of hours. I've a box canyon about half a mile west where they can graze some because it's sheltered and the grass is tall. I'm going to take a couple of horses over there and leave them. I'll be back by noon, if you'd like to have that stew warmed up." He gave a nod toward the stove.

"Don't worry. I'll have dinner ready when you get back."

"I'll bring more wood in and fill the water buckets before I go." Elisha put on his coat and gloves, and left.

Within a few minutes, he had the wood piled near the stove and the fireplace, and two buckets of water fetched for her. He usually shaved most days, but he'd forego the ritual for today.

The sky was clear and the wind had died down, and he didn't want to delay. The temperature was well below freezing, but without the wind. He rode into the box canyon leading the two horses and past the barrier he'd put up. The horses would be able to get to the tall grass with no problem, and the springs flowed in spite of the cold weather. The horses could gather under the trees to get out of the weather. He took the bridles off and slapped their rumps. They ran off as if looking forward to the freedom of the canyon.

Elisha was thankful he'd found the box canyon. He'd only need to check on them every few days, and it made his work a little easier. He had in mind to go get some more of the Jamison's things when he could get a full day and would take his three extra horses to use as packhorses if he couldn't use the wagon. He'd have to see how much snow was on the ground.

As he rode back to the barn, Elisha thought about his situation. Henry and Susana Jamison would be with him until he could get them down to the ranch. It could be three or four months before the trail cleared up enough for the trip. The winter had just started and it would only get worse. If they were careful, they had enough food to last them through the winter. He could also supplement their food with killing a deer or two. He'd even butcher a cow, if it came to it.

Elisha had to make some changes at the cabin to give Susana some privacy. And a bunk would help him to sleep better. He could always build another bunk and put it into the loft, but that meant climbing up and down the ladder several times a night to keep the fire going, especially with Henry Jamison so ill. No, it was better if he stayed closer to the fireplace. The floor would have to do until he could build another bunk to place to the side of the fireplace.

Elisha didn't mind the extra work of taking in and caring for the Jamisons, but he wanted to get a plan in his mind. He owed it to Mr. Weathers to do his job, but normally that meant being away from the cabin overnight at least once a week. How could he leave Susana alone with her ill grandfather?

Having a young woman's touch around the place, along with hot meals sure felt good. Elisha even enjoyed their time at the table and reading the Bible. Although he'd read through the Bible several times over the years, there were parts of it that scared him and parts of it that gave him comfort; but mostly, he didn't understand it.

Elisha took some rope and nails with him as he headed from the barn to the cabin where he found a hot dinner waiting for him. The deep aroma of cooked meat hung in the air. His stomach growled. Had he been this hungry before he smelled dinner?

Susana had cut some meat off the venison hanging in the barn. It must have been an effort for her, as it was frozen. He was surprised she had even found it. Now it sat in the Dutch oven on the table. The carrots and potatoes from Nate and Smithy's garden surrounded the roast venison. She'd also warmed the leftover biscuits.

Susana sat across from him with her head slightly bowed and her eyes cast down. "Would you mind saying a blessing for our meal?" She then looked up at him with her lovely green eyes and a blush showing on her cheeks.

Elisha thought of the times he'd heard Mr. Weathers praying over the meals. "No, I don't mind." He bowed his head.

"Father, we thank you for this meal and for Miss Jamison for preparing it. Thank you for the warm cabin where we can be safe. Please tell us how to help Mr. Jamison, and let him get well soon. In the name of Jesus, Amen."

He looked up at Susana. "Was that all right?"

"What do you mean?" She frowned as she considered his question.

"I've never said a prayer aloud before. Was it all right?" He was sure she'd let him know if he might not have done it right.

"That was perfect." Susana nodded and smiled. "Thank you and please call me Susana." She ladled a large helping of the roast meat and vegetables onto his plate.

He added a couple of biscuits that he covered with the rich gravy Susana had made from the roast.

"How is your grandfather?" He asked between bites.

"This morning he woke for a while and took some broth, but he soon tired and went back to sleep. I'm concerned that he isn't any better and he's sleeping so much."

Elisha nodded. He had no thoughts on how to comfort her and no idea how to help her grandfather. All he could do was make sure the cabin was warm and that Susana had plenty of water.

"You tell me if I can do anything to help. And you don't need to tire yourself out cooking for me. I can manage."

"Oh, I don't mind the cooking. In fact, it's a relief. It gives me something to do besides sitting by Grandfather's side. It's little enough I can do for you for taking us in. I know what would've become of us if you hadn't come along as the answer to our prayers. We owe you our lives."

Embarrassed she had spoken so directly, he struggled with what to say. "You don't owe me anything, Miss Jamison, I mean Susana. Anyone would've done the same thing if they'd found you."

"That may be true, but I don't think many would have done it with such grace as you have. You are a kind, gentle man, Elisha Evans."

Elisha could only stare at her. Her last words had been spoken with a look that seemed years older than her age.

"Grandfather said this morning that it was a blessing you found us and not some rapscallion. He thinks you're a good man, a strong man. He's a good judge of character."

Elisha had never had anyone tell him he was kind, gentle, strong, and good, at least not all in the same conversation. He had never stopped to think seriously about what kind of man he was. He needed to be honest with her about all of his shortcomings and failures, but was almost too embarrassed to speak.

Instead, he stood and then started the task he'd given himself. He put up a rope across the southwest corner of the cabin and secured an old blanket on it. Pulled back during the day, the makeshift curtain could close off the corner when Susana wanted some privacy. He removed the various sacks and bundles that had accumulated in the corner, then relocated her bunk behind the curtain. He then stored all of his things up in the loft and placed her things by the bed.

When he finished, Susana had a private bedroom behind the blanket. While he'd been working, Susana cleared the dinner away. When she finished, she sat in a chair next to her grandfather. She sponged his brow with a cloth from a basin of warm water.

Elisha liked that she'd let him get on with his project without giving advice or even protesting. It made sense that she needed a place for herself, and in the one room cabin, this was the best that Elisha could do.

He spent the rest of the short day bringing in wood and water, then worked on chores in the barn. The sun had set and darkness fallen by the time he made his way back to the cabin. He stepped in to find supper warmed up and on the table waiting for him. They ate the last of the stew and cornbread.

Susana explained that she saved the venison roast for the next day. After supper, she again asked him to read from the Bible.

Elisha was happy to oblige. He took the Bible from its place on the shelf, then set it on the table and let it fall open in front of him. The book of John. Elisha found the beginning of the first chapter and read aloud. After he'd read several chapters, he heard Mr. Jamison stirring on the bunk and stopped his reading.

Susana got up and went over to her grandfather. "Are you all right, Grandfather?" She straightened his covers.

"Yes child. I've been listening to Elisha read from John. It's a comfort. He reads so well."

"Yes, he does." Susana looked over at Elisha and smiled.

"Can you get me some water, honey?"

As she gave him some water, he looked over at the curtain and the bunk. "I see that you've been busy, Elisha. Thank you for thinking of my Susana."

"I should have thought of it earlier, sir. I'm not used to a woman about the place."

The old man nodded. "We've put you in a difficult spot, but you've handled it well. You have my gratitude." His weakened voice sounded even older than the last time Elisha had heard him talk.

"It's no problem. We'll manage fine, and we'll get you back on your feet before you know it." He spoke to assure Susana as much as the old man.

The old man looked back at Elisha as if assessing him. With a nod, he relaxed back on the pillow and closed his eyes.

The next day continued clear and cold. Elisha decided that if he was going to the wagon for the Jamison's things he might as well get it done. After doing the morning chores and eating breakfast, he told Susana what he intended to do. Since he'd be out all day, he asked her to make him some sandwiches with the leftover biscuits and roast. By the time he had hitched up the horses to the ranch wagon and saddled Shadow, she came out of the cabin wrapped in a blanket and handed him a packet of sandwiches wrapped in a flour sack.

"Take care of yourself and get back by dark if you can." Her eyes were big and she had the same expression of concern she'd had the first time he'd ridden off for the day.

Elisha wanted to say something to take away that expression of fear. Not being used to talking much to women, he had a hard time thinking what best to say. "It'll take me most of the day to ride there and back. I'll try hard to make it back before dark. Bolt the door and stay in the cabin." He awkwardly patted her shoulder and then mounted his horse. Yanking on the lead ropes of the horses hitched to the wagon, he started out.

* * *

Susana watched the cowhand ride away. She entered the cabin and then bolted the door. She could still feel where he had patted her shoulder. There was a lonely shyness about the man.

The cabin seemed lonelier with Elisha gone. She checked on her grandfather. He was asleep again. Looking around the cabin, she wondered what to do with herself. It wasn't messy and everything was clean. The man who lived here made an effort to keep things orderly. Susana admitted to herself that he was handsome. She liked how his black hair curled, and his dark eyes often saw right through her. He had such a direct way of looking at her.

Her grandfather stirred and called out to her. "Susana, you there?"

She went over and sat in the chair beside the bunk. "I'm here."

He usually smiled at her, but now he looked at her seriously, as if wanting an answer to something.

"Granddaughter, I need to talk to you; I'm not sure you're ready. You're growing up, but you're still a child. I'm afraid that you've got to grow up in a hurry now."

"What is it?" She gently rubbed the dry, loose flesh of his old hand. She liked when he called her, Granddaughter. It was always said like a blessing.

"I'm going to say what needs to be said, honey. I love you enough to do that. I'm dying and I know it. My heart is slowly giving out and I don't have much time."

"No, Grandfather, please don't say that." She started to cry, because no matter how much she wished it were a lie, she knew it was true.

"You got to be brave and turn to the Lord. He'll walk with us through this. He won't leave you alone. I'm holding fast to that truth." The ring of assurance in his voice gave her courage.

"I will too, then. God loves you Grandfather, and maybe He wants you in heaven, but I need you here."

"It's in the Lord's hands. We need to prepare and that's what I want to talk to you about. I'm going to be gone in a day or two, and you're going to be alone with this stranger. He seems like a good man. He's been very kind to us."

"Will he let me stay here?" When her grandfather died, she would be on her own.

"That's what we need to ask him. I want you to do something that I would never ask you to do under any other circumstance." The old man could hardly talk and she could tell it was a strain.

"Ask me, and then you need some rest."

"Don't worry about me, honey. I'll have all the rest I need soon. Let me say what I must. You're old enough to know that when a man and woman are together that often things happen that they didn't intend. Elisha is a grown man. He's not a boy and he hasn't been around a woman for months. I'm a man, Susana; I know what I'm talking about. As good a man as he might be, after I'm gone, he's going see you in a different way. He's going to want what he doesn't have a right to have. It's not fair to put him in that situation.

Do you know at all what I am talking about?" He gazed at her with a look that seemed to plead for understanding.

"Yes, you mean that he's going to want to make love to me." She felt her cheeks burning. She had never talked about such things with her grandfather before. "Are you sure? He might not even like me."

"You're still such a child." The old man sighed. "It doesn't matter necessarily if he likes you. With the two of you here alone in one room, it'll happen, and I want to protect you. I've already seen how he looks at you and tries not to look. But he's simply a normal man."

"What should I do?" She pressed her hand against her chest. Her heart felt like it wanted to jump out.

"First, we have to trust the Lord to be with you always. Second, we need to do what we can to protect you spiritually. I want to ask Elisha if he'll let me marry the two of you in the next day or so."

CHAPTER SIX

"Marry? But that's for people who are in love. I don't even know him and he's so old." Susana couldn't imagine being married, especially to this stranger, even if he was tall and ruggedly handsome.

Her grandfather's chin trembled and he closed his eyes against the tears threatening to flood down his cheeks. It was almost too much for her and Susana cupped her hands over her face to keep from seeing her grandfather's pain.

Then the old man's hand gently patted her arm. "I know, honey, I know, and I wish it could be different. He seems old to you now, but in a year or so, he won't seem so old. Will you do it for me?" His voice was low and his eyes softened as he looked at her with the sweet smile that he seemed to reserve for her.

Everything within her rebelled at such a thought. Her words came out in a rush. "What will it mean if I marry him? Will I have to let him be with me like a husband?" She knew some of what that meant but the thought of this stranger touching her filled Susana with fear.

"Yes, honey, you will. It won't be fair otherwise. He's a man and if he marries you, he'll expect certain things. You'll have to allow him his pleasure, and I can only pray that you'll come to take pleasure in it too. I fear it'll happen whether you marry or not, and at least this way it'll be acceptable to God."

Susana jumped to her feet and paced back and forth between the bed and the table. "But Grandfather, there must be another way. Maybe the weather will get better and he can take me to a town. Surely there is something else." She tried to keep her voice from quivering. With her grandfather so ill, arguing with him was the last thing she wanted to do. But the alternative was to give in and do as he asked.

The old man coughed and struggled to get his breath. "If you could get to a town where people could care for you that would be a blessing. But think about where we are. Where is the nearest town? How deep is the snow already? I fear that's not possible. We have to look at what is possible and do what will protect you."

She sat in the chair by the bed. "Can we ask him again whether he can get us to a town? Maybe there would be a doctor that could help you." She wiped her eyes.

Her grandfather lay with his eyes closed and breathing with shallow gasps. Then he opened his eyes and gazed at her with a look of love. "I wish that could be possible. I want to stay and make sure you're safe. But I can feel that there isn't time. I'll be going home to God soon."

Susana wanted to reassure her beloved grandfather that she could take care of herself. But could she? The wood crackled in the fireplace and she looked around the bare cabin. The snow was already two or more feet deep outside the door. What was it like in the hills and mountains? What choice did she have?

Forcing her breathing to come slowly to keep from sobbing, Susana suddenly felt years older. "It'll be hard, but if it's what you think best, Grandfather, then I'll agree to marry him. Do you think he'll give me some time to get used to him?"

"I'll ask that of him. If he's a person of his word, and we have no evidence that he isn't, then he'll give you some time. But I'll need to talk to him soon as possible as I'm not sure how much time God will grant me." His breath rattling in his chest, Susana's grandfather collapsed back in his bed and looked at Susana through half-shut eyes. "Now give me a kiss and let me rest a bit."

"I love you, Grandfather." She kissed him on the cheek and pulled up the covers to his chin. If possible, he looked even more fragile than he had when they began to talk. It was as if she could see the life slowly leaving his body.

Susana could hardly imagine what her grandfather was asking of her. And he asked even more of Elisha. What if he didn't like her? She had no idea how to give him pleasure as her grandfather said. Hopefully, Elisha would know.

She made some venison broth with dumplings to have ready when Elisha returned. Then, she sat by her grandfather and prayed for him over the next couple of hours. When her grandfather woke she was able to feed him some of the broth and dumplings.

"Honey, let's talk some more."

"Yes sir. But can I ask about something?" Susana's cheeks flushed and she hoped he didn't see her embarrassment.

"Of course, you ask me anything you want, Granddaughter."

"You mentioned before about me giving Elisha pleasure. Can you tell me how I'm to do that?" She needed to know all she could before her grandfather died. Then, she'd have no one to ask.

"This is when you should be talking to your mother but bless your heart, she isn't here. So, I guess I need to tell you some things." The old man closed his eyes and took a moment, as if praying for wisdom.

They talked for the next several hours, with frequent periods of rest for the weak old man. Her grandfather told her things that she had trouble accepting, but he always told her the truth. She asked him questions she would never have thought possible for her to ask any man. Besides the physical intimacy that he prepared her for, he talked about how to live at peace with a man. He also talked to her about how to live as a faithful Christian in front of a man who was not a Christian.

"You have to pray every day that Elisha will come to faith and belief. Don't ever give up. You don't preach at him, but if he asks a question, you have an answer. You know many Scriptures, and you can lead him to a greater knowledge of God. Do it with respect, because that's what God commands. No matter what Elisha does, you decide in your heart to love him with the love of the Lord. Love is a feeling and it's wonderful. But love is also a decision that will carry you through bad times." The old man gasped for breath.

"Shh. Don't use up all your strength. Thank you for telling me all these things." She wiped his brow with a cold cloth and held a cup of water to his chapped lips.

After he swallowed some of the water, he pushed the cup away. "Who else should I use my strength for but you, my precious little one? Elisha is a man used to doing hard work and living a hard life. What you can give him besides love is kindness, gentleness, admiration. He probably hasn't had much of that in his life. All men need and want that. Be sweet and kind to him." The old man paused and took several shallow breaths before he was able to continue. "Serve him well, and if he has the kind of heart that I think he has, he'll return your kind deeds a hundred fold. More than anything else, he needs to see you loving God. I know it's a lot to ask of you, but do you think you can do these things?"

"Yes, I can show him my love for God and be kind to him. You've shown me how." She leaned forward and kissed him on the forehead.

"Then I think I'll rest awhile." The old man closed his eyes and sighed.

Susana set the table for supper and waited for Elisha to return. She tensed whenever she thought about the tall, dark haired man who would possibly soon be her husband. The thoughts of how to find a way to avoid marrying this cowhand kept playing round and round.

She prayed and asked God to give her peace of mind and acceptance of this man. She sensed God's peace and felt herself relax. Taking a deep breath, she waited for her future husband to come home.

* * *

Elisha rode directly to the wagon stopping only once to rest the horses. The further east he traveled, the less snow there was on the ground. The wind had blown it away, or the frigid dry air had evaporated much of it. The Jamison's wagon stood with the white canvas of the cover sagging from the weight of the snow. Although it had only been a few days, it looked abandoned for months. He wasted no time and quickly packed everything from the wagon onto the ranch wagon. He made his way back to the cabin riding Shadow and leading the horses pulling the wagon full of furniture and things.

When he got home, he unloaded the trunks and furniture into the barn. He had no idea what Susana would do with all of the stuff, but for now, it would be under cover.

With the last trunk carried into the barn, his back went into spasms and he fell to his knees. The pain had been building for hours as he had loaded the furniture onto the wagon. Holding on to a post, he pulled himself up and stood breathing slowly until the spasms stopped. All he wanted was his old strength back and to be able to do a man's day of work. Would his back ever completely heal?

Fearful of another spasm, he lifted the small bureau and carried it to the cabin, thinking Susana could use it by the side of her bunk to keep her things in and to hold a lantern at night.

Susana swung open the door to let him enter the cabin. Her eyes stretched wide and she broke into a wide grin. "Oh, Elisha, thank you so much for bringing our things." She backed out of the way for him to place the bureau by her bunk.

Elisha liked that she was pleased. "Thought you could use it."

"Yes, it'll be very nice to have a place to put things." She opened a drawer and examined what was inside.

He hadn't thought about it being packed full. That explained why it had seemed heavier than expected. Elisha shrugged off her thanks as though moving a wagonload of stuff was an everyday occurrence. He didn't let her know of his pain and how worn out he was. Hazing cows back across the creek was a lot easier.

He went out to the barn and took care of the horses before heading back to the cabin for supper and another quiet evening with his companions. They were no longer visitors. He now had two people living at the cabin with him for the winter. It wasn't an unpleasant thought—to know someone was watching for him at the end of the day.

During the night, Elisha woke to find Susana adding wood to the stove. He could hear Mr. Jamison's harsh breathing.

"Is your grandfather worse?" He kept his voice at a low whisper.

"Yes, I'm going to warm some broth and try to get him to swallow it." She added the last log cradled in her arm, then stirred the contents of a pot warming on the stove.

"Elisha, you there?" The frail, crackly voice called through the dim light in the room.

Elisha moved closer and knelt by Mr. Jamison's bed. The old man looked almost translucent. He was dying and Elisha sensed that he knew it.

"Please, sit by the bed, Elisha. We need to talk." The old man reached up and with a surprisingly strong hand grasped Elisha's arm. "Susana, please sit down by me, but let me talk to Elisha."

Elisha dragged two chairs across the rough floor and pulled them up close to the bed so he and Susana could sit down. Then, he took Mr. Jamison's hand.

The old preacher frowned and looked at Elisha with a clear, piercing look that reminded Elisha of the look of a hawk as it searched for its prey. "Elisha, I'm dying. The only way I'll know Susana is all right is to ask an enormous favor from you."

"Sure, Mr. Jamison, what might that be?"

"I want you to let me marry you and Susana tonight." Beneath shaggy white eyebrows, the old man's eyes bore into Elisha's.

Elisha fell back in his chair. The old man's request knocked all the air out of him. He never expected such a request. He wanted to stop the old man before he said anything further, but he was numb and his mouth wouldn't work.

"When I'm dead, you and Susana will be left here alone and you're two healthy people. I can't leave my granddaughter in a situation that might put her in danger spiritually, and I can't leave you with the growing frustration of being alone with a lovely young woman. The only answer that will work is for me to marry you, and for you to promise to stay true to that." The old man spoke with an authority of one who knew what he said was the truth.

Elisha felt his face burning. What was the old man asking of him? Get married? To this girl that he didn't even know? He couldn't support a wife. Maybe someday but all he had to offer a girl now was hard work. Didn't Mr. Jamison understand that? And what would Mr. Weathers say? What of his responsibility to his boss?

Elisha was acutely aware of Susana beside him. Why hadn't she spoken up and opposed this? Maybe she liked the idea. The urge to look at her and gauge her thoughts pushed through, but he couldn't bring himself to move.

Mr. Jameson wheezed as he struggled to draw in a deep breath. "I know it's asking a lot, but look at it from my side. You're a good man. I can tell. You told me you'd never been married. You're old enough to know what you're doing. You can't find a better young lady than Susana." The old man stopped talking.

Elisha was fearful he'd stopped breathing, but then saw the slow rise and fall of the preacher's chest. Dumbfounded was the only word Elisha could think of that described how he felt at that moment. He finally glanced over at Susana, afraid of what he might see on her face. He expected shock or revulsion at the idea that she marry a cowhand she hardly knew.

Instead, she sat quietly with her hands folded in her lap. Tears spilled down her cheeks, and the muscles of her throat worked up and down as if she tried not to cry.

Elisha breathed deeply and looked her in the eyes. "Your grandfather has already talked to you?"

She returned his gaze with a calm directness. "Yes sir, today while you were out, we talked about it a lot. He thinks it's the only way to protect me. I know he's dying and I'll do what he thinks best."

"Do you want to marry me?" He had to ask her.

She looked back at him. "No, I don't want to marry you. I don't want to marry anyone. It's nothing against you because I don't know you."

"Then...?"

"But my grandfather is a wise man and he says there is no other way. I'll do what he says for me to do." Again, she blinked to hold back the tears. "Can you give Grandfather a way to get us to a town, or will we truly be trapped here for the next several months? Surely there's a way to get out of the mountains." There were deep furrows between her eyes and the distress he saw pleaded with him to find a way.

"I need time to think." Elisha turned back to the old man. "Give me some time before I give you an answer." He ran his hand through his hair in frustration.

"Yes, son, take some time to think about it. But I can't tell you how much time I have." The old man patted Elisha's arm and looked at him with almost a look of pity.

Elisha stood and put on his coat, gloves, and hat. Lighting a lantern he left the cabin and walked to the barn. He could hardly get his mind on what was happening. In the barn, he walked back and forth in the small space not taken up with stalls. The horses looked at him almost with a questioning look.

What did it mean to marry this girl? He would have to find a way to support her and could they even live in peace together? He had found her pleasant enough in the two days he had known her and she was pretty. But what would it be like to live day after day with her?

He stopped pacing and stroked Jasper's neck. "Hey, Jasper, maybe I should be asking what will it be like for her to have to live with me? What do I have to offer as a husband?" He picked up a brush and started brushing Jasper. The horse lowered his head as if enjoying the attention. "But on the other hand, what does it mean for the old man to die and the two of us to be here by ourselves? I'm already thinking about her too much. What's it going to be like with the two of us alone?" The horse looked around at him and snorted.

Elisha laid his head on horse's flank and closed his eyes. How did he make such a decision? He wouldn't tell the old man he would do it and later go back on it. When he gave his word, he kept it.

Could he get them out of the mountains? He thought of the way south to the ranch headquarters. If they had a couple of weeks with no snow, he might make it. Then he shook his head, not with the sick old man. They might all die.

No, the girl and the old man, as long as he lived, would be with Elisha at the cabin for at least four, maybe five months.

The old man was right. To marry Susana was the only way to protect the girl.

Was he man enough to do what he needed to do as a husband? He would have to try.

Elisha had made his decision ... marry Susana.

He was cold and tired as he struggled back to the cabin. It was snowing again.

Susana was sitting by her grandfather with her head on his arm. When he came in and brushed the snow off, she sat up and looked at him.

"How is he?" He struggled out of his gloves and coat.

"He is drifting in and out of sleep. He was asking for you a few minutes ago."

Elisha walked over to the stove, poured a cup of coffee, and drank it down in a couple of swallows. The hot coffee hit his stomach and gave a sense of warmth.

"I've made a decision. If you agree, I'll marry you. I can't get you out of the mountains and I think your grandfather knows that he only has a few days. If it weren't for that, I'd say we need to wait." He sat in the chair next to her. "What do you think?"

She moved her legs a bit away from his as they sat next to the old man's bunk. "If you agree, but you have to be sure. I don't want you to regret your decision later." Her words came softly. "I know it's a big thing to ask of you, a stranger."

"But how can you trust that I can be a proper husband? That I'll be good to you?" He wasn't sure of the answers himself.

"There comes a time when you have to trust that God will protect you. I think you'll keep your word. If you promise Grandfather, we're trusting you'll do what you promised."

Amazing. Such trust for a God he didn't even really know and a trust of him, an ordinary cowhand. Mr. Jamison was doing what was right as he saw it. He was trying to protect his granddaughter's honor, and trust that he was also putting her in the hands of someone who would protect her. This old preacher really was placing his greatest treasure into Elisha's hands. Did Elisha have it in him to be worthy of that honor?

As he looked at the dying old man, trying to do one last thing to care for his granddaughter, he couldn't refuse. He didn't know how he'd care for a wife and he couldn't imagine what Mr. Weathers would say when he found out.

Mr. Jamison coughed and gasped for breath. "Elisha, I don't want to rush you, but I don't know how much time I have."

Elisha really wished he knew how to pray. This wasn't something to take lightly. He took a deep breath, looked from Susana to the old man.

"Mr. Jamison, I'll marry Susana. I'll try to be a good husband to her. I promise to protect and provide for her." He couldn't believe what he was agreeing to, or what it meant for his future.

"Thank you, son. You'll be helping an old man die in peace. Susana, honey, go get my Bible."

Susana brought the well-used Bible from the bureau. She laid it in her grandfather's hands. He stroked it slowly as though it were an old friend.

"Open it up for me, Susana. Please." Susana quickly did his bidding.

"Now both of you sit real close to me." When they had both leaned in toward him, he took their hands and enfolded them over the open Bible.

"As a preacher of the gospel I now declare that Susana Mary Jamison and Elisha Evans are here with me to be joined in holy wedlock. As it was written in the book of Ruth so many centuries ago, 'Whither thou goes I will go and your people will be my people and your God will be my God.' Do you, Susana, agree to take Elisha as your husband?"

Susana didn't look at Elisha but kept her gaze on her beloved grandfather. She said softly, "I do."

"And do you, Elisha, say the same promise and agree to protect and provide for Susana as your wife all the days of your life?" The old man's voice seemed stronger.

Elisha looked at the girl next to him. When her grandfather died, she'd be alone. He didn't want that for her. He hardly knew what it would mean for her to be his wife, but he could promise to protect her. He turned back and looked the old preacher straight in the eye.

"I do," he promised.

"Then as a preacher of the gospel of Christ, and with God as our witness, I declare you man and wife." The old man intoned. "Susana, find the pen and ink, and I'll witness your marriage in the front of the Bible."

Susana went to the bureau, and then brought back a little bottle of ink and a pen. Dipping it carefully into the ink, she handed the pen to her grandfather. With an effort, he steadied his hand and wrote in the Bible under the record of Susana's birth.

"Now I want you both to sign it. You first, Elisha."

With the pen in his hand, Elisha's eyes scanned over the page and he read what Mr. Jameson had written.

I, Henry Jamison, have performed the wedding of Elisha Evans and Susana Mary Jamison this date, December 23, 1872.

Elisha signed his name, and then he handed the Bible and pen to Susana who also signed.

Mr. Jamison closed the Bible and handed it to Susana.

"Let me rest awhile, and then I got some things I want to say to you, Elisha." The old man closed his eyes and lay back.

Elisha stood and looked down at Susana, feeling as if there was something he should say to her.

She looked up at him. She seemed very calm.

"Susana, I know this isn't what you wanted, and it's hardly what a girl dreams of for her wedding. Know that I'm a man of my word, and I'll do everything in my power to protect and provide for you. I think we should take care of your grandfather for now, and talk about other things later."

"Thank you. I do believe you'll keep your promise to me, to Grandfather, and to God."

The night had faded and the sun peeked over the mountains. Elisha pulled on his coat, hat, and gloves to tend to the horses. He wanted some time alone to think. Susana didn't seem to mind that he left the cabin so quickly.

He took his time mucking out the barn. He didn't move any faster when feeding and watering the horses. The day was clear and cold. Elisha should have been out working the cattle, but he didn't want to leave Susana alone in case her grandfather died. He stood still in the barn. What difference did it make that he and Susana were now husband and wife? It didn't make any difference.

Before asking her for more than companionship, he had to give her time. He hadn't expected to have a wife anytime soon anyway, so could be patient with his young bride. Elisha had no idea what life would be like in the future, but he'd keep his promise to Susana.

Elisha headed back to the cabin. He crossed the threshold greeted by the smell of fried salt pork. A plate of eggs and biscuits waited for him at the small table. He was hungry, and thankful, as he sat at the table to eat.

Susana didn't want to eat. She sat by her grandfather's bed holding his hand. Toward the middle of the morning, he roused again and called for Elisha.

"Susana, honey, I know it is cold outside, but would you mind going out to the barn? Let me talk to Elisha alone for a while." The old man asked.

"It's a clear day, Grandfather. I'll go out for a walk." She put on her grandfather's coat and wrapped a shawl around her head. She looked over at Elisha. "You'll call me if need be?"

Elisha opened the door for her. "I promise to fetch you if he needs you." He returned to sit in the chair and waited for the old man to speak.

"Elisha, how old are you?"

"I'll be twenty-six on my birthday in March."

"Well, Susana turned sixteen in October, but in some ways, she's younger than her years. She's never been away from her folks, and they always lived a quiet, simple life. She's pure and innocent. You understand what I'm telling you?"

"I think I do, Mr. Jamison. You're telling me she's still a child in some ways, and not yet introduced to being a woman." His face heated as he spoke.

"Good, you understand. How about you, Elisha, do you have a lot of experience with women?"

"No sir, I don't." It was the truth. He definitely liked women but had never wanted to visit the women in town like some of the other cowhands. His mother's voice had been with him urging him to treat women with respect always.

"Well, let me tell you how to keep a woman happy."

Elisha wasn't sure what the old man was about to tell him. He didn't know if he was ready for what was to come. He shifted in his chair as if bracing himself.

"Her grandmother and I were married for over fifty years, and I can tell you some things." The old man smiled at the memory of his wife and began to talk.

Elisha was amazed at the detailed and intimate advice the old man gave him. The old man encouraged Elisha to be gentle and patient with his young bride. He asked him to take his time when demanding of Susana what he had a right to ask as a husband.

"She's so young and all this has been a shock to her. Give her some time, and I promise you, the wait will be worth it." The old man barely got his words out. "You know, Elisha, the word gentle in the original Greek language means strength under control. You're a strong young man, but when it comes to your dealings with your wife, you keep that strength under control. Always be kind, gentle, and patient with her."

"I promise you I'll treat her with respect and patience." Elisha could tell that the old man was tired, as his breathing seemed more difficult. "Let me call Susana back in, so she can sit with you."

He went to the door and called to Susana who came in, hung up her coat, and then sat by her grandfather.

Through the rest of the day and into the night, the old man gradually sank into a restless sleep. It was as if the effort to make sure Susana and Elisha were married had used up the last of his energy.

Elisha sat in the chair next to Susana, not talking, late into the night.

About midnight, the old man stopped breathing.

Elisha braced himself as Susana realized that her grandfather was gone.

She sobbed as she stroked her grandfather's face. "Oh, Grandfather. What am I going to do? What am I going to do without you?" She fell against his chest, hot tears falling onto his lifeless body, her whole being shaking with sobs.

After a few minutes, Elisha put his arms around her and drew her close to him.

She resisted at first and then collapsed against him as she sobbed.

He didn't have the words to comfort her. But sensed that she had to release her grief, which had been a palpable thing in the cabin for her grandfather's last hours on earth.

Elisha rocked Susana for a couple of hours as she cried off and on. Finally, she wore herself out with her grief, and he felt her slump in his arms and he looked down to find she had fallen asleep. He brushed the hair that was wet from her tears back from her face, glad that she slept. At least for a time, she wasn't feeling the terrible pain of the loss of her grandfather. He could barely stand to hear her cry and he wanted to make it all right for her. As he remembered his own grief at the death of his mother when only a boy, he knew nothing would make it all right, not for a long time.

Elisha stood with her cradled in his arms and looked at her face, now calm in sleep. Was this beautiful creature truly his bride? Gently he laid her onto her bunk and then covered her with blankets.

He combed the old man's hair and beard, and then wrapped him in a blanket. In the morning, he and Susana would need to bury her grandfather. Digging a grave through the snowy, frozen ground would be quite a job, but Elisha had to do it. He didn't know what shape Susana would be in when she awoke, but he'd ask her, as gently as he could, where she wanted the grave.

He glanced at the calendar, Christmas Day. He wouldn't mention what day it was until Susana spoke of it.

Elisha spread out his bedroll, then he lay down in front of the fire, but he didn't sleep. He'd keep a vigil and be there for Susana when she woke and realized it was not a bad dream. Her grandfather was dead and she was married to a cowhand. He shook his head, still not quiet believing that he was married. He couldn't imagine how it would seem to Susana. It wasn't how he had ever envisioned getting married.

Elisha pushed himself up from his bedroll at dawn. He put on the coffee as Susana stirred in her bunk. Her muffled cry tugged at his heart. She must have remembered that her grandfather had passed in the night.

Elisha took a few long strides and was by her side. He sat on the side of the bunk, took her into his arms, and rocked her again. Her tears moistened through his shirt at the shoulder. He let her cry until she grew quiet. He looked down at her.

She met his gaze, her eyes red and puffy.

"Are you ready to talk about burying your grandfather?" The look of pain on her face was awful for Elisha to take, but he had to ask.

"Yes, we have to do it, and grandfather would want us not to take too long." Her voice was muffled, as she pressed her face into his chest.

"I've got some ideas of where to dig the grave, but I want you to choose. Let's get our coats on, and go look for a place. You decide, and then I'll start digging."

"I'm sorry that you have to do it by yourself. We keep making difficulties for you."

"You know I don't mind doing this for your grandfather. He was a good man."

After putting on their coats and gloves, they walked out to a spot above the cabin, below the ridge toward the west. It was on a slight rise with a grove of trees around it. Susana nodded. This would do.

Elisha gathered wood and placed it where he would have to dig. After feeding the hot fire for an hour, he raked the hot coals away from the ground hoping it had thawed enough. He got his shovel and pick out of the barn, and began to dig. It took him most of the day to thaw the ground, dig it out, and then start the fire again. It became easier when he got below the freeze line in the ground

Susana sat by her grandfather's body in the cabin and waited while Elisha worked.

The sun was low in the western sky when they carried the old man's body wrapped in a blanket across the snow and lowered the corpse into the grave. Breathing heavily, Elisha and Susanna stood looking down at her grandfather's remains.

She handed Elisha her grandfather's Bible. "Would you read Psalms twenty-three and then read from First Corinthians chapter thirteen?"

Elisha fumbled through the pages and found the twenty-third Psalm. He began to read, "The LORD is my shepherd ..." He read it to the end

Elisha could imagine the old man nodding as he listened to the Psalm being read. He understood why Susana wanted him to read it because it fit the faith of the old man.

He flipped the pages of the Bible until he came to the book of First Corinthians and found chapter thirteen. Again, he began to read aloud. "Love is patient, love is kind.... It always protects...Love never fails." As he read he wondered if the words describing love was for the old man or for him.

Elisha looked over at Susana. He hoped he read it in a way that was appropriate.

She sobbed quietly into her handkerchief.

He took her hand and held it as he prayed aloud, "God in Heaven, we send this fine, old man, Henry Jamison, to you. Take him in and take care of him. Be with Susana and me. Help me protect her and take away her grief. I don't know what else to say, God. You know me. I'm not used to praying. Help me take care of Susana. In the name of Jesus, Amen."

Letting go of Susana's hand, he handed her the Bible. "You should go back to the cabin while I fill in the grave." He hated for her to have to see it being filled in. The temperature was also too cold for her to stand around outside.

"May I simply stand here?" Her voice quivered on the edge of sobs.

"Of course, I'll hurry." He shoveled the dirt into the grave, covering the old man's body. He looked up at Susana. He couldn't blame her for wanting to stay with him. The cabin must be too empty for her now.

Elisha was exhausted after he finished filling in the grave and his back had been in spasms off and on all afternoon. Also, he hadn't had anything to eat through the day. He asked Susana if she'd prepare something while he took care of the horses. She agreed and made her way to the cabin while he went to the barn.

When he stepped into the cabin, Susana had put a meal of oatmeal and biscuits together. Elisha sat down and ate without talking. When he finished, he put on his coat again and opened the door to leave.

"Where are you going?" She stood by the table, wringing her hands.

Elisha heard the panic in Susana's voice. "I need to get some more wood and fill the water bucket. Go ahead and clear up the supper things and by the time you're finished I'll be done too."

Elisha carried in several loads of wood because he'd let the woodbin get low. He brought in two buckets of water. He was so tired he swayed on his feet and he didn't know how much longer he could stand with the searing pain across his lower back.

He gripped the back of a chair to steady himself. "Would you like for us to read some out of the Bible?" That wasn't what he wanted. All he wanted was to lie down, and finally get some rest, but he didn't want to leave Susana sitting by herself.

"Thank you, Elisha. If you don't mind, I only want to go to bed. It's been a hard day."

"I'll be right here if you need anything." Elisha pulled his bedroll down from the loft and rolled it out on the floor in front of the fireplace. Susana didn't say anything about him using the bunk where her grandfather had died less than twenty-four hours before. He'd let it ride for a few days, and then probably start using the bunk. For this evening, he'd sleep on the floor again. After adding a couple logs to the fire, he pulled the blanket up to his chin and was soon asleep.

* * *

Susana dressed for bed. She had to admit that she was relieved. She had been afraid Elisha would want something from her now that her grandfather was gone. Pulling the covers up and curling into a tight, little ball, she cried softly, missing her grandfather, and in fear of what was to come.

Elisha had the right to come to her bed anytime. Would he come that night? Then she heard him breathing beyond the curtain. He was asleep. Maybe she had some time yet.

She understood why her grandfather wanted her to marry this cowhand, but what would her life be like now? It scared her to think of being a wife.

Then she remembered one of her mama's favorite verses from Timothy, "For God hath not given us a spirit of fear, but of power, of love, and of self-discipline." Susanna acknowledged her fear. She whispered in the dark. "Get thee behind me Satan. God will be my power and love and He will see me through even this marriage."

During the night Susana woke to a strange sound, as if the cabin was moaning. She lay listening and then she heard it again. It was Elisha moaning in his sleep. She wondered if she should get up and see if he was in need some way. Maybe he was having a nightmare. Then she heard him get up and add more wood to the fire. Why would such a strong man be groaning in his sleep? There was so much she didn't know about this man who was now her husband.

* * *

The next morning Susana was silent and Elisha let her be. The cabin seemed much quieter now that the old man was gone. Elisha needed to get back to his work, but he couldn't leave Susana alone in the cabin, not yet. It would be too lonely for her and he couldn't forget the look of fear when he had left the evening before to get wood. No, he couldn't leave her all day alone in the cabin.

As he finished eating he said, "I've got to ride out and check on the horses in the box canyon then patrol along the creek to the west. What do you think about riding along with me?" He hoped the suggestion wouldn't offend her. It wasn't what a young girl normally would do.

Susanna looked at him across the table. "I'd like that, if I won't be a bother."

"No, you won't be a bother. In fact, it'll be nice to have someone with me. Could you pack us some food to take with us for our dinner? And you need to dress as warm as you can. It gets cold sitting in the saddle. While you're getting ready I'll go saddle the horses." Elisha put on his coat, gloves, and scarf and then headed out to the barn.

He saddled Shadow for himself and Jasper for Susana, as he was an easier ride. He didn't know what to do about a sidesaddle for Susana. He only had his saddle and the one from the Jamison's, which was a regular one. She had ridden well enough when he had rescued them and he assumed she was willing again to ride astride.

When he came back to the cabin leading the horses, she came out. She was dressed in her brown dress with the baggy pants, wooly chaps, and boots. She had also put on her grandfather's coat and gloves. The outfit was much more practical for riding than just her dress. Elisha managed not to grin, as he found her to be cute as a button in her riding outfit.

Elisha helped her mount her horse. He checked the length of the stirrups and then adjusted them. "Stay up close behind me and let the bay have his way. He knows how to herd the cattle. You be sure to stay in the saddle." Then he mounted Shadow.

Elisha first rode to the box canyon and checked on the two horses there. The day passed quickly as he trailed and drove back the cattle that had drifted north of the creek. He kept a close watch on Susana and was pleased to find that she was an experienced rider.

Susana let the bay have his head and work the cattle. Not once during the long workday did she complain but followed his lead.

Elisha turned toward the cabin a couple of hours before sundown so they could get back before dark. He didn't want to make the day too hard for Susana.

* * *

Susana had been both exhilarated and terrified with the day of riding, although it wore her out. She wasn't about to tell this man she was tired. It helped to be out in the fresh air and not sit in the cabin thinking of her grandfather. And what it meant to be married to this man.

Off and on all day she thought about the fact that they were now married and that he had certain rights. Several times that day she had tried to push away the worry, but it always came back—like now. As they headed back to the cabin she thought of a way that might help discourage him from demanding of her what she didn't yet want to give—she'd get the other bunk ready for him. Maybe he would be content with that. She dismounted at the cabin door, and Elisha took the horses on to the barn.

* * *

When Elisha came inside, Susana had pulled the mattress off the bunk where her grandfather had laid. She pulled it to the door.

"Here, what are you trying to do?"

"I want to get this outside, empty it, and put fresh hay in it. There is no reason for you to sleep on the floor when there is a perfectly good bed. But it needs some fresh hay."

"Oh. Well, let me do that for you." He took it from her, carried it out to the corral, and emptied it, then filled it with fresh hay. He carried the mattress back into the cabin and placed it on the bunk.

Susana nudged him out of the way and made up the bed with the blankets she'd shaken out.

Elisha sensed this was something she wanted to do for him, so he backed out of her way.

He was relieved that he didn't have to sleep on the hard floor. It also told him that she wasn't ready for any other sleeping arrangement. He had promised to give her time and he would keep his promise.

CHAPTER SEVEN

Elisha carried Susana's trunks into the cabin. It took several trips from the barn as she had four of them.

Susana looked up from washing down the table when he entered the cabin with the last trunk. Her eyes opened wide, she dropped the dishrag, and put her hands together like a child presented with a gift.

He grinned as he set it down in the middle of the cabin. "Put your things wherever you want. And if I can do something, tell me what to do." He rubbed the small of his back.

"Thanks. It'll be good to have my things around me."

"I don't mind helping. It makes for something different to do than chasing cows."

"Do you mind bringing in the rocking chair?"

"That's my next trip from the barn." He strolled to the barn and hefted the rocking chair from the wagon. After the heavy trunks, it was light and easy to carry.

In the cabin, he set the rocker down by the fireplace.

Susana stood by the table and unpacked one of the trunks. White china dishes with little red and blue flowers painted on them sat on the table.

"What do you want to do with the dishes?" Elisha walked over to the table and picked up a dainty cup. He carefully placed it back on the table afraid it would break in his hands.

"I'm not sure where to put the china. They do make a bright pretty look."

Elisha glanced around. "What if I hang some shelves there by the fireplace?"

"Oh, that would be nice."

Elisha went back to the barn and found a couple of boards and nails. He returned to the cabin and nailed the shelves up on the wall, attaching support pieces underneath. "You want me to help you put up the dishes?"

Susana carried several china dishes to the shelves and began to place them. "Yes, if you will bring them to me, I'll arrange them."

With some trepidation, he picked up a stack of plates and handed them to her. The feel of her fingers as they slide across his as she took them left a tingling. As he handed china plates, cups, and saucers to her, he took his time and handed them piece by piece. The sensation of feeling her touch was too tempting to hurry. He then moved to the tea set. Susana gave him no indication that she was reacting to his touch.

Elisha looked at bright, colorful dishes and the rocking chair by the fireplace. He smiled. It felt like a home. The first time he had felt like he had a home since before his parents had died. He remembered the warm safe feeling of sitting by the fireplace watching his mother prepare supper. Hoping Susana didn't notice he wiped his eyes that were suddenly wet.

Susana closed the trunk. "Would you put this empty trunk up in the loft? Or, wherever you think would be a good place to store it."

"I think for now the loft might be best." After locating a place for it, he climbed down the ladder to find Susana making a dried apple pie.

"Making a pie?" He grinned, as he smelled the cinnamon she sprinkled over the dried apple slices.

She smiled back. "I thought maybe you earned a sweet for all the work you've done today."

"That sounds like good wages for very little work." His mouth salivated at the thought of the pie.

The cabin had a more homey air. Not at all like the bunkhouses where he had spent his last twelve years. Those had been bare, crowded, and dirty. This was so much better, all because Susana was there. Elisha sat in the rocking chair by the fireplace and watched her move about the cabin. He liked having her there, and the constant feeling of loneliness receded.

* * *

During that first week after her grandfather's death, Susana tried to hide her crying from Elisha, but especially in the long evenings, she couldn't stop the tears from flowing. She noticed that when she couldn't hold the tears in that Elisha would duck his head and get busy with braiding on a hide rope that was an ongoing activity. But he would look up at her in quick glances and frown as if he wanted to say something but couldn't find the words.

She missed her grandfather, but his passing also brought back the grief of her parents and siblings all dying from diphtheria within a week of each other. Each night she cried herself to sleep missing her family and waiting for Elisha. A part of her dreaded his coming to her bed, because of her fear of what it would be like. Would he be kind and gentle? Would he expect her to know more how to respond to him than she knew? Then, again, she wondered if her grandfather was right and that there would be a time when she would be eager for Elisha to come to her and claim his pleasure. But he didn't come.

Glad that Elisha let her ride out with him to work the cattle, she didn't know what she would have done all day alone in the cabin.

Elisha told her about the trees, animals, and land, which made their time interesting as they rode out each day. As she asked questions, he revealed more about himself and the work he had done working on ranches and taking herds to the railways.

Thankful for her health and strength, she found the work tiring but not excessively and it made it possible for her to sleep. The first few nights the nightmares came and she woke in the dark with a sense of being alone. Then she would hear Elisha's steady, deep breathing as he slept a few feet away. She began to take comfort in the sound. He promised to give her time and to protect her, and so far, he had kept his word.

They rode out each day over the next week as the weather held clear.

After they sat down to eat breakfast at the end of the week, Elisha said, "Today I think we should stay around the cabin. I need to do some work in the barn and get more wood chopped while we have a break in the weather."

"Oh, that would be great. I can clean the cabin. Do you have anything bigger than these pots? I need to wash some clothes."

"There's a wash tub in the barn. I'll bring it in." Elisha looked around the cabin. It looked clean to him, but he wore the same shirt for the third week in a row. "I'll go get the tub."

When he brought it into the cabin, she clapped her hands in delight. "Why didn't you tell me you had a sit bath tub? I've so wanted to bathe. Now we both can have one." Sparkling green eyes and a broad smile told of her delight and brightened the whole room.

He should have brought the tub in to her sooner, but with all the work, he hadn't really thought about it. And, he sure could use a bath, as he hadn't bathed except for a spit-bath since the creek got too cold to go for a swim.

Susana had him put the tub by the fireplace. "Let me get some clothes washed first. Then we bathe." Susana handed the bucket to him. "Do you mind bringing in the water?"

Elisha took the bucket and grinned. "Do I need a bath that bad?"

Susana smiled. "Yes, you do, and so do I."

He carried buckets of water into the cabin and Susana washed their clothes with the lye soap Elisha had brought up from the ranch. She hung their clean clothing to dry on the guide rope between the barn and cabin. Although they initially froze, the dry mountain air soon caused the clothes to begin to dry.

They emptied the tub of dirty water off to the side of the yard.

With his back aching more with each bucket of water, he poured the last one into the tub.

Elisha's gaze fell upon his wife. She would want privacy. He cleared his throat. "I have work to do in the barn." He backed toward the door, grabbed his coat, hat, and gloves off the hooks, and quickly stepped out of the cabin.

"I'll call you when it's your turn." She yelled after him as he bolted along the path to the barn. The definite hint of laughter laced her voice and followed him like a fluttering bird.

Elisha busied himself mending a piece of frayed brow band on one of the bridles. No sense dwelling on what was happening in the cabin. He took the brow band and cut it loose from the ring. He folded it back around the ring, then started to sew it back together. But his thoughts slipped back to the cabin. Would Susana dip her toe into the water to test its warmth? Or would she step into the tub? A flush rose up his neck to his cheeks. Shaking his head to get his mind back to the bridle, he kept his thoughts under control for a few minutes before they slipped back in the cabin. It wasn't wrong for a husband to think such things, but the guilt still weighed in on him. He had too much imagination. He took a tighter hold of the leather and jabbed the needle through with a harder push. Ouch. The end of the needle had penetrated his thumb. Elisha found himself going back and forth between thoughts of the bathing tub and trying to repair the bridle. After an hour, Susana called to him. With a sigh, he tossed the bridle down. It still wasn't repaired.

He too wanted privacy for his bath, but didn't know exactly how to tell Susana. When he entered the cabin, he didn't see her, then realized she was behind the curtain. The steam still rolled through the air above the tub of hot water.

"If you don't mind, I'll sit here on my bed." She spoke from behind the curtain. "It's too cold to be outside with wet hair."

"All right." Elisha hurried to shed his clothes. He couldn't remember bathing with a woman in the same room since he was a very small boy. Another thing he'd have to get used to, not that he wasn't willing to try.

Being in the same room without a stitch of clothing on brought an urgency to rush through his bath. He wasn't sure whether his face flushed from the hot water or from his thoughts. For a married couple to be so shy with one another was indeed a strange thing. But someday, maybe one day soon, that would change. He could hope.

He relaxed in the hot water as his muscles loosened and some of the ache in his back diminished. After he had bathed and rinsed off, he stepped out of the tub, dried off with the towel Susana left for him, and then dressed in the clean clothes. She had brought in a shirt and pants for him, although the pants were still slightly damp.

He ran his fingers through his wet hair. "I'm finished with my bath."

Susana pulled the curtain back, and stood before him with her hair still damp and hanging loose. He'd only seen her hair in a braid, until now. Undone and freshly washed, its soft brown and gold color tantalized him. Her tresses flowed down her back almost to her waist. Elisha caught his breath. He had never seen anyone so lovely.

As if she could read his thoughts, Susana ducked her head and quickly busied herself with cleaning up the clothes he'd dropped on the floor. She then wiped up water they had both spilled.

Elisha stood there, watching her move. Then getting control of his thoughts, he fetched the bucket and emptied the tub out into the yard. He figured that with a woman in the house his frequency of bathing was sure to increase so he stored the tub in the loft.

His mind started to wander the same paths as earlier, but he shook the thoughts off. How would he keep his thoughts under control and honor his promise to her grandfather? He needed to keep his word, he just hadn't known how hard that might really be.

As Susana started supper, Elisha went to the barn to take care of the horses. On his way back, he stopped and gathered the dry clothes, and took them into the cabin. He lowered his face and sniffed the bundle in his arms. The clothes had a fresh, clean smell to them.

Susana stood by the stove stirring a pot of stew. "You didn't have to bring in the wash. Here, put the clothes on the bunk. I'll put them away."

"I was already out in the cold, so there's no need for you to get cold also." He took his coat, hat, and gloves off. He stood with his back to the fireplace and his hands behind him to warm them. The smell of the stew bubbling on the stove and cornbread baking was enough to set his stomach to growling. He noticed with regret that she had braided her hair again.

"Well, thanks anyway. Go ahead and sit down. Supper is ready." She placed the pan of cornbread on the table next to the pot of stew.

Elisha marveled at how natural it felt to have a beautiful woman, his wife, prepare food for him. A bath, laundry done, and fresh cornbread—what more could a man want? Well, there was more. But he'd promised to be patient.

After they'd eaten supper, Susana walked over to the shelf of books and pulled the Bible off. "Would you read to me?"

"Of course. What do you want me to read?"

"Would you finish reading the book of John?"

He finished reading the book of John and then they went to bed, each in their own bunk.

* * *

That night Susana turned over again trying to find a comfortable spot in her bed to relax and fall asleep. Thoughts of the day's events flooded her mind: being around Elisha as he helped with filling the tub, watching Elisha bolt out of the cabin with his cheeks flaming red, and listening to the mellow deep sound of his voice as they exchanged small talk. She enjoyed the calm day of getting chores done and being around Elisha. She admitted to herself that she was growing to like this man. But did he like her? She didn't know, as he didn't talk about his feelings.

Over the last week, they talked about their lives. What her grandfather said was true. Elisha had had a hard life growing up. He had received very little kindness or gentleness. He responded so quickly to any fun and laughed easily with her. As she did each night, she waited for him to come to her, but he didn't. Did he not want her there? Did he regret marrying her? Did he not like her or think her a little bit pretty? He didn't even seem to want to kiss her. As she lay in her bunk, listening to him breathe in his sleep, she was glad he gave her time, but his eyes at times seemed to be saying something different.

She had seen him look at her with such a longing gaze, as if he wanted to reach out and touch her, that she somehow knew he saw her as a desirable woman. However, he made no move toward her. She remembered him holding her and rocking while she sobbed. His arms had felt safe and secure. She lightly touched her lips. What would his lips feel like on hers? With that thought, she drifted off to sleep.

For the first time Susana woke before Elisha. She dressed and then began to prepare breakfast. She looked at him lying sprawled out on his bunk and realized it was the first time she had seen him asleep. His black, curly hair was all tousled, much like that of a little boy. The urge to go over and push his curls into some sort of order rushed through her, but she kept her feet planted where she stood.

Her gaze roamed over his face. High cheekbones rested above a strong jaw and chin. As he lay asleep on his stomach, his broad muscled shoulders were evident beneath his undershirt as the blanket only covered him to his waist. She thought of how he looked riding or chopping wood, tall, over six feet but with a slender frame with the narrow hips of a rider and broad muscled shoulders. She even found his faint smell of sweat, horse, and lye soap very masculine. He was truly handsome with his well-shaped eyebrows and long, dark eyelashes. His dark curly hair matched his dark brown eyes. Did he know how handsome he was? She was amazed, and she realized with surprise, happy that this man was her husband. If he would only tell her how he felt about her.

She turned back to the table and taking the dough she had mixed up the evening before and left to rise overnight, she began to knead. She sang softly to herself, and then heard him turn in the bed.

* * *

Elisha woke and stretched. It had been a good night of sound sleep and he could feel the difference on his back. The bath definitely helped.

Susana was already up and preparing breakfast. She was at the table kneading bread and singing softly to herself an old hymn, "Amazing Grace."

As Elisha lay listening to her, memories flooded him of his boyhood. His mother had sung in the kitchen every morning as he woke up to the smell of fresh coffee.

Susana flipped the dough and continued to knead it in a pushing motion away from her body.

Elisha watched the calm way she worked and felt such a need to provide for Susana and to keep her safe that tears come to his eyes. He shook his head. Why did he have such strong feelings from hearing her singing a song? He wiped his eyes. When he looked up, he found his wife watching him.

With a calm, serene look, she stood for a few moments gazing at him, and then she smiled. "Morning sleepyhead. This is the first morning I've seen you still abed with daylight come."

"Morning yourself." Elisha realized the truth of what she said.

Susana turned back to her kneading.

He swung his feet to the floor. He had his drawers on but no pants! Jerking the covers back up to his chest, he grabbed the pair of pants and overshirt lying at the end of the bed. Under the security of the covers, he pulled his clothes on. Only after he'd dressed did he throw back the covers. He glanced toward Susana to see if she was watching him. With a sigh of relief, he found that she was busy with her bread making. He stomped into his boots. Had she seen anything? Why he was concerned he didn't know, because he'd be all right with her seeing him.

He poured hot water into the basin to wash and shave. As he looked in the mirror, he caught a glimpse of Susana standing by the table watching him with a look of gentleness, like he had seen on the faces of cowhands as they cared for their favorite horses that had been injured. There was a slight smile on her face as if she saw something that pleased her. Not having much experience with girls, he wasn't sure what it meant, but maybe he could start showing her how he felt about her. He was startled at his thoughts. When had he begun to care about her so much – to love her maybe? And could she ever come to love him? He pushed the thoughts aside. It was still too soon.

Elisha pulled himself from the cabin to the barn using the rope that had become a lifeline. It was the only guide in the blowing snow. Once inside the barn, he shook the snow off his coat. The horses were doing well. Their body heat kept the barn at a reasonable temperature. He gave them water and feed.

As he petted the horses and let them nuzzle his face, Elisha worried about the horses left in the box canyon, but they would probably be all right.

Elisha fought to keep his feet as he made his way around to the east side of the cabin where he had the wood stacked to the roof. He slapped his gloved hands against his chest to get some circulation going in his fingers. The howling wind made it seem colder than it really was. He was glad he hadn't let Susana leave the cabin during this second major snowstorm with such bitter cold. It was an effort for him to go back and forth to the barn and to bring in wood. He filled his arms with as much wood as he could carry.

Before Elisha entered the cabin, he stomped his feet to get the snow off his boots. Then he pushed open the door and walked inside. "It's a cold day and the snow is up to the eaves on the west side of the cabin." He told Susana. "Except to get wood, or take care of the horses, we're pretty much snowbound. I can't even go check on the cattle until this wind dies down. You can't see where you're going."

"Then we'll stay in today. You can read a book aloud for me." She tilted her head.

"Can't you read?" He stacked the wood by the fireplace.

She smiled as she put the last of the breakfast dishes back on the shelf. "Of course I can read, but it's more enjoyable to hear you read."

"How far did you get in school?" He got one of the books down to read to her. He didn't mind reading aloud, but was curious about her life.

"I never really went to school much, but both my parents taught me. I had a lot of schooling, always at home. Mama would have us do chores in the morning, and then after dinner we studied for a couple of hours. Papa taught us to do our sums."

"Your folks must have been educated people." She talked some of her family but not much and he didn't ask because it seemed to pain her.

"They were. What about you? How far did you get in school?" She finished washing down the table.

"I got to go to school for about three years off and on, but that ended when I was twelve and my folks died." Even now, he could hardly bear to think of that sad, lonely time.

"You were twelve when your parents died? Where did you live after that?" Susana hung up the dishcloth and came over to the table.

"A neighbor family took me in for a couple of years and I worked for my keep on their farm." It sounded simple but it had been backbreaking work from before dawn until late evening. "Then I hired on with a rancher when I was fifteen. I've worked cattle ever since." For some reason he wanted to tell her things about himself he usually didn't talk about. She had a way of leaning forward with her eyes opened wide, as though what he told her was the most interesting thing she'd ever heard. He liked that.

She sat at the table across from him. "I've never read much, except for the Bible. We didn't have many books. Of course, there was no money to buy any."

"As I worked different places and met different cowhands, there was always someone wanting to trade a book. So I got to read a lot." Elisha looked over to the shelf of books. "And now with Mr. Weathers encouraging me to read his books, I can't get enough." He picked up the book.

Susana sat with her hands folded on the table and smiled at him. "I'm glad because I like to hear you read."

Elisha opened the book, The *History of the Decline and Fall of the Roman Empire* by Edward Gibbon. He wasn't too sure it was something of interest to Susana, but he enjoyed learning of history and faraway places. He began to read.

She sat and listened with occasional nods and frowns as she followed the reading with apparent interest.

He read a couple of chapters before returning the book to the shelf.

Susana went to her bureau, and from one of the drawers pulled out a small delicately carved box. She placed it on the table in front of Elisha. "Do you know how to play chess?"

"No, I've watched men in the bunkhouses play it, but I've never learned. Can you teach me?" He hoped he could learn to play the game. As he watched cowhands play, it always looked difficult.

"Grandfather and I played a lot. This was his set. His father brought it over from England." Susana unfolded the small board and set up the pieces.

Elisha enjoyed listening to Susana's warm voice explaining the chess moves and pieces. Elisha was enthralled with the animation of her hands and the light in her lovely green eyes as she explained the movement of the chess pieces. He wanted to reach out, and take her hands into his and tell her how he felt about her. But he was afraid of how she would respond. How could he know when she was ready to hear of his feelings? With a sigh he brought his thoughts back to the game, which he wanted to win. Susana was always a couple of moves ahead of him. They spent the rest of the day without Elisha winning, but he felt rewarded by hearing her laugh.

The next evening after supper, Elisha lingered over a second cup of coffee.

Susana cleared the dishes and washed them. She then sat at the table with her own cup of coffee. "Tell me what you think you'd do if you no longer worked for Mr. Weathers."

He raised his eyebrows. Should he tell her of the land to the northwest? After all, she was his wife. "There's land north of here that I'd like to claim someday to start a place of my own."

"That sounds like a good idea. Tell me about it." Susana leaned forward holding him in her gaze.

The shine in her eyes and the way she leaned in to hear him encouraged him to go on. "It's located north up behind the ridge about ten miles. I want to build a house there and buy some cattle." He ducked his head after he finished speaking. He had no way to make those dreams come true.

"Tell me more about the land, Elisha."

He looked up at her and told her about the large valley with the springs and creek running through it. Then about the other two valleys that ran further west. "No one seems to have found it yet. If I can get it in the next couple of years it would make a great ranch."

"How big a house will you build? And you will have to build a barn and corrals, of course."

Elisha stared at her. Susana didn't see it as a dream, but as a reality. As he began to talk about the possibilities with her, it seemed more real for him. What Susana lacked because of her youth, she made up for in her enthusiasm. She probably didn't realize the years of hard work it would take, but she seemed to have no doubt that he could do it. Someone believed in him. And that filled his heart with confidence that one day he would have his ranch.

~ ~ ~

The end of January had warmed, although the temperature held below freezing during the day.

Elisha was content with Susana riding out with him. He feared it was too much work for her, but he wouldn't have left her day after day by herself at the cabin. Their working together was not only useful, but enjoyable for him. As he thought back to his fear of spending the winter along, he wanted to laugh aloud at how different things were now that Susana was there by his side.

They were able to patrol most of the area he was responsible for by putting in long days. They didn't find many cattle north of the creek, which he attributed to the wind having been mostly out of the north, and the cattle would have drifted more toward the south in front of the wind. It was hard, cold work and hard on the horses.

They had had five days of clearer weather, and he decided to ride east of the cabin. The wind kicked up and the temperature started dropping. Elisha brought his horse to a stop and looked around. He glanced over at Susana who sat quietly on her horse waiting for his guidance.

There were no sounds and even the birds were silent. The horses had their heads up and ears pointed forward as if on alert for something. The clouds rolled in from the west. Elisha looked at his young bride who sat shivering in the saddle. They needed to get to the cover of the cabin as quickly as possible with no time to waste.

"The weather is about to close in on us. Keep up close behind me, we're heading back," he yelled back to her. He kicked Shadow in the ribs and heard Jasper following behind them. He had to get Susana back to the cabin and safety.

By the time they got back to the cabin, the snow fell as thick as a drawn curtain and the temperature had dropped at least thirty degrees.

He helped Susana out of the saddle. "Get into the cabin, and stoke up the fires. I'll take care of the horses."

"All right, but please hurry." Her teeth chattered. She pushed through the cabin door and closed it behind her.

As he finished with the horses in the barn, he heard a noise out at the corral. He went out to find the brown mare and the gray gelding standing there with their heads hanging down and their rumps to the wind. He didn't know how they got out of the box canyon, but was glad because he sensed the weather was about to turn dangerously cold. For a few days, it wouldn't hurt to have all six horses in the barn, adding their warmth together. He led them inside, and he could have sworn they seemed grateful to enter their stalls.

Elisha pulled himself along, glad he had the rope to guide him to the cabin. The snow fell so thick that he couldn't see the cabin from the barn. Covered with snow and shivering uncontrollably, he staggered into the cabin and slammed the door behind him.

Susana rushed over to brush the snow off. "Sit by the fire in the rocking chair." She then poured him a cup of hot coffee and handed it to him.

"Thanks," he said when he could talk without shivering. "I'm afraid we're in for a cold one."

"Yes, I can feel it coming under the door and in from around the windows. This is the coldest I've felt in the cabin. Here, let me have your coat and gloves, and put this blanket around you." After she wrapped the blanket around Elisha, she felt his hands and cheeks. "You feel like ice. Move closer to the fire."

A tingling started in his belly at her fussing over him. He warmed at the feel of her soft hand on his cheeks. He wanted to take her hand, press it to his cheek, and hold it there. Instead, he wrapped the blanket tighter around himself and watched the sway of her skirt as she turned to get another blanket off her bed.

His stare continued as she pulled the blanket up around her shoulders and wrapped it around her slender body. He turned his head away, but he wanted to look back at her. He had to put his mind on something else.

Susana put out the plates and cups. "I'm glad I made enough stew yesterday to last us a couple days. It'll be hot in a few minutes and will warm us up." She served the hot stew, then took the warm cornbread out of the oven.

They sat at the table still snuggled tight in their blankets. On impulse, Elisha reached over and took her hand as he bowed to ask the blessing for the meal. He also asked for protection for themselves and the horses through the storm and thanks for the warm safe cabin. After he'd said amen, Elisha held Susana's hand for a few seconds longer. She hadn't pulled away, her small soft hand rested in his large calloused one. He released it, and then picked up his fork to eat. But his eyes remained on hers, and for a lingering moment they held one another's gaze.

As they ate, the windows shuddered against the heavy gusts of wind. After dinner, Susana cleared away their plates, and then Elisha read to her from the Bible for a while.

With the weather being so cold, Elisha suggested they go to bed to get warm. He took the smooth, flat stones, each about the size of a loaf of bread, and heated them by the fireplace. He wrapped them in a wolf pelt and placed one at the foot of each of their beds under the covers. When they went to bed, at least their feet warmed.

Through the years, Elisha had developed the ability to tell his mind to wake up every few hours to feed the fire, and tonight it would be a necessity. He'd need to keep both the stove and the fireplace burning. With all the wood he'd stacked up on either side of the fireplace over the last few weeks, they could last several days without bringing in more. Elisha would still have to go out and care for the horses in the morning.

Elisha fell asleep thinking about the touch from Susana's hand on his cheek.

* * *

Susana lay in bed and kept her feet against the wolf's pelt, which warmed them. But the rest of her body was cold. She pulled the blanket tighter around her shivering body and slid her hands under her arms to warm them enough to fall asleep. Thoughts of the last month drifted through her mind. She enjoyed sharing the cabin with Elisha. They worked hard, and she was often exhausted, but they also had fun. She liked that he always thanked her for her cooking and seemed pleased with the help she gave him driving the cattle. She often found herself doing things to see his smile. He could look so serious sometimes, but when he smiled, well, it lit up his whole face, and he was just plain handsome.

The cold air came in a draft through her blankets. Susana shivered unable to stop. She hadn't enough covers on her bed the whole time she'd been at the cabin. She hadn't said anything to Elisha, but this night she was so cold, she couldn't ignore it any longer. His body would be so warm, if only he wasn't so far away in the other bunk. How nice it would be to curl up against him and let his body warm hers.

She heard him get up and put more logs on the fire. Their fire never went out. He did everything with such ease and grace of movement. She liked to watch him ride because the movements of his body were fluid as he maneuvered his horse.

Why was she thinking such thoughts? She wasn't sure, but she couldn't go to sleep because she was too cold and his warm body was so close by in the next bunk. Elisha's rhythmic breathing told her he'd fallen back to sleep.

Well, it's silly to lie under too few covers and die of cold. What would happen if she went to his bunk and asked to share it with him? He might think he could claim his pleasure. What if she let Elisha kiss her and to touch her? Her stomach did a flip of excitement at the thought. Well, eventually it would happen, and it might as well be now. After all, he was her husband. Maybe it would be easier if she went to him instead of waiting, as she did every night.

Lifting up a prayer that God would be with her and give her wisdom, Susana slid from under her blanket, padded quickly across the cold floor, and knelt by Elisha's bunk.

She shook his shoulder. "Elisha, wake up."

CHAPTER EIGHT

Elisha awoke in the dark to the sound of Susana calling his name. "What is it? What's the matter?" He rose up on one elbow. The glow from the fireplace illuminated her soft outline. What was she doing kneeling by his bunk? Was she sick?

"I'm so cold, I can't get warm. May I bring my cover and get into bed with you?" Her soft voice made the request sound so simple.

Suddenly wide-awake, he pulled his covers back. "Sure." He pushed himself out of bed and stood next to it, cold air rushing over his body. He tried not to stare at her as she stood there in her thin nightgown. "Here, you're shivering. Get in bed and I'll get your covers. I need to feed the fire anyway."

Dressed in his long johns and socks, Elisha watched her curl up in his bed as he put the covers back over her. He grabbed the thin quilts off her bunk and threw them over his own. He was surprised how little she had. A pang of guilt stabbed through him for not noticing her lack of sufficient covers. No wonder she was cold.

Elisha moved quickly for the air in the cabin was well below freezing. He added logs to the fireplace and stove. When the flame was ablaze, he hurried back, and slid under the covers trying not to touch Susana, but truthfully, that was all he wanted to do.

* * *

Susana snuggled down beside him, the bed luxuriously warm from his body.

Elisha lay on his side away from her as if he hesitated to be close to her in the narrow bunk. What she should do? Shifting a little, she inched closer to him and felt the warmth of his body. She hesitated then slid her hand until she felt his arm, and pulled it toward her body, wrapping it around her waist. The warmth radiating from him felt wonderful. His arm around her waist gave her a surprisingly secure feeling. It tightened ever so gently around her. She felt his chest moving with his breathing. Then there was a soft touch on the top of her head as he kissed her hair. She looked up at him and could make out his face in the firelight. His dark eyes gazed at her with a look of one wanting.

"May I kiss you, Susana?" His voice came to her smooth and deep.

Was this the time that he would ask for his rights as a husband? Was she ready? She nodded.

He lowered his face and his lips gently brushed across hers. Then, he pressed his mouth to hers.

* * *

Elisha couldn't believe she was actually in his bed, his arm around her body, and he had kissed her. Did he dare hope that they could now become truly man and wife? He wanted to engulf her in his love, but he also wanted to hear she was ready.

"Are you all right for me to love you?" He didn't know of any other way to ask her.

She looked up at him with a clear gaze. "Is that what my grandfather called taking your pleasure?"

"I suppose it is." Elisha smiled. "I would really like to take my pleasure, and to give you pleasure."

"Yes, I'm ready." She returned his smile.

Slowly and cautiously, Elisha began to make love to his bride, and she with the inexperience of innocence responded to his love.

~ ~ ~

Elisha woke with his arm asleep from holding Susana, but he didn't want to wake her, so he lay still. The pre-dawn grayness brought a slight glow of light into the cabin. Through the window, he watched the snow fall. The memory of the night before flooded in and he wanted to shout for joy.

The fire was a bed of hot coals. He needed to add wood. Even with the fires burning, Elisha could see his breath misting in the cabin's cold air. Moving as quietly as possible, he slid out of the warm bed and rushed to throw logs in the fireplace, making sure they caught by nesting them in the hot coals. He then fed wood to the stove. The logs started to sizzle and pop. The water in the bucket on the floor not far from the stove was frozen. He pulled it closer to the stove to melt. By the time he was done, his teeth chattered uncontrollably. He turned back to his bed.

Susana, awake, held up the covers, inviting him back.

He slipped back under the covers and enjoyed the warmth of her body pressed next to his. They didn't talk, but lay there holding each other. Elisha couldn't remember a time when he'd been more blissfully content.

Susana relaxed. Her breathing evened out and she drifted back to sleep.

Elisha lay awake and watched her. He found himself tracing her eyebrows with his finger and pushing back some curls from around her face. Her hair spread over the pillow. He remembered the night before when he had loosened the braid and ran his fingers through her hair. He wanted to bury his face in it now, but caught himself. Had it actually happened? At first he'd thought it must be a dream, but seeing her invite him back to bed as she had and the way she snuggled against him, assured him it had been no dream.

With a sigh of regret, he slid out of bed and dressed. Time to start his workday.

Fortunately, he had the horses to care for, because he needed to get out of the cabin and think about what had occurred during the night. He felt his spirits soar. He had wanted this to happen but didn't know how to bring it about. Her coming to his bed felt as if she had given him a gift. They were now truly husband and wife.

Even with two sets of clothes, his coat, gloves, and wrapping his hat on with a wool scarf, the penetrating cold wind between the cabin to the barn was like icy fangs penetrating his flesh. He pulled himself along the guide rope to the barn through four feet of snow.

The horses looked at him with misery in their eyes. The barn was cold, but with their long, winter coats, they would survive under shelter. The wind blew from the north, and he hoped the cattle had drifted south and that none had gone north of Pinto Creek. Between the wind, cold, and snow he couldn't have reached them, and even if he did, there was nothing he could do for the animals in this frigid weather.

The water coming into the barn flowed as usual, which amazed Elisha. He gave each of the horses a bucket of water and some fresh hay. Getting back to the cabin was easier since the wind blew against his back and pushed him along. He was eager to get back to Susana.

When he entered the cabin, the temperature difference between the outside and inside was enough almost to make him lose his breath with the relief of getting out of the cold. The thermometer that Mr. Weathers had given him showed twenty degrees below zero.

Susana was dressed, but still had a blanket wrapped around her.

He stood with his back leaned against the door, the snow melting off his hat, coat, and boots. Never had he felt such cold.

"What's the matter?" Susana rushed over to him with a look of concern.

"Sooo coold," was all he could get out, as he was shivering so hard.

"Oh my, let me help you." She tugged off his gloves and his hat, and then rubbed his icy cold hands. "Your hands are frozen. Here, turn around and get out of your coat." She pulled off his coat.

"Go on and sit by the fire. I have the coffee made; I'll get you a cup."

Elisha moved the chair close to the fire, sat, and stretched his hands out to the heat.

He smiled his thanks when she brought the cup of hot coffee, then wrapped his cold fingers around its warmth.

"This could get to be a habit." As cold as he was, a warm feeling filled him at having someone who truly welcomed him home.

Susana returned his smile and let her hand rest on his cheek. "It's the least I can do to help when you have to go out in such bitter cold. I made some oatmeal and biscuits. Are you ready to eat?"

"Always." Elisha laughed. "Haven't you noticed?"

After breakfast, they played a game of chess. Susana won. There wasn't a lot they could do with such cold, except stay in and pass the time. Elisha thought it would warm up some with daylight, but the cold was unrelenting.

After dinner, Elisha took the book, *Travels to the Westward of the Allegany Mountains, in the States of the Ohio, Kentucky, and Tennessee, in the Year 1802* off the shelf.

"Would you like for me to read to you from this book? We haven't read it yet."

"Yes, that'd be nice, but could we wrap up in our blankets in bed? It's too cold to just sit."

Elisha looked at her. "Sure." Spending the afternoon lying next to his wife sounded like a fine idea to him.

He added logs to the fire and the stove and lit the lantern. The cabin grew darker as the clouds thickened. He took one of the stones he'd reheated and wrapped it in the wolf pelt.

Susana already lay under the covers of his bunk with her back toward the wall.

Elisha put the heated stone under the covers, then sat on the edge of the bed and pulled off his boots. Holding the book, he slid under the covers.

Susana snuggled comfortably into the curve of his arm with her head on his chest. "Now read to me."

They spent most of the afternoon taking turns reading aloud to each other. It seemed so natural to Elisha to lie there with Susana's head on his chest.

Later that afternoon Elisha gathered some of the old newspapers that Mr. Weathers had sent to him and stuffed them around the edges of the windows to seal them against the cold air. He had meant to do it for several days but with so much work, he had not gotten around to it. He also put a wolf pelt at the base of the door to try to block any drafts.

~ ~ ~

The bitter cold lasted for six days, and Elisha needed to check on the cattle. But the weather was too severe to take Susana out in such cold, and he didn't want to leave her alone at the cabin. The thermometer registered around thirty degrees below zero in the mornings. So, they stayed home and passed the time together reading, talking, playing chess, and loving each other.

Their food lasted, although Elisha would need to do some hunting in the next few weeks to supplement it with some meat. He still hesitated to kill one of Mr. Weathers' cows, but Elisha would not be surprised to find some frozen cattle after the storm. In the meantime, he and Susana were relatively warm and well fed.

During the next week, Elisha woke in the mornings with more contentment than ever before. He wanted to tell Susana that he loved her, but he had never declared that to anyone, not since he was a small child, and that to his mother. He wasn't sure he knew how.

A few mornings after they had truly become husband and wife, Susana woke and smiled up at him. "Morning, my love."

Elisha swallowed the lump in his throat. "Morning, my love." There, he said it. How simple it had been. The overpowering sense of wanting to provide for her and keep her safe filled his being.

"I do love you, Elisha." She reached up and pulled his head down so she could kiss him.

"And, I love you." He kissed her back.

He couldn't believe how easy it was to say to her that he loved her. And he meant it. Elisha hadn't fully understood the depths of his solitary existence until Susana filled his life with her love.

He remembered the chapter on love, the one Susana had him read at her grandfather's burial. He reached to the shelf above their heads and pulled down the Bible.

"What was that chapter you asked me to read at your grandfather's grave?"

"You mean the one on love?"

"Yes, that one. Tell me where to find it."

"First Corinthians thirteen. Will you read it to me?"

Elisha flipped the pages until he found it. As he read it aloud, he realized more than ever what it said about how to love someone. He wanted to have that kind of love for Susana.

Elisha remembered that dark night when Henry Jamison had asked him to marry Susana. He often thought of the wisdom of the old man's words and the gift he'd given to Elisha and Susana by leaving them free to share their love without guilt or reservation.

~ ~ ~

Elisha marked the calendar Susana had made for them from a notebook. He carefully crossed out the date, February 15th, and then slide into bed.

Susana snuggled close. "How long will winter last? I've never been in the mountains in winter before."

"Well, we're in the middle of February. Last year we had an early spring. I came up here the first week of March and the snow was almost all melted. But I don't think it will come that early this year." Elisha pulled the covers up closer around the back of her neck.

"How can you tell?"

"I can't really. I have a sense that we'll have more cold weather yet."

"Well, I hope you're wrong. I'm tired of being cold. I'm ready for spring."

Elisha wrapped his arms around her and pulled her tight. "In the meantime, let me keep you warm."

* * *

Susana found herself smiling often. Being loved by her husband had opened a whole new world for her. She truly felt like a wife and she noticed that Elisha seemed much more relaxed.

The continued cold and snow was a challenge and she liked the days when they stayed at the cabin. There wasn't much she could do to expand the meals she prepared, but Elisha didn't seem to mind. He appreciated whatever she prepared for him with a word of thanks.

She had fallen in love with this cowhand. It surprised her how easily it had happened. And he loved her. She could only give thanks to God for the blessing of such a good husband, one who was kind and gentle to her. More than anything, she wanted to show Elisha her love for God, and help him to come to believe and trust. It gave her such comfort and she wanted that for him.

"What you thinking about?" Elisha sat by the fireplace braiding a rope with narrow strips of hide.

His question startled her from her deep thoughts. "I was thinking about how much has happened in a few months."

He stopped his braiding and looked at her. "What were your thoughts?" His dark eyes widened and a furrow appeared between his eyebrows.

She realized he wasn't sure what she thought of the direction their lives had taken. "I was thinking that although I miss my grandfather and wish he could be here to share my happiness, that I'm having the best days of my life, now, here with you." She moved over to stand by him and put her arm around his shoulder as he sat in the chair.

He put his arm around her waist. His look cleared and he smiled. "I definitely can say this is the best time of my life."

Susana looked at his glittering dark eyes and broad smile. He looked so happy. It gave her a warm feeling to know that she had something to do with that.

He tightened his hold around her waist. "I know a lot has happened and that it's been hard on you."

"No harder than it's been on you. It's different than anything I've ever done before but I find that I like riding out and working the cattle and I do it well." She grinned at her bold statement.

"Yes, you're a good cowhand." He drew her around until she sat on his lap. "When I met you at the wagon looking like a boy, I never would have thought you would be working cattle with me. Or, that you would be married to me!"

"But God knew his plans for us and I am so thankful that you rode into my life that day." She kissed him softly. "Don't you think it's time for bed?"

* * *

After another week of being snowbound in the cabin except for tending to the horses, Elisha made the decision to ride out. The sky was clear even if the temperature was single digit and the world was snow covered. It was already the third week of February and winter showed no signs of going away.

He braced himself as he sat at the table drinking another cup of steaming hot coffee. Susana was clearing up the breakfast dishes at the dry sink.

"I'm going to ride west for a couple of hours. I should be back by the middle of the afternoon."

She swung around and glared at him. "What do you mean? Shouldn't you be saying we are riding out?"

Elisha took a deep breath. This is what he had feared. "It's too cold for you to ride out with me. You stay here in the cabin where it's warm. I'm sure you can find plenty to do."

"Staying warm is not the problem. I can't bear to be here all alone all day with you gone." She pushed some stray curls back from her face. "No, I'm coming with you."

Frustrated at his need to keep her safe, he really wanted her with him. "Now Susana, I'm the man and I decide. You're not going."

She came over to where he sat at the kitchen table. Putting her hands on each side of his face, she kissed him until he could feel it to the bottom of his feet. When she finally released his lips, she said. "I'll wrap some sandwiches and meet you at the barn. You go saddle the horses."

So they bundled up and rode with the intent of checking along Pinto Creek. Elisha was learning the strength of resolve that his little woman was made of. He wasn't sure what they could do if he found cattle in distress.

Elisha turned in the saddle and yelled back at Susana. "Stay up close and try to keep Jasper in the trail that Shadow is making through the snow."

She waved at him and he thought he saw a smile but it was hard to tell with her face partly covered by the wool scarf tied over her hat and under her chin.

Up ahead he saw a couple of cows up close to some big boulders protected by trees. As he surveyed the area, he decided that they were as sheltered there as anywhere and he bypassed them.

As they rode up a ways from the creek through the forest, it was easier going for the horses. The snow had not accumulated as deeply but they risked the occasional clump of snow falling from the tree branches and landing on them.

Elisha noticed that Shadow had his head up and ears pricked. From behind, he heard Jasper tromping skittishly and then snorting. He jerked his head around trying to see what disturbed the horses.

A scream filled his ears as a weight knocked him from his saddle. As he hit the snow covered frozen ground pain exploded in his lower back. But there was no time to even react for as he rolled in the snow, he recognized that he had a mountain lion rolling with him. Putting his arm up to protect his face, Elisha felt the searing clamp of iron jaws locking on his arm through his coat and shirt. As he struggled to keep the animal from getting loose from his arm, he tried to reach his revolver with his other hand. If the cougar got loose from his arm, his throat was the next target. He felt streaks of pain from his leg where the back claws of the animal carved their way down his thigh.

The low growl of the fury of the cat filled his ears along with screams from Susana. When his strength started to fade, he managed to grip the revolver with his free hand and brought the gun up pressing against the light-cinnamon colored fur. He pulled the trigger repeatedly, the sound of the gunfire drowning out even Susana's screams.

The weight of the big animal relaxed against him and the jaws gave up their hold on his arm. Breathing hard in the cold air, Elisha lay for a moment to get a hold of himself. It had happened so quickly and unexpectedly that he was only now hit by the fear. Susana? What had happened to Susana?

He pushed the dead mountain lion away and struggled to his knees in the snow. Again he felt a weight on him, only this time it was his wife's arms hugging him with more strength than he would have guessed her capable.

"Elisha! Elisha! Are you all right?" She then held his face between her gloved hands with tears running down her face.

He put his uninjured arm around her. "I'm all right. A little torn up. How about you?"

"I'm fine. Only it scared me so bad. What is that?" She looked at the dead animal.

Elisha struggled to his feet pulling her with him. "It's only an old mountain lion who thought he had found his dinner." He wanted to make light of it to relieve her fear. His arm throbbed through the feel of wetness that was his blood. They needed to get back to the cabin and out of the cold. Only the thickness of his coat had saved him from more injury from the claws of the cougar. He shuddered to think what might have happened if the animal had gotten his jaw loose from his arm. The mountain lion was a good five and half feet long and probably weighted close to a hundred pounds.

She had tied Jasper's reins to a tree branch. "Did you see which way Shadow went?"

"He took off toward the cabin, I think." She stepped back from him and then seemed to notice for the first time the blood soaked tears in his coat sleeve. "Elisha, you're hurt."

"Yeah, that old lion got his teeth into my arm pretty good. Can I use your scarf to wrap it until we get back to the cabin?"

She took the scarf off and wound it tightly around his arm. "Are you hurt anywhere else?"

Elisha looked down at his leg, where blood ran down his left pants leg where the feet of the mountain lion clawed through the fabric to his flesh. He reached down, picked up a large handful of snow, and packed it against his leg.

"Let's ride double on Jasper and get back to the cabin. Probably Shadow will be waiting at the barn." He mounted the saddle after calming Jasper down some. The horse trembled, as the smell of the cougar was strong. With his uninjured arm, he helped Susana swing up behind him. She encircled his waist with her arms as if she would never let go again.

"It's all right, honey. We'll make it back to the cabin and you can help me bandage my arm and leg." He could feel her shivering against his back.

"What if I had lost you? Oh, Elisha, what would I do if anything happened to you?" Her voice sounded full of tears.

"You're not going to lose me. I'm not going to be easy for you to get rid of, ever."

Jasper struggled to make it through the snow with the extra burden. Elisha had to pay attention to follow the tracks left by Shadow through the forest. It took an hour to get back to the cabin where they found Shadow standing at the barn door, waiting for them.

"I hate to ask it, but would you put up the horses? I'm a little lightheaded." He feared he would pass out before he got into the cabin.

"Let's get you inside and take a look at your arm. The horses will be all right for a few minutes." Susana slid off Jasper holding onto the stirrup. "Can you dismount?"

He kicked his feet out of the stirrups, and using his one good arm, lowered himself to the ground. His left leg didn't seem to want to hold him but he managed to stagger into the cabin leaning on Susana's shoulders. Susana guided him toward the bed and he slumped down onto it, his head reeling.

"I'd feel better if you would put Shadow and Jasper into the barn. There might be other critters after us." He wished he could eat his words. A wide-eyed look of fear flooded Susana's face. "There's probably no worry. Don't look like that, honey."

"I'll get the fires stoked up and then tend to the horses. You rest 'till I get back." Her voice subdued, she quickly placed logs on top of the coals in the fireplace and the stove.

After she left the cabin, Elisha unbuttoned his coat. Carefully he slid the coat from his bleeding arm, his teeth clenched at the pain, both from his wounds and his lower back. The fall from the horse had stirred up spasms that he had hoped were behind him.

It was easier to tear the bloody torn shirtsleeve off and throw it on the floor, but he pulled his undershirt over his head. The clearly defined teeth marks on his arm oozed blood. The flesh around the marks was swollen and angry red.

Susana came back into the cabin, bringing with her a blast of cold air. "The horses are unsaddled and happily munching hay. Now let's take care of you." She took her coat and hung it on the hook by the door.

Elisha sat on the edge of the bed, watching his beautiful young wife as she gathered clean rags and soap, and poured water into the kettle to heat. What if that attack had killed him? What would she have done? He hadn't told her how to get down to the ranch. She needed a map just in case. Getting control of his thoughts, he made himself breathe slowly and relax. Fear and pain could get him in knots quicker than anything. And he was afraid, not for himself, but for this woman he had promised to protect.

Susana spread a flour sack towel on the table. "Can you walk enough to sit by the table? I can take care of your arm better there."

"Sure." He slowly got to his feet and feeling more than a little woozy, fell onto the seat. "If you can clean it up and wrap it tight, it should be all right."

She examined the teeth marks on his arm. "Some of these are clear to the bone. I'm so thankful it wasn't worse. Now hold still while I wash the wounds and wrap it up, and then I'll do the same with your leg."

Elisha took his mind off the pain of her washing the arm, then the leg wounds by watching her move, and noticing how the light reflected off her hair. As Susana knelt beside him and finished tying the bandage on his thigh, he placed his hand on her hair and stroked it.

She looked up at him with wide-eyed seriousness. "How do you feel?"

He lifted her chin and bent to kiss her. "I'm tired and a little shivery. I think I'll lie down for a while." He kissed her again. "It's worth getting bit by a mountain lion if you're going to take care of me."

Susana smiled at him. She jumped up and pulled him to his feet. "Come on and lie down. I'll get some dinner going, you rest and eat, and then you'll be all right."

Elisha had meant to simply rest a bit and then go make sure the horses were all right. But he fell asleep.

It was dark outside when he woke, and he had slept the day away. His arm throbbed and felt swollen.

Susana set in the rocking chair by the side of the bed. She stitched on his coat sleeve that she had evidently washed of the blood and dried.

When she noticed that he was awake, she asked, "How are you?"

"I'm all right." He didn't want to move and if he was truthful with her, he felt awful.

Susana reached over and placed her hand on his forehead and neck. "You have a fever. Let me look at your arm." She put aside the coat and sewing kit. When she unwound the bandage around his arm, it revealed a swollen forearm with angry looking flesh around the puncture wounds.

"What can we do for the fever?" Elisha asked.

"I'm not sure but you need to stay in bed and let your body heal. For your arm I'm going to make a poultice after we soak it in hot water to try to draw out the infection."

Susana took a towel and dipped it in hot water boiling on the stove. Using a piece of oilcloth to keep the hot wet cloth away from his chest, she wrapped the hot towel around his arm then wrapped it with the oilcloth.

Elisha wanted to yell at her to remove it at first as it hurt like the dickens, but as his skin got somewhat used to the heat, the arm began to feel better.

After several minutes and the wet towel had cooled, she removed it, then placed a poultice of bread soaked in hot canned milk on the wounds and wrapped them with the oilcloth.

"We should leave that for several hours and let it draw out the infection and inflammation." She pulled the blankets up over his chest and arm.

Elisha hated that she had to take care of him, but until the arm healed there wasn't much he could do and he had to admit that taking a few days to rest was what his back needed.

* * *

Susana was scared as she looked at her young husband lying in the bed. He was the strong one and to see him hurt twisted at her heart. She tried to think what her mother had done for fever when she was a child. Then she remembered the apple tea.

They still had several apples wrapped in straw among the foodstuff. She peeled and cored three of them and placed them in a pan of water on the stove and let it come to a simmer. When the apples were nice and mushy, she carefully drained the water through a thin piece of clean cloth into a fruit jar.

Hearing muttering from Elisha, she turned from the table to see him slinging the covers off and twisting around on the bed. She moved to the bed and put her hand on his forehead, which was hot to the touch.

He looked up at her with fever bright eyes. "I'm so hot."

"Yes, your fever has gone up. Let me get a wet cloth." She took a cloth and wet it in the water from the bucket she had brought in from the water trough. It was icy cold. She laid the cloth over Elisha's brow and eyes. "How does that feel?"

He seemed to relax. "That's better. Sorry to be such a bother for you." His voiced was slurred.

"Who else should I take care of?" She took some of the apple tea that was still hot, added some honey, and sat down on the bed next to Elisha.

"Here, drink some of this. It'll help." She helped him raise his head and held the cup to his lips.

"That's tasty," he said after a few sips, "What is it?"

"It's apple tea. My mother used to make it for the children to drink when they had a fever." She blinked back tears at the memory. How she wished for her mother now.

He sipped on the apple tea until the cup was empty. He lay back down, then he began to shiver.

Susana pulled the covers back over him and watched as he drifted off to sleep.

The next three days were hard for Susana as she took care of her hurt husband, feed and watered the horses, and prayed. But on the morning of the fourth day Elisha woke with no fever.

"How do you feel?" She smoothed the hair back from his brow.

"Like I might survive that old mountain lion. I'm weak this morning but hungry." He did look much better to her.

She examined the wounds on the arm and thigh. They had started to heal and were no longer red and inflamed. Her prayers of thanksgiving continued for several days.

Soon he was up and about, as if the attack had not happened. The only reminders were scars. He unsaddled the horses, fed them, and rubbed then down with an old feed sack. Susana was preparing supper. All afternoon he had been thinking of what he should do to protect Susana if something happened to him.

After he finished his supper, he got the tanned hide map out and a piece of paper and their pen. "Sit at the table with me."

Susana put the dishcloth down and sat at the clean table. "What is it?"

Elisha took her hand. "I don't want to scare you but after this last week, and the cougar, I need to know that you can get to the ranch headquarters without me."

Susana gripped his hand and looked at him with wide unblinking eyes. "Why would I go to there without you?"

"I might not be able to go. Something might happen to me. You know there is always that chance. I just need to know you have a map and good directions."

She shook her head. "This is a waste of time. Nothing is going to happen."

He grinned at how fiercely she spoke, as if that would make it so. "Indulge me. It's important to me."

Still frowning, she nodded. "All right, if it will make you feel better."

"Okay, let's look at the map first." He showed her all the landmarks he could remember and how far from each one. "If I had thought I would have to explain it to someone, I would have paid more attention on my trips to the ranch. Now repeat back to me how to get there without looking at the map."

"I really won't need to know this, but all right." She repeated what he said to his satisfaction.

"Now let me describe exactly who works at the ranch so you will recognize them." He described each person at the ranch.

"I'm not going to have to use this map because nothing will happen to you." She prayed that was the truth.

"Well, just in case I want you to have it." He handed her the map.

"Thank you for wanting to take care of me. I appreciate it." She carefully folded it and put it in the top drawer of the bureau with the intent that she would never use it.

CHAPTER NINE

Cold held the land prisoner until the last week of February. They rode out and searched for cattle as they could. But Elisha made it short days and returned early to the cabin to try to protect Susana from the weather. Every time they rode out Elisha kept a watch on the clouds and the animals to warn them of the next storm.

On the last day of that month, Elisha awoke to the sound of dripping water. When he opened the door, a warm Chinook wind blew from the southwest. It had pushed the temperature above freezing. The snowdrifts started to melt and little streams of water ran off the downward slope to the creeks.

"Susana! Susana! The snow's melting! Get up ... get up. Winter's almost over!"

Elisha grabbed Susana's hands, pulled her out of bed, and they danced and twirled around the cabin. "We'll be free of the cabin!"

Of course, the clear day was likely a reprieve. No doubt, they would have more snow before spring made a permanent appearance, but for now it was melting. Elisha's gaze roamed across the snow covered land outside. He only hoped that they'd seen the last of the arctic cold.

They packed a lunch and headed out to check on the cattle to the west. Elisha tried to put the cougar attack out of his mind, but found himself anxiously watching for tracks. But he didn't mention it to Susana. He saw no sense in both of them worrying about it.

Following cattle tracks in the snow, they rode into the breaks that led up to the ridge. There they found bunches of cattle that had drifted north. The cattle huddled up against the ridge, heads facing away from the wind. Elisha and Susana hazed them back to Pinto Creek, but when they got there, they found the creek running full from the melting snow.

"We can continue to bunch the cattle by the creek." Elisha looked out over the valley. "I think there should be enough grazing to hold them in the area."

"How long until the creek falls and we can herd them across?" Susana kept her horse close to Shadow.

"Well, if we don't have any rain they should be able to cross in two or three days."

A movement to his left caught his attention and he turned quickly. A wolf ran through the trees. He pulled his rifle out of the scabbard. "I am going to try to kill those wolves or they'll get at these cattle. Stay here and I'll be back soon."

Elisha listened to the creak of his saddle as he rode slowly into the trees and stopped. Nothing moved in the icy silence and for a moment sat his horse while his breath made puffs of steam in the cold air. Then, he swung down. His boots crunched in the deep snow and Elisha stood there, his Henry repeating rifle heavy in his hands. Then, with a loud click, he chambered a cartridge into the barrel.

Something moved in the brush ahead of him and four big wolves edged through trees toward a small bunch of cattle up against the creek. Elisha threw off his gloves and braced the rifle against his shoulder. He would only have one shot per wolf, if that, before they would disappear back into the forest. Steadying his grip and lining up the sight, he pulled the trigger as fast as his finger would work.

Pow-WHOOP of the rifle was loud to his ears but the forest and snow quickly absorbed the echoing vibration. As the sound died away, four wolves lay dead with blood staining the white snow red. His breathing was rugged from having held his breath and his hands shook from the suddenness of the shooting. He put on his gloves and sheathed the Henry.

He regretted having to kill the fine animals, but if not culled, they would kill more cattle than the ranch could afford to lose. Elisha had several pelts curing on the barn wall, since the wolves over the last several months had been numerous—which told him that they'd had plenty of food the year before. Hurrying in the cold, Elisha skinned the wolves and packed the skins on the back of his saddle. Other animals would take care of the carcasses.

Then he rejoined Susana where she waited for him by the creek.

She had bunched the cattle closer to the water. When she heard Shadow coming from the forest, she turned Jasper toward him. "You got them?"

He noted that her eyes were wide and her face pale, and he regretted that she was out in this cold waiting while he killed and skinned the wolves. But he didn't know what else to do. "Yeah, I got them. For now that's all there are, I hope." He maneuvered Shadow until he could reach out and touch her face. "I'm sorry to have left you here waiting."

"No, that's what you needed to do. It seemed like a lot of rifle shots. I'm not used to animals being killed."

"Let's head back to the cabin. We've done enough for today."

~ ~ ~

The warmer weather held for several days before the sky filled with gray clouds and the snow returned. During those days, Elisha and Susana rode out and worked the breaks and canyons to the west and south of the cabin. Elisha looked toward the blocked snow-filled high passes up over the mountains. He was eager to ride up through the pass into the big valley with Susana.

Elisha enjoyed working with Susana by his side, and the days passed easier, even though there was much to do. Susana was surprisingly resilient for such a small person, but Elisha was fearful that she'd do too much. He was amazed at how responsible and protective he felt for her.

Susana was quick to point out things of interest and to find enjoyment and laughter in the workday. He liked to hear her laughter floating through the air. Even if he didn't know what amused her, he found himself smiling just at the sound.

Elisha rode up next to Susana. "What are you laughing at now?"

"See those rabbit tracks, they were so cute as they managed to run across the snow. I had to laugh." Susana smiled at him. "Don't you find rabbits cute?"

"Well, that's not exactly how I've normally thought of them, so I'll take your word for it." Elisha grinned at her bright, animated face. Laughing over rabbits, who would have thought of such a thing.

When the temperature dropped, the run-off from the snow decreased and lessened the creek's flow. Elisha took the opportunity to push the cattle south of the creek. He hadn't thought much about the ranch headquarters in weeks while he'd been so enthralled with Susana and coping with day-to-day necessities. However, with the coming change in the weather, his boss would expect him at the ranch. He'd need to go as soon as the winter weather broke enough for the passes to clear for travel.

What would his boss think about his line rider having found a wife, and such a young one, during the winter? Elisha didn't know if Mr. Weathers would even allow him to keep his job now that he was a married man. Many of the ranchers didn't want married riders. Depending on the snowfall, Elisha figured he had about a month before he was due at the ranch. Mr. Weathers had stocked him up with enough food for one person. He wouldn't know that Elisha needed to stock up again so desperately.

Elisha made the decision not to share any of his concerns with Susana. Glad that the way south was still block, he wanted to enjoy the time they had together before they had to face the outside world.

~ ~ ~

At dawn one morning toward the end of March, Elisha and Susana were in bed holding one another. The weather had warmed and Elisha threw the covers back. He looked at his beautiful wife lying so peacefully with him.

He pushed back a strand of hair from her face. "Do you know what today is?"

"It's Saturday, the 28th of March, I think." She looked up at him with a puzzled frown. "You want me to look at the calendar?"

"No, it's the 28th of March. It's also my birthday." He grinned at her. "I'm twenty-six today. How's that for an old man?"

Susana sat up in bed and punched him on the shoulder. "Why didn't you tell me? We've got to plan a celebration."

Elisha laughed. "You being here with me is the best celebration I could have."

"I'll think of something special for supper."

"Well, I'd planned to start east and move cattle. Isn't that special enough?"

"Oh, you!" Susana sat up and swung her bare feet down to the floor.

He pulled her down to him. "Don't I get a good morning kiss for my birthday?"

"You get more than that." She smiled and gave him his first birthday gift of the day.

~ ~ ~

Even though they got a late start, they spent the day riding east, herding cattle. When they got back to the cabin, Susana fried the last of the venison with the last of the potatoes and onions, then made biscuits. The flour bin was almost empty. For several weeks, they had been out of sugar, so she couldn't bake a cake. She opened the last two cans of peaches as his special birthday treat.

"It's time that we talked about my reporting in at the ranch." Elisha finished the last of the peaches and licked his spoon. "We're low on grub and Mr. Weathers is probably past expecting me." He didn't want to go down to the ranch. Married life with his bride was too enjoyable, but he had to go.

Susana's brow creased as she shot him a look of concern. "You do plan for me to come with you? You aren't going to leave me here alone, are you?"

Elisha laughed. "Honey, I wouldn't leave you behind for anything you can name." He took her hand. "Whether you know it or not, you and I are tied at the hip from now on, and it would take a lot for me to decide to leave you behind."

"Then that's all right." She smiled and gazed into Elisha eyes with a look of one who had no doubts of his protection, and gave her full trust. "When do we go?"

Elisha inclined his head. She didn't understand that Mr. Weathers might not be pleased that she was with him. He decided not to tell her and they would deal with things as they came. He didn't want that look of trust to change.

"Let's plan to leave the day after tomorrow if the weather holds. Tomorrow I'm going to work on the barrier to the box canyon. We'll need to leave the extra horses there. I don't want to take the wagon this trip. I don't know what shape the trail's in. We'll each lead a horse, and if we need more pack horses when we come back I can get them at the ranch."

"What do we need to take?" Her eyes sparkled.

"Clothes and food for two or three days. We need to dress warm. The trail through the hills will probably still have some snow on it."

"I'll stay here at the cabin tomorrow and wash clothes. And I think we should both bathe tomorrow since we're going visiting." Susana was in high spirits.

Elisha laughed at her. "Those old boys down at the ranch won't care if we have on clean clothes or if we bathed the night before."

"Well, I care, Elisha Evans. We'll dress in clean clothes and our hair will be shining." There was sternness to her voice that he'd never heard before.

Elisha expected to hear her foot stomping on the floor as she put it down. He got up and gave her a big, swinging hug. "You tell me what to do and I'll do it."

Susana laughed as Elisha swung her in a circle in the middle of the cabin. "All right, so I'm excited about seeing people and taking a trip."

Elisha set her on her feet and looked down into her animated, smiling face. She looked like a little girl promised a treat. For months, it had just been the two of them, cooped up in the cabin and he had been so content with no regard of what it might be like for her. Guilt tagged at him that he hadn't stopped to think that she might miss having other people about. He couldn't have done any different, but at least he should have realized what she might be going through.

He got the tally book and pencil, then the notebook and the pen and ink, and sat down at the table. "We need to have this in order to show Mr. Weathers the work we've done. He'll expect us to have our lists ready. I'll list the tools and supplies for the work. If you don't mind, you list what we need as far as food." He told her about the large storerooms.

What would Sam Weathers think about Susana? He ran his hand through his hair, then rubbed the back of his neck. Then Elisha had another thought that made him want to forget the trip. Where would they sleep? Susana couldn't stay in the bunkhouse, and he couldn't assume they could stay in the ranch house. He thought of the barn loft and decided that for a couple of nights they could manage there.

What if Mr. Weathers fired him? His stomach felt queasy. Elisha sat looking at his list without seeing it. Mr. Weathers owed him at least three hundred dollars, counting the money he'd asked his boss to hold for him. Susana had a little money from her grandfather, but he wouldn't let her touch that except for special things she wanted for herself or for their own home someday. That was her money, and he'd provide what she needed from his work. They could manage if they had to for a while, but it was not enough to start their own place with any cattle.

Elisha wrote a couple items on his list and then sat and chewed on the pencil. What did he want to happen with Mr. Weathers? He looked around at the cabin and then at Susana who was busily writing a long grocery list with the pen and ink. He wanted to come back to the cabin and work for Mr. Weathers another year and save his money. In another year, he might be able to save as much as six hundred dollars all together. Even though six hundred dollars wasn't a lot, it was more than most young couples had to start with.

His father had provided for his family by working the farm. Elisha determined to provide for Susana one way or another. Even if it wasn't what he wanted to do, there was nothing wrong with being a farmer. Elisha looked at his rope-calloused hands. He was a cattleman, and working with cattle and horses was all he'd ever done since he left the farm many years before. He put the list and pencil away. His thoughts wouldn't settle on making the list of supplies.

Elisha lay awake far into the night, holding his sleeping Susana in his arms as he contemplated what the future held for them. He'd always gone from job to job, only responsible for himself. How differently he thought now that he was responsible for Susana. She'd become a grown woman during their time together, but he still thought of her as young and vulnerable.

She seldom spoke of her parents or of her grandfather, except to tell stories from her childhood. Susana seemed at peace with the loss. He thought that her belief that they would all be in heaven together someday gave her that peace. And he found himself more and more comforted by such a thought.

As he lay in the dark next to his wife, he realized that she was now his family and he was hers. It was a new thought to think that he had a family, and someday they would have children. Elisha wanted to have children, more for Susana's sake than his own. She was such a loving, giving person, and Elisha was sure she'd be a wonderful mother. He wanted to wait until she was older and they had their own place, but it was in the Lord's hands. There was only one way he knew not to start a family, and he wasn't willing to do that. And when they were blessed with children he wanted to provide for them. All of these thoughts and more whirled through his mind as he finally drifted off to sleep.

The next morning Susana rose early and had Elisha carry in buckets of water for her washing. He was glad to finally to ride off, unconcerned about leaving her for a few hours since the box canyon was less than a mile from the cabin.

When he arrived at the box canyon, he worked to strengthen the barrier. Elisha added rocks to each end of the barrier and cut more logs to make it higher. He took down part of the fence he'd put up to divide the canyon. The horses could graze on all of the grass growing there, at least until the middle of the summer. Then in July, he'd again block off half to start growing some taller grass for the winter, assuming they'd be there.

Bowing his head, he stood next to the tall barrier. He wanted to pray. Did he have the right to ask for help with something as simple as where he wanted to work? There was so much he didn't know or understand about God. The Bible reading and talking to Susana helped. Taking off his hat, he took the chance that the God he had prayed to at breakfast was still listening. He prayed that whatever worked out, he and Susana would be all right together.

Elisha put the bay in the stall of the barn and then walked toward the cabin. Looking around he felt a sense of home. He pulled out a handkerchief and wiped his face and neck. The day had been one of hard work and now he looked forward to a nice meal and quiet evening with his waiting wife. He wished they didn't have to return to the ranch headquarters. Pushing the door open, he stepped into the cabin.

The first thing he saw was Susana dragging the tub closer to the fireplace.

She lowered the tub, walked up to him, and kissed him. "I'm so happy you're home, my love."

Elisha kissed her back, "I'm happy to see you too. You're serious about the bath, then?"

"You want to carry in the water for the bath before you eat or after?" Susana wanted to know, with a smile.

"It looks like you got supper ready. I'm ready to eat."

"I don't know why I even ask," Susana said with a laugh, "you are always ready to eat. But, you don't gain weight. Where does all that food go?"

"Guess I work it off." Elisha sat at the table and took Susana's hand for the blessing.

"Father, please be with us as we go to the ranch. Your will be done in all that happens. Bless this food and bless Susana for preparing it for me. Help us be better people and be obedient to you. In the name of Jesus. Amen."

Elisha passed his plate for Susana fill with the salt pork and gravy. He then snagged two of the biscuits.

Susana took a smaller portion and they both ate quietly for several minutes.

Elisha glanced up from eating to find Susana looking at him intently. "What?"

"Your hair has really grown over the winter."

"Yes?" Elisha didn't know what she was leading to, but sensed some question.

"Would you let me cut your hair? I always cut my grandfather's hair."

Elisha assumed he would have to wait until they got to the ranch and Smithy would cut his hair. "What would you cut it with? My straight razor?"

"No, my sewing scissors." She stood, then walked over to the bureau and pulled a small box out of the drawer from which she took a pair of scissors.

"Well, if you want to I guess it won't hurt." Elisha wasn't sure it was the best idea, but if it pleased his wife, he was willing to take a chance. He wasn't sure how much of a chance it would be.

"Let's get it cut before you bathe. That way you can wash the hair off, too." She pulled a chair toward the middle of the room. "Take off your shirt."

"Let me finish my food first."

"I'm sorry. Of course, finish eating. It'll be fun to cut your hair." Susana cocked her head to the side as she examined his hair.

Elisha ate the last bite of biscuit from his plate, stood, then pulled his shirt over his head. He sat in the chair and Susana tied a flour sack towel around his neck.

"Now, sit real still." Susana spent the next ten minutes cutting his hair. So many long clumps of black hair fell to the floor as Susana plied her scissors to his hair. Glancing covertly at the fallen hair on the floor, Elisha worried he'd be bald by the time she finished.

She combed his hair and took off the towel. "There, that looks better."

Elisha walked over to the washstand and held up the mirror. He turned his head from side to side for a better look. He smiled and nodded. She'd done a good job. Susana had cut his hair above his ears and left his sideburns short. He ran his fingers through his short curls, musing that his head felt lighter.

"Thanks, Susana, that's as good a haircut as I've ever had. You just got a new job, personal barber to one Elisha Evans."

"Now, let's get some water heating up." Susana swept up the hair that had fallen to the floor.

Elisha didn't mind getting his haircut and bathing. He'd gotten used to Susana's level of cleanliness, and filling the tub at least three times a week was part of it. Except for summers when he swam daily in the creek, Elisha had never bathed so much.

Even as a child, his mother had only made him bathe once a week on Saturday night. He liked the feel of clean clothes on a clean body. He especially liked the smell of Susana's hair as she came to bed with it still damp from drying it in front of the fireplace on a cold night. Little things he'd never appreciated before he now associated with his life with Susana.

Before heading to bed, Elisha packed what they would need if they had to camp out one night. Elisha also put the books they had read in a gunnysack, ready to exchange at the ranch house.

Neither of them slept well, but for different reasons; he suspected Susana had trouble going to sleep because she was so excited.

Elisha couldn't seem to stop his mind from worrying about the reception Mr. Weathers would give them. Turning over he punched his pillow and tried to relax. He needed to get some sleep.

It was still dark when Elisha woke. He could tell from her breathing that Susana was also awake. He turned to her and reached out to pull her close.

"You awake?" He ran his fingers through her hair.

"I've been awake for awhile. I can't go back to sleep."

"Well, we might as well get up and get ready for our trip." Elisha gave her a kiss and then swung his legs over the edge of the bed.

After dressing in her pants and shirt, Susana used the last of the flour to make a batch of biscuits, half to eat at breakfast and the other half to take with them. She also warmed the last of the salt pork, then packed it to make sandwiches for the noon stop.

Elisha had already taken the brown mare and the gray gelding to the box canyon and turned them loose behind the barrier. He saddled Jasper for Susana and Shadow for himself. He put their packs on the chestnut. The roan and dapple horses had a lead rope on them that Elisha would tie on his saddle horn. He hoped they would return with the horses laden with packs. Elisha made sure the fires in the fireplace and stove were out.

Susana straightened up the cabin including making their bed.

"Are you expecting visitors while we're gone?" he asked her, puzzled about her extra cleaning.

"You never can tell who might stop by," she replied with a smile. "It's best to leave the place in the shape we want to come back to, especially since we'll have all those extra supplies to put away when we return."

Elisha sighed. *I hope we'll be returning.*

As the sky turned light in the east, they mounted up and headed south. The morning air was cold, so they wore their coats and gloves. They stopped for a bite to eat at noon and let the horses rest, the temperature had warmed, and they shed their coats. There was snow still under the evergreens, but in the open areas, the snow had melted. All of the creeks ran full, and several small waterfalls that hadn't been there in the fall spilled into the creek. Traveling took longer than he'd hoped. They had to stop several times to clear tree limbs and rocks off the trail. At least, the snow hadn't delayed them, as he'd feared it might.

"How far is it now?" Susana asked, as they remounted after eating their noon meal.

Elisha guided Shadow along the trail, ducking his head to avoid a low branch. "We should make it before dark."

"Well, before we get there we need to stop." Susana ducked her head at the same branch even though she was in no danger of hitting it.

"Why?" Elisha turned in the saddle and looked back at her.

"I want to change from these pants into my dress. I can't meet your friends dressed like this."

Elisha's eyes drank in the sight of her. She looked sweet in her baggy pants. He guessed that, as a girl, she wanted to make a good impression when she met his friends, and the baggy pants weren't exactly proper.

"We'll stop before we start down the last hill into the valley," he promised her. Elisha thought about it as they rode down the twisty trail through the forest. As far as he was concerned, Susana looked beautiful no matter what she wore. He stopped the horses when they were about two miles from the ranch house.

As she changed into her best weekday dress and petticoats, Elisha packed her baggy pants and shirt in the pack. She undid her braid and started to brush her hair out.

"Here, let me brush it." Elisha took the brush from her and ran it through her hair. "Your hair is shining with soft waves and looks beautiful."

"Thank you, Elisha." She made a small braid on each side of her head, then pulled them together at the back of her head and tied them with a ribbon. It gave an illusion that she was wearing a crown.

"Well, you look lovely. You were right about changing into your dress. I don't see how the fellows at the ranch can help but be enchanted by you, and I don't often use that word." He shook his head in amazement. He,

Elisha Evans, had a wife, one of great beauty. He didn't know about the fellas at the ranch, but he was enchanted.

Elisha gave her a kiss, helped her back on her horse, and mounted his for the last couple of miles of the trip. Please God, Mr. Weathers would accept Elisha's new bride. And maybe, Elisha would still have a job

CHAPTER TEN

The ranch lay beyond the next ridge and once over the crest, it would be downhill all the way. And, there would be no turning back.

Elisha, with Susana riding up close, rode to the top of the hill and looked down on the ranch in the middle of the valley. Glad to see it while at the same time his stomach churned and his palms sweated with his concern for their reception.

Several horses trotted around inside the corral while a small herd of cattle grazed in a large field by the creek. A few men relaxed on the bunkhouse porch and several ambled across the yard.

Elisha glanced at Susana and smiled. Then, he reached out and took her hand.

Susana frowned. "You're trembling."

"I know," Elisha said. "I'm wondering what Mr. Weathers will think about us being married."

Susana's frown deepened. "No matter what he says, the important thing is that we're together." She gave him a quick squeeze of his hand.

Elisha sat a little straighter in his saddle and held his head a little higher as he led his little caravan down the hill.

When they rode into the yard, Josh waved at them. "Hey, it's Elisha!"

Red and Abe strolled toward them, grinning.

Jim, Frank, and Albert waved from the bench where they sat, up against the bunkhouse.

Josh came to an abrupt stop and stared. "My word, Elisha, who is that with you?"

The others also stared at Susana with their mouths open and their eyes wide staring, as if she'd dropped from the moon.

"Howdy." Elisha dismounted. "Good to see you all. I want you to meet somebody." Elisha stepped over to Susana and helped her down from her horse. He turned back to the men.

They each stood with their eyes wide open, and then they whipped off their hats as if they had just remembered their manners.

Glad now that Susana had made him stop for her change into the dress, because she looked like a lady, and the men would treat her like one.

"Boys, let me introduce you to Susana, my wife." Elisha started to tell her their names, but she held out her hand first to Red.

"You must be Red, the foreman. I'm sorry I don't know your full name. Elisha refers to you as Red."

His face turned the color of his hair. "Howdy, ma'am, it's okay if you call me Red, too."

"And you must be Abe and Josh." She put out her hand for them to shake.

They each took her hand, as hesitantly as if she'd been made of china. "Howdy, ma'am."

Jim, Frank, and Albert gathered around to greet Susana, who called them all by name.

Elisha had never seen such a bunch of self-conscious men.

"Is the boss in the front room?" At their nods, he handed the horses' reins over to Josh and Red. "Then I'll take Susana in and introduce her to Mr. Weathers."

The men all ducked their heads and stood around watching while he escorted his young wife to the front door.

He knocked, opened the door, and looked in. Mr. Weathers sat at his desk. Elisha guided Susana into the room.

Mr. Weathers abruptly came to his feet and walked around the desk. "Well, hello."

"This is Susana, my wife. This is Mr. Weathers, the owner of the J Bar C ranch."

Mr. Weathers shook her extended hand. "Come in and sit down." He showed her to one of the chairs in front of the fireplace. As she sat down, he turned to Elisha and shook his hand as well. "Elisha, you look none the worse for wear. Glad you made it through the winter. Sit down and tell me what's going on here."

Elisha sat and cleared his throat. "Yes, I need to tell you what's happened and how I came back from a winter alone in the mountains with a wife." Elisha could hear the nervousness in his own voice.

Susana looked at him with a frown.

Elisha told Mr. Weathers how he had found Susana and her grandfather, of Henry Jamison's insistence that he marry Elisha and Susana, and then about the old man's death.

"He married us on December 23rd, about three months ago. At first, we didn't know each other, but it's turned out better than I could've imagined. I quickly grew to love Susana and I believe she's come to love me." He glanced at Susana and found her looking up at him with her eyes shining.

She reached over and took Elisha's hand. Susana smiled at Mr. Weathers. "My grandfather was a preacher of the gospel, and he wanted to leave me protected, so he asked Elisha to become responsible for me by taking me as his wife. I bless him every day for that gift. And now Elisha is letting me meet his friends he's told me so much about."

Mr. Weathers's broad smile turned his face into a mass of wrinkles and his blue eyes were alive with twinkles that Elisha had never noticed before. Elisha relaxed for the first time in days.

The older man didn't take his eyes off Susana and he continued to nod and smile. Elisha knew the feeling of being smitten by the loveliness that was Susana.

"We need to get our pack and bedrolls—" Elisha halted when Mr. Weathers held up a hand to interrupt him.

"The boys will bring those in for you. Let me show you to your room." He got up and called out for Nate.

Nate arrived, and Elisha knew from the way he nodded at him, then at Susana that he'd already heard they had a woman in the house.

"Nate, we got guests, Elisha, and his wife, Susana," Mr. Weathers said in his booming voice. "Freshen up the spare bedroom for them and get some hot water for them to wash up."

Elisha opened his mouth to protest, but Mr. Weathers stopped him. "Of course, you'll stay here in the house. We got a nice spare bedroom that I think will do."

"I'm sure it'll be fine." Susana smiled at Nate and Mr. Weathers.

Elisha breathed a sigh of relief that he didn't have to take Susana to the barn loft for the night.

"Elisha, get your little bride settled, and then we'll have supper together."

Nate led them through one of the doors leading from the front room into a spacious bedroom nicely furnished with a double bed covered with a colorful quilt, chest of drawers, washstand with a pitcher and bowl, two straight chairs, and a braided rug. There was an oil lamp on the chest by the bed.

Susana glanced around. "Mr. Nate, this is a lovely room."

"Call me Nate. I'm glad you like it." He picked up the pitcher on his way out. "I'll bring you hot water to freshen up."

As he left, Josh came in with their things and placed them on the floor at the end of the bed.

"I guess I won't get to hear you snoring tonight in the bunkhouse, Elisha." Josh had gotten over his shock and returned to his usual, cheerful self.

"You certainly will not see Elisha in the bunkhouse," Susana confirmed with a laugh.

Josh backed out of the room as Nate returned with the pitcher of hot water. "I'll see you all at supper."

Nate put down the pitcher on the washstand. "Come to the kitchen when you're ready." He left, closing the door behind him.

Elisha took off his coat and hung it, along with his hat, on a wooden hook by the door. He told Susana to wash up first.

She splashed water on her face and used a towel to pat her face dry. "You were right. All these men are lovely."

"That isn't how I'd describe them." He laughed. "But I'm glad you like them. They're certainly taken with you." Elisha relaxed from the stress he had been feeling about how Mr. Weathers would react to Susana. He didn't know if he still had a job but he was more hopeful.

"Isn't this a nice room? Is this were you stayed when you were here before?"

"I've never seen this room before. I stayed in the bunkhouse with the rest of the men. I think the only reason I'm in this room now is because of your charm, Mrs. Evans."

"Well, we'll be very comfortable here."

As they entered the kitchen, all the men stood behind their chairs waiting for them.

Mr. Weathers came over, escorted Susana to the chair to his left, and waved Elisha to sit next to her.

Susana looked around at the men. "Please, sit down, gentlemen."

Elisha could tell that the men had slicked down their hair and brushed off their clothes in honor of having a woman in their presence. It was a wonder, what being around a lady did for their manners. They all sat down at the table laden with food and waited for Mr. Weathers to give the blessing.

"Heavenly Father, we thank you for the blessings of this day and for keeping everyone safe. We thank you for the return, in good health, of Elisha, and for the blessing of Susana coming into this house. We thank you for the bounty of this meal and the hands that prepared it. In the name of Jesus the Christ, Amen."

As the men served themselves from the bowls and platters of food, Elisha saw Susana reach over and place her hand on Mr. Weathers' arm.

"Now I know where Elisha learned to give the blessing for the food. Thank you for teaching him."

"I'm glad to know that he learned." He looked over at Elisha, and then back to Susana and smiled. "He's a good man and I'm guessing that he's found a good wife."

Elisha found it hard to suppress a smile as a warm glow filled him at Mr. Weathers's words.

Susana placed her hand on Elisha's arm. "I'm going to try very hard to be a good wife, but I've so much to learn."

"Be patient with him. We men have some rough edges, and we need a gentle hand to help smooth them out." Mr. Weathers passed a platter of fried steak to her.

As usual, the men took eating seriously after a hard day of ranch work and didn't talk much. Nate and Smithy kept the food coming until everyone had their fill, and then Nate served dried apple pie.

Nate placed a generous sized piece of pie in front of Susana.

She took a fork of apples and crust and ate it slowly with Nate and Smithy watching. "Mmmm...this the best dried apple pie I have ever had. You gentlemen are to be complimented for such a wonderful meal, and especially this pie." She ate another generous forkful.

Nate and Smith rewarded her praise with shy smiles and soft, "Thank you, ma'am."

When dinner was over, Elisha looked around the table. "You fellows mind if Susana sets out on the front porch?" He turned to her and said, "Most evenings when the weather is warm the riders sit around and relax a bit before bedtime. Mr. Weathers and I need to talk."

Susana smiled at the men. "That would be lovely. I look forward to getting better acquainted with your friends."

They all stood, and Abe offered his arm to Susana. He escorted her out to the porch with the men following along behind.

Elisha was proud of the way his young wife accepted Abe's arm and serenely walked out to the porch as though having five men as an escort was an everyday thing.

"Red, Elisha, let's go talk." Mr. Weathers walked over to his desk with Red following him.

"Sure thing, Mr. Weathers. Let me go get the ledger and lists." Elisha went into the bedroom and retrieved them. On impulse, he picked up Mr. Jamison's Bible. As he was leaving the room, he took Susana's coat and stepped out on the porch.

Susana sat in a rocker with the five men seated and standing in a circle around her. "Thank you, Elisha." She smiled up at him, taking the coat. "It is chilly out here."

"Now you fellows take care of Susana."

They all nodded their heads and mumbled.

"Sure."

"Of course"

"Glad to."

Elisha went back into the front room, chuckling.

"What's so funny?" Red asked.

Elisha took the chair next to him. "I've never seen such a bunch of moonstruck fellows in my life." Elisha laughed. "Susana has them eating out of her hand and doesn't even know it. She's just being her usual self."

"Well, you know most of those boys haven't been to town since last fall and haven't seen a woman for months," Mr. Weathers said. "Then you come waltzing in here with the prettiest little thing that we have seen in years. What do you expect?" He joined Red and Elisha in laughter.

Red shook his head in amazement. "I never saw anyone so lucky; the only woman in a hundred miles and she lands at your feet."

Elisha thought on that. Maybe blessed was a better way to look at it. He'd felt unlucky when he'd arrived at the ranch the year before. His life had changed so much since then.

Before giving his report to Mr. Weathers, he gave them more details about finding Susana and her grandfather. Mr. Weathers asked several questions about the death of Mr. Jamison, and about where Elisha had buried the old man.

"Wasn't it kind of sudden to decide to marry the girl, and especially since she's a lot younger than you are?" Mr. Weathers asked bluntly.

Elisha needed to explain as fully as possible to his boss. "Mr. Jamison was a preacher and a strong believer in doing the Christian thing. He knew that if he died, he'd have to trust that I'd do the right thing by Susana. At first, I didn't understand what he meant by protecting her spiritually if we were married. Now I do. It would've been hard on both of us to be together and unmarried in the cabin for all these months, alone. Susana is a Christian, and she'd have done what was right, but it wouldn't have been easy."

Elisha felt the heat rising up his neck and then his cheeks. He felt embarrassed to talk like this in front of Red and Mr. Weathers. But he wanted them to understand. "Anyway, I don't regret marrying her. We've come to care for each other and all I want to do now is to protect and provide for her. I know she's young, and I'm trying to be considerate of that." Elisha waited for Mr. Weathers to respond, but the room remained quiet for a moment.

"Elisha," Mr. Weathers said in a voice much quieter than normal. "Thank you for explaining that to us. I respect what you've done for Susana, and I know that you'll keep your word to her grandfather. In fact, I think you did the only honorable thing a real man could have done."

"You are so right." Red nodded in agreement.

"Here is Mr. Jamison's Bible. He wrote it down official, for he wanted it done proper." Elisha opened the Bible to the front page where they had all signed under the notation of the birth of Susana.

"Then that's all right." Mr. Weathers took the Bible. For some reason he had to take out his handkerchief and wipe his eyes and blow his nose. "Well, let's hear how my cattle are doing up in the north corner of the ranch."

Elisha opened the ledger and told him about the work over the winter. He had a count of all of the cattle he'd hazed back across Pinto Creek and the number of cattle he'd found dead after the hard freeze.

"I expected to lose some." Mr. Weathers nodded his head at the number of dead cattle. "But to lose only eight head is not bad. We lost that many down here. It was a bad spell, but the loss was a lot less because you moved the cattle back south. We lost five times that many last year, plus having to send a crew up to move the other cattle back down which took a week."

"It really was fortunate that we had you up there," Red said. "This winter was the first in several years that we've been able to keep someone at the line cabin."

Elisha welcomed the approval, but felt he needed to let them know of Susana's work. "Susana has ridden out with me every day since she came at the end of December. I couldn't leave her at the cabin by herself after her grandfather died, and she wanted to ride with me. She was a big help. Having two riders keeping the cattle moved back south really made a difference."

"I'm amazed that she's strong enough to be working cattle; she's such a little thing," Mr. Weathers said.

Elisha smiled. "She may be small, but she's stronger than she looks. Also, she can ride as good as me."

"Have you seen any Indian signs?" Red asked.

"No, I've kept an eye out for tracks, but haven't seen any. I've not ridden up north beyond the ridge much."

"We haven't been bothered here either, but the Utes and the Arapahos are said to be moving out against the army this spring, so we're keeping a sharp lookout," Red shifted in his chair and crossed his legs at the ankle.

"I thought the Utes were more to the west." Elisha leaned forward.

"They are mostly, but last time the boys were in town there was talk of raids further east than their normal range. We need to keep a watch. Now, tell me what supplies you need," Mr. Weathers raised his hand, palm forward. "Although, I may be jumping ahead too fast. What with having a wife now, you may not want to keep working the north section. If you don't, I can understand, and we'll have you work here."

He needed to be sure he understood. "You mean that you'd take me on as a hand here at the ranch?"

"If that's what you want. I can see how being isolated up at the cabin might not be best for you and Susana. You've done a good job this year, and

I don't want to lose you as a hand. Now if you and Susana have other plans, I'll understand."

"We've got contracts from Chicago to ship all the cattle we can send," Red said. "The boss and I have been talking about getting a couple more riders. We got a place for you, if you decide to come down and work here. Of course, we can still use you up at the north range. We need someone up there. Look at how much work it's taken for you this year to keep the cattle pushed back onto J Bar C range."

Elisha's relief was great, but he managed not to show it. What would it mean to be at the ranch headquarters, especially for Susana? He wanted to return to the cabin. It was a decision he'd leave to Susana. If she wanted to move down to the ranch headquarters, then that was what he'd do.

"Let me think about it and I'll let you know tomorrow, if that's all right."

"Sure. Why don't you and Susana plan to stay a couple of days, rest up, and then decide? I know the boys would like to have you around for a while."

Elisha laughed. "Well, at least have Susana around. I don't think I count much in there."

"That's what usually happens when you got a pretty woman around a bunch of lonely men. Now, here's another thought. I'm sending some boys into Cedar Ridge in a couple of days to pick up a wagon and supplies. Maybe it would be nice for you and Susana to go along. She might like to get to town and get some things at the general store."

Elisha was surprised at the idea. "I'll ask her. Thanks."

"If you went you could get some household stuff. Things that a woman might want that us bachelors don't think about. I remember my wife used to get doodads at the store when we went in to town I'd never have thought of. When I noticed the pretty ribbon Mrs. Evans was wearing, I remembered that was something my wife would have bought for our daughter," Mr. Weathers said with a far-away look in his eyes. His voice remained soft. "Your Susana has brightened up the place. And we're glad to have her. You're staying in my daughter Christine's room. My son's name is Joseph. So you see where I got the name for the ranch."

Elisha saw a different side of Mr. Weathers, one that made him seem less remote. Knowing that he'd suffered loss that he'd suffered seemed to bring him closer to where Elisha lived. Elisha didn't have to lose Susana to understand what a loss that would be to his life.

"Well, boys, it's getting toward my bedtime." Mr. Weathers stood and walked around the desk to stand by Red and Elisha. "We'll talk more tomorrow. We're surely glad to have you here, Elisha. The surprise of Susana, well, I don't have words for that." He walked him toward the front door. "You let us know if there is anything Susana needs, you hear? A good wife is a precious thing."

Going out onto the porch where Susana listened with rapt attention to one of the men tell a story, Mr. Weathers bid his goodnight to her and headed back into the house.

Susana stood and thanked the men for visiting with her and told them she'd see them in the morning. Taking Elisha's arm, they went into the house to their bedroom.

Later, in bed, Elisha told her what Mr. Weathers had said about his work and the choice they had of staying at the cabin or moving down to the ranch headquarters.

"What do you want to do?"

"No. The decision is yours. I want to do whatever you want."

"Well, staying here would be nice in some ways. I like all these boys."

Elisha smiled at that since 'these boys' were all older than she was.

"But I also like our cabin and working together there. It's nice being the two of us." She snuggled up closer to him and rested her head on his chest. "I can be happy at either place as long as I'm with you. You decide where you want to work and that's what we'll do."

He gave her a long hug and sighed. "You are so good to me, Susana. What other wife would be content in a place like the cabin?"

"You like being on your own and being responsible for the work. That's really where you want to work, isn't it?"

"Yes, I'd like to go back to the cabin and work for maybe another year. Then we can see about getting a place of our own."

"Elisha, if I've anything to do with it, that's what you shall have, a place of your own." Susana spoke fiercely.

He returned her kiss. "Then we're in agreement?"

She nodded.

"I'll tell Mr. Weathers that we'll return to the cabin on Pinto Creek. No doubts at all?" He wanted to make sure that it was what Susana wanted and that she wasn't willing to do it simply to please him.

"I can't wait to get home to the cabin."

"Well, can you wait a week or so?" Before she could answer, he then told her of the offer for them to take a trip to Cedar Ridge.

"Oh Elisha, that will be such fun! When do we go?" Her excitement spread over to him.

Elisha grinned at her. He couldn't remember when he had last felt that kind of excitement. He had grown up at the age of twelve when his father died. There hadn't been much fun in his life.

They were nearly ten years difference in age. Susana, after all, was still young and energetic, while he felt like a much older man. Going to town would be a nice break, especially with Susana, but he didn't really care much for towns. To her it was an exciting prospect.

Elisha wanted to take her to town and tell her to buy whatever she wanted. But, he also wanted to save his money.

"We'll leave in a couple of days with some of the riders from the ranch. I'll ask Mr. Weathers for some of my wages, so you can buy some things."

"I could use some material to make another dress. Mine are getting too tight across the top for some reason, but other than that, I don't need much. We should save our money for your ranch."

"For our ranch," he corrected her. "And we can spend a little on material for a new dress. Maybe new boots for you, too." He stroked his wife's hair as he thought about what the day had brought. He felt her relax as she drifted off to sleep and he soon followed.

~ ~ ~

The next morning, Elisha woke before daylight, quietly dressed, and slipped out of the house, carrying his shaving gear and coat. As he expected, the bucket of hot water was already by the shelf at the back of the bunkhouse. He quickly washed up and shaved. He stored his shaving gear in his coat pocket and put his coat on against the chill of the morning air. He went to the corral and mucked it out. In a few minutes, he heard Abe up in the loft.

"Hey Elisha, I can't believe my eyes. What are you doing up so early and not still with that pretty, little wife?" he called down softly.

"Well someone had to get some work done around this place today with all of you cowhands asleep past daybreak."

Abe pushed another bale of hay down into the corral. Elisha spread the hay out for the twelve head of horses milling about. He met Abe coming out of the barn. They walked back down to the basin by the bunkhouse to wash their hands before going into the kitchen.

Elisha sat at the kitchen table with his first cup of coffee. "Think you might have time today to help me do some shoeing?" He turned to Abe.

"I don't see why not. I'll check with Red and see which horses he plans to send on the trip to town, maybe we can do all the horses together."

Elisha nodded. "That would be a fair trade."

Soon the other men ambled into the kitchen, and Nate and Smithy set bowls and platters of food on the table. Elisha slipped out of the kitchen. He found Mr. Weathers seated at his desk. He went over and sat in one of the chairs.

Mr. Weathers looked up with a smile and a greeting. "Morning. Did you'll sleep all right?"

"We slept very well. In fact I'm about to go see if Susana is still asleep. I wanted to let her rest a little longer because we've put in some pretty hard days."

"I forgot to ask you last night about how you're feeling. How's your back?"

"My back is much better. The bad spasms have mostly gone away. My lower back gets to hurting bad pretty often, but nothing I can't deal with," Elisha responded, feeling that Mr. Weathers had a right to know.

"I'm glad to hear that it's better. I'm hopeful that given more time it'll heal completely."

"I wanted to let you know that Susana and I talked a long time last night. We've decided we'll work either here or at the cabin. We'll go with whatever you want. However, we'd rather go back up to the cabin." He waited for a response.

"Well, now that's fine. I'd love to have you both around here more often, but I'm relieved that you want to continue the work up at the cabin. That's where I need you." He sat back for a moment. "Let's do it this way. You'll go back to the cabin for the summer and we'll reconsider in the fall. If you decide it would be best to stay down here through the worst of the winter because of Susana, then that's what we'll do. Now, I hope you've decided to take that trip into town."

"Yes, sir, we have and I'd like to pull out some of my wages, so I can get a few things for Susana while we're in town. She wants material for a new dress or two and she needs new boots."

"Of course, how much do you need?"

"Well, with staying in a hotel, food and purchases I guess about fifty dollars would be more than enough. I'd rather go with too much than too little. That's if you have that much on hand."

"Now, I take care of hotel and food when I send my men to town. In fact, I think it might be best if you got what you want at the general store and put it on my bill. Then when you get back we can figure it out." Mr. Weathers opened one of the drawers on the desk and pulled out a metal box, opened it, counted out fifty dollars in tens, then handed it to Elisha. "Here's the fifty. I'd rather you didn't spend it unless you have to. You and Susana talk about what you want up at the cabin to make it more of a home for Susana. What we don't have here we'll get in town."

Elisha put the money in his pocket and thanked his boss. "You're being more than generous and I appreciate it. I'll go check on Susana. I plan to help Abe shoe horses today, and I want Susana to take it easy if you don't mind her staying around the house."

"Mind? Why I think that's a great idea. It'll be fine seeing a young woman about the house." Mr. Weathers stood, then headed to the kitchen. "You all come in to breakfast when you're ready."

Elisha eased open the bedroom door. Susana pulled on her boots.

"Morning, sleepyhead." He went over and kissed her.

"Why didn't you wake me?" She kissed him back. "I felt so foolish waking up in that bed by myself and it full daylight."

"Well, I thought you could use the sleep. Come on. Breakfast is ready and the hands are already at the table. By the way, I told Mr. Weathers that we would work at the cabin, at least for the summer, and that we would take the trip to town."

"Then it's all settled?"

"It's settled." He took her hand as they walked toward the kitchen. All the worry and the anxious feelings were gone. Elisha's heart hadn't been this light in years. He smiled down at Susana and she rewarded him with a brilliant smile in return. What more could a man ask for?

Through the open kitchen door, green fields shimmered in the sunlight. But high above dark clouds swirled around the mountain peaks.

After breakfast, Mr. Weathers signaled Elisha to follow him. "Come into the front room. There are some things I need to say."

After he was seated at his desk, he said, "Elisha, I've decided to send Abe and Josh to town. I've got a Moline chuck wagon on order from Herman Jones and need you all to get it back to the ranch. The bank is set to pay Herman when my representative gives the word, so all you have to do is make sure it's in good shape. I want you to handle that for me."

"You don't want Abe to do that?"

"Abe doesn't like to be in charge and Josh is too young. I figure you can handle it. I'll send a list of supplies for the ranch. Normally, I send the boys in with an empty wagon, but this time you won't take the wagon. You'll take extra horses into town and you'll load the new chuckwagon with supplies and drive it back."

"Yes, sir, I can handle that."

"And another thing, I need you to keep Josh in check. He has a tendency to get too exuberant when he's in town. Not every time, but he's been known to drink too much and get a little rowdy. He's a good boy and I want him back at the ranch without getting into trouble. Try to keep him out of the saloons." Mr. Weathers leaned back in his chair and rubbed the back of his neck. "I know it might be better not to let Josh make the trip to town at all. But I figure that if I hold the reins too tight, he'll want to break loose even more. So, I let him go and hope that he makes it back without getting into too much trouble."

"I'll do what I can, but I'm not sure how." This would be an opportunity to accomplish something he had been thinking on for months. While in town he could check on filing on the land north of Weathers's ranch. It almost took his breath away to think on it.

After a day of shoeing horses and getting lists together, the next morning they prepared to leave for the trip to town. Because they needed to take horses with them to pull back the new wagon, Elisha, Josh, and Abe would each ride a horse and lead two others that would make up the team for the wagon. Susana would ride a buckskin Abe suggested because of its easy gait.

With the horses saddled, Elisha waited for Susana.

Susana came out the door onto the front porch of the house. She'd tucked her loose shirt into her full skirt and the baggy pants underneath. She wore a pair of worn boots. The long thick braid of her light brown hair hung down her back. An old Stetson sat atop her head.

The hands stood around to see them off, trying not to stare.

Elisha grinned at her as he took her packed saddlebags. "You ready to go?"

"I'm ready. Can you help me mount?" Susana seemed unaware of the attention she received.

Elisha tied the saddlebags onto the back of her saddle and then helped his wife onto her mount. The pants and loose shirt made for a more convenient and comfortable ride for her.

~ ~ ~

Because they paced the horses, it took two full days to make the trip to town. The second afternoon, while they were still about three hours from Cedar Ridge, Elisha dropped back and rode beside Josh. Abe moved up to ride beside Susana.

Elisha spoke in a low voice so Susana and Abe couldn't hear. "I got a favor to ask."

"Sure," Josh said, twisting in his saddle to look at Elisha. "What can I do for you?"

"I know you're looking forward to a good time in town, and I want you to enjoy yourself. But I don't want you drinking too much. We represent the ranch, but more than that, we got Susana with us." He looked over at Josh to see if the younger man resented what he'd said.

Josh glanced down at the ground, then looked at Elisha and shook his head. "I'll try not to drink too much and whoop and holler, but I can't promise anything."

"Also, I need you to help me with Susana tomorrow. She's going shopping so she'll be wandering around town. I can't be with her because I have to get Mr. Weathers' orders filled and see about the new wagon with Abe. Would you mind trailing after Susana and make sure no one bothers her?"

"Bothers her? Do you expect trouble?" Josh whipped his head back around to frowned at Elisha.

"No more than what usually follows a young, pretty girl who is too friendly and innocent. It's a Saturday and all the ranch hands will be in town." Elisha laughed. "Susana hasn't been on her own much, and she thinks everyone is good and kind. She doesn't understand how some men can be toward a woman when she's walking through town. I don't want her bothered if she wants to go shopping without me."

"Well, don't you worry, she won't be bothered one bit tomorrow. Not with me looking after her," Josh said emphatically, a determined look on his young face.

"Thanks. I thought I could trust you to help me out." Elisha would hate to be the person Josh might target as bothering Susana. This tall, strong young man was bigger than most riders. Susana would be taken care of like a she-bear watching its cub.

As the group rode, Elisha found it easy to get Josh to talk about himself and his past.

"I don't remember my mother. After my gambler father rode off and left me on the streets of Abilene, Kansas when I was eleven years old, Mr. Weathers found me begging for food. " Josh talked about his past as if it were no big deal. "It wasn't too long after Mr. Weathers' wife and daughter had died. Mr. Weathers asked me to come back to his ranch and work. I've been with him ever since. The ranch is the only home I've ever had."

The young man now seemed to include Elisha and Susana in that loyalty. In a way, it looked like Susana was becoming the sister Josh never had. Elisha enjoyed getting to know him. And even though the young cowhand might have a little wild streak, Josh rose a few notches in Elisha's regard.

Arriving in town before dark on the second day of travel, they left their horses at a large livery stable, then made their way to the hotel on Main Street.

Elisha led the weary group through the hotel door. They were dusty and ready to clean up. The line rider stepped up to the front desk.

A clerk peered over his spectacles. "Rooms for you folks?"

Elisha gave a nod. "We need two of your best rooms and hot water for baths as soon as possible."

"Yes sir." He pushed the hotel registry toward Elisha. "Sign here." The thin man then watched closely as each signed his name. Turning the book back to face him, he read the names.

"Mr. and Mrs. Elisha Evans from the J Bar C. That's Mr. Sam Weathers' ranch. Plus two cowhands. He keeps a running tab here at the hotel." The man sprang into action and retrieved keys from a box on the wall behind him. "You go along to your rooms, and I'll have the hot water sent up for the baths. The dining room is through there when you're ready to eat." He pointed toward an open area across the room.

Elisha handed a room key to Abe and Josh and told them he and Susana would meet them in an hour in the lobby. Then, they would eat together in the hotel dining room.

He and Susana mounted the stairs and took the room at the back of the long hallway. A double bed and a washstand near the window furnished the room. They set their saddlebags down on the floor.

Susana unpacked her dress and petticoat. She fussed with the dress. "It's so wrinkled. Do you think anyone will notice?"

Elisha wisely kept his mouth shut about no one caring how her dress looked. Someone knocked on the door. He was relieved for it rescued from having to respond to Susana's comment. He opened the door and found a young girl in the hallway.

"Sir, I've filled the bathtub with hot water for the Madam. It's down the hall here."

Elisha went downstairs to wait for his wife. In the lobby, Elisha found Josh sitting by the window. He dropped into the wingback chair next to Josh, glad to have some time to relax.

"Where's Abe?"

"He's resting up. He'll be down in time for supper. I was too excited to stay up in the room." He looked around. "Where's Susana?"

"She's changing into a dress and freshening up." Elisha stretched out his legs and slid down in the comfortable chair, which felt like heaven after days in a hard saddle. He rested his head back against the upholstery. "Before she comes down, I want to give you some money for tomorrow."

Elisha pulled out his wallet, then gave Josh twenty dollars. "Pay attention when you take Susana shopping tomorrow. If she looks twice at something, but doesn't buy it, you buy it for her. I don't want you to tell her. Have it put with the ranch supplies."

"All right." Josh took the money and put it into his pocket. "But why wouldn't you give the money to Susana?"

"I've given her money to spend, but she knows that we're saving for a place of our own someday. Knowing her, she won't spend much. I want her to have some of the things she wants."

"I'll try, but I hope I don't mess it up. I'm not that good at knowing that someone wants something if they don't come right out and say it."

"You'll do fine."

When Abe and Susana joined them, they headed to the dining room to eat. It was a large room with about a dozen tables with white tablecloths, which impressed Elisha. About half of them had customers seated at them in the midst of eating.

It was a pleasant meal, made brighter by Susana and Josh's exuberance. Their mealtime was filled with talk and laughter. Josh related funny stories about the ranch hands and Susana giggled so much she had to put a napkin to her mouth.

Abe didn't say much, but he seemed to enjoy the two younger people.

Elisha also enjoyed Josh and Susana as they talked about what they wanted to see and do in town. He never had a time when he felt free to be young and enjoy living. Life had always been full of work and getting by.

The more he was around Susana and her joy of life, the more the hard years seemed to drop away.

As soon as dinner was over, Josh and Abe excused themselves and set out to see the sights of town. Elisha flagged a waiter and asked him to have a bellboy bring hot water to the bathing room. Tired from their travel, Elisha and Susana returned to their room after supper.

Later, he and Susana lay in the bed and listened to the hum of the town noise.

"After we eat breakfast, you go shopping with Josh." Elisha stroked Susana's hair.

"What do you mean? Where will you be?"

"I'm going to the land office to ask about filing a claim on the upper valley." He couldn't believe he had said it. "I have enough money and I want to file on the land before someone else does."

"But you told Mr. Weathers that you would continue to work at the cabin."

"And I'm going to do that. I can also go up to the valley every once in a while and start building a cabin," Elisha explained.

"I thought you had to live on the land if you filed on it."

"I'll find out about that, but I think you have a couple of years to make improvements. And we can go live on it some in our time off from working with Mr. Weathers."

"Well, you know that whatever you decide, I'm going to be there with you."

Elisha took her into his arms and pressed his face into her hair. "And with you there beside me, I can build us a good ranch. It'll take some time. I promise I'll make a good home place for you and for our children."

She laughed softly. "And how do you plan to go about providing me with those children?"

He kissed her softly and then showed her.

~ ~ ~

Saturday morning after breakfast in the hotel dining room, Elisha sent Josh and Susana to start her shopping. Then, he told Abe he'd meet him at the wagon yard where the local carpenter built wagons, surreys, and buckboards. Mr. Weathers had ordered a basic Moline chuck wagon to be shipped in by train, but had wanted some extras added on by Herman Jones.

After the others left, Elisha walked down to the land office, which was a few doors from the hotel.

Elisha stepped into the land office and moved over to the counter. As he watched, an older man seated at a desk behind the counter who glanced up then smoothed back his short gray hair.

"Can I help you?" The man stood up from his stool and thumbed his suspenders back over his shoulders as he shuffled over to the counter. He squinted up at Elisha.

"I want to file on some land." Elisha looked at a large map of the Colorado Territory on the wall behind the man. "But I'm not sure exactly where it's located."

"I'm Cullen Fredericks, the land agent for the government." He turned and waved at the large map hanging on the back wall of the office. "Well, we can find it on this, and that will give me the coordinates to find it in detail on the official register."

"I'm Elisha Evans." He shook hands with the man. "Can I come around and take a closer look at the map?"

"Sure, that's the best way to orient yourself. Have you ever seen a full map of this part of the territory?" Fredericks asked.

"No, I've ridden it, but I haven't seen a proper map."

Elisha found the valley of the J Bar C headquarters and traced his way north with his finger until he knew where the upper valley was. Elisha tapped on the map.

"That's the area that I'm interested in filing on. Can you tell me if it's available?"

"That's pretty wild country up there and not really near to anything." Fredericks pulled out a big book of section maps, flipped through several pages, and then showed Elisha the area he'd pointed out on the big map. "Now to the south, but quite a ways, is the J Bar C. Weathers has filed on his place and a couple of boys also filed and then sold their land to Weathers. But no one has filed anywhere in that north area."

Elisha carefully examined the map, then pointed to a particular section. "That's the area I want to file on."

The area was only part of what he wanted for his ranch, but it was the most important. It contained the main source of water for the big valley. The creek that wandered through the valley originated from a large spring back in a cave that flowed year round. The hundred and sixty acres that Elisha wanted to file on would cover most of the major springs he'd found in the western part of the valley.

"All right, fill out this application." He handed Elisha a piece of paper. "That'll be ten dollars. You can start to improve on the land. Now you know you have to live on the land at least part of the year, build a dwelling, plant a crop, and in five years the land title will be yours free and clear."

Elisha filled out the application. "What happens if I only live on the land part of the time until I can get a house and barn built? I'd like to spend most of my time building the house and planting this year, but I'll be working some for the J Bar C to keep a little money coming in until I can work my own land full time. Is that a problem?"

"Well, back in Washington, D. C. where they made the Homestead Act, I'm not sure what they would tell you. You build a house and barn, get a crop in, and come back in five years with two witnesses that say you have done that, and I'll make sure you get the deed. You look like a solid, serious citizen, and I don't know many folks that would want that remote area."

"What if something happened to me? Can my wife continue the claim?"

"Sure, and even your children if both of you was to die. But we'll hope that don't happen."

Elisha took ten dollars from his wallet and handed it to the man with the completed application. Fredericks wrote out a receipt and gave it to him.

"You hang on to this. Its proof you filed on the land and paid for it. Now let me mark on this map in the book so no one else can claim this section." Fredericks took a pencil and shaded over the section of land that Elisha was claiming. Then he took his pen and wrote Elisha's full name in an official ledger book, along with the description of his claim.

"I suggest you stake out your claim, so folks will know that section is taken. Although I don't expect you'll have many neighbors anytime soon. I recommend you get some iron stakes down at the general store, as they'll last much longer than the plain, wooden ones."

"I will, and thanks for suggesting it." Elisha shook hands with the man.

"I hope it'll be a good place for you and your family." Fredericks walked Elisha to the door of the land office.

Elisha headed down the street toward the wagon yard to meet Abe. He had the sense that he'd done something monumental for his future. He probably would've put off filing a claim for another year, except he wanted to provide something more for Susana.

Beside a big, canvas-covered wagon, Abe spoke with a man wearing overalls. "Here he is now," Abe said and turned to Elisha. "This is Herman Jones. He owns this wagon yard."

Elisha shook hands with the middle-aged man and noted the strength of his grip. Mr. Jones wasn't tall, but the broadness of his shoulders gave an impression of being taller than he was.

"The wagon is ready if you want to look it over. It came in on the train about two weeks ago, and I've outfitted it the way Mr. Weathers ordered. Abe said that you would officially take possession of it for Mr. Weathers."

"He did, did he?" Elisha grinned at Abe. Abe could have taken possession as well as Elisha. "Well, I'd better look it over to make sure it's what the boss wants."

He commented on the good workmanship, but pointed out that the wheels needed more tallow, the grease rendered from cow's fat. It would keep the wheels from freezing up from the dust and sand of the journey home. Abe nodded his agreement, and Jones said he'd get right to it and have the wagon ready by noon. This wagon was expensive and would have to last for several years. Elisha hoped someday to have a need for such a wagon on his own place.

"Mr. Weathers told me that when he sent someone to pick up and sign for the wagon, the bank would pay me. Is that still the plan?" asked Jones.

"Yes, I'll sign for Mr. Weathers. Then, you present the signed bill to the bank and get paid."

He and Abe left Jones to finish adding more tallow to the wheels while they went in search of Susana and Josh. The sun hung straight above them.

Abe told Elisha that he had left the lists for ranch supplies at the general store first thing that morning and the supplies would be ready by the middle of the afternoon.

They found Josh and Susana in the lobby of the hotel, waiting for them. Susana's eyes sparkled and Josh grinned.

"Didn't you buy anything?" Elisha was surprised not to see any packages.

"We've already put them in our room," Susana's brow knit with concern. "I'm afraid I spent too much money, but, oh my, there were an awful lot of nice things in that store."

Josh shook his head. "You really didn't buy much."

"Well, I bought plenty."

"Did you buy anything, Josh?" Elisha asked and raised his eyebrows in innocence.

"Yeah, I bought several things that'll be with the ranch stuff." Josh winked at Elisha.

"Let's go in and eat dinner. We got a wagon to load this afternoon." Elisha took Susana's hand and led the way into the dining room.

After they sat down in the dining room and ordered their food, Susana touched Elisha on the arm and he looked over at her.

"They have a church," she said. "They'll be having services in the morning at ten. May we go?" She looked up at Elisha with excited expectation.

Looking at her pretty face, aglow with finding a church, Elisha knew that whether he wanted to go or not, he'd take her.

"Sure, we can go." His reward was her brilliant smile. "I thought we might start out for the ranch in the morning, but Mr. Weathers told us to stay a couple of days. We can start out tomorrow afternoon, travel for a few hours, and then camp." Elisha turned to Abe. "If we did that, we could travel most of the way on Monday. We'd get into the ranch by the middle of the day on Tuesday, and still have time to unload in daylight."

Susana turned to Abe and Josh. "You'll come to church with us, won't you?"

Josh looked flustered, as if he didn't know what to say. "I've never been to church, Susana. I don't rightly know if I know how or not."

"Oh, that's no problem." She was quick to tell him. "You'll be with us and you'll be fine."

"I think it would be right nice to go to church with you all," Abe said solemnly. "You'll be all right, Josh. I'll tell you what to do."

"Then it's settled. We'll meet for breakfast, go to church, eat dinner, and then start for home."

Elisha laughed. "Fellows, now that Susana has tomorrow all planned out, let's talk about what we need to do this afternoon."

"Well, if you all don't mind, I think I'd like to go up to our room and rest a bit. I'm feeling tired," Susana said.

"Are you all right?" He'd never known Susana to tire so quickly.

"Oh yes, I think it's all of the excitement of being in town. I didn't sleep well last night."

"You rest all afternoon if you want. We have to go get the wagon loaded and see about the horses. That'll take up most of the afternoon. Then I'll come back, and we can take a walk around town before supper."

They left and Susana went upstairs to lie down.

The three men headed back to the wagon yard.

"I did like you told me to," Josh said. "I watched what Susana looked at and then put back. Once I figured out what she really wanted, I had the store lady put it aside with the ranch items. It wasn't really that much."

"Thanks, I appreciate you doing that. When we get to the store and start going over the ranch list for loading, you can show me what you put aside. I'll see if we can afford it." Elisha tipped his hat at a lady they walked past.

"What kind of stuff was it?" Abe asked.

"Oh, material for dresses, hair ribbons, lace, a pair of boots for herself, some things for the cabin. Some dishes, a couple of quilts. Oh, I don't know what all. Just stuff like that."

Abe grunted and said, "Well, we'll see about it."

Elisha looked at Abe and wondered what he meant. It was for him to decide to buy something for his wife or not, not Abe, but he didn't say anything.

"You didn't have any problems with any of the men on the street, did you?" Elisha asked, although if there had been, he thought Josh would have told him first thing.

"No problems. Because you warned me, I was on the lookout. I had no idea so many men looked after a woman walking down the street that way. I stayed up close to Susana and tried to look fierce, and it worked. I don't know what might have happened if I hadn't been with her because, like you said, she's so friendly to everyone."

"Were you expecting trouble?" Abe raised his eyebrows as he looked at Elisha.

"Not really, but I wanted to make sure that nothing happened." Elisha turned to Josh and patted him on the back, "so I asked Josh to look out for her."

"Here's the money you gave me. I didn't spend any of it because everything is with the ranch supplies." Josh handed Elisha the twenty-five dollars.

Elisha put the money back into his billfold. "Guess I'll have to settle up with the store keep."

They walked into the wagon yard and found the wagon ready to go, as well as the new set of harness. They hitched the horses and pulled the wagon up to the back of the store by the loading platform.

Elisha entered the general store and saw that it was several stores in one: a general store with dry goods and groceries, a hardware store, and a ranch and farm implements store. The aisles were narrow, and items were stacked from floor to ceiling.

A short, bald headed man stood behind the counter in the general store.

"I'm Elisha Evans. We're here to load the supplies for the J Bar C.

"Hello fellows. I'm Milburn Black and this is my wife, Agnes."

Elisha looked around and all he could see was confusion. But when someone asked for something, Agnes seemed to know exactly where to find it.

Milburn checked off items from the ranch list.

Abe and Josh packed the big wagon. They packed some of the bigger items first: five sacks of flour weighing a hundred pounds each, a hundred pounds of cornmeal, three hundred pounds of sugar, twenty pounds of baking powder, and on and on the supplies went. The ranch required a lot of food to feed ten people for three months. The last thing to be packed was a crate of eggs, with each one wrapped in paper.

Then Milburn remembered to get a sack of mail that belonged to the ranch. The store also contained the local post office.

When they had the wagon packed, Elisha hadn't seen the things for Susana. "Mr. Black, I believe you put aside some things for my wife this morning?"

"Yes, we did. They've already been loaded, I believe." He turned and called to his wife. "Agnes, the things for Mrs. Evans?"

Agnes Black came over and smiled at Elisha. "She's going to be so surprised when she opens her packages at home."

"I hope so. But, I'm not sure we can afford everything that got set aside."

"I've got the list here, and it comes to fifteen dollars. Is that all right?" Agnes gave Elisha a piece of paper.

Elisha laughed with relief. "I thought it might be a lot more. We can afford that."

"Good. I liked your wife, Mr. Evans, and I'm glad she's going to get a few things she wants." She looked thoughtful. "I've something else I know she'd like, but it's expensive."

"What is that, ma'am?"

She took him to the part of the store where they had all of the fabrics and ribbons displayed. In a walnut cabinet, she showed him a machine.

"A Singer sewing machine," she said proudly, "the latest thing to help ladies to make their own dresses, their husband's shirts, and even quilts. I've got one and it's a wonder."

Elisha eyed it, afraid to know the answer to his next question. "How much does something like this cost?" he asked, thinking about a birthday present for Susana.

"Well, I've got to admit that this is not a new one. A woman, traveling through with her family, ran out of money. She sold the sewing machine to me in exchange for food. I've tried it out and it works perfectly. New, this sewing machine would cost you a hundred dollars."

A hundred dollars would buy a couple of good horses and more, Elisha thought.

"But because the lady had used it, I can let you have it for twenty dollars."

"You think my wife would like to have something like this?" Elisha rubbed the back of his neck, trying to think.

"I know she would. She spent a great deal of time looking at dress and shirt goods. She now has enough for three dresses and several shirts, and this is the very thing she needs to get all that sewn up." Agnes stood with a confident look on her face.

"All right." After all, he couldn't resist that kind of logic. "I'll get this...what did you call this thing?"

Agnes laughed. "This is a genuine Singer sewing machine."

Elisha reached into his pocket to pull out his wallet, but Abe reminded him that Mr. Weathers had said everything was to go on the ranch account, and that Elisha would settle later with Mr. Weathers. Elisha felt like he'd entered another world, full of things he knew nothing about. He certainly had never imagined buying a sewing machine when he walked through the door of the store. Would Susana know how to operate it? He sure didn't.

Abe and Josh wrapped the sewing machine in the walnut cabinet in a piece of canvas, tied it up, and then loaded it onto the wagon.

As they were ready to take the heavily loaded wagon back to the yard where Herman Jones would let it stay in the barn until they left the next day, Agnes came up and handed Elisha a box.

"Your wife will need extra thread and things. I made her a sewing kit and added an extra pair of scissors as a gift. Tell her it's from Mr. Black and me, and good luck with her new sewing machine."

Elisha thanked her for her generosity. Agnes could have sold the machine for a lot more than twenty dollars. Elisha shook his head and grinned. His wife's charms appeared to affect everyone.

After making sure to park the wagon back in the barn at Herman Jones' wagon yard, they parted ways. Abe and Josh went to do more exploring of the town.

Elisha returned to the hotel to see if Susana wanted to go for the walk he'd promised her. He knocked on the door, then went ahead and opened it. "Hey, Susana, it's only me."

Susana sat in the hotel room waiting for him. She'd been reading her Bible, which she did most days.

He covered the distance between them and bent to give her a kiss. "Did you get some rest?"

"Yes, I actually fell asleep for over two hours. I don't know what has gotten into me being so tired all of a sudden. Did you get the supplies loaded?"

"We're all ready to start out tomorrow afternoon. It's a big wagon and fully loaded, so we'll travel slowly. We have six horses to pull at any one time, so it shouldn't be a problem."

"This has been so much fun, Elisha. Thanks for bringing me."

"Mr. Weathers is the one who offered for us to come. You can thank him when we get back. You want to go for that walk before supper?"

"Oh yes, let me get my boots and jacket on."

They went down to the lobby, and Elisha told the room clerk that they would be leaving the next afternoon after lunch. He also asked for directions to the church building and the residential part of the town.

Elisha took Susana's hand and pulled it through his arm as he escorted her out the door of the hotel and turned away from the business part of the town. Soon they were walking on a street a couple of blocks behind the hotel. Elisha wanted to get an idea where the church building was and figured that was as good a direction to walk. They passed by several homes with picket fences and flowers planted in the yards. The spring flowers were starting to bloom, and the afternoon was pleasant and cool.

"I filed on the land," he said after they walked for a few minutes in silence.

"Oh, you did it." Susana looked up at him with shining eyes. "You've really started."

"Started what?"

"Started building your ranch. This is the first step and I'm so proud of you."

"It's our ranch." He smiled at her. "It's going to be for both of us. You're right, filing on the land is a beginning." He kept his hand over hers as it rested on his arm, and pulled her closer. "It'll be years of hard work and a lot of unknowns. As I looked on the map at the land office I realized how isolated the ranch will be. Do I really have the right to take you so far from town and all the things that make for an easier life?"

"Aren't you forgetting something?" She cocked her head at him coquettishly.

"What is that, my love?"

"We are tied at the hip, and if you are going to be up in that valley starting a ranch, then that's where I'm going to be, and I'll not have any argument about it."

"Thank you. You're what gives me the strength to step out and do this."

"I'll always be here to give you what I can. Don't you ever forget."

They walked full circle and were back at the front of the hotel as the evening started to grow dark.

"Ready to go in and eat?"

"Yes, I'm starved."

"Let's keep the filing on the land between you and me. There's nothing wrong with telling Abe and Josh, but I'd rather not talk about what we plan until we have things further along."

Susana looked up at him with a frown. "I think I understand. You're right." She smiled that devastatingly beautiful smile and his heart turned over at the sight of it. "You and me, when we're ready, right?"

Elisha couldn't find the words to express how that felt to him. How his life had changed in the last few months. To have such oneness with someone so beautiful, both physically and spiritually, was such a surprise after the loneliness in his life a year ago.

"Elisha? What are you thinking?"

"How beautiful you are in the twilight. Let's go get Josh and Abe and eat. I'm hungry."

CHAPTER ELEVEN

Elisha was glad to see Sunday morning come with a bright, clear blue sky and the warming temperatures of a spring day. A good day to be outside and to travel. Susana was more talkative than usual at breakfast and her face was bright and animated. Elisha guessed she was excited about going to the church service. He listened to her talking and couldn't keep a smile from his face. She was happy, and he'd been a part of bringing that about.

Josh was unusually quiet and Abe was his usual self. Josh and Abe had stayed up late the night before, seeing what the town had to offer, but Elisha got no hint that they had been involved in drinking too much. Elisha guessed that Josh was a little concerned about going to a church service for the first time. He was such an outgoing young man. Elisha forgot sometimes what a restricted life he'd lived. Except for a few trips to the Cedar Ridge, Josh told him he had spent the last seven years on the J Bar C.

Elisha noticed that Josh and Abe had on clean clothes, had shaved, and brushed off their hats and boots, which he had done out of respect for the church service. Susana wore a pretty, light green dress. She'd brushed her hair and now it shone in the sunlight.

They walked together to the church service, and as they approached the little white, wooden building, Elisha was relieved to see other men dressed in ranching wear. A few of the men wore black broadcloth suits, and several of the women had stylist dresses with matching hats.

Elisha estimated that there were about forty people waiting for the service to start and many said, 'Hello" as the little group entered the church. Elisha was not sure how long he could stay around so many people. He quickly forgot their names, his hands felt wet, and he wiped them on his pants before he shook anyone's hand. He looked over at Josh and Abe. They also seemed uncomfortable with all the attention.

Susana smiled and talked, as if in her natural element.

The church service began with a prayer by Milburn Black, followed by the reading of a Scripture. Then a young man dressed like a cowhand led the group in several hymns in a strong, tenor voice.

Susana's clear soprano joined in, and to his surprise Abe's deep bass followed. Elisha looked over at Josh, caught his eye, shrugged, and grinned. Even though he didn't know the hymns and couldn't join in, Elisha didn't feel like an outsider. He closed his eyes for a moment and listened.

An elderly man, who reminded Elisha of Susana's grandfather, stepped into the pulpit. He'd chosen a few of Jesus' parables to talk about, and pointed out how they applied to his congregation's lives. The way he laid out the Scripture and then found ways to explain it in terms of events were things Elisha could understand. The lesson was over before Elisha was ready for it to end. Again, the young cowhand led them in a couple of hymns.

Two men rose from their seats and stood before the congregation. One of the men said a prayer and then they passed a plate holding pieces of flatbread. The people in front of them each took a small piece. Now what? Elisha thought. He didn't understand what they were doing, so he passed the plate on to Susana who took a small piece of the flatbread and ate it before giving it to Abe who also took a piece and passed it on. One the two men at the front then said another prayer. This time they passed two goblets and each person took a small sip of the dark liquid. Curious, Elisha looked carefully at it and then passed the goblet to Susana. He would ask her later to explain it, as it was something new to him.

To Elisha's surprise, Cullen Fredericks stood at the front of the group and talked about people and their prayer needs. Then Fredericks nodded toward Elisha and Susana and welcomed them as visitors. He also acknowledged Abe and Josh, telling everyone to be sure to welcome them, which most of the people had already done. "Now, please stand for our closing prayer," he said and bowed his head.

After a few words, Mr. Frederick said, "Amen." Voices murmured and gradually grew louder as people turned in their pews and began leaving the church building. When a few men and women told Elisha how glad they were to see him, his mouth felt like dust and he began wiping his hands on his trousers again.

They walked back to the hotel, and Elisha suggested that they eat before changing into their traveling clothes. He led them into the dining room and chose a round table that would seat six people easily. After they sat at the table, he noticed several others from the congregation coming in.

Cullen Fredericks entered with a young girl, who looked to be about sixteen. She had long curly blonde hair cascading down her back and held back from her face with a ribbon that matched her white dress with little pink flowers on it. Her deep blue eyes were bright and sparkling as she laughed at something Cullen Fredericks said.

From the moment she walked into the dining room, Josh stared at her.

Elisha waved to Cullen.

He walked up to their table with the young girl following. "Elisha Evans, I'd like to meet your wife. And I'd like to introduce my daughter, Mary."

The J Bar C men stood, shook hands with Mr. Fredericks, and nodded at his daughter.

Elisha made the introductions and asked Fredericks to join them for dinner.

As they settled back in their chairs, Josh sat across from Mary, which seemed all right with them because they kept sneaking looks at each other and smiling.

Elisha was a little concerned that Mr. Frederick might talk about his filing on the land, but they spoke in generalities about other things. A pleasant hour and a half passed eating fried chicken, boiled potatoes, canned green beans, biscuits, gravy, and apple pie and conversing with as a group of friends.

Fredericks was the first to get up. "Well, we need to get going." He pulled back Mary's chair as she rose. "Thanks for letting us eat with you all. Maybe we'll see you the next time you make it to town," Fredericks said to Elisha as he shook hands.

Fredericks walked quickly out of the dining room and on through the lobby. Mary hung back and let Josh escort her out of the hotel.

Elisha turned to Abe and Susana. "It's a little later than I thought we'd leave town, but we'll go ahead like we planned and start back for the ranch this afternoon."

Susana nodded. "I hope we haven't lost Josh."

They arranged to meet at the wagon, and Elisha and Susana went upstairs to change clothes and pack. Elisha was relieved to start out for the ranch. A little bit of town went a long way for him. But he was glad he had been able to give Susana a chance to attend church services. He knew how much it meant to her.

As they walked toward the wagon yard, Josh came running up behind them.

"So you decided to come with us?" Elisha asked, grinning.

"Sorry, but Mary let me walk her home," Josh said with a hint of pride.

"She seemed very nice and so pretty." Susana smiled at him.

"Yes, she is." Josh agreed.

"And we got to get on the road home. Sorry, Josh," Elisha said in understanding.

"Well, maybe I can get Mr. Weathers to let me come back to town next trip. Mary said I could call."

"I hope so. That would be nice for you." Susana linked her arm with Josh's. "See what can happen if you go to church?"

When they got to the wagon yard, Abe already had their saddle horses ready and waited for Elisha and Josh to help get the six horses hitched up to the wagon.

Just when they were ready to pull out, Milburn and Agnes Black came up to the wagon carrying two crates of chickens.

"Here you go, Abe. I promised you some chickens to take to the ranch, and we almost forgot," Milburn said.

Abe managed to find a place in the wagon for the crates. "Thanks folks. Nate and Smithy will be glad to have these chickens."

Milburn and Agnes waved goodbye as Abe got the wagon started up and they began the trip back to the ranch.

The two-day trip was uneventful but the heavily loaded wagon slowed them down. Elisha was glad it didn't rain, although with the waterproof canvas over the bows of the new wagon tied down tightly, their cargo was secure.

Elisha was content to ride back to the ranch, although he did get a little tired of Josh's mooning over Mary. He remembered the first time he thought he loved a girl. There was little likelihood that Josh would see Mary anytime soon. Well, at least he had someone to think about.

Elisha, used to Susana's talking as they rode, puzzled over her quietness. She rode so easy and confident beside him. Maybe the reason she was so quiet had something to do with Josh and Abe being with them.

Around noon, they pulled into the yard of the J Bar C. Elisha took in the sight of the ranch as he dismounted and then helped Susana. He liked the sense of being in the midst of familiar surroundings, kind of like coming home.

Nate and Smithy came from the house to greet them.

"Glad you all made it. We're starting to get low on some things, like coffee. It don't do to run out of coffee," Nate said.

Abe scratched the side of his head. "Where is everyone?"

"Mr. Weathers and the rest of the hands are out with the south herd doing the branding. I'm sure they're missing you boys. Especially you, Josh." Nate replied.

"Well, here are some chickens that Milburn Black sent you. I'm glad to get rid of them. They're noisy, smelly creatures." Abe handed the crates of chickens down to Nate and Smithy.

"This is great. Now we can have our own eggs." Nate set the crate of chickens on the ground.

"Yeah and something else to take care of." Smithy placed the second crate by the first.

"Is that because you're the one that will get to feed them and clean up after them?" Elisha asked.

"Exactly right. I've always managed to talk Nate out of getting any chickens until now. Oh well, I do like to cook with eggs." Smithy grinned.

"Miss Susana, you go on in and I'll bring you some hot water to wash up with. You boys tend the horses and wash up and we'll have dinner ready in about twenty minutes," Nate said.

"That sounds good. I'll bring your valise in later, Susana. You go on into the house." Elisha looked at her tired face. Had the trip been too hard for her?

"Thanks. Nate, I would like to wash up some." Susana walked toward the house looking like she had to drag herself along.

Nate and Smithy had a meal on the table by the time the horses were unhitched and everyone washed up.

Elisha liked sitting around the kitchen table again and eating Nate and Smithy's delicious, plain food.

"Susana, you look tired. Why don't you go rest this afternoon?" Elisha suggested. "We can handle the packing."

"It would feel good to lie down for a little while." Susana sighed.

Elisha accompanied her to the bedroom and kissed her. "Have a good rest. I'll come in after we finish the unloading and repacking."

"Thanks for understanding." She gave him another kiss.

They divided the supplies between what Elisha and Susana would take back to the cabin and supplies for the ranch. Since Elisha hadn't brought the wagon down, all of their supplies had to be crammed into packs the horses could handle. The sewing machine was a challenge, but Elisha finally figured out how to tie it onto the pack. He wanted to start back to the cabin early the next morning, so he spent the afternoon getting everything ready. Mr. Weathers and the hands rode in tired and hungry an hour before dark.

Nate and Smithy put together a bountiful meal of roast beef and vegetables that Elisha gave his full attention to, as did the other men.

Susana had put on her light green dress. She had a new, matching ribbon to hold her hair back, loosely flowing down her back. Elisha thought she looked especially beautiful, although still tired, in spite of resting most of the afternoon.

After supper, Mr. Weathers asked Elisha to meet with him in the front room.

Susana again went out to the porch and sat with the hands. Her laughter came in from the porch as he and Mr. Weathers talked about the work on the north range.

Elisha asked what he owed Mr. Weathers for the things he and Susana bought in town.

"Oh, it's not much, Elisha. Let me figure a bit from this list sent by Milburn Black. Let's see . . . some dress goods, ribbons, and this sewing machine, whatever that is."

Elisha explained what it was and that he was giving it to Susana as an early birthday present.

"Well, that's something, a machine that you can have in your own house and sews clothes for you. Now who would have thought up something like that?" Mr. Weathers shook his head in amazement.

Elisha thought it was amazing also, but what astounded him more was that Agnes Black had talked him into buying it.

"There are other household goods that Susana picked out. There were a couple of hand-stitched quilts, and actually I'm not sure what else there was. They need to be on the list that I'm paying for and not for the ranch."

"Now how do you figure that, Elisha? I provide what my crew needs in the way of living."

"Well sir, I feel like Susana and I need to be accumulating some things of our own. One day we hope to have our own place, and we'll need household goods."

"I see. Tell you what I'll do, I'll pay for them now, and you can use them as needed. When you decide to move on to your own place, I'll make you a good deal on whatever you want to take. Does that seem fair?"

"That's more than fair. In a way, it's a relief, because I think Susana is worrying about spending too much and not saving. I can tell her its ranch policy, and maybe she'll not be concerned."

"Elisha, I like that little wife of yours, and of course, you too." He laughed. "And if I can do something to reduce her worry about things, you let me know." Mr. Weathers sat thinking for a minute. "I know you said that you had talked it over with her, but if it gets too rough up at the cabin, I want your word that you'll bring her on down here, whether she wants to come or not. I want your promise on that. I'll not be a part of a woman suffering needlessly."

"I can make that promise willingly."

"Well, I'm off to bed and we'll see you off in the morning."

Elisha strolled out to the porch. The men listened as Abe and Susana softly sang a hymn for them. He sat on the steps, watching the faces of the cowhands soften as they listened to the singing.

CHAPTER TWELVE

Elisha watched as the gray light of dawn crept through the bedroom window. His usual time to wake. Glancing at the sleeping form of his wife, he reveled in her porcelain skin, her arching eyebrows, her soft lips, and her loosely flowing brown hair spread out over the pillow. He felt a surge of energy as he remembered that he was taking his bride back to the cabin today. Elisha carefully slid out of bed to let her rest as much as possible before they started back. He opened the door of the bedroom to find a pitcher of hot water. Elisha smiled at Nate or Smithy already up doing their jobs.

He quickly washed up, went to start saddling the horses. He found Abe already at work. They tied the mounts Elisha had brought down from the cabin to the corral fence and packed them for the trip back up the mountain.

Back in the house, Elisha found Susana sitting at the table sipping coffee and talking with Nate and Smithy. Soon all of the hands had gathered around the table, waiting for Mr. Weathers to say the blessing. At the 'amen' Elisha looked at the table and licked his lips. Nate and Smithy outdid themselves with pan-fried ham, eggs, gravy, biscuits, fried potatoes, and a special treat of pancakes and syrup.

Elisha filled his plate and ate with gusto. When his plate was empty, he looked around and saw that there was plenty of food for another plateful. As he used his biscuit to sop up the last of his gravy, he felt full and had probably eaten more than his share. Looking at Susana who still seemed tired, he knew he could make it the rest of the day without another hot meal.

~ ~ ~

As Elisha tightened the girth on his saddle, Nate and Smithy came out of the house carrying a gunnysack. "Here's some grub for your journey."

Smithy nodded. "Susana, we don't want you to have to cook when you get to the cabin. There's roast beef sandwiches made with bread baked yesterday, plus two, whole, dried peach pies for you Elisha, knowing how much you appreciate our cooking."

Elisha tied the gunnysack onto his saddlebags behind his saddle. "Thanks, we appreciate it."

Susana gave each of the older men a hug. "You are a blessing. I won't have to worry about dinner or supper."

After they said, "Good-bye," Elisha and Susana mounted their horses and started up the wagon trail toward the cabin. He led the packhorses with Susana riding alongside. He thought about the time at the ranch and in town. The trip to town had cemented deep friendships with Abe and Josh. If Elisha didn't want to go back to the cabin, Mr. Weathers was willing to find a place for him at the ranch headquarters. Nevertheless, he was also glad to be riding back home with Susana by his side. He liked the life they'd made, the two of them working together.

The chill of evening was already on the land when they came up over the rise, then looked down on the cabin and barn in the valley up against the far ridge. Elisha exhaled and the tension drained away. They were home.

Once at the cabin, Elisha helped Susana dismount. "You go on in and start a fire to get the chill out of the cabin. I'll be in as soon as I take care of the horses."

Susana hugged him. "Welcome home. I'm so glad to be back."

He grinned at her. "Me too."

Elisha unloaded the packs in the barn and then turned the horses into the corral. He carried their duffel bags and saddlebags into the cabin.

Susana had lit a lamp and had a fire started in the stove. She'd set water to heating.

He put the saddlebags down on the table. "I'll bring in the rest of the things tomorrow. They'll be fine in the barn for tonight." Elisha stood by the fire rubbing his aching back.

"Good idea. Then I can be of more help. Tonight all I want to do is go to bed. I'm really tired for some reason."

She did look more tired than usual after a day of riding. He stepped over to where she was standing by the stove and put his arms around her.

Elisha brushed her hair away from her face. "We can eat up the last of what Nate sent and get on to bed. No need to cook anything."

She laid her head against his chest. "Are you sure? I don't mind fixing you some hot supper, although I'm not really hungry."

"I'm sure. I like Nate's sandwiches and pie. It'll be plenty. But you sure you don't want any?"

"No, my stomach hasn't been happy with me for a couple of days. I don't know what the problem is. Maybe if I get a good night's sleep in our own bed I'll feel better in the morning."

Elisha was concerned, but didn't have a solution other than getting her to rest more. While he sat at the table and ate the last of Nate's sandwiches and half a dried peach pie, Susana put on her nightgown, and then went to bed. After awhile, he went to the bed and found her already asleep. He pulled off his clothes and boots. What would he do if she got sick? He turned the lantern off, slipped in beside her, and then prayed that she'd be all right the next morning.

Elisha woke before daylight to find the other side of the bed empty. When he looked around the cabin, he didn't see her. Remembering how tired she had looked the evening before, he quickly dressed, walked outside, and saw her standing bent over at the far side of the yard. He swiftly went over to her and heard the sound of her being sick.

"What's wrong?" Elisha put his arms around her to give her support. "Why are you sick? You didn't even eat last night."

"I don't know." She raised her head and rested it on his chest. "I've been feeling sick every morning for over a week now."

"Why didn't you tell me?"

"Well, it's not very attractive, now is it? And besides, what can you do about it?"

"I can hold your head and be sympathetic." Elisha brushed her hair from her face. "Are you all right now? It's chilly out here and you aren't dressed." She wore only her thin nightgown, and she was barefoot.

"Yes, it's better now. Let's go back in." She continued to lean against him.

Elisha picked her up and carried her back into the cabin. He put her on the bed and pulled the covers up to her chin, then lit a fire in the stove. It would warm up later in the morning, but it was still chilly.

He stared at Susana, lying in the bed with her eyes closed, looking small, and pale. Suddenly Elisha gasped and his eyes opened wide! He grasped the edge of the table with the dizziness of the thought.

Could it be that she was with child?

Elisha didn't know much about such things, but the possibility existed. There had been a rancher's wife where he had worked once who had pretty much the same symptoms as Susana, and she had a baby girl about eight months later.

A child! He found himself grinning, and then frowning. A shiver went down his spine. How was he going to take care of her and a baby? Moving slowly with his thoughts a turmoil, Elisha poured water into the coffee pot.

He'd have to take her back to Mr. Weathers's house. Almost forgetting to put in the coffee, he reached up to the upper shelve for the bag of Arbuckle coffee.

Going outside to the stacks of cut firewood, he stared at the creek. What if the trip would hurt the baby, or worse, hurt Susana? Shaking himself, he brought in an arm full of wood and then refilled the water bucket from the trough.

After setting the bucket of water down by the stove, Elisha slipped quietly over to her and sat on the side of the bed. He pushed Susana's hair away from her face.

She opened her eyes and smiled up at him. "Why such a serious face, my love? I'm all right now, just being lazy."

"Susana, could you be expecting a child?" He drew his words out slowly.

Her eyes widened, and she drew in her breath. "Is that what's happening?"

"It might be." He stroked her cheek.

"Oh, Elisha, that would be wonderful!" She exclaimed with a sunburst of a smile. "Oh my, wouldn't that be something?" She sat up and flung her arms around him in her joy. "Aren't you glad, Elisha?"

He gathered her up into his arms and buried his face into her hair.

"Why, Elisha," she pulled back to look at him. "You're crying. Don't you want a child?"

He struggled to get his voice under control. "Susana, I want a child with you more than anything. It's so surprising. I wasn't expecting it so soon." He wiped his sleeve across his eyes but more tears fell.

He didn't tell her that it also filled him with such fear. Everyone knew that women sometimes died giving birth, and the two of them were so isolated, without another woman nearby. There wasn't even a woman down at the ranch. He could hardly imagine what it would be like.

When he could speak again without the tears, he asked, "When do you think it will come?" He tightened his arms around her.

"Well, you know it takes nine months if everything goes all right."

"Don't say that!" He swallowed down a sob. "It has to go all right."

"It'll go all right." She pulled away from his arms and took his hand. "Having a baby is a natural thing. Many women have babies. If I count from my last monthly time, I believe this may be a Christmas baby. Won't that be a nice present?" She sighed with a smile.

"We're heading back to the ranch as soon as you can travel." He tightened his arms around her again as if that could protect her.

"We are not. We are going to do our work here, and then we'll see what we need to do in the fall."

"But Susana, what if you need help?"

"Then you'll help me. I don't know everything about having a baby, but I do know that most of the time before they are birthed the mothers feel fine and can go about their chores. That's what I plan to do. Feeling sick in the mornings is no reason to change our plans."

From her expression, he could tell this wasn't the time to argue with her. "All right, we'll see how it goes, but before the baby is born we're heading down to the ranch headquarters, and that's final."

"Yes Elisha," she said sweetly, as she beamed at him. "Now you go ahead and take care of the horses and bring in the supplies. I'll get breakfast going. I'm hungry." She pushed him away and swung her legs out of bed.

Elisha did as he was told. He went out to the barn, and fed and watered the horses. Then he tackled the packs, bringing in all the parcels for Susana and the food first. After that, he stored the other supplies in the loft. He left the sewing machine in the barn.

By the time he'd carried the last gunnysack of foodstuff into the cabin, Susana had a hot breakfast of fried ham, gravy, and biscuits on the table. Elisha washed his hands in the basin on the washstand inside the door and then sat down at the table with her.

Taking her hands across the table, he bowed his head. "God, we thank you for the safe trip and the nights rest. Thank you for this meal and bless Susana. Take care of her and if we are truly expecting, bless the child. Please, God, keep her safe and help me to know what to do. In the name of Jesus, Amen." When he raised his head, Susana looked at him with tears in her eyes.

"Thank you. So it's true. We're going to have a baby?"

"That's the only thing I can figure out. We'll know for sure in about eight or nine months."

"If it's truly happening, we'll know for sure long before that. You know that I'm going to get big and fat and ugly and all those things that happen to women while waiting for the baby to be birthed."

With her shining face and her trim figure, he couldn't imagine her fat and ugly. "You take care of having the baby, and I'll tell you when you get fat and ugly," he teased.

"Can we stay around the cabin and get settled again, or do we need to head out and start checking the cattle today?" She passed him more hot biscuits.

"We'll take today to get things squared away here, and then tomorrow I'll ride out. You're going to stay here and take care of yourself." He wanted to keep her safe.

"It'll be fine for me to ride if we don't make it more than a normal day and are back at the cabin before dark. Having a baby isn't going to make me a frail, delicate woman. I'd rather ride out with you than be lonely all day here by myself."

"How do you know that riding won't hurt you or the baby?"

"If I feel like it's hurting me, I won't ride. I promise that I'll tell you if I shouldn't ride out. I don't want to hurt our baby any more than you do."

Susana put the food away and washed the dishes while Elisha sorted through their supplies. He stacked several packages on the table that felt like dress goods.

"What are those?" Susana picked up one of the packages and felt of it.

"Open it and see." Elisha grinned.

Susana undid the string around the brown paper wrapped package and revealed several pieces of yard goods. Looking up at Elisha, she stood still for a moment. "Elisha Evans, what did you do? This is the cloth I looked at with Mrs. Black at the store. How did it get into our stuff?"

"Maybe an angel put it there?" Elisha grinned. He wondered what Josh would think of being called an angel.

As she unwrapped several of the parcels, Susana laughed with delight as things were revealed that she'd wished for at the store. "This is the fabric for a couple of shirts for you, and black broad cloth to make you a suit. I can't believe you bought all this for us."

"A suit! I don't need a suit. Where would I wear it? And besides that, do you know how to sew one?" Elisha thought of the sewing machine out in the barn. Maybe she really did need it.

"Oh, don't you worry. I know how to sew you a suit. I helped my mother sew for my father. She made all his shirts and his suit."

Elisha lifted a larger paper wrapped parcel from beside the door where he had left it the night before and placed it on the table.

Susana immediately unwrapped it and found the two quilts she'd admired. "The wedding ring quilt and the star of Texas quilt. Agnes Black told me that a lady on a ranch out from Cedar Ridge made these quilts and Agnes sells them for her. Look at these perfect stitches. This is fine work."

Susana held up the quilts for him to examine. "Oh Elisha, these will make the cabin look so pretty." She took the quilts and spread them over the bunk. "We never had much need for quilts where we lived in California. But these will be useful, especially through the cold nights."

"Well, if we are going to have pretty quilts, then maybe I should move the bunks to the loft and set up your bedstead. And the truth be told, that bunk is a little crowded for the two of us."

Susana smiled. "Don't you mean the three of us?"

Elisha looked around the cabin. His first proper home. How was it going to hold more stuff, like a cradle? This was so much better than any bunkhouse. Yeah, he liked being married and living here with Susana.

Elisha looked at his slender wife, who carried his child. How his life had changed again.

"What are you thinking?" Susana turned toward him from where she was arranging cans of food on the open shelves.

He tilted his head at her. "Why do you ask?"

"You're looking at me so strangely."

"I was thinking of the marvel of having a child. And with a family, I've got to get our own place as soon as I can."

Susana put her hand on his arm. "I want our own place, too. But wherever you are, that's where I'm going to be content. And that goes for the baby also."

After a full day of sorting and arranging things, carrying in wood, cleaning out the hearth, mucking out the barn, checking on the horses left in the box canyon and setting up the bedstead, Elisha was ready to sit quietly with Susana. After supper, he read to her.

As he put the Bible away, he said, "I need to go out to the barn for something. I'll be right back."

She didn't question it. "I'll start some dough rising for the morning while you're gone."

Elisha headed out to the barn. Once he got there, he decided to pitch more hay down for the horses and to rub down Jasper who he had ridden all day. Then he unwrapped the sewing machine in its cabinet. It looked like it made the trip without damage. He carried it to the cabin door and set it down. Peeking into the cabin, he saw Susana put a cloth over the bowl of dough.

"Susana, I've got a surprise for you," he said through the open door. "But I want you to close your eyes while I bring it in."

She looked puzzled, but complied.

He brought the sewing machine in and then placed it next to the bureau.

"You can open your eyes now."

Susana opened her eyes and looked at him and then at the small cabinet he'd placed by the bureau, with its metal base with a treadle wheel and a foot pedal that bespoke of many garments to come.

"What is it?"

"Come and look." He removed the wooden cover to reveal the sewing machine.

Susana came over to look closer. "Well, my goodness, it's a sewing machine! Wherever did you get this?"

"I got it from Agnes Black as an early birthday present for you. What do you think? Can you use it?"

"Use it! Of course, I can use it, but it must have cost a lot of money. Can we afford it?"

"Agnes gave us a good price for it because she'd got it in exchange for food from some lady passing through with her family. She promised me that it works." He gave her the box of different colored threads, scissors, and other things that Agnes has sent with the sewing machine. "You do know how to work it, don't you?"

"Yes, one of our neighbors had one and she let me use it. I learned all about how to operate it. It's not hard," she assured him.

He let out a sigh of relief. Knowing she could use it and seeing her excitement gave him a warm feeling inside.

"Oh Elisha, with the baby coming I can make everything we need for him. Thank you so much."

She hugged him and then kissed him with what started as a simple thank you kiss, but it soon turned into a long passionate kiss that started his blood to pounding. He pulled away from her with a shake of his head.

"What's the matter, Elisha?" she asked, pulling him back to her.

"Not with the baby coming, we can't," he said, resisting her.

"What do you mean? The baby won't be here for months. It won't hurt the baby for you to make love to me." She pulled him toward the bed.

He hoped she was right.

CHAPTER THIRTEEN

How long can I keep doing this? She gently caressed her stomach. Susana steadied Jasper as they hazed a bunch of cows back toward the creek. Elisha was on Shadow and doing most of the work.

Hey, baby, you riding comfortable? Rubbing her stomach, which was only slightly rounded, she thought of her unborn child. With so many hours in the saddle, this baby had to be a good rider.

She watched her husband as he rode up beside her. It took away her breath when she watched the way he moved in the saddle. The way he became one with his horse and seemed to turn in concert. She liked to watch as he threw out his lariat and snagged a cow that didn't want to be driven. His muscles rippled under his shirt across his broad back and the tendons stood out on his exposed arms where he had his shirtsleeves rolled up.

"You doing all right?"

"Of course, I'm all right." She smiled at him. Did he know he was so handsome, especially when he worried about her?

"You'll tell me when you get tired?" He leaned across and took her hand.

"Yes, my husband. I promise. Now let's get these cows across the creek." Susana was more tired than she had been before she knew she was expecting a child. A child. The thought still sent a shiver through her. The thought of the birthing and the care for the infant concerned her, but not enough to take away the joy of her becoming a mother. She leaned over and gave him a kiss.

"Let's head back to the cabin," Elisha suggested.

"But there's hours of daylight still." Susana turned to look at him.

"I know, but let's make it a shorter day. We've done enough and besides that I'm hungry."

"You're always hungry. All right, let's get back to the cabin and I'll have more time to prepare supper." Was he really that hungry? Or, wanting it a shorter workday for her? She didn't mind because she was tired. She still was sick every morning and didn't sleep well. But she didn't want to use it as an excuse.

~ ~ ~

Susana looked at Elisha over her cup of coffee as they lingered over breakfast. "Elisha, shouldn't you be riding out to the west and spending the night?"

"It'll be all right." He poured himself another half cup of coffee.

"Tell me the truth. Are you not doing your usual patrol because of me?"

He glanced down and over to the left as if thinking of what to say, then sighed. "I can't lie to you. Yes, I guess I am. I don't want you to have to sleep on the ground overnight."

"But I can sleep in a bedroll on the ground and it won't hurt the baby." She had a frown and there was an edge to her voice.

Elisha frowned back at her. "How do you know it won't hurt you or the baby? This is all as new to you as it is to me."

"I just know. I'm not hurting and not being sick. What makes you think it will hurt me?"

He shook his head and stared down at the table.

Susana didn't want to be the reason he didn't get his work done, but she didn't want to argue with him either. She got up from the table and started packing their bedroll.

"What are you doing?" Elisha also left the table and stood by her.

"I'm going to go patrol to the western boundary. What are you going to do?" She glanced sideways at him and allowed a slight smile to escape.

He shook his head at her. "I guess I'll ride along with you."

She could hear the frustration and maybe a little anger in his voice. Was she stepping over her boundary as a wife? Maybe she should give in to him as her husband, but maybe they should ride out and then they both could see if it hurt her. Susana said a silent prayer that she was making the decision God wanted her to make.

~ ~ ~

Even though the trip tired Susana, she enjoyed their two days trip to the west, especially the way Elisha took care of her. Camping overnight wasn't too difficult. She did enjoy the snuggling with Elisha after they combined their bedrolls and gazing up at the stars.

The first morning she had woke in the cool mountain air and poked her head out of the bedroll. She watched as Elisha put pieces of wood on the fire, filled the coffeepot, and added the Arbuckle coffee, walked over to the spring, and refilled the water bucket. She really didn't want to get up, but if she didn't stir soon he would have all the camp chores done.

Elisha squatted by the open fire and put salt pork in the hot skillet. He turned toward her. "Morning, sleepyhead. Aren't you going to get up?"

"Morning yourself. You let me sleep."

He grinned. "You and the baby."

Susana rubbed her stomach, thankful that she was no longer sick every morning.

Elisha came over to the bedroll and surprised her by lying down next to her. Taking her face between his hands, he kissed her and then wrapped his arms around her. She felt warm and secure with the tightness of his embrace.

"I love you," she smiled.

"I love you." Elisha's voice was muffled as he had his face in her hair. He gave her a last kiss and jumped up to return to his breakfast preparations. In a minute, he was back with a cup of fresh, hot coffee. "Here you go, my lady."

Susana giggled. "Thank you, kind sir." She sat up and took the cup.

"I'll pack up and saddle the horses. You rest until I get us ready to start out."

"I can help. I'm not an invalid." She hoped she didn't sound ungrateful. To be cared for so completely did feel good.

"I know you're able to do what you want. But let me have the fun of doing for you. It's the least I can do." He handed her a plate filled with fried salt port, gravy, and warmed up biscuits. Then he got a plate of food for himself.

As he said a prayer of thanks for the food and the night's rest, Susana thanked God for such a caring husband who wanted to make her life easier.

Susana looked out over the snow-capped mountains in the distance bright with the morning sun and the green meadow where they had camped. Tiny wildflowers spread out like a carpet as far as she could see. The sound of birds made an orchestra and an occasional snort from the horses vied for attention. How could she be more blessed?

~ ~ ~

After that trip, she could tell that Elisha began to plan the work as it needed to get done, rather than hesitating because of her condition.

The week before they were due to return to the ranch, they loaded a couple of horses with packs for being away for five days. They rode over the ridge and through the mountain pass to the land Elisha had filed on. He helped his wife to dismount, and they stood with their backs to the wind.

Elisha, shading his eyes against the sun, gazed over his land with a look of love he might one day bestow on his own son; this was his, his to nurture, his to make prosperous.

He turned to smile at his wife. "I want to pace off the hundred sixty acres. The law says we have to stake out the land we filed on so no one else will try to claim it. I know it won't be exact, but it'll be close enough." He extracted a bundle of metal stakes from his saddlebags. "Here, you carry these stakes and hand them to me as I hammer them in."

"Do we cover them up?" Susana cradled the stakes, holding one out to him.

"I wouldn't think so, but we need to try to remember where we put them." He hammered in the first stake.

The sound gave her a feeling of real satisfaction. The shining in his eyes and the way he lifted his head as he stood straight and tall to look out over the land told her far more than any words ever could what it meant to him.

After he had the four corners of the land staked out, they went to the bench of land on the northwest side of the big valley. About fifteen miles long and varying in width from a mile to five miles wide, the valley ran east and west. Through the center of the valley, a large stream flowed with areas of open meadows and deep forest. In the distance toward the west were the snow-covered peaks of the high mountains.

"Here is where I thought we would build the house. Put the front door on the south side. What do you think?"

Susana looked around her, and then stepped to what would be the location of the front of the house. "I love this view. It's going to be a beautiful home for our family."

Elisha came over to her and hugged her. "Yes, this'll be our home. Let's step off the size of the house with two rooms, and I'll get some large stones to mark the four corners. I plan to build it so we can add on later as we need more room."

~ ~ ~

As the month ended, it was again time to head back down to the ranch headquarters. Susana wondered what Mr. Weathers would think of their expecting a baby.

Elisha brought up the question. "We need to decide whether we are going to tell the boss about the baby. What do you think?"

"Why shouldn't we?" She lifted her eyebrows at him.

"What if Mr. Weathers doesn't want us to come back to the cabin? He might worry about you and the baby."

"I hadn't thought about that. As long as we are getting the work done, why does anyone besides us need to know about the baby?"

"Tell you what we'll do. If they ask, we'll tell them the truth. But if they don't ask, we'll wait until later."

Susana was glad that Elisha intended to be honest with Mr. Weathers, but she also wanted to stay at the cabin through the summer.

* * *

Elisha and Susana rode down to the ranch headquarters to replenish their supplies the first week of May. He was glad Susana was over her sickness. Elisha thought he could feel a slight rounding of her stomach, but when she was dressed, it didn't show.

When he made his list of supplies for Mr. Weathers, Susana added several yards of muslin cotton and other pieces of fabric. Because it was Susana, Mr. Weathers didn't question the request.

Elisha gave his monthly report to Mr. Weathers after supper.

"I want you to be more diligent." Mr. Weathers said. "We've seen several sets of tracks of unshod horses on the ranch. We got a report from a rider who rode through that he had heard of Indian attacks along the northern wagon route."

"That's northeast of where I found Henry Jamison, Susana, and their wagon. I've planned to return to the abandoned wagon to retrieve the wheels and the wood from the wagon bed, but haven't gotten around to it."

"It might not be a bad idea to remove all trace of the wagon, but be cautious when you venture into that area. Ride with your rifle ready and don't take any chances."

"With Susana to consider chances are the last thing I'm going to take," Elisha assured his boss.

~ ~ ~

Elisha had packed the wagon so they could sleep in it and he took two days to return home to make it easier on Susana.

The first evening back at the cabin they went to bed early.

"How are you feeling?" Elisha lay on his back with Susana's head on his chest and his arms around her.

"I'm tired, but not more than usual. Why do you ask?" She looked up at him.

"I worry about you. I wanted to be sure you made the trip in the wagon all right." He ran his fingers through her hair, which flowed loose down her back.

"Well, don't worry except maybe that I'm getting fat and I've been so hungry lately."

"What do you mean, you're getting fat?" She didn't feel fat to him.

"Feel. It's starting to get bigger." She took his hand and placed it on her stomach.

He laid his hand across the warm skin of her stomach and noticed a slight rounding that had not been there before. Was this really his child that was growing? So, it wasn't a dream. They truly would be parents in a few short months. He shook his head at the wonder of it. He would soon be a father.

~ ~ ~

One evening, a month later, Elisha sat at the table braiding a lariat and Susana lounged on the bed with her back against the headboard, her legs stretched out, sewing on a little sleeve of a nightgown for the baby.

"Oh, Elisha, come here!"

He dropped the lariat. The urgency in her voice pulled him to her side in two strides. "What's wrong?"

"Put your hand here on my stomach."

"What is it?" A flutter moved under his hand.

"It's our baby moving."

The awe of feeling his child move was like nothing he'd ever experienced before. This small being growing inside of his wife's body was already his child. Protectiveness overwhelmed him. Tears filled his eyes. He rubbed them with his shirtsleeve. "Can you believe it? Our child—I never expected to ever have anything like this, a wife, a child, and land of our own so soon. I've never allowed myself to dream of so much, and now it's happening."

"And you deserve it, my love. You're such a good man, and you're going to be the best father."

"I want to be a good father. I hardly remember my own father and I've never been around children much." He rubbed his eyes and the bridge of his nose. "What if I mess up? What if this child sees through me and knows how much I don't know about things."

"I think you know more than you give yourself credit for. You wait and see. You're going to be a wonderful father."

He planned to do his best to be a good father, but he couldn't see how Susana could be so sure.

~ ~ ~

They worked through the summer months keeping the cattle shifted to the south. But each month they spent several days working on their own land. They camped by the stream that gurgled its way down the valley and the next morning Elisha told Susana that the first thing he needed to do was dig a well. He began to dig the soil loose.

When he stopped for a break and rested for a few minutes. "It's a lot of hard work to dig a well, but I've never liked to haul water, especially in the winter." He took another drink from the canteen Susana offered. "It's also a great safety if we get attacked by Indians. With food stored in the house and water handy, we could survive any attack."

Susana's eyes grew wide. "You think we might be attacked?"

"It's not likely since we're off the beaten trail, but it's always a possibility. We need to be prepared."

"When do you think you'll get the cabin built? I know it'll take a while, but I'm anxious to see it all finished."

"Don't get too anxious. It'll take about two years to build the cabin at the rate I'm going with this well."

"I see what hard work you're doing to get the well dug, and moving all those stones you've gathered for the foundation of the cabin. I wish I could help more. I see how bad your back gets to hurting you. And my rubbing it at night doesn't seem to help that much."

"You watch and keep the canteen filled. I won't have you doing any heavy lifting with the baby."

"Well, I'll go start some supper to have ready while you finish up for this evening. At least I can feed you." She kissed him and strolled back to their camp area.

Climbing down into the deepening well and hauling up buckets of soil was exhausting. He didn't tell Susana how he felt almost physically ill because of fear when he was at the bottom of the well. He had never liked to be hemmed in and thoughts of the well collapsing invaded his sleep as nightmares.

"You're not eating. Aren't you hungry?" Susana sat on the blanket by the campfire.

He shook his head to stop thinking of the bottom of the well. "I'm not as hungry as usual."

"Is your back hurting?"

Elisha nodded. He didn't usually tell her when his back hurt but she was getting good at guessing.

"Please eat your supper and then I'll rub some liniment into your back. Maybe that will help."

She sounded so distressed he decided to do what she wanted to sooth her. "That would be nice." He shoveled a big spoonful of the beans and ham into his mouth.

After he had cleaned his plate, Susana stood and went over to their packs and took out a flat brown tin. "Take your overshirt and undershirt off then lay on your stomach on your bedroll."

Elisha grinned at her. "Yes, ma'am." He pulled his overshirt over his head and winced. His back was close to going into one of the spasms. It was with relief that he laid on his bedroll.

Susana sat by him and began to rub the liniment into his lower back in rhythmic strokes.

Elisha felt the muscles start to relax a bit. He closed his eyes and listened to her humming as she massaged deeper and deeper. He drifted off to sleep.

The next morning he tied a rope around a tree and then around his waist as he readied to continue digging the well. "After I get down to the bottom of the well, you lower the basket full of stones down. The easiest way for you to do that is to wrap the rope around the pommel of Shadow's saddle. Keep the rope taut and lower the basket over the lip of the well, and then have Shadow walk toward the well until I yell for you to stop. That way the horse is taking the weight of the stones and not you." He paused, not wanting to tell her what else he needed her to do. "If I holler or you hear dirt falling, wrap this other rope that I have around my waist around the pommel of the saddle and have Shadow back up from the well as fast as you can."

"Do you have to go back down?" Susana gripped Elisha's arm.

He patted her hand. "Don't worry. The bottom is getting muddy. I'm almost deep enough. I need to line it with the stones. I've got enough poles framing it to keep it safe." He could only hope he was telling the truth.

Elisha slowly backed down into the well holding on to the rope. At the bottom, he found the soil had turned to mud with a couple of inches of standing water. After Susana lowered the basket, he placed the stones around the wall of the well, and then sent the basket back up for more stones. He hated to ask Susana to handle the stones that were the size of a large loaf of bread, but he could get the work done so much quicker with her help.

By the middle of the afternoon, he had the well completely lined with stones. In spite of the pain in his back, he made his way down the well to dig deeper into the mud. He was probably down about seventy-five feet and had to take a lantern down to be able to see. Elisha had to concentrate on taking steady breaths and couldn't keep his hands from shaking. He hated being down in the well.

As he dug into the mud and filled the bucket that was tied to the second rope, suddenly the well started to fill with water. He had struck an underground spring or stream.

"Susana, pull me up, pull me up!" Forgetting the shovel and the bucket, he tried to climb the rope but kept slipping. Just as his head was about to go under the water filling the well he felt the rope tighten. Elisha held on with a grip of desperation until he was at the top of the well, and then dragged onto the grass.

"Whoa, Shadow, Whoa! Good boy." Susana ran down the taut rope to where Elisha, wet and miserable, stretched out on the grass. "Are you all right?"

Elisha lay on the ground not wanting to move. His back was in spasms and the pain was like a knife.

"Elisha, speak to me!" Tears ran down her face. She sat on the ground and lifted his head onto her lap. Stroking his hair she wailed, "Speak to me!"

Taking a breath, Elisha was able to speak. "I'm all right...just a spasm. Don't cry."

"You scared me so. What happened? You're soaking wet." She wiped mud and water off his face.

"We have a well full of water, or I think it will stay full of water." He hoped the well was built strong enough to contain the water and that the source would be continual. He actually felt rather pleased in spite of the damage he had done his back. He'd never dug a well by himself before and now he could start building the house.

The next morning they packed their stuff and loaded the horses. They had been away from their work for five days and Elisha knew that was as long as he could justify.

"The next time we come up I'll build a well house. For now I've covered it with logs to protect it."

Susana gazed around the valley. "I can really see it. Now that we have something as permanent as a well, it seems so much more real. This will be our home someday."

Elisha kissed her and then helped her mount. "Someday, but for now we must get back to work for Mr. Weathers."

~ ~ ~

They made two trips to the abandoned wagon. On the first trip, they brought back the four wheels. They were still in good shape. Elisha took the wagon apart bit by bit. By the time fall came around, he had it down to the last part of the bed, the axles, and tongue. He was tempted to leave the rest. However, Mr. Weathers was right, leaving no evidence of the wagon was the safest thing to do. But it would have to be another trip.

The trips to the ranch headquarters seemed to come more quickly each month as the summer passed. They kept putting off telling Mr. Weathers and the others about the baby. Elisha didn't think anyone suspected. Susana always put her petticoats and dress on before they arrived at the ranch headquarters.

Each time they returned to the cabin with a full wagon. The loft filled little by little with food supplies by the time the cool days of fall arrived.

Susana had picked up the fabric she ordered from town with the other supplies. She began to make more things in preparation for the baby. How she knew how to do all of the sewing was a marvel to Elisha.

Elisha had put off discussing the actual birth with Susana, but now was the time to talk about it.

"We need to go down to the ranch headquarters for the winter."

She leaned forward in the rocking chair where she sat sewing. "You think we should have the baby there?"

"Yes, it'll be better for you and for the baby. Nate is real good at doctoring. I'll do what I can, but he's actually helped his wife deliver a baby."

"Then you need to learn from Nate. You might want to know how to birth a baby sometime." She cocked her head and grinned.

He shifted in his chair where he sat at the table working on the ledger. "I'll learn if I must." The thought of delivering a baby by himself didn't sit too well.

"I know that God will be with me." No longer grinning and with a slight frown, Susana leaned back in the chair. "But I'm a little scared about the birthing."

He slipped out of the chair, knelt by her, and put his arms around her. "You're going to be fine." If only he could be certain of his own words.

"When we go down next week for our September supplies I don't think we'll have a choice, but to tell them."

"Ma'am," he cocked his head and laughed, "I don't think we'll have to tell them. Surely they'll figure it out, considering how you're looking."

"Are you saying I'm looking ugly?" She pushed him away and pursed her lips into a definite pout.

"You can only look lovely, but you also look like you're with child."

* * *

When September's trip to the ranch came Susana found it easier to ride astride her horse than in the hard wagon seat, but Elisha had to help her mount and dismount. They made it a two-day trip again and arrived at the ranch headquarters after noon.

Nate and Smithy were the only ones at the house. All the other men were out rounding up the herd and holding it for the shipment to Chicago.

The Evans' didn't have to tell the two cooks about the baby. They both stared at Susana's stomach, then they both blushed and quickly looked away.

"Won't Sam be surprised," Nate hugged Susana.

"And pleased," Smithy added. "He sure does like babies."

"I hope so since we're having one." Elisha smiled at them. "Is it all right if Susana goes in and gets some rest before supper?"

"Sure, we've had your room ready for a couple of days, since we've been expecting you all." Nate held the door open for her.

Susana headed inside while Elisha took care of the horses.

He'd entered the front door on his way to check on Susana when a thunder of horse hooves beat across the ranch yard. The riders had returned.

Elisha opened the door and entered their room. He held his wife's gaze for a moment. She was so precious, such a gift. "You ready to face Mr. Weathers?"

"I'm ready. Are you?" She smoothed her dress over her definitely rounded stomach.

"Well, seeing as I don't know how he'll respond to our having a baby, I'm not sure."

"And what do you plan to do about it if he doesn't approve?" She asked with a laugh.

"I guess go ahead and have the baby."

They heard the sound of boots heels hitting the floor from the front room and Elisha assumed it was Mr. Weathers. Elisha took Susana's hand and they walked out of the bedroom.

They quietly stepped over to the desk where Mr. Weathers sat. They waited for him.

He looked up and then stared at Susana. He sprang up from his chair, came around the desk, and gave her a great big, fatherly hug.

"My word, Susana, you are a surprise. Is this what I think it is?"

"Yes, Mr. Weathers, we're having a baby." She looked up at him and then quickly looked down at her hands that were resting on her stomach.

Mr. Weathers turned to Elisha and shook his hand. "Congratulations son. Don't you beat all? How long have you known?"

Elisha admitted that they had known since April.

"Well, why didn't you two say something?"

"With Susana expecting, we thought you might be concerned about us working up at the cabin." Elisha looked over at Susana. She never looked more radiant than she did at that moment, and his chest puffed with pride. It wouldn't matter whether or not the boss liked the situation, he was a happy man.

"You're probably right. And I'm concerned, but my, you look lovely, Susana, and the picture of health."

"I am, Mr. Weathers. I'm doing very well."

"Are you planning on going back to the cabin?"

"If it's all right with you, we thought we would go back to the cabin until the end of October or middle of November," Elisha answered. "When it looks like winter is about to close in, we'd like to come down and have the baby here. We think it's due about the middle of December, but we're not exactly sure when. I want to leave it to Susana, and how she's feeling about traveling. If she wants to come sooner, I'm open to it. I want her and the baby safe."

"I want you two to know that if there is anything you need, or I can do for you, tell me. My home here is yours. It'll be wonderful to have a baby about the place. Wait until the hands find out. That baby is sure going to have a lot of uncles." Mr. Weathers' eyes shown and his deep booming laugh filled the room.

They heard the supper bell and boots scuffing as the crew gathered in the kitchen.

"Let's go see how the hands react to this news. I think you'll find they'll be pleased." Mr. Weathers offered his arm to Susana to escort her into the kitchen, and Elisha followed closely behind in anticipation of sharing the news.

For men who ordinarily were polite around Susana, they did a lot of staring. Elisha moved to their usual place and held the chair out for Susana.

She smiled at the men and sat graciously. "Yes, I'm having a baby, and you all are going to be uncles."

The men laughed and congratulated them as well as each other.

Josh's face lit up with a big smile. "An uncle, well I'll be, I've never been an uncle before." He turned to Abe, "What does an uncle do?"

"I'll tell you later. Right now let's listen to the prayer and eat."

Mr. Weathers' prayer for the meal included a request for special care for Susana and the baby.

Elisha, hearing the concern in Mr. Weathers' voice, felt a lump in his throat. It was good to have folks who cared about what happened to him and his family.

The crew wouldn't let Susana lift a finger for the next two days. Out of her earshot, they gave Elisha a lot of ribbing about becoming a father. They were expressing their friendship, so he took it all in stride.

Mr. Weathers took extra care with the supplies. He wanted to make life easier for Susana, as she waited for the baby to arrive.

The only other major news around the ranch came from Josh.

They lingered at the breakfast table. The other cowhands had headed out to their work.

Josh cleared his throat. "I've made it to town once a month since April." His face was a bright red. "I've been calling on Mary."

"Oh, Josh. That's wonderful. She seemed like such a lovely girl." Susana patted his hand.

"Well, her father said that I could come call at their house. Then he said I could sit with her at church. But she's too young and ladylike to go anywhere alone with me." Josh ducked his head.

Elisha worked at not laughing at Josh's embarrassment. "Sounds like it's going well."

Josh nodded. "Yes, it is. She's so friendly...and pretty."

Susana smiled at him. "If she is meant to be someone special for you, it will work out. Take your time."

Josh frowned. "But should I assume that something will come of it. I don't have much to offer her."

"If you truly care for Mary, then you keep seeing her. She would be fortunate to find as fine a young man as you. Just be patient."

"Thanks, Susana. That's what I'm trying to do." Josh stood and turned to Elisha. "I thought we'd get the wagon loaded this morning."

Elisha stood and put a hand on Susana's shoulder. "We'll get everything done and you rest. Read or something."

Susana patted his hand on her shoulder. "That's what I plan to do."

Elisha understood Josh's concern of providing for a wife, as he didn't have much prospects of a place of his own. If he'd waited to marry Susana until he could afford it, it probably wouldn't have happened.

Before Elisha and Susana left for the trip back up to the cabin, Mr. Weathers took Elisha aside. "We keep getting lots of rumors, and we saw tracks last week over at the northeast boundary. I know I've told you before but I want to remind you to be extra vigilant when riding out from the cabin and not to leave Susana if you can help it." Mr. Weathers leaned forward and looked at him with an unusual intensity. "You place yours and Susana's safety above protecting the cabin or cattle."

"You don't have to worry; Susana will always be my first concern."

"For the first of October, why don't I send Josh and Abe up with the supplies? That way you wouldn't have to make the trip down here. Then the first of November, you can plan to move down here for the winter."

"Thanks. That will make it easier for Susana. Coming back down in early November should put us here in plenty of time for the birth of the baby."

Elisha was grateful to have such a boss. It made it easy to leave the next day knowing they had a place to return to for the birth of the baby.

CHAPTER FOURTEEN

Elisha stood by the corral fence and glanced up and down the valley. September! One of his favorite months. He gazed at the trees in the distance, surprised again by the variety of colors God painted the leaves.

Jasper poked his head over the top rail of the fence and huffed at him.

Elisha laughed and rubbed the horse between the eyes. That was Jasper's way of asking for a cube of sugar or an apple. "Sorry, old boy, I don't have a treat for you."

He saddled Jasper and Shadow for the day's work. How could he convince Susana to stay at the cabin? It had to be difficult for her to ride all day. Course, if he were truthful, he didn't want to ride out without her.

Susana came out of the cabin and walked up to the corral. His heart skipped a beat and he held his breath at the sight of his petite wife dressed in one of his shirts. She also had on a long skirt she had made to accommodate her expanding waist. She wore the skirt over a pair of his old pants. Elisha understood her need to maintain propriety by wearing the skirt even though he was the only one to see her. He grinned. She was just so cute.

"So you won't stay home?" he asked, knowing her answer in advance.

"Please don't make me. I feel fine. I just look awful."

"You couldn't look awful if you tried." He made sure Jasper was tied up to the rail, and then he picked Susana up and lifted her into the saddle. She no longer could mount and dismount without his help. He didn't tell her what it did to his lower back.

They spent the day working along the creek west of the cabin. As they found small groups of cattle and hazed them back across the creek, Elisha stopped and rested the horses several times.

In the early afternoon, he dismounted, guided Jasper close to a large boulder, and helped Susana dismount. It was easier on his back than lifting her.

"Are the horses tired again?" She asked, with a sideways glance at him.

He grinned. Not for the first time, he wondered whether she could read his mind. "Yeah, the horses are tired. We can take a few minutes to rest."

"Good."

Her easy agreement worried him. Was the riding finally getting to her?

Elisha looked at the position of the sun. It was four fingers above the horizon, the middle of the afternoon. They would head back to the cabin.

He turned to tell Susana and didn't see her. His stomach knotted up as he looked around searching for her. Then he stepped around a large boulder and found her. She was slumped on the grass on her side asleep with her head resting on her right arm and holding a yellow wildflower in her left hand, which rested on the mossy grass. He let her sleep.

Elisha moved the horses to a better patch of grass, staked them, and returned to his sleeping wife. What was he doing letting her work cattle? But how could he stop her? She wasn't exactly docile. He liked that she had a mind of her own, but sometimes...

She seemed to be fine as long as they stopped and rested a couple of times throughout the day. Torn between the need to do his job and making sure Susana was safe, he still was too uneasy to leave her by herself. There was no guarantee that a stray war party might not stumble upon the cabin.

Maybe it was time he took her down to the ranch. He had to make a decision that Susana wasn't going to like.

Sighing, he gently shook her awake. "Honey, we need to get going."

She sat up and stretched her arms high over her head in a big yawn. "That felt good. I needed a little nap."

Elisha brought Jasper up to the large boulder and helped her mount. He then swung up into the saddle and turned the horse toward the cabin. He glanced back at her, she hadn't protested their starting back so early.

Following the faint trail they had made in their goings and coming, Elisha rode down to the creek. If they crossed it a couple of times as it meandered through the valley, they saved at least a mile in their return to the cabin.

Elisha held Shadow back and let Jasper enter the creek first. It was only about two feet deep with various sized rocks scattered on the bottom.

Jasper had crossed it a hundred times, but this afternoon he stumbled and almost went down. Susana was throw back and forth in the saddle but managed to hang on to the pommel with both hands.

"Susana!" Elisha kicked Shadow into the creek and was by Jasper's side in seconds. They walked the horses together to the other side of the creek.

"Are you all right?" He leaned across from where he sat in the saddle on Shadow, and put his arm around her waist.

Her eyes were opened wide and her breathing seemed labored. She had her hand on her stomach. In a shaky voice she said, "I'm fine. It startled me."

Elisha fought to get his trembling body under control and wanted to shout at her to be careful. It wasn't reasonable to yell at her because of his feelings. It wasn't her fault and she didn't seem to be harmed. He took a deep breath and let it out slowly. "It scared me, what might have happened."

Susana smiled at him and took his hand. "Nothing bad happened. Don't look so worried. I'm all right."

The rest of the journey back to the cabin Elisha rode slowly and was never more than a foot or two away from her. It took him awhile to get his breathing under control.

~ ~ ~

Abe and Josh brought up the supplies the first week of October and stayed overnight.

The next day, Elisha and Susana sat on the bench outside the cabin and watched the two men ride out of sight to the south. Elisha slipped his arm around her shoulder and pulled her close. "Honey, I'm going to go saddle up and ride out, but I've decided you're not going with me."

She opened her mouth as if to speak.

Elisha raised his hand to stop her. "Now, hear me out. I know you're willing to keep working, but I'm not willing to take the chance of your falling. Last week when your horse stumbled and you almost fell, well, it scared me."

"But Elisha, that's not likely to happen again."

"I've made up my mind. You're not riding out to work the cattle. It's too close to the time for the baby to come, and I can't stand the thought of something happening to you or the baby." Elisha looked at her with the sternest expression he could manage. He wasn't going to argue about it.

"I don't like this. I don't want to spend all day with you away. I like being with you too much." She leaned against him. "Although I have to confess, it's been getting harder and harder to make it through a whole day. I know you've been stopping to rest the horses more than usual. Also, I've noticed you're making the work days shorter and coming back to the cabin earlier. I love it that you want to protect me."

She pulled his arm around her waist, so his hand rested on her stomach. He felt the tiny flutters of movement. He was getting more and more anxious to meet this child.

"The little fellow is certainly active this morning." He laughed. How many men got to sit with a beautiful, young wife, looking at the grandeur of snow-capped mountains, and feel the growing life of his child?

"Yes, he's getting more and more active. I think maybe staying off a horse for a day or two won't hurt me. I've a lot of sewing to do, and I can take my time getting meals ready. Yes, my husband, you're right. Go do your work, and I'll be content to wait for you, or, almost content. I'll miss you." She smiled up at him and he kissed her. She pushed him away. "Go on now and get saddled up. I'll get sandwiches ready."

With one last kiss, he stood and ambled to the barn to saddle up the bay. Going back to the cabin to collect the sandwiches, he checked that the woodbin and the water buckets were full. He also made sure Susana's rifle was loaded. He placed it on the rack by the door.

"If you have any problems, you fire the rifle two times and then wait a couple of minutes and fire again. I should hear it. I'm not going too far today." He kissed Susana and stood with his arms around her until she pushed him away.

"Go on, the sooner you start, the sooner you'll be back. And hurry back," she said.

He gave her another quick kiss, swung up into the saddle, and rode off before he could change his mind.

~ ~ ~

A few days before the end of October, Elisha sat eating his supper. He needed to make a last swing to the east if he was to be fair to Mr. Weathers, but he didn't want to do it.

After he cleaned his plate, he shifted in his chair. "Honey, I need to make one last trip to the eastern boundary before we head down to the ranch headquarters for the winter."

She poured him another cup of coffee. "Is that a problem? You sound worried."

"The problem is that to ride all the way to the east boundary and chase whatever cows I find back south, I have to camp overnight. It will take at least two days. I don't like the thought of leaving you here alone overnight." He sipped some of the coffee. "Do you think you'll be all right if I head out tomorrow, sleep out over night, and get back the next day? I hate to do it, but if I could do one more swing of the eastern bluffs, I'd feel better about it not getting done again until spring."

"Of course, I'll be fine. I have things to do before we leave, and I still have sewing to do. I'd rather you were here at night, but I understand the need to see to the eastern boundary."

He looked into her eyes, but he saw no concern. She wasn't the least bit afraid, but he wished he felt as confident.

"Since I'll be close to the wagon, I'll swing by and get what's left of it. There's the last of the boards from the wagon bed, the axles, and the tongue. I'll get back as early as I can. Next week we'll pack up and head south to the ranch." Elisha packed his bedroll for the trip and   Susana put together a packet of food for him to take.

~ ~ ~

The next morning he left at daybreak, taking a couple of horses with him to carry back the rest of the old wagon. By changing from one horse to another, he made it to the eastern boundary by the bluffs by mid-afternoon. He let the horses rest for a short while, then rode to the meadow where he had found Henry Jamison and Susana almost a year ago.

What was left of the old wagon was still there. He off loaded his pack and saddle by the side of the old campfire. After he staked the horses close by, they grazed on the tall grass in the meadow. They had drunk fully at the last creek they had crossed so Elisha was not pressed to take them down to the creek.

He stood and looked around the meadow. The leaves on the trees that surrounded the meadow were the colors of fall. The grass was already loosing the green of summer. The sound of a hawk added to the noise of the breeze through the leaves. As Elisha surveyed the meadow, he felt his aloneness, and he missed the sound of Susana's voice.

With a couple of hours before dark, he began to take the last of the wagon apart. He took the boards off the center brace that ran the length of the old wagon. The piece of wood was extremely heavy that ran the length of the bottom of the wagon bed to which the axles were attached. Much heavier than he expected. It appeared hollowed out with a wood plug firmly hammered into the end. Elisha pried the plug out and reached into the hollow piece of timber. He pulled a rawhide sack out. He sat hard on the ground, and then untied the drawstring. He poured its contents into his hand.

He counted fifty gold coins!

Not believing what he found, he tipped the piece of timber up and emptied out more sacks. There were fifty of the small bags. Elisha only opened a few, but they all held either gold nuggets or gold coins.

Susana once told him her father had panned for gold, and been paid in gold at his store. There had also been a farm. After her parents had died, her grandfather sold the farm and the store. She'd had no idea what became of the money. She thought her grandfather used all the money to buy the team and wagon.

The gold now belonged to Susana, and it was a fortune. It could go a long way toward helping them with the ranch. Elisha sat still on the hard ground staring at the gold. Susana now had the choice to stay with him, or to take the gold and go back east to live an easier life. Elisha's heart thumped hard against his chest. He didn't want to lose her. He could bury the gold and not tell Susana about his find. Would she leave him and take their baby with her? He also couldn't stand the uncertainty of what she'd do if she had the choice.

After he had the last of the wagon taken apart, he built a fire and heated some beans and salt pork for supper. Thoughts of what he had found were foremost in his mind. He cut and gathered several armloads of the tall grass and made a place to spread his bedroll. When he lay down for the night as full darkness fell on the land, he breathed in the sweet smell of the grass on which he lay.

Elisha tried to sleep but woke often through the long night. Each time he woke, he thought about the gold. What would Susana do with it? Shifting to ease his aching back, he waited for sleep.

The next morning he loaded the packhorses with the axles, tongue, and last of the timber from the wagon. He put the gold in a couple of packs in front of and behind the saddle on Shadow. It made for a heavy weight for the horse after Elisha got into the saddle, but it was only about fifteen miles to the cabin, and he planned to ride easy.

He was almost to the edge of the meadow when he looked back at the far edge to the east and saw four Utes sitting on their horses, watching him. They didn't look like a hunting party and they carried their bows and arrows at the ready. He didn't want to fight them, but they might not give him a choice.

When the Utes saw that he'd seen them, they let out war whoops and urged their horses into a run at him.

Elisha decided not to wait around, and kicked Shadow hard in the ribs and let out a yell at the packhorses. He made a break for the forest, hoping he could get enough of a start to evade the four Indians behind him. He might have one advantage. Having ridden the area often, he knew the lay of the land. Of course, the Indians might also know the trails.

Reluctantly, he let go of the lead on the packhorses. He hated to lose the horses, but he had to survive. He kicked Shadow again. He had to evade these Utes and make sure he didn't lead them to the cabin and Susana. He would die first.

The Utes didn't stop for the packhorses, but rode past them and let loose their arrows at Elisha. He ducked at the sound of the arrows whizzing by. They didn't seem to have a rifle, for which he was thankful.

Elisha ran Shadow up a ravine, then they crested a ridge. He twisted from a blow to the left side of his back that almost unseated him from his saddle. A searing pain radiated and grew in intensity. He grabbed for the pommel, letting the horse have his head. Shadow ran all out and soon was in a full gallop.

He was hard hit with an arrow in his back just under his ribs. Elisha fought to hang onto his horse. The wetness flowing down his leg told him how much he was bleeding. The pain spread with each pound of the horse's hooves. Could he pull ahead enough to get clear of his attackers? Shadow raced along the edge of a deep ravine, then lost footing and fell toward the edge.

The falling horse threw Elisha out of the saddle and he tumbled down the ravine, banging against rocks and crashing through brush. The arrow in his back caught on something and broke off. A wave of agony swept through him. He tumbled out of control down the steep ravine. He bounced off the large boulders and brush along the way. Susana, alone! His head smashed into something, a burst of pain, and thought faded.

* * *

When Elisha rode away from the cabin, Susana watched him until he was out of sight beyond the trees. Two days without Elisha! A cold tingling ran up and down her spine and the hair at the back of her neck stood up.

What if something happened to him? She shook her head and walked back into the cabin.

Busyness was an answer to worry. She got down the tub from the loft and began to carry in water to do the wash. Get the wash done first and then scrub the cabin floor. Plenty of things to keep her mind occupied.

By dark, she sighed in exhaustion as she rubbed her aching back. But she had a clean cabin and clean clothes. Where had Elisha camped? Was he safe? Were the horses okay? Was he cold? He was all she could think about. She woke often, as every sound was too loud. The night was long.

In the morning, Susana woke and reached over for Elisha but he wasn't there. He wouldn't be back until the afternoon. Yawning, she got out of bed. Might as well do something useful while she waited for Elisha to return. After caring for the horses and eating some oatmeal, she opened up the sewing machine.

By the middle of the afternoon, she had Elisha's suit cut out and ready to sew. She needed him there to try it on before she went further with the sewing. Putting the sewing machine away, she prepared supper in case Elisha got back a little early. She smiled at the thought of how hungry he would be. He was always ready to eat.

The afternoon passed slowly and still no Elisha. Susana slipped into her coat and stood in front of the cabin, searching the eastern horizon. Disappointed, she went to the barn to take care of the horses. She then brought in several armloads of wood. The baby was active and kicked her the whole time. "It's all right, baby. Papa will be home soon."

Susana spent the evening rocking in her mother's chair and reading her Bible. And she prayed. *Oh, God, let Elisha be all right. Please, bring him home.*

When she became so exhausted she could no longer sit up, she curled up in the empty bed.

"Elisha, I need you to get home." She pulled his pillow into her arms and inhaled his scent, and then she began to cry. What if he never came back?

CHAPTER FIFTEEN

Elisha woke cold and his bed felt lumpy. Then the pain hit him. Elisha fought awareness as he struggled to stay asleep and avoid the pain that filled his body. Sleep, he mumbled to himself, stay asleep. He groaned. The pain forced itself again into his consciousness. He opened his eyes to darkness. His back and left side was a mass of hurt. Agony pulsed in his left leg like a living thing. He tried to move, but the pain caught him and nearly stopped his breathing.

This wasn't his bed. Where was he? The memory of what had happened seeped into his mind. Small pains shot throughout his body. In his right leg, pain pulsed harshly. He gingerly felt of his leg. His pants were torn and saturated with blood. He could only guess that his flesh underneath was torn. His head felt like it would fall off from the searing pain. He relaxed and rested his cheek against the dirt and leaves. It was easier than fighting the pain.

Susana, he couldn't leave her alone.

The moon shone full and white against the dark, cloudless sky, and he could make out trees and brush in its light. And then he remembered the Utes and the gold and the chase and the arrow. Had the shrubs and trees hidden him from the Utes. Or had they thought him dead? For whatever reason, they were gone, and he seemed to be alone. He could hear nothing that sounded like a horse. They must have taken Shadow.

A pang of regret spiraled through him—the gold was gone. He'd known about it for such a short time, he felt no real loss. He did feel the loss of Shadow, the canteen of water that was on the saddle—and his rifle. Feeling around the ground, his hand slid over the cold steel of his revolver, still tied down in his holster.

As he tried to take shallow breaths against the pain, he didn't want to move. But with Susana back at the cabin alone, there was no other choice. He had to get back to her. Crawling to a small pine tree, he pulled himself up to his feet almost screaming from the agony in his chest and he almost fell. As he steadied himself, something sharp poked against his left arm.

Rubbing his right hand carefully along his ribs, he found an arrowhead protruding from below his rib cage on the left. Touching it sent excruciating pain clear through to his back. He could pull it out, but what would that do to him inside? Maybe the bleeding would start again. Could he stand the pain of pulling it out? No, leave it along for now.

He had to move. There was no other way if he wanted to get back to Susana. Letting go of the pine tree, Elisha hitched himself along, following the bottom of the ravine. Elisha stepped carefully, as the thought of what it would be like to fall on the point of the arrow left him breaking into a sweat.

Every movement of his leg sent a searing pain shooting up his thigh. He focused on placing one foot in front of the other. Gradually, the darkness faded and morning came. Elisha could see his leg and the six-inch bleeding gash on his thigh through the tear in his pants. There didn't seem to be a broken bone, only the severe cut. He took his bandana from around his neck and tied it around his leg. His thirst fought against the pain for his attention. Putting a pebble in his mouth to suck on helped the thirst, Elisha couldn't let either keep him from taking his next step.

By midmorning, he could barely inch himself along and held onto trees to keep himself upright. His feet almost didn't clear the ground as he shuffled through the forest. He tripped over a branch and slammed into the ground, managing to hit on his right side. As least, he hadn't fallen on the point of the arrow. Weakness spread throughout his body. He felt a sense of life ebbing. *Susana, my love, I'm sorry. I tried.* His mind wandered in and out of consciousness.

* * *

Susana woke early with one thought on her mind, *Elisha, where are you?*

She went to the barn and took care of the horses again. On her way back to the cabin, she brought in fresh water. Every time she turned, she stared to the east, looking for a rider on a big black horse. Elisha wouldn't have left her alone a second night if he had any choice. Something was very wrong.

Another evening passed slowly as she sat in the rocker and tried to read her Bible. The words blurred through her tears.

"Lord, help me, help Elisha. I don't know what to pray. Oh, Lord, help me." She hugged her stomach as a way to hold her baby while she cried and begged God to bring Elisha home.

* * *

Something nuzzled his neck. Elisha raised his hand to slap off whatever was there. Shadow! The big black horse nuzzled him again. Could he climb into the saddle? Grabbing a stirrup, he used it to help him stand. How the animal came to be here, he could only guess. Somehow, the horse had evaded the Utes, found Elisha's trail, and followed it.

Gritting his teeth and stifling a moan against the living agony in his chest, Elisha pulled himself into the saddle with the last of his strength. The canteen still hung on the saddle horn. He took a long swig of water, hung the canteen back up, and then tied his hands to the saddle horn with the reins. Could he remain conscious? He mustn't fall off the horse, as he'd never get back on again. He urged Shadow westward toward home.

Drifting in and out of consciousness, Elisha trusted the horse to know the way back to the cabin. Sometime later, the dark surrounded him again. Shadow walked far into the night.

Elisha woke to find the horse stopped by a stream. A light shown through the trees. The cabin! He prodded the horse to wade across the creek. After what seemed like another hour, they stopped outside the cabin door. Elisha wanted to call out to Susana but the pain in his chest refused to let him take enough air to do more than breathe. Weakly he plucked at the reins with his fingers, finally untying the reins tied around his wrists.

* * *

Susana sat in her rocking chair, her hands busy with crocheting, when she stopped rocking and cocked her head to listen but all she heard was silence. The night birds had stopped their singing and the wind no longer whispered in the pines. Then, she heard a faint, clop, clop.

"Elisha!" she screamed. She ran to the door and flung it open. The light from the lantern in the cabin shown on her husband. His clothes were torn and dried blood and dirt covered him.

"Susana..." Holding on to the pommel of the saddle, Elisha slid off his horse.

Susana recovered in time to rush to his side and she took some of his weight to steady him enough that he managed to land on his feet. Straining under his weight leaning on her, she helped him stumble into the cabin to the bed, and let him fall onto it.

"Oh, Elisha, you're hurt!"

"I'm here...it'll be all right now. Go put the horse in the barn." He spoke in a hoarse voice.

"Who cares about a horse? It's you I've got to see about." She tried to open his coat.

He pushed her hands away. "The horse. . . put him in the barn ... bring in the rifle."

She hated to leave him but he wouldn't be easy until she put the horse away. It didn't make sense. She grabbed a lantern and led Shadow into the barn. After she undid the cinch, the saddle and pack fell to the floor with a thud. She'd no idea what was in the pack, but it was too heavy for her to lift. The other horses he had taken were nowhere to be seen. She led the horse into a stall, gave him a bucket of water and some feed, a hug around neck to thank him for bringing Elisha home, then closed the barn door behind her, and tucked the rifle underneath her arm.

When she entered the cabin, Susana could hear Elisha breathing raggedly, and saw that he plucked at his left side. He was no longer conscious. While the water heated, she retrieved some of the cotton fabric she'd cut in preparation for the baby. She then poured hot water into the basin and sat by Elisha on the bed.

Susana cut his shirt, undershirt, and pants away from the wound in his chest. She examined the end of the arrow protruding from Elisha's chest, then cried softly. The wound was bloody and seeping. The flesh was swollen and angry inflamed looking around the shaft of the arrow. At least what protruded from the wound on his back was only a small round stick looking. Shuddering Susana faced that she had to get the arrow out. If she pulled it straight out from the chest wound maybe it wouldn't do too much more damage. Lord, please give me courage to do what will help Elisha.

She tried to get a hold on the end of the arrowhead, but with the continual seeping of blood, her hand kept slipping off. She wrapped a cloth around the end of the arrow so she could grasp it tighter. Grasping it firmly with one hand, she pressed down on Elisha's ribs with the other. She pulled on the arrow but it refused to move.

Elisha moaned and tried to pull away from her. She was hurting him but the arrow had to come out.

Gritting her teeth, she repositioned her knee on his chest and jerked on the arrow as hard as she could.

At first, it resisted as if it were a living thing. As she strained to pull on the arrow there was a sucking sound and then the arrow slipped out of his lower chest. As the arrow left his body, Elisha screamed and struggled to push Susana's hand away from his chest. Too weak to push her off, his hands kept pushing at her and then he was quiet. With the arrow out, she washed the wound with lye soap and hot water, then packed it to stop the bleeding with clean cloths and bound his chest.

Next, she cut away his pants leg to expose the ugly tear down his thigh. As she wiped the area around the jagged tearing of the flesh, she caught glimpses of white bone. Gently pushing the flesh together, the two rugged edges kept separating. Susana took a shaky breath. She had to sew it up. Getting her sewing needle and thread, she held the edges together and sewed as if it were a seam in a shirt. Several times she had to stop until she could stop her hands from trembling so. Finally, she had it stitched together and bandaged.

The wound on his head was swollen and bleeding slightly. It was a good-sized bump but the cut was only an inch long. She decided to leave it along with a simple bandage. After washing it, she put a bandage on it to stop the bleeding, but didn't know what else she could do.

She removed Elisha's bloody, torn clothes, then washed the many scrapes and scratches all over his body. It hurt her to wash his hands with the fingernails torn and caked with dirt. How far he had crawled, she couldn't imagine. But he had made it back to her.

She pulled the covers up over his chest, and then laid her hand on his brow. He was hot to the touch. Susana didn't know much about such serious wounds. Her father had helped take care of injured people and she was thankful she remembered any of it.

Elisha's body would have to fight off any infection. She'd done what she could. Now she had to watch and wait to see if he was strong enough to win the battle.

Since the time she'd helped Elisha into the cabin, she hadn't let herself think about how bad his injuries were. With his wounds cared for, her body began to tremble and she fought not to throw up. She wanted to shake him and tell him not to be hurt. It was too hard for her with the baby coming.

Swallowing hard, she forced herself to check on Elisha. Her husband would want her to be strong, and the only way she could do that was to depend on God to give her the strength, will, and determination to survive and save Elisha.

She knew what the arrow meant. It was also obvious from the scrapes and scratches that he'd fallen many times. As she thought about what had happened to him, she understood why he wanted the horse put in the barn. The Indians could be following him. She checked Elisha's rifle to make sure it was loaded and stood it against the wall nearby.

She checked the barred door and closed all the inside shutters. Taking their three rifles, she made sure they were loaded, and placed them by the door and the windows. She laid the revolver on the bureau where she could easily grab it from the rocking chair. She didn't know what else she could do to protect them and their household but pray. She pulled the rocking chair up to the bed so she could sit close enough to her husband to touch him.

Elisha mumbled and moaned occasionally.

Susana wanted to take his pain and make it her own. She wanted do anything to relieve his suffering, but she couldn't. She could only sit in the rocking chair with a blanket around her shoulders and begin a vigil for him—and she prayed.

Susana dozed off and on for an hour or two. Toward dawn, she woke. Elisha's eyes were open.

"Elisha? Do you hear me?" she asked softly. Even though his eyes were open, she could tell he wasn't seeing her. She touched his forehead. His skin was hot under her hand.

He tried to lick his lips, and she guessed he was thirsty.

She held a cup of water to his lips. He didn't seem to know how to drink from it, so she took a spoon and let the water slowly flow in between his slightly opened lips. After a bit, he swallowed. She poured another spoonful of water, which he swallowed. He closed his eyes and fell asleep or unconscious, she couldn't tell. Whatever it was, it was a dark journey away from her.

Susana undid the bandage around his chest and looked at the two wounds, one in the back where the arrow had entered his body and the one in his lower left chest where she had pulled it out. The skin was red and angry looking around the wounds and hot to the touch, and still bled slightly. Taking a clean cloth, she washed the wounds and redid the bandage. The leg didn't look much better, still red and angry looking, but had stopped bleeding. She also cleaned it again. After peeking underneath the bandage on his head, she decided to leave the head wound alone, as it seemed to be healing.

Elisha stirred restlessly as she cleaned and bandaged the wounds, but he didn't waken.

Susana stretched her back. She opened a couple of the shutters on the windows. The sun was high and filled the cabin with light. The horses needed to be fed and watered, but she decided they could wait until later in the day. Peeking out the loopholes under the windows and those next to the door, she saw nothing unusual. If anyone had followed him, they might be out there, out of her sight but she needed water.

With a bucket in one hand and the rifle in the other, she headed outside, filled the bucket with fresh water, and then returned to the cabin. At least they had plenty of wood in the cabin, enough to last several days. Although the nights were growing colder, the days were warm enough to do without a fire.

Encouraged that no one had appeared at her first appearance outside, Susana fed the horses and mucked out their stalls. Afterwards she boiled some beef to make broth, and tried to persuade Elisha to take nourishment spoon by spoon. By afternoon, exhausted, she sat in the rocking chair by her husband's bed.

Elisha tossed and turned in pain and fever.

Susana could only sit, watch, and pray. As the evening shadows darkened the cabin, Susana wiped the sweat from Elisha's face with a wet cloth. What if he died? The ranch headquarters was a full day's ride away. She couldn't leave Elisha and she couldn't load him into the wagon. And she doubted he would survive the trip.

~ ~ ~

Susana looked at the calendar. Two weeks had passed while Elisha drifted somewhere in that twilight world of pain, fever, and semi-consciousness. She could not be any more exhausted or concerned for her husband.

He wasn't aware of her presence, even though there were times when his eyes were open. Try as she might, she couldn't get him to eat. He'd only swallow the water and broth. He lost weight and faded before her eyes.

She wouldn't let herself think of him dying. He had to live. She had come to love him so much, and the thought of not having him was unbearable. Although she tried to remain strong, she couldn't stop the tears of fear.

Susana woke from dozing in the rocking chair in the middle of the night. She heard Elisha talking from the fever.

"Put it away...the gold...Susana? Where are you? Susana..." His voice faded. Suddenly he tried to sit up. "Where is it? Susana...the gold."

He was talking so crazy. It was the fever. She put her hand on his forehead and whispered softly to him. "It's all right. You're home, honey. Don't take on so."

Then his rambling and restlessness diminished for a while.

Only able to sleep in snatches of time, Susana almost felt too tired to comfort her husband. She lay on the bed beside him and put her arms around him to hold him as tightly as she could, as if that would hold him here with her. Soon he was asleep or unconscious; she didn't know which. She allowed herself to drift into a troubled sleep.

* * *

Elisha woke as if from a deep, dark place and looked to see Susana lying next to him. Had he been in a fight? His body ached all over. He raised his hand to his face and rubbed a beard of at least two weeks growth. Where had that come from? The last he remembered, he'd been clean-shaven. Just lifting his hand was difficult.

Then he remembered the Utes and his horse finding him. But he couldn't remember returning to the cabin.

He tried to speak, but nothing came out. Reaching over he placed his hand on Susana's head.

She awoke with a jerk, sat up, and looked into his eyes. "Elisha? Are you awake?"

He cleared his throat and was able to whisper. "I'm not sure."

"How are you?" She placed her hand on his forehead. It was wet with sweat, but cool to the touch. "Thank God the fever's gone."

"How long have I been out?" Why was speaking such an effort?

"It's been fifteen days since you got home. You had me so worried."

"Where am I hurt?" He touched his head and the healing scar. "Can I have some water?"

Susana got up awkwardly and got a cup of water. She held it to Elisha's lips.

He was able to drink most of it. He tried to hold the cup, but his hands didn't have any strength. "Sorry. I should be helping you."

"Don't you be sorry, Elisha. You're here and that's all that matters to me."

"Has it been that bad?" But he could tell that it had by the weariness in her face.

"Yes, my love, it's been that bad, but you're getting better." Susana started to cry softly.

"Tell me about it." He wanted to reach up, wrap his arms around her, and hold her tight, but he didn't have the strength, so he stroked her arm with his finger.

"You didn't come back. I waited all night and then all the next day, and you didn't come. Late that night, I begged God to keep you safe and bring you back to me. Then I heard your horse outside the door. I opened the door and you were sitting on your horse, covered in blood. I was so frightened." She sniffled and wiped her nose with her handkerchief.

His precious bride looked so vulnerable. How he wanted to protect her, and here he lay, flat on his back.

Speaking hoarsely from his dry throat, he told her what he remembered. "I was leaving the meadow with the pack horses loaded ... the Utes came at me. I remember ... being hit with the arrow. Then Shadow threw me into a ravine." He paused and swallowed. "I came to in the dark and the Indians were gone. I walked and walked before I passed out. Shadow found me and I got in the saddle. I don't remember much after that."

"I got the arrow out and sewed up your leg."

"My leg? I don't remember hurting my leg."

"And you hit your head hard. I think it was that and the fever that has made you so sick these last couple of weeks. How are you feeling now?" She wiped his face with a wet cloth.

"Thanks, that feels good. I'm not in much pain... except for my chest, but I haven't tried to move. I feel sort of like I'm floating, and I've no strength."

"Well, I'm not surprised. You haven't eaten anything except beef broth and a little soup the whole time."

He looked at her and could only guess what the last two weeks had been like for her. She seemed so slender everywhere except for her belly, which was huge.

"How are you?" He tried to sit up but couldn't do it. "How is the baby?"

"I'm fine, a little tired. And I guess the baby is all right. He's kicking a lot." She gave him a wan smile.

"Are you sure the baby is a he?" Elisha smiled. Even with the pain and sick feeling, he felt a rush of joy at the coming child.

"If this is a girl, she's not going to be dainty, I can tell you that for sure. Not with the kicks I'm feeling."

"We were supposed to be at the ranch house by now. They'll look for us and begin to worry." He hoped they would be worried enough to come searching for them. He and Susana needed help. Frustrated at his weakness and not even being able to breathe deeply without an agonizing pain in his chest. How was he to take care of his wife and get them on the trail when he couldn't even leave his bed?

"I hope so. Maybe one of them will come up the trail." Susana pushed some curls back from her face.

It surprised Elisha that it looked as if she hadn't combed her hair in days. That wasn't like her.

"How's the weather?" He thought of the need to make it down to the ranch headquarters before the winter storms.

"It snowed about three inches yesterday."

"No, it's too early!" He hadn't meant to sound so anxious. His wife didn't need any more worry. His sense of panic was strong enough for the both of them.

Susana put her face against his. "Please don't worry. Now that you're better, we'll be all right. It's an early snow and will melt by tomorrow. We've time to make it down to the ranch house. The baby won't come for another month."

Elisha remembered the gold he'd found. "Did you unload the pack or was there even a pack still on the horse?"

"I'm sorry, Elisha, I know you like for things to be kept neat in the barn. I undid the cinch, and let the saddle and pack drop to the floor. I haven't taken the time to pick them up. They're still lying where they dropped off the horse."

"Don't worry about it. You don't need to be lifting that saddle. As long as it's out of the weather, it's all right. Did you look in the packs?"

"No, I haven't touched them. Does it matter?" She had a puzzled frown.

"Let me tell you what I found, and then you tell me if it matters. I took the bed of the wagon apart and found all these little rawhide sacks of gold. In the pack out on the barn floor is a fortune in gold. I guess it's what your grandfather got from the sale of your folks' place, and the store. It belongs to you." His dry throat closed on his last words, begging for more water.

Susana sat on the edge of the bed looking at him with big, round eyes. "I can't believe it. I thought it took all of the money to buy the wagon to get us back to Ohio." She shook her head as if amazed.

"I know that's what you believed and that's what I thought too. Can you get me some more water, please?"

Susana got up and got him another cup of water. After she helped him drink it, she sat again on the bed.

"Why do you think Grandfather didn't tell us? Do you think he forgot?"

"I'm not sure. We may never know. But it's your inheritance. When I can I'll hide it somewhere, at least off the barn floor."

"This has been a strange couple of weeks." Susana shook her head. "First, you're hurt, and now you tell me we've got lots of gold. I'm not sure what God is trying to tell us with all of this."

"You're a wonder, Susana. Only you would try to figure out God's plan in all of this when you've been told you're rich."

"Well, having some gold is nice, but not near as nice as having you well and strong, my love." She kissed him lightly on his dry, chapped lips. "I'm going to warm some soup. You need to eat to get your strength back."

He wanted to tell her not to bother, that he wasn't hungry, but he knew she was right. He had to get his strength back as quickly as possible. They had to go down to the ranch soon to beat the coming snow. How could he feel so exhausted after a little talking? He closed his eyes and drifted into sleep.

The next morning, he ran his hand over his chest and could fell every rib. How much weight had he lost? Even his arms seemed smaller. His muscles felt like they turned to jelly. Would he ever feel right again?

But Elisha felt the need to get up and begin to function. "Susana, help me sit up. I need to get to moving."

"Are you sure?" Susana wiped her hands on the dishcloth.

Putting her arm around his shoulders, she heaved. Elisha managed not to groan from the stab of intense pain in his chest, as he struggled to a sitting position. The room swayed and he couldn't hold his head up. He fell back on the bed.

How could it be that he couldn't even sit up? "Sorry, honey, I can't do it." He struggled for breath.

Susana wiped the sweat from his face. "It's all right. Give yourself a few more days. You'll soon be better." She smiled and nodded, even as she frowned.

CHAPTER SIXTEEN

Gold coins clinked and jingled in a cascade of yellow dreams until dawn's soft light woke Susana to the sounds of morning. Gentle snores came from Elisha's side of the bed, so she quickly dressed and left the cabin. In the coolness of the morning, Susana walked across to the barn and took care of the horses. With that chore done, she opened the pack that had lain on the floor of the barn for the last two weeks. Opening one of the rawhide sacks, she fingered the gold coins. The heaviness of the gold surprised her. She liked the pretty, yellow color. What did it mean to her and Elisha? Glancing at Shadow, munching away in his stall, Susana realized how much she owed to the horse, he'd borne home his master, plus a fortune in gold.

She said a prayer of thanksgiving, both for her grandfather's efforts to secure the gold and for God providing for them in an unexpected way. They could begin to build their ranch. Now she could really be of help to Elisha. He had to get well. She couldn't do it alone. Bowing her head, she gave a prayer of thanks.

"Father in Heaven, thank you for the effort of my parents and grandfather to provide for me. Thank you for bringing Elisha home and help him to heal. Father, guide us to know how best to use this gift of the gold. Watch over our growing baby. In the name of Jesus, the Christ. Amen"

Opening her eyes and raising her head, she glanced around the barn and decided to store the gold behind the feed bin. There was enough space behind it to drop the leather sacks. With the weight of each of the small pouches, she could carry only three or four at a time. By the time she had the last leather sack placed behind the wooden feed bin, she was breathing hard and holding her stomach. Storing the two empty packs on a shelf, it was a relief that the job was done, she walked from the barn to the cabin.

After she took off her coat and hung it on the hook by the door, then she perched on the edge of her husband's bed. "I found the gold. I put it behind the feed bin."

Elisha reached up and stroked her cheek. "That should be as good a place to hide it as any other. It's not like anyone will be searching for it."

She pressed his hand against her face. "I opened one of the sacks and fingered the gold. It didn't seem real somehow."

Elisha smiled at her. "It's real."

~ ~ ~

Two days later, as the darkness of night arrived, it started to snow again. Susana sat in the rocking chair, hemming a little dress for the baby.

Elisha drifted off to sleep again as he had off and on all day. Susana felt concern at his slow recovery, but as long as Elisha seemed better, she had hope. She kept praying.

The sound of horses outside startled her. Indians?

Shaking Elisha on the shoulder to wake him, she said quietly, "Someone is out in the yard."

Elisha struggled to sit up. "Give me the revolver. Get a rifle and stand by the door but don't open it."

Susana placed the revolver in his hand and put one of the rifles on his bed. "Could it be the Indians?"

"I don't know. If it is are you ready to fight?" The effort to sit up and hold the revolver left Elisha's hand shaking. Sweat beaded on his forehead.

She looked at her husband and then at the weapon by the door. The feel of kicks from her baby decided her. "Yes, I'll fight for you and the baby."

Elisha nodded. "Get your rifle and listen at the door."

Susana picked up the rifle by the door, and then leaned toward it to listen to the sound of approaching footsteps crunching in the snow. A loud knock on the door startled her and she jumped.

"Elisha, Susana, you home?" A deep voice bellowed.

She recognized Abe's voice on the other side of the door.

With a sob, Susana set the rifle against the wall and then removed the bar from the door and swung it open.

Abe and Josh, illuminated by the lantern light from the within the cabin, stood in the snow, grinning at her.

Susana stepped into the snow and flung herself into Abe's arms. "Oh, you've come, you've come."

Abe put his arms around her. "Now, honey, it's all right. We're here. What's happened?"

"We need help. Oh, you've come!"

Abe guided Susana back inside the cabin.

Josh followed closely and shut the door to keep in the warmth.

She wiped her eyes with her handkerchief.

The men looked over at Elisha lying in the bed.

"Hey boys, glad you could come." Elisha lay back against the pillow, let the revolver drop to the quilt, and waved weakly.

"We got worried, and Mr. Weathers told us to come on up and meet you coming down," Josh struggled out of his coat. "We got real bothered when we didn't meet up."

"What's happened, Elisha?" Abe asked.

Susana sank down into the rocking chair, feeling as if her legs would no longer hold her.

"Ran into some Utes about three weeks ago, they wanted to fight, and they won." Elisha handed the revolver to Abe who placed it on the bureau. "Susana has had a bad time of it, and then it snowed."

"How bad are you hurt? Can you ride in the wagon if we load you up?" Abe bent over to look closer at Elisha.

"You help me into the wagon and I'll make it. We need to get Susana down to the ranch house."

"He had an arrow all the way through his chest," Susana held her stomach and gently rocked. "His head was hurt bad, and he has a wound in his leg. He's only been out of the fever for three days. Until then, he didn't even know me."

"I can't seem to get any strength going yet. I tried to make it out of bed and walk today, and I couldn't do it."

Abe looked thoughtful. "You shouldn't push it after that kind of wound. Josh and I'll look after things now, but we need to start down the mountain at first light. More snow is coming, and this may be our only chance."

Abe turned to Josh. "Go take care of our horses and see what needs doing out in the barn. I'll rustle us up some grub."

"Oh, Abe, how thoughtless of me," Susana struggled out of the rocking chair. "You must be hungry. I'll start supper." She was so glad to see the two men. With the way Abe took charge, she sensed a burden lifting.

"No, Susana, you let me do that. You have more important things to do. You need to gather what you want to take down to the ranch. We may not be able to return here before spring, so we need to take everything you want to keep safe. We have to start out as soon after first light as we can. A storm is coming."

"All right. Prepare whatever you can find, and I'll pack." Susana looked around the cabin, and then started taking their clothes off the hooks and folding them. With the possibility of not returning until spring, she'd need to pack everything she could, including the things she'd made for the baby.

Abe poured water into the basin, washed his hands, and then started making biscuits, frying ham, and gravy. He had a meal on the table by the time Josh came stomping in the house, brushing the snow off his shoulders.

Josh, Abe, and Susana sat at the table and ate quickly with little talk.

Elisha had refused any food and lay propped up in the bed with his eyes closed, his breathing rugged.

Susana looked over at Elisha and then turned to Abe. "You think we can make it to the ranch tomorrow?"

"We need to try. You all can't make it here through winter. There's already some snow on the trail and the clouds were awfully heavy. " Abe took another biscuit.

"How is Elisha really?" Josh whispered to Susana.

"He's so much better, but he's sleeping a lot. I had no idea he wouldn't be up and moving around by now. He still hasn't healed. His wounds are still draining. The one in his chest is the worst. It worries me that he is still so sick and in such constant pain."

"Nate and Smithy are both good hands with fixing up wounded men. Don't worry, we'll make it down the mountain. When do you think the baby will come?" Abe asked.

"The baby should come in about three weeks. I've been making some clothes for him. I need to take those with me. I'd like to take the sewing machine Elisha gave me if we can." She looked around the cabin, their home. What else to take? She almost didn't have energy to think about it.

Abe finished sopping up his gravy with the last of the biscuit. "Sure, that's no problem. What else?"

"How much will the wagon hold?"

"You tell us and we'll pack it down the mountain," Abe promised. "Between the wagon and the extra horses, we can pack everything."

Susana rubbed her lower back. "The most important thing is to get Elisha down to the ranch without hurting him anymore than necessary. He's been in so much pain." She looked over at Elisha laying so still n the big bed. "Could one of you go into the loft and bring down my trunks?"

Josh broke another biscuit apart and covered it with gravy. "Sure, I'll do that as soon as I finish eating. What about your horses?"

"Four horses are in the box canyon and two are in the barn. The Indians got two of the horses when they shot Elisha."

Swallowing the last of his biscuit, Josh rose from the table. "I'll go for the horses in the canyon at first light. Then we can load and head out. If we pack all the horses, we can take everything and have room in the wagon for Elisha to ride lying down."

Abe gathered up the dishes and sat them in the dry sink. "Good idea. Now Susana, I want to look at Elisha's wounds."

"Oh, Abe, it is so good to have you here. I did the best I could, but I don't know what else to do. You give me hope." Susana hugged the cowhand.

Abe hugged her back and patted her on the shoulder. "Now, now, it's going to be all right. We need to see to Elisha, get some sleep, and ride down to the ranch tomorrow."

As they approached the bed, Elisha opened his eyes.

"I need to look at your wounds." Abe pulled back the covers. He unwrapped the bandage around Elisha's chest and lifted the cloth from the exit wound. "The wound is still red around the edges and oozing slightly tells me this needs some attention for sure. Now let me look at your back." Abe carefully helped Elisha roll onto his side.

Susana bit her lip as she saw the look of pain that Elisha tried to hide.

"Sorry that I'm hurting you. The good news is that this wound on your back is much more healed and closed up." Abe gently helped Elisha roll onto his back.

Susana pulled the quilt back toward the foot of the bed so Abe could look at the leg wound.

Abe unwrapped the bandage and looked at the gash in Elisha's leg. "This is about halfway healed. The top part of it is still raw and swollen. This head wound is scabbed over and looks to be healing." Abe wrapped the bandages tight, with Susana's help. "Was there any blood in your ears that you know of?"

"You'd have to ask Susana. I wasn't very conscious."

"Not that I noticed." Susana stood at the end of the bed wringing her hands.

"That's good. Then maybe your skull isn't cracked. That chest wound doesn't look good. Nate and Smithy know how to doctor. They'll get you better." Abe pulled the covers back up to Elisha's shoulders.

Abe turned to Susana. "Now what can Josh and me do to help you pack?"

"Well, there're the dishes and the china. I can do the clothes and the baby's things." Susana tried to think but she couldn't seem to hold a thought long enough to get anything done.

Josh grabbed one of the trunks and started wrapping the china dishes with the paper and clothes he found in the trunk.

Abe started packing the pots and pans. "I'll leave the skillet and coffee pot out for the morning," he said, "There's not a lot of food left. We should leave it. We have always left some food here in case someone came along and needed help."

Susana sat down in the rocker. She was feeling more and more exhausted. "What about our furniture? Can we take it with us?"

Abe asked, "What furniture do you want to take?"

"Well, I'd like to take the rocking chair, the little lamp table, bureau, the bedstead, and the sewing machine. The bunks, table, and chairs belong with the cabin." She glanced with fondness at the few pieces of furniture that were all she had left from her parents.

"Don't worry, Susana, we'll be able to load everything. But we need to get to bed now and get some rest," Abe assured her.

"You all are such an answer to my prayers. Do you mind sleeping in the loft?"

"Not at all, it's warmer up there than on the floor down here." Josh picked up their bedrolls and climbed up the ladder to the loft.

"Susana," Elisha spoke barely above a whisper.

She immediately went to him. "Yes Elisha?"

"I want to speak to Abe," he lifted his hand and then let it fall back on the quilt.

Susana waved Abe over.

He leaned over the bed to listen to what Elisha wanted to tell him.

"Abe, out in the barn there are sacks of gold coins that belong to Susana. We need to take them with us." Elisha spoke in a low weak voice so that Abe had to lean farther over the bed.

"Where in the barn?" Abe didn't seem to be surprised.

"Behind the feed bin is where Susana said she put it."

"Don't worry. We'll find it. You try to sleep and be ready to travel tomorrow." Abe assured him, patting his shoulder.

"I'm really glad you're here." Elisha put his hand on Abe's arm.

"I'm glad we came on up. Don't worry, Josh and me will take care of everything." Abe motioned for Susana to walk over to the loft ladder. "Elisha's chest looks bad. I'm not sure we should even move him. But we have to with the snow coming."

"Can he die, Abe?" Susana could feel her insides trembling from the fear.

Abe patted her shoulder. "We'll do everything thing we can to get him to help tomorrow. Just pray tonight and try to get some rest. Tomorrow will be a tiring day."

Susana blinked back tears and nodded.

Abe climbed the ladder into the loft.

Susana went back to the bed and pulled Elisha's covers up, tucked them in, and gave him a light kiss. "Rest easy now, God has sent us help. We'll be down at the ranch by tomorrow night. Then you'll soon be better."

"I'm so sorry I can't help you," he whispered.

She packed a few more things and then lay down beside Elisha.

He looked even more ill than he had earlier in the day. They had to get him to help.

Thank you, Lord, for bringing Abe and Josh to help us. Please, heavenly Father, heal Elisha and protect our baby.

* * *

Elisha woke at the sound of Abe climbing down the ladder from the loft and guessed that dawn was near. He lay still, not wanting to antagonize the pain in his chest. Each day he woke hoping to feel better, but like this morning, he felt desperately ill. The thought of the trip down the mountain to the ranch was enough to make him break out in a sweat.

Abe made coffee. The good smell of the boiling coffee filled the cabin.

Josh soon came down the ladder from the loft, too, with their bedrolls, which he carried outside.

Elisha glanced down at Susana lying beside him and found her gazing at him. "Morning sweetheart."

She sat up and pushed her hair back from her eyes. "How are you this morning?"

"I'm all right." He didn't want her worrying anymore than necessary. Glancing at her stomach, he wondered if it could be possible that it was bigger than yesterday.

Susana climbed out of bed and dressed behind the curtain. She then got Elisha's clothes together and laid them on the bed.

Elisha wanted to jump out of bed and dress. He struggled to sit up, but finally leaned back against the headboard. All he could do was watch as the others moved about the cabin, making breakfast and packing the last of their belongings. He plucked at the quilt with a sense of helplessness. What use was he to anyone if he couldn't even get out of bed and dress?

By the time Josh came back into the cabin, breakfast was on the table.

Susana took a plate over to Elisha. "Try to eat, sweetheart."

"I will." Elisha nibbled at the food and drank a little coffee. However, before he had eaten much his energy was gone and he leaned back against the headboard with a sigh. He never remembered a time he couldn't eat a plate of food, not even when the time his horse fell on him.

Josh and Abe, on the other hand, ate like men who planned to put in a hard day's work.

Abe took his coat off the hook. "Josh, let's hitch up the wagon and pull it up to the cabin. I'll start loading, and you go fetch the horses in the box canyon. Time you get back we'll be ready to help Elisha into the wagon, get the packs on the horses, and ride out."

Josh stuffed another biscuit into his mouth and put on his coat and hat. "I'm on my way," he said, and headed out the door.

Elisha watched Susana pour hot water from the kettle into the basin. She washed the dishes from breakfast and set them on the shelf by the stove. She packed the left over biscuits and ham into a gunnysack, along with some cornbread and the makings of coffee for their lunch.

When she finished her task, she looked at him. "You ready to put some clothes on?"

"Not sure, but I suspect there's no choice." He hated that she had to help him.

Elisha determined to make it as easy as possible on Susana. As she helped him sit up and swing his legs to side of the bed, he broke into a sweat and bit his lip to keep from moaning.

Susana put his shirt over his head and guided his arms into the sleeves. "I'm sorry, love. I know it hurts."

Elisha gritted his teeth. "Let's get it done."

She struggled to pull on Elisha's pants as Abe entered the cabin.

He stepped over to the bed. "Susana, you get your things together and I'll help Elisha get dressed."

Elisha was exhausted by the time he was dressed. "Thanks, Abe. I'll find a way to repay you someday for all your help."

"Why, Elisha, no need for thanks. You'd do the same for me. By the way, those packages that were in the barn are now in the wagon. Can you sit at the table for a bit? I need to take the bed apart."

"You'll have to help me over there. I think I can sit up if I have the table to lean on."

Abe easily helped Elisha stand and walked him over to the chair.

At the table, Elisha could barely sit without falling over.

Elisha fought the weakness and the pain and tried to stay alert. But he sensed his fever returning and found it hard to focus.

Abe carried the straw-filled ticking with all the blankets from Elisha and Susana's bed out to the wagon. He returned and took the bed frame apart and carried it out.

Abe stepped back into the cabin with Josh following him and walked to the table.

"You ready, Elisha?"

"As ready as I can get." Elisha steeled himself for what was to come.

"Here, let's put your coat and hat on." Josh held Elisha's coat up to make it easier to slip on.

With the help of the two men, Elisha made it into the wagon.

Abe covered him with the blankets and quilts. "Sorry we hurt you, Elisha. We tried to be easy."

"Not your fault." Elisha tried to keep the sound of the pain out of his voice.

"This mattress will be the smoothest ride in the wagon and will protect you from the wind. I won't be surprised if we have snow all the way down. The mattress is big enough for Susana to rest here with you," Abe said, "I don't like how she looks this morning."

"I know. She's exhausted from worry and it's not good for the baby." Elisha looked up at a sky full of low-hanging dull gray clouds and felt the tiny spitting snowflakes.

He turned to watch Susana walk into the cabin. What was she thinking? That possibly was their last look at the cabin where they had started a life together? Elisha's heart grew heavy at the thought.

Abe helped Susana into the wagon. She sank down into the blankets beside Elisha with a sigh.

He took her hand. "Lord, give us a safe trip. Be with Susana and the baby. Thank you for the blessings of Abe, Josh, and Mr. Weathers offering us a place. In the name of Jesus, Amen."

Elisha squeezed Susana's hand. He felt wretched. *Lord, don't let me die before I see my baby.*

CHAPTER SEVENTEEN

Elisha woke to the cold touch of snowflakes on his face. He took shallow short breaths against the pain in his chest and in this white land the air was like icicles sliding into his lungs. Why couldn't he stay awake? He kept drifting in and out of sleep. Too weak to talk, he grit his teeth and dealt silently with the bouncing, which jabbed him with every jolt of the wheel. The creaking of the wagon and the hoof beats and the whinnying of the horses pounded into his consciousness and left him exhausted.

What felt like hours later, the motion of the vehicle stopped and Susana stirred next to him. Her face looked pinched and her jaw clenched. "Susana. You all right?" Elisha managed to ask in a whisper.

She slipped out from under the covers, and stood in the wagon. "I need to walk a bit."

Abe stood by the wagon wheel and gave her a hand to steady her as she climbed down to the snow covered ground.

"Are we almost there?" Elisha asked.

Susana walked away from the wagon.

Abe stepped up on the wheel. "We've stopped to rest the horses a bit and Susana said she needed to walk around. She's hurting, I think. I'm sending Josh on to the ranch. We have about an hour before we arrive. I want Mr. Weathers to know we're coming."

"That's a good idea." Elisha tugged the blankets tighter around his shoulders and pulled his hat down. The weather had grown colder and a dusting of snow covered the quilts and their coats and hats. He watched Susana as she slowly walked by the side of the trail. He should be walking with her to give comfort.

Susana bent over and clutched at her stomach. "Abe... Abe!"

He rushed over to her. "What is it? Susana?"

"I think the baby is coming."

"I'm not surprised after what you've been through." Abe put his arm around her and walked her toward the wagon. "Do you think you can make it to the ranch house? We're only about an hour out."

"I'll make it. Let's get going." With Abe's help, she climbed back into the wagon.

Elisha struggled to sit up. "What's wrong?"

She smiled. "I think I'm about to have a baby."

"You mean, now?" Elisha fought to keep the panic out of his voice.

"I think so. I'll try to wait until we get to the ranch house. That would be easier, but if not, Abe can help me. For now, will you hold me?"

Elisha wrapped his arms about her as she lay down next to him. He could do that for her.

She stiffened and he could see the pain the flitted across her face. He wanted to take the pain from her, but all he could do was stroke her back until she relaxed. *Lord, take away her pain and help us reach the ranch for the birth. Please, Lord.*

* * *

Josh sat on his horse, holding the lead ropes to the four horses he was guiding, waiting for Abe to start the wagon down the trail. Could he help Abe with the birth of a baby? The thought made him want to throw up. He would help if he had to, but he would rather not.

He looked at Elisha lying in front of the furniture in the wagon. Josh was more concerned than he'd let on to Susana or Abe. He'd never been around anyone so ill. Elisha looked awful. He'd lost so much weight and his eyes sank back into his head. If they could get to the ranch, Mr. Weathers would know what to do. Josh was sure of it.

Abe helped Susana back into the wagon, then turned to Josh. "Tie the packhorses to the back of the wagon, and ride on in. Tell Sam and the men we're coming."

Abe wanted all the help he could get when they arrived. Josh hurried to tie all the packhorses to the tailgate of the wagon, and then mounted his horse.

Josh settled into the saddle, waved at Abe, and urged his horse into as quick a gait as he dared on the snow-covered ground. He took it easy over slick areas and snow-filled ruts; as a result, it was almost dark when he rode into the ranch yard. Jumping off his horse, he ran into the kitchen, where he found all the men gathered around the supper table.

"Josh, what's wrong?" Mr. Weathers lunged to his feet.

"I'll explain... in a minute, but first, Jim, Albert go get a couple of lanterns. Saddle your horses, and ride up to meet Abe. He's driving the wagon. He needs some light on the trail. Go now! Quick! No time to explain. You'll find out why later." Josh stood bent over pulling in deep gulps of air.

Jim and Albert left the kitchen with Frank hurrying behind to saddle the horses.

When he could speak easier, Josh said, "Abe's got Elisha and Susana both in the wagon. Elisha fought with the Utes and is bad hurt. He can hardly get around yet, and the baby's about to come." He stopped to catch his breath again.

Mr. Weathers stepped toward Josh. "You mean she's having the baby now?"

"Yeah, Abe hopes he can make it to the ranch before she does. She's been having bad pain for a couple of hours how."

Mr. Weathers nodded at Nate. "You take charge of this. You know a whole lot more about arrow wounds and birthing babies than I do."

Nate turned to Smithy. "I'll get some water boiling and Smithy, you go get an oilcloth and put it on the bed in their room. Sam, we need to get that room warmed up—fast. A roaring fire in the front room fireplace and the stove should do the job. We're going to have a baby." He turned to Josh. "What about Elisha?"

"He had an arrow through his body from back to front here." Josh pointed to spots on his own back and lower chest. "He took a bad hit to his head and a gash on his leg. Susana said he lost a lot of blood. He's weaker than a newborn foal, can't even walk by himself. Abe looked at his wound and said the one in his lower left chest is bad."

Nate turned to Red. "You think you could get a bunk moved into that bedroom and made up for Elisha?"

"Sure, but he can have my room," Red offered.

"I know you'd give up your room for him, but I think he's going to want to be with Susana during this time. What do you think?" Nate asked.

"You're right. I'll go get the bunk moved right now." Red got up and headed out the kitchen door.

Mr. Weathers put a cup of coffee in front of Josh, and then dished up a plate of food. "You might as well eat up. I've a feeling it's going to be a long night around here."

Josh almost felt guilty to be eating with all that was going on, but he was hungry.

He had cleaned his plate when he heard the wagon roll into the yard and stop at the front porch. He stood and went with the other men to meet the wagon to do what they could to help.

"I'm so glad you're here," Mr. Weathers said as he climbed up on the wagon wheel. He patted Susana on the shoulder and shook hands with Elisha.

"We're glad to be here. Thanks for sending Abe and Josh," Elisha's voice could barely be heard, it was so weak.

Josh climbed into the wagon. "You all right for me to lift you down to Red?" he asked Susana.

"Thank you, Josh." She wrapped her arms around his neck as he put an arm around her waist and one under her legs. Josh carefully lifted her and then lowered her over the side of the wagon into Red's waiting arms.

Red carried her through the front door as if she was a small child. Nate and Smithy followed them into the house.

Josh looked down at Elisha. "You ready?"

Elisha nodded. "Just get me out of the wagon and onto my feet."

Abe and Josh lifted Elisha and lowered him out of the wagon to where Mr. Weathers waited. Elisha would have fallen if the older man hadn't held him around his waist and put Elisha's arm around his shoulder.

Josh jumped down and put Elisha's other arm across his shoulder. If it had been him, he would have let everyone know of his pain. But not Elisha, he clenched his jaw. Slowly Mr. Weathers and Josh helped him walk through the front door, across to the bedroom, and then helped him sit on the bunk across the room from the bed where Susana was lying.

Josh glanced over to where Susana lay with her eyes shut. She looked to be in terrible pain to him. He wanted to help, but he was glad when Nate told them to leave. How could these men act as if it was a normal happening? Well, he supposed having a baby was.

He went out to the wagon where Abe was unloading the trunks.

"Here Josh, take this valise and haversack to the bedroom. I saw Susana pack her things and the baby's thing into these bags."

Josh grabbed the luggage and sat them just inside the bedroom door. "These have Susana's things." He told Nate. Josh didn't linger.

Abe motioned for Josh to help with the last pack from the wagon. "Where do we put this?" Josh asked.

"These two packs go on the floor behind Mr. Weathers's desk." Abe lifted one of the packs with a grunt.

Josh hefted the other. No wonder Abe had let out a grunt, it was heavy. With muscles straining, Josh followed Abe into the front room and deposited the pack on the floor next the wall behind the big desk.

With the wagon unloaded and the horses in the barn, the men went to the kitchen to wait on news from the bedroom.

* * *

Elisha sighed and let his body relax as he felt the relief of making it to the ranch as the weight of a boulder rolling away. Only to himself did he admit how scared he had been for Susana with him too weak to protect her. Now if he died others would be there to help her.

Nate took charge and the others seemed glad to let him. "Everyone out except for Smithy. Sam, you stay close if we need you." The men left the bedroom.

Nate gently helped Susana get undressed and into the nightgown, he found in her valise. She was in such pain she didn't seem to care who was there.

Smithy helped Elisha out of his coat.

Elisha managed not to groan from the pain of removing his coat. All he wanted to do was lie down. "Smithy, help me to the chair there, by Susana." He had to be with Susana during her time. When Elisha, with the older man's help, made it to her side, she was in the midst of another birthing pain.

Elisha took her hand, held it in both of his. "My love, I'm here." He leaned on the side of the bed so it would bear most of his weight. Although it was all he could do to sit up, he still kept his eyes on Susana's.

"Oh, Elisha, it hurts so bad. Don't leave me." She cried out and almost crushed his hand with her grip.

"I won't leave you. You go ahead and holler, or whatever you need to do." He felt sick and weak, but he was going to be strong for his Susana. Nothing would keep him from being with her now, not even his own pain.

Within a few minutes, Susana screamed again. The pain seemed to come in waves.

Elisha could hardly bear it and he didn't know how she did.

"Can't you do something for her?" he begged Nate.

Wiping Susana's face with a wet cloth, Nate shook his head. "I know it seems bad, but she's doing fine. It won't be long now."

"Don't worry, Elisha, Nate had helped dozens of babies come into the world. You know he used to be a doctor's helper and almost a doctor hisself." Smithy ripped a large piece of cloth into strips. "And I helped my wife in birthing eight of our children."

Elisha nodded and took a shallow breathe. At least Susana had help they could trust.

At Susana's next birthing pain, her cries for relief were so severe he almost wept. He vowed he'd never be responsible for putting her in such a condition again.

Then Elisha heard a small cry, sort of like a little kitten.

Susana relaxed with her eyes closed and breathed deeply. Then another pain, but nothing like as before.

Nate cut the cord separating the baby from its mother and tied something around it.

"It's a boy, Elisha." Nate held the tiny infant so Elisha could see his son. The baby looked awful to Elisha, like a newborn calf.

Nate held the tiny infant in one hand and used the other to wipe it clean with a towel.

Elisha reached over and kissed Susana lightly on the lips.

She opened her eyes.

"Did you hear, my love? We have a son." His heart thumped in his chest and he couldn't stop grinning. What a feeling! He had a son!

She smiled. "Thank God. Is he all right?"

"Give us a few minutes to get you and the baby cleaned up and then you can hold him." Nate handed the baby to Smithy and then quickly cleaned the bed, laying a clean sheet under Susana, and turned away while she changed into the clean nightgown he handed her.

Smithy gave the baby a wash in the basin of warm water, then diapered and swaddled him. He handed the baby back to Nate.

Elisha held Susana's hand and grinned.

"You want to hold your son, Mrs. Evans?" Nate smiled as he place the tiny bundle into Susana's arms.

"Oh, yes please. Hello little one. Welcome to God's great earth."

Elisha looked at the perfect little face, and then he looked up at Nate. "Thank you."

Nate rubbed his eyes with his sleeve. "It was my privilege. He's a beautiful baby."

As Susana held their little son, Elisha couldn't hold back the tears that slid down his cheeks. God had let him see his son, and his wife had survived the birth. *Thank you, God, Thank you for answering my prayers.*

* * *

When the gray dawn broke through the night, Nate sent Smithy to tell the exhausted men sitting in the kitchen about the baby boy, and that they could come into the bedroom and see the baby.

One by one, the men filed silently into the room.

Susana looked pale and tired, but she smiled as she held up their son for the men to see. The baby had a little, scrunched-up red face and no hair.

"Say hello to our son, Samuel Henry Evans," Elisha said

"Oh my," Mr. Weathers took out his handkerchief and wiped his eyes. "What a blessing God has given this house. The birth of a healthy baby boy. Congratulations to you both."

Red leaned forward. "Now, that's a handsome baby."

Josh looked at Red and then back at the baby. "Do all new babies look like that? He's awfully little and ..."

"Haven't you ever seen a baby before?" Abe asked.

"No, not up close like this."

Susana ran her finger along the baby's cheek. "Don't worry Josh. He'll grow."

Elisha smiled. "I wondered the same thing, Josh. Nate promises me that in a day or so he'll look a lot different."

Nate nodded. "Remember he's only about two hours old. Give him time to get used to being in the world."

Susana kissed her son on his wrinkled forehead. "He's absolutely beautiful."

The men all murmured in agreement.

Then Nate shooed them out of the room. "Sam, don't you think we better go on now and let Susana rest. You'll get to see the baby a lot from now on." He and Smithy gathered up the soiled linens and followed the other men out.

With the room empty except for their little family, Elisha took his wife's hand. "Thank you, Susana. You're wonderful, and our baby is beautiful."

"Oh Elisha, isn't he? I feel so blessed that we made it here and that he's all right." She glowed with a happiness that overshadowed the fatigue and pain of the night.

"Well, we can relax for awhile now and get back on our feet. You don't have to do anything but take care of the baby and get your strength back."

She ran her fingers along his jaw. "And how about you, my love? How are you doing? You look so tired and thin."

Elisha laughed. "I've never been so happy or so tired in my life. This thing of having a baby is hard work."

Susana laughed back at him. "I didn't see you doing much. I was doing all the hard work from my side of things."

"I know and I pray that I don't ever put you through anything like that again."

"Elisha, you didn't put me through anything. We both made the choice and I, for one, plan to do it again, probably several times if the Lord is willing."

Elisha reached over, pulled her face toward his, and kissed her. "You are so much braver than I am."

The baby scrunched up his face and gave a little cry. Susana looked at Elisha. "What do I do?"

"Maybe he's hungry." Elisha looked at his son. What an amazing thing to be looking at his own son!

"Yes, he sure is." Blushing a little, Susana pulled down her gown and positioned the baby to her breast so he could nurse. When a soft knock came at the door several minutes later, the baby had fallen asleep.

Susana covered herself and pulled up the blanket. "Come in," she called.

Nate stepped into the bedroom. "How are you folks doing? I heard the little fellow." He came over to the bed.

"You need your rest while you can, Miss Susana. You want me to settle him here on the bed and let him sleep? He'll let you know when he needs feeding." Nate made a little bed with a quilt next to Susana on the big bed and gently laid the sleeping baby on it. He took a little blue and white baby afghan out of the valise and used it as a cover for the swaddled baby.

"I finished crocheting that day before yesterday." Susana yawned. "I'm so tired. I think I'll rest a bit." She lay back on the pillows, relaxed, and closed her eyes.

Nate left the room quietly.

Elisha held her hand as she drifted into a deep sleep. Then he laid his head on his arm, as he leaned against the bed.

He felt wretched.

CHAPTER EIGHTEEN

"You all right?" Nate's voice brought Elisha back to awareness. "Elisha?"

Elisha raised his head off his arm and looked at Susana, who appeared to be deep in sleep. "I'm all right. Had to rest a minute." Had he been asleep or had he passed out?

"Why don't I get you back to the bunk and look at your wounds?" Nate put his arm around Elisha's waist and helped him stand and over to the bunk.

Elisha sat on the edge of the bunk, fumbling with the buttons on his shirt. How useless he was that he couldn't even unbutton a shirt? He looked up into Nate's wise, old eyes.

"It's like I'm dying inside. I feel awful and the pain is bad. Help me, Nate. I need to get well for my family." Elisha could hear the weakness in his own voice.

"I'll do my best," Nate patted him on the shoulder. "Let's see what's going on." Nate pulled the cotton shirt up over Elisha's head and threw it in a corner.

Elisha looked at the crumpled shirt. The left side was wet and bloody from the drainage seeping through the bandage. Was he still bleeding that much?

With slow, deliberate movements, Nate unwound the bloody bandage from Elisha's chest. "Let's see what we have here. This wound here in your back where the arrow went in is red and tender but closed up and healing."

Elisha closed his eyes and his head drooped down almost to his chest. If only he could lie down. "That's good?" He could barely hear his own voice, but there was no strength to speak louder.

"Yes, that's good. Here, lie down and let me pull these pants off." He then helped Elisha lay back on the bunk and slide off his pants.

The relief of relaxing on the bunk after the long night left Elisha feeling like a dead squirrel.

He heard Nate's voice as if through a fog. "This wound in your chest is still bloody, draining pus, and raw looking. I don't see any healing even starting. It's about three inches wide. I think that's from the infection as I can't imagine the arrowhead being that wide."

Elisha opened his eyes and looked at Nate. "You'll have to ask Susana about what the wound was like at first. I don't remember." It felt like a crater now. How could it be only a few inches when it consumed his whole chest?

"Well, it doesn't matter. We need to get it to healing now. It's too large to cauterize and I'm not sure that's even a good practice." Nate took the bandage off the thigh. It was also wet and stained from drainage. "If I'd realized you were this bad off, I'd of let Smithy help Susana. I would have dressed these wounds last night, at least with clean bandages."

Elisha weakly shook his head. "No, Susana is more important." And his son coming into the world. That mattered more than his surviving. He couldn't give in to this drifting feeling. He wanted to live.

"But this one here on your chest is real bad." He looked thoughtfully at Elisha. "You won't like what I'm about to suggest, but I think it needs to be done."

"Will it help me get back on my feet faster?" He would agree to anything if it helped him get well.

"I think so, but I can't promise. The wound is festering and that's poisoning your body. We need to clean it out, let it bleed, and put a poultice on it. If we don't clean it out, I think you'll die. I have some prickly pear with some other herbs that I use for the men when they cut themselves and the wound festers. The prickly pear will draw out the poison so it can start to heal. If we don't do something, it'll continue to worsen. That's why you're still feeling so poorly. Your body is full of poison."

Elisha was too tired to care what Nate would do. He wanted some relief. "You do what you think best...I can't go on like this."

Nate put his hand on Elisha's forehead. "You have a high fever." He looked over at Susana sleeping in the next bed. "I'd say we should move you to another room but I fear it's not safe. We need to get it done. I'll go prepare what I need and ask Sam and Josh to help me" He gently pulled a quilt up to Elisha's chin.

What if he died? What about Susana and little Samuel? He would have to depend on Mr. Weathers to care for them. She had the gold and wouldn't want for anything. Would she remarry if he died? She deserved someone who could take her back east and give her an easier life. Elisha had thought he couldn't feel any worse, but the thought that his son might not grow up in the west, or know his father, pulled him even further into despair. He had to live.

Nate returned with Mr. Weathers and Josh. "Elisha, this is going to hurt bad, and I've asked Sam and Josh to hold you still. You understand what I got to do?"

Elisha nodded. "Susana..." He mustn't let her know what they were doing to him. He had to be quiet, if he could. The pain was so bad now, what would it be like when Nate stabbed him with that knife in his hand? Did he have the strength to be brave enough for what was coming?

Mr. Weathers took his hand. "We'll do this quick and quiet."

Nate took a piece of rolled-up leather out of his pocket. "Put this between your teeth and bite down on it as hard as you need to against the pain."

"Wait." Elisha looked deep into Mr. Weathers's eyes. "Promise me that if I don't make it, you'll take care of Susana and the baby. Please."

"Now, Elisha, you don't need to worry. You're going to be fine." Mr. Weathers gripped Elisha's shoulder. "But if it'll make you feel better, I promise. You don't even have to ask."

"Thanks." Elisha tried to smile at the older man in appreciation, but feared it came out more as a grimace. Yes, he could trust Mr. Weathers to care for his family. But he wanted to take care of them himself.

"All right, no more talking. Open your mouth." Nate put the piece of rolled up leather between Elisha's teeth. "Bear down on that when you need to."

Nate picked up the knife he had placed on a cloth on the chair. "Josh, you stand at the end of the bed, cross Elisha's legs at the ankles, and bear down with your full weight. I need him still. And Sam, you stand at the head of the bed and pull Elisha's arms across and up, until his hands are at his shoulders. Then you bear down your full weight on his crossed arms. If you let go he'll try to get the knife."

"I understand." Mr. Weathers took Elisha's arms, folded them high on his chest, and pressed down with his full weight. "Elisha, I'm probably going to hurt you, but I'm not letting go."

Elisha thought he wasn't going to be able to breathe from the weight of Mr. Weathers. Then he truly couldn't breathe, as he watched Nate thrust the knife into his chest. Nate pushed it in further and Elisha felt as if it was coming out his back. A hot fire of agony spread through his chest and he tried to heave his body away.

Nate kept his knee pressed on Elisha's ribs as he twisted the knife.

Clenching his teeth against the roll of leather was all that kept the scream in his chest from escaping. He had the sensation of something pouring out of his body, and a pressure in his chest lessened.

Nate withdrew the bloody knife, dropped it on the chair, and picked up a bunch of wet clothes. He started cleaning up the blood and pus that poured from the wound.

Elisha collapsed onto the bunk as the agony lessened, his body covered in sweat. Would the pain ever end?

"Quick," Nate told Josh. "Reach me that bottle of alcohol."

Josh picked up the bottle, unscrewed the top, and handed it to Nate. He then took hold of Elisha's legs again.

Elisha looked at the bottle of alcohol and knew what was coming. He bit down on the roll of rawhide, steeling himself to take the pain.

Nate poured a liberal amount of the alcohol into the raw flesh of Elisha's wound. Elisha's body gave another heave and he thrashed his head from side to side, staring into Mr. Weathers' eyes as if they were his lifeline against the living agony in his chest.

Mr. Weathers' face was pale and covered with sweat, but he held Elisha down firmly.

Nate put some of the crushed prickly pear paste on a clean cloth, pressed it to the wound, and then tied it on with a narrow length of cloth.

"We might as well get the leg done." He removed his knee from Elisha's ribs. "You men hold him down for a few more minutes." Nate looked closely at Elisha's face. "You're doing good, son. We'll be done in a few minutes, and then you can rest."

Elisha tried to nod, but all he could manage to do was breathe.

Mr. Weathers released the pressure he'd been applying to Elisha's arms. Elisha gave a small nod and took a deep breath. More agonizing pain was coming. He had to go through it, if he wanted to get past whatever was keeping him from getting well. Could he be strong in front of these men? That was crazy. These men wanted to help him. But he would take the pain in silence, so he bit down on the leather and tried to hide the agony.

"All right, men, hold him down again." Nate turned his attention to the wound on the leg. "The skin around the stitches is red and angry looking. Part of the wound has started to heal. The cut has gone through to the bone at the top and is still an open wound." Nate cut the stitches and removed them.

Elisha braced himself as he watched Nate put the point of the knife into the top edge of the wound, and going into the flesh about two inches, twisted the knife before removing it. The nerves around the traumatized flesh screamed. Elisha's body tried to pull away from the knife, as if it had a mind of its own.

As the blood and pus flowed from the wound, Josh and Mr. Weathers held him down.

This time he clenched his jaw as hard as he could, but he had run out of strength to fight. He couldn't keep a deep moan from escaping. Tears of pain slid down the sides of his face.

Nate poured alcohol into the wound, pressed the cloth with the crushed prickly pear poultice into it, and tied it tightly onto the leg.

Nate soaked a clean cloth with the cool water. "You men can let go," he said. He took the rawhide out of Elisha's mouth, then wiped Elisha's sweaty face, chest, and arms with the cool wet cloth.

"It's done, Elisha." Nate patted his shoulder. "Sorry we had to hurt you like that, but it had to be done."

"You rest easy now and try to sleep." Mr. Weathers' voice choked up. "Don't worry about anything. We're going to be right here to take care of you and your little family."

Elisha regarded the three men who looked at him with such concern. The pain was still there but so much better that he could barely speak.

"Thanks. Sorry I gave you a hard time." For some reason he was freezing, and his whole body trembled.

"You did fine, Elisha. I'm going to make you some willow bark tea with some laudanum, and I want you to drink it. It'll help you sleep. Sam, you get some covers on him and I'll get some hot tea to warm him up. He's reacting to what we did to him." Nate turned and left the room.

Elisha couldn't stop the shivering that took over his whole body. The quilts Mr. Weathers put over him didn't seem to help.

In a few minutes, Nate returned with a cup of hot tea, into which he poured some white powder.

"Drink this down." Nate lifted Elisha's head and put the cup up to his mouth. His teeth chattered against the porcelain rim.

Elisha swallowed a mouthful of the bitter tea, and then tried to pull away, but Nate gave him no choice by keeping the liquid flowing into his mouth. So he drank the whole cupful of bitter tasting brew.

Elisha felt his stomach heaving, almost to the point of throwing up. But he was warmer and the trembling lessened. He took a deep breath, and for the first time in weeks wasn't attacked by an intense pain in his chest. The pain was more manageable. Elisha relaxed. He began to drift away. He vaguely heard Mr. Weathers, Nate, and Josh talking as if far away in a long tunnel.

"Are you all right, Josh? You're awfully pale." Mr. Weathers asked.

Elisha waited for Josh to speak but he didn't seem to be there. Then as if it were an echo he heard Josh say, "I'm all right. I just never experienced anything like that before. I could have sworn that knife went into my own flesh, as it went into Elisha's chest. I really care about Elisha and Susana and it tears me up to see them so hurt. They're my family." Elisha almost didn't recognize the voice, it was quivering so much.

Mr. Weathers spoke again but to Elisha it seemed he was floating above him. "I know how you feel, son. We would've taken the hurt for them if we could. Elisha's going to need all of us to help him get back on his feet. I feel responsible because he got hurt taking care of my property. Nothing I own is worth losing a man like Elisha." Elisha focused on Mr. Weathers and saw him pat Josh on the shoulder. "Nate, do you think Elisha will survive this? He lost a lot of blood and is now losing more."

Elisha wanted to sit up and yell at them. Of course, he was going to live, but his body wouldn't move, and he couldn't seem to keep a focus on what was said. So tired, he let the talk float over him as he watched.

"I won't lie to you. He's bad hurt. If he can fight through until some real healing starts, he has a chance. I wish I could have gotten to the wound about three weeks ago. All I know to do now is keep it clean and draining, and pray." Nate sounded like the old man he was, especially after a night of no sleep.

Mr. Weathers nodded. "I'll do some praying while I take the first watch. For as long as you think they need it, I want one of us sitting right here."

"I'll take the second watch." Josh rubbed the back of his neck and around to his jaw that needed a shave. "Why didn't you give Elisha the white powder to start with if it would make him sleep? Why make him go through all that pain?"

Nate gathered up the basin, dirty bandages, and knife. "It won't put a person under deep enough to keep them from awaking with the type of pain you just saw, Josh. It'll help him, now that the pain is less. I think he's been in terrible pain for days from that infection. He may sleep all day and night, which won't hurt him. Now I'm going to get some rest myself. When Susana or the baby wakes, call me."

Elisha heard the men leave the room, and then he sensed someone sitting down in the chair by his bunk. When had he closed his eyes? He struggled to open them. Mr. Weathers sat next to him holding his Bible.

"You don't have to stay with me." Elisha tried to speak clearly, but for some reason his words slurred.

"You rest easy, son. I'm going to be right here with you." Mr. Weathers pulled up the covers around Elisha's chin and tucked them in. Elisha thought of his father tucking him in when he was a small boy, and the thought comforted him as he drifted into the open arms of a painless sleep.

CHAPTER NINETEEN

Susana woke to the sound of her baby's cries. Her eyes searched until she saw him, at the foot of the bed, having his diaper changed by Nate. She smiled and sighed. The birthing had been worth it, just to see her little son.

Nate smiled at her from the foot of the bed. Her baby pumped his fists and legs. "This little fella needed his diaper changed."

"Was that why he's crying?" Susana sat up and anxiously examined her baby.

Nate lifted the baby and laid him into her arms. "My misses always said that an infant liked to hear its momma's heart beat." He laid the crocheted afghan over Susana's shoulder to give her privacy.

She guided little Sam to his meal and relaxed as she cuddled him close to her heart. She remembered her mother holding her little sister in the same way. If only her mother could have seen her grandson.

Susana glanced over at where her sleeping husband lay and frowned. Josh sat next to the bed, reading a newspaper. "Nate, why is Elisha still sleeping? Is he worse?"

Nate patted her arm. "I had to open the wounds to get them bleeding and draining, and his fever is fairly high. I don't want him thrashing around too much, so I gave him something to help him sleep. Josh is there to make sure he doesn't aggravate his wound."

Josh looked up from his paper. "It's all right, Susana. He's sound asleep and seems to be resting easy without pain."

"When I finish feeding the baby, I want to sit with him." Susana gently rubbed her baby's back as he nursed.

Nate nodded. "I figured. Josh, you can go on. Susana can sit with Elisha."

"Let me know what I can do to help." Josh left the bedroom.

"Thank you, Nate. You're a good doctor." She blinked rapidly to keep the tears of thanksgiving back. God had answered her prayers and provided help both, for her and Elisha.

"I was almost a doctor once upon a time. I'm glad what I know can be of help to those I care about." He left the bedroom as Susana went over and sat by Elisha.

* * *

Elisha rose from sleep as from a deep well. He looked at the lamp-lit room and the black night beyond the window. Time was confused and had been for the last few weeks. But his mind was clearer than it had been in weeks. He raised his arm to rub his face, but even that small effort left him almost unable to move. How could his once strong body be so weak? Across from him, Abe dozed in the chair by his bunk. Elisha appreciated the men's effort, but was he still so ill that he needed watching?

He looked at Susana and took in the miracle of his wife holding his son. She was so beautiful. Could he keep his family together?

"Hello sweetheart." Susana smiled at him. "How do you feel?"

Elisha smiled back. "I'm better, I think. How are you?"

"I'm doing well and so is little Sam."

Nate came in carrying a tray. "I need to change the poultice again."

Abe woke with a jerk and stood up. "You need me? I could use some coffee."

"You go on to bed. Sam will be here to take your place." Nate set the tray on the chair that Abe had just vacated.

"I'll try to take it easy. I know this will hurt." Nate pulled the covers back and began to remove the bandage.

"Just do what you have to." Elisha had come to dread Nate's ministrations. When Nate pulled the bandage back and eased the poultice off, Elisha sucked in his breath at the flash of searing pain. Beads of sweat formed on his face.

"Sorry." Nate wiped the wound. "The wound has stopped draining and looks better." Nate applied a new poultice pack.

Elisha hadn't been hurting much until Nate started cleaning the wound. Now it was as if a branding iron pressed against his chest.

"I want you to drink this tea." Nate handed Elisha a cup of bitter tea.

Elisha downed it, and then laid back, knowing that he'd soon be asleep.

Nate crossed over to Susana where she had just finished changing the baby. "He'll settle down for the next two or three hours and then will want to eat again."

Susana smiled. "I'm sure I'll wake when he starts crying."

"I know you will. This little cowhand has a good set of lungs."

There was a tap on the door and Mr. Weathers entered the room. Carrying his Bible, he settled himself in the chair next to Elisha's bed. "I'm glad to see you awake, Elisha. How are you feeling?"

"I'm weak as a newborn kitten, but I feel better." Elisha lay still feeling sick but thankful for the lessening of the pain. He sensed a change in his body, a sense of healing. If he could just get some strength, he could get back to work. What was Mr. Weathers thinking of his missing so many days of work? But he had to take it slow, there was no other choice.

Mr. Weathers opened his Bible and began to read as Elisha drifted toward sleep.

* * *

Elisha took another week before he could walk slowly from the bedroom to the front room to sit for a while. He felt uneasy, as if he was doing something wrong by not being at work.

"Here, sit in this chair, son. It's comfortable." Mr. Weathers stood from behind his desk and crossed the room.

Elisha made it to the chair in front of the fireplace. "Thought I'd get out of that bedroom for awhile. I'm tired of lying around." Elisha didn't tell him how shaky he felt. Just getting his shirt and pants on had taken almost all his energy. He looked at Mr. Weathers, trying to tell what he was thinking. Did his boss understand how much of an effort it had taken just to survive the last few weeks? Elisha was so tired of feeling sick and dealing with the pain. He had never felt so useless in his life.

"I think Susana is in the kitchen helping with dinner. The baby is sleeping." Elisha was glad to be sitting in the front room.

"She doesn't have to work in the kitchen but she said she would be happier to keep busy." Mr. Weathers leaned back in his chair. "Smithy is handling the washing. It is a marvel how much laundry that baby can make."

~ ~ ~

That evening Elisha sat in the front room with Susana and most of the crew. The cheerfulness of the fire in the big fireplace drew everyone to that end of the room. Outside it was cold and snowy.

Albert, Jim, and Frank entered from the kitchen carrying two cradles. They set them down in front of Elisha and Susana.

"Oh, these are beautiful." Susana leaned over and ran her hand over the polished golden oak wood of the identical cradles. "How wonderful."

"Thank you, fellas. This is real nice." Elisha ran his hand over the beautifully carved oak wood, and then covered Susana's hand. He appreciated what the men had done. Why hadn't he been able to make the cradle himself? Another thing that the Ute's arrow had taken away from him.

"Why two cradles?" Mr. Weathers said as he leaned an elbow against the hearth and looked on with amused interest.

The men looked at each other sheepishly, and then to Mr. Weathers.

Albert ran his finger around the inside of his collar. "Well, boss. We thought if we made one and it was in the bedroom, we wouldn't see much of the baby. But, if we made one for the front room too, then maybe Susana would put the baby in here sometimes and we could visit the little fella."

"We'll be quiet and not wake him. We promise," Jim shifted from foot to foot.

Elisha and Susana looked at each other and laughed gently.

"That was real smart of you boys." Elisha was just beginning to realize how much having the baby at the ranch meant to these lonely men.

Susana stepped up to each man and kissed him on the cheek. "Thank you so much. So thoughtful and such beautiful cradles."

~ ~ ~

Over the next few weeks, Elisha watched as the men kept their word and tiptoed in to gaze on the sleeping baby whenever they had an opportunity. If they came in for a meal and the baby was asleep, they only whispered, and if anyone did speak too loudly, the looks and shushing were fierce.

Elisha shook his head and chuckled to himself. He'd never seen cowhands act quite like this before.

~ ~ ~

After breakfast one day a month later, Mr. Weathers had given the men their instructions and as usual had not included Elisha. He watched the men saddle up and head out. The gray clouds hung low and the air carried the feel of snow.

Elisha made up his mind and headed back to the bedroom. He didn't want to argue with anyone about his decision to leave the house. Of course, he'd have to deal with Susana.

He opened the bedroom door and found Susana dressing baby. He leaned over the end of the bed where his son lay. What was this little person thinking as he looked up at his father with such big eyes? Elisha glanced at his pretty wife, handling the baby as if she had done it for years. What a miracle God had given to them in their son.

Sam kicked his legs up in the air and flailed his arms. When Elisha held out his finger, the baby grabbed it with his tiny hand. Would his son grow up to have such big hands? *Hold on, little cowhand. Your pa is here.*

"A strong grasp for such a little fellow." Elisha couldn't help but smile at his son. Yes, he would teach him to be strong and make sure nothing hurt him. If God would just help him be the father that such a child deserved.

"He's growing every day. It's amazing. Only four weeks old and already he looks so different." Elisha heard a mother's pride.

Elisha took his coat from the hook, and then pulled it on. He shoved his hat onto his head.

Susana picked up little Sam and cocked her head at Elisha. "What are you doing?"

Elisha braced himself for the argument to come. "I'm going to take a walk this morning."

"Are you sure you're up to it?" She raised her eyebrows and then frowned.

"I won't be out long." Elisha kissed her and exited the room before she could say more. He left by the front door so he could avoid Nate and Smithy in the kitchen.

As he stepped off the front porch, he took a deep breath—and caught his breath from painful pressure in his chest. He hadn't expected it to be so cold. He glanced up at the clouds, which threatened to release snow at any minute.

Elisha took his time walking to the corral behind the barn. This must be what it felt like to be an old man. The short walk from the house to the barn left him with nothing but the desire to sit down. He turned toward the bunkhouse. Would his body ever get back to the strength he had before his meeting with the Utes?

He shuffled toward the bench in front of the bunkhouse. Suddenly his back went into spasm and he couldn't breathe. Collapsing to his knees, he caught himself from falling flat by putting out his arms. The impact of his hands with the ground jerked his torso and a stabbing pain went through his chest.

"Elisha! What are you doing out here?" Abe came out of the bunkhouse and knelt by him.

Clenching his jaw, Elisha tried to relax his back. "Help me to the bench."

Abe aided Elisha to stand and then eased him onto the bench.

"I was just getting some air." His legs trembled. "Didn't expect to have a problem. Let me just sit here and get my breath." Disgusted with himself for falling, he tried to relax his back. What a worthless excuse for a man he'd become. Couldn't even take a little walk without falling. How could he expect Susana to want to stay with him when he had become so weak and useless?

Abe sat next to Elisha and looked out over the pasture toward the south. "It's been a year and half since you rode down that trail for the first time. Amazing what all has happened since."

Elisha slipped his hands under his armpits. He had forgotten his gloves. "It doesn't seem that long and yet it seems like years." Had it only been less than a year since he met Susana?

"You been through a lot in a year and half, married, getting hurt, and now a baby." Abe settled his hat more securely on his head.

Yes, his life had definitely changed. A wife and a baby. If he could only hold on to them.

A tight band squeezed his chest, whether from breathing the cold air or from dread, he wasn't sure. An old fear rose to haunt him: Would Susana want to stay with him now that she had the gold?

"What's the matter? You're looking awfully peaked all of a sudden." Abe put his hand on Elisha's shoulder. "Maybe you better get back to the house and get out of this cold."

Elisha nodded, and then pushed himself up to stand. He's come to the point that he couldn't tell whether it was the weather or the fear of losing Susana that made him colder. "Maybe you're right, Abe. This is long enough for the first time."

"Can you make it back to the house? I'll walk with you. Let's go to the kitchen and see if Nate has some fresh coffee." Abe walked slowly matching Elisha's slower stride across the yard.

Elisha appreciated Abe's gesture of friendship, but he wished there weren't a need for it. "Abe, don't tell anyone about my fall back there. Especially don't tell Susana."

"All right, if you don't want me to, but you just take it easy. Give yourself time."

A short walk to the bunkhouse and back had exhausted him. He wanted so bad to saddle a horse and ride out with his old strength.

In the kitchen, he accepted a cup of hot coffee from Nate and found he could barely lift the cup to his lips, most of his strength spent from his tiny sojourn to the bunkhouse.

Susana walked in from the front room. "How was your walk?" She sat next to Elisha and laid her hand on his arm.

"It was good. Winter is definitely just over the hill. Little Sam asleep?" He sipped his coffee and warmth radiated through him.

"Yes, I put him down in the front room near the fire. He'll probably sleep a couple of hours." Susana pushed a curl back from her forehead.

Elisha looked at his beautiful wife and a longing stirred within him. He wanted to hold her close again. Then he lifted his cup of coffee and pain shot through his arm to his chest. Turning away, he stared out the window.

CHAPTER TWENTY

"Josh, wait a minute." Elisha stood by the door leading to the front room as the other men left the kitchen after breakfast. "I have a favor to ask." He realized he had his fist clenched. Why was he so tense about asking for help to saddle a horse? He felt ready to ride, but the lifting of the saddle was still beyond him.

Josh shrugged into his coat and grabbed his hat. "Sure, what can I do for you?"

"I want to ride today, but I don't know that I can lift a saddle. Would you saddle the bay mare for me?" Elisha hated to ask for help, but he also didn't want to tear open the chest wound that was finally healing.

"When do you want the horse ready?" Josh pushed his hat on.

"Now. I'll get my coat and meet you at the corral."

Elisha went to the bedroom to fetch his coat, gloves, and hat where he found Susana rocking the baby while she nursed him.

"I'll be back in a little while." He hurried from the room before Susana could ask him what he planned to do.

When he got to the corral, Josh had two horses saddled.

Elisha put his foot in the stirrup and pulled himself up, being careful to pull with his right arm.

Josh swung into the saddle. "You mind if I ride along with you?"

Elisha glanced at his friend. "You think I might need some help?"

"Well, if you fall off, who's going to catch the horse?" The hint of a grin played at the corners of Josh's mouth.

Elisha grinned. "As weak as I feel, I may fall off."

They rode the horses slowly south until they could see the cattle that the cowhands had bunched up along the south ridge.

Thirty minutes was all it took for Elisha to know he had ridden far enough. How could his legs be so weak?

"You ready to head back?" Josh reined his horse to a stop.

"Yeah, this is far enough." Elisha turned the bay mare back toward the barn. He held her to a slow walk.

Josh rode slouched in his saddle. "Remember, this is your first time out. You'll get your strength back."

Elisha looked at the young cowhand. "You trying to be encouraging?"

"Yeah." Josh grinned. "How am I doing?"

"You're doing good. I want to push it. I hate hanging around the house all day. But this is a start."

"Don't push yourself too hard." Josh rubbed his horse's neck. "And let me handle your saddle for the next couple of weeks."

"I always know I can count on you." Such a loyal friend was hard to find.

When they got back to the corral, Elisha dismounted carefully and stood on legs that wanted to fold under him. He was glad to let Josh take care of the unsaddling.

"Go on into the house and get warm." Josh led the bay mare into the corral.

Elisha strolled to the house, entering through the front door.

Mr. Weathers sat back in his desk chair. "Did you have a good ride?"

"Slow, but good." Elisha took off his coat and hat and left them on a chair.

"Come on over here and sit awhile." Mr. Weathers waved him toward one of the overstuffed chairs by the fireplace with a big fire blazing.

Elisha sat down and stretched his legs toward the fire. It felt good after the cold of the ride.

"Red told me you asked Josh to saddle up for you." Mr. Weathers stood and moved to the other chair in front of the fireplace.

"Yes, sir. Hope you don't mind. He rode with me." Elisha grinned at his boss. "He was afraid I'd fall off, and to tell you the truth, if the horse had acted up, I would have. My legs are awfully weak."

Mr. Weathers chuckled. "That's to be expected for the first time back in the saddle after almost two months in bed. But you'll get your strength back in no time."

Elisha leaned forward and held his hands up closer to the fire. "It's frustrating not to be able to get back to work sooner. You're being patient about it."

"Now, don't you worry. You'll be back to work when you can. I'd like us to talk about that. With shipping twice a year to meet the contract from Chicago, I need more help here at the ranch. Red can take care of the north herd. What do you think about taking the south one for me? That would give me more freedom to go between the two."

Elisha felt a twinge of regret that he and Susana wouldn't be going back up to the cabin. But with the baby, he didn't see how they could work there any longer. This was a good job offer.

"That'd be fine. What about where we'll live?" Elisha didn't want to assume that they would live in the ranch house.

"That's all settled. You'll stay in the house. We have the room, and besides, I like having Susana and little Sam around. Of course, I like you being around too."

Elisha smiled. "Don't worry, boss. I know who's more important. I appreciate you letting us stay here." Elisha rubbed the back of his neck. "It's only fair to tell you about our plans. Last spring, I filed on the land about fifteen miles north of the ridge beyond the cabin."

Mr. Weathers' eyebrows shot up. "You mean that big valley?"

"Yes, sir. When we'd take a couple of days off, I'd work at digging a well and gathering rocks for a foundation for the house. Susana and I have talked about it, and if you're willing, we'd like to work here another couple of years so we can gradually build the house and barn." Elisha held his breath, waiting.

Mr. Weathers gazed into the fire and stroked his chin for a few moments. "I've been up through that area. I hunted up there the year before my son left. It's good land, although high up in the mountains. But the grass is good and that valley is sheltered with a good source of water." Mr. Weathers looked directly at Elisha. "Tell you what. Let's agree that you'll work here for the next two to three years. In the meantime, you go up to your place every few months and work on building a house and barn. Maybe some of the hands can help and even me."

"You do beat all, Mr. Weathers." Elisha shook his head. "That's a generous offer."

"Well, you and Susana have become like family. You've been more than fair in your work for me. The least I can do is help you all get your own place someday."

"It's a dream I've had for a long time. I just hope it can happen." Could he trust Mr. Weathers with his fears?

Mr. Weathers frowned. "What would keep it from happening? You've filed on the land. And Susana shared with me about the gold, which is sitting in that cabinet there."

"Well, that gold is Susana's, and I'm not real sure she wants to live in such a remote place. She only married me to please her grandfather. I'm afraid she may not want to stay married to me if it means living in such a hard place." Elisha wiped the sweat from his forehead as he finished.

"I can understand your fear." Mr. Weathers leaned forward. "But I don't think you have to worry about it. What has Susana said?"

"I haven't talked to her about it." Elisha shook his head. "I'm not sure how to go about it."

"Is this why you've been feeling so down? Or is there something more?"

"You've noticed?" Elisha raised his eyebrows and leaned back. "I thought I hid it."

"Well, I've gotten to know you pretty well. Since getting hurt, you've been a lot quieter and thoughtful. I didn't know if coming so close to death, or something else, was bothering you." Mr. Weathers reached over and put another log on the fire.

Elisha looked at the floor for a couple of minutes, and then raised his head. "I've done a lot of thinking about who I am and what I want to become. With my folks dying when I was twelve, I've not had anyone to talk to about important things." He took a deep breath. "Since knowing Susana and you, I've been reading my Bible a lot. I've always believed in God, knew about Jesus and tried to live a good honest life. But as I've read the book of Acts and the books of John and others, I've come to realize that God wants more from me than just being honest."

Mr. Weathers nodded. "What do you think it is that God wants?"

"I think he wants me to become his son, to become a Christian." Elisha rubbed his forehead. He thought hard to try to explain things he had never talked about before. "I read about Paul and how he was told to be baptized to wash away his sins. Then I read about Jesus baptized to fulfill all righteousness. I think to myself, if God asks it of them, is he also asking it of me? I especially looked at that verse in Acts chapter two where it says to repent and be baptized so you can get your sins forgiven."

"What is it you think God is saying to you?" Mr. Weathers spoke softly.

Elisha took another deep breath, as breathing didn't seem so easy. "I need to have my sins washed away so that I can be righteous before God. So I can say I'm His child and have a hope of heaven."

Mr. Weathers nodded. "How do you think you do that?"

"I saw some people baptized in a town one time a few years ago. At the time, I didn't have any idea why they did it. They went down to the river with the preacher, he prayed and then lowered them into the river. I think that's what Jesus did, and Paul, and everyone else in the Bible that it says got baptized. I want to be a Christian like you and Susana and her grandfather. She told me her grandfather baptized her when she was only fourteen years old. And you see how she lives her life as a Christian. She's so happy and content. I want that, too." Elisha felt his cheeks getting hot. He had never talked like this to anyone before.

Mr. Weathers took out his handkerchief, wiped his eyes, and then blew his nose. "That's as good a way of saying what God wants as any preacher I've ever heard. You do understand what God is asking of you."

"I don't know how to ask it or if it's all right, but would you help me get baptized?" Elisha hoped he wasn't being too presumptuous, but there was no one else he could turn to.

Mr. Weathers smiled. "I'd be honored to help you get baptized. It's been twenty-five years ago that I was baptized myself down at the creek."

Elisha shifted in the chair. "Only problem is, what if I can't live good enough to stay a Christian? I don't know that I can be perfect." This was his biggest fear. How could a man be perfect?

Mr. Weathers gave a soft chuckle. "Don't worry about it. You won't stay perfect. None of us do. But when you're baptized, you come under the cover of the atoning blood of Christ that he shed on the cross for you. As long as you're trying and repentant, God looks at you through that cleansing blood and sees you as perfect. But God can't do that until you are washed in the blood."

A weight lifted from Elisha. At last he understood. He could do it. Be the man that God wanted. "When can you help me get baptized? I don't want to wait."

The dinner bell sounded. How could the morning have passed so fast?

Mr. Weathers stood and put out his hand to Elisha. "If you're sure you're ready, let's go eat dinner and then invite whoever wants to come down to the creek to witness your becoming a Christian. I know Susana will want to do that." He smiled. "'Course, that water will be cold."

"That's all right. I suspect the Jordan River was cold when Jesus was baptized."

"We'll have a lot of time to talk this winter both about the things of God and about your plans for the future. But for now, you take what time you need to get your strength back."

With a sigh of relief, Elisha shook his boss's hand. With winter come, it was a comfort to know he had a warm place for his wife and baby. What would the spring bring?

Mr. Weathers and Elisha walked toward the kitchen. "I'm proud of you, son. You've come to this decision all on your own from reading your Bible."

When they entered the kitchen, all the hands and Susana waited for them.

After Mr. Weathers and Elisha had taken a seat, Elisha cleared his throat. "I'd like to say something before the prayer." He looked around at everyone at the table. "I've come to understand my need to wash away my sins and become a Christian. I've asked Mr. Weathers to baptize me this afternoon down at the creek. I invite all of you to come be there as witnesses." He looked sideways at Susana and was surprised to see tears flooding her eyes. He turned to her. "What's the matter? Why are you crying?"

She smiled through the tears flowing down her cheeks. "I'm so happy."

After the meal, Mr. Weathers had Abe and Josh hitch up the horses to the buggy. The men saddled their horses and mounted up for the mile ride down to the creek.

Susana wrapped the baby in several blankets and put on her grandfather's coat.

Elisha put on some old clothes and his moccasins. He shrugged into his coat and hat, and went out and helped Susana, who carried little Sam into the buggy. Nervous but determined, he climbed up on the seat for the ride down to the creek.

When they arrived at the creek, Elisha gave Susana a hand as she stepped out of the buggy. Nate asked to hold the baby so Susana could stand close to the creek bank and observe.

Mr. Weathers walked with Elisha into the cold creek water until they stood waist deep. He put his hand on Elisha's back and raised his other hand toward heaven. "Do you, Elisha Evans, believe in God and promise to serve Him all the days of your life?"

Elisha shivered. Was it from the cold water or from the step he was taking? "I do."

"Do you believe that Jesus is the son of God, that he died and was raised on the third day?" Mr. Weathers's voice boomed across the water.

"I do." Elisha took in the sight of his wife and friends all standing on the bank of creek. What a group of witnesses: a wife, a son, and friends. He then looked up into the clear blue sky, turning his face toward God.

"Then I baptize you in the name of the Father, the Son, and the Holy Spirit for the forgiveness of your sins, and may you receive the gift of the Holy Spirit. Amen." Mr. Weathers tipped Elisha back and submersed him in the cold creek water, and then quickly brought him back up.

Elisha came out of the water with a smile and then he gave Mr. Weathers a wet hug in his joy. He shook with cold, but warmth in his inner being spread. He was now right with God.

When he reached the shore of the creek, Susana flung her arms around him. "Oh, Elisha. Thank God." He hugged her back, feeling the warmth of her body through his soaked clothing.

Abe put a blanket around them, and handed one to Mr. Weathers.

"Let's get back to the house before we all catch cold," Nate said as he handed little Sam back to Susana.

Josh rode his horse alongside the buggy for the short distance back to the barn. "Elisha, would you mind us talking sometime about why you did what you did? I'd like to know."

Elisha looked at the young man who had become such a good friend. "I'll be glad to talk about it with you."

CHAPTER TWENTY-ONE

After supper, Elisha followed Susana to the bedroom tired from the day. All he wanted to do was go to bed. The excitement of becoming a Christian and the satisfaction of riding for the first time in two months left him both emotionally and physically wrung out.

In the bedroom, Susana prepared the baby for sleep.

Elisha sat on the chair and pulled his boots off.

"You headed to bed so soon?" Susana picked the baby up and walked toward the rocking chair.

"Yeah, I'm tired." Elisha undressed and slipped under the covers and watched Susana.

She settled in the rocking chair to nurse little Sam.

"I talked to Mr. Weathers today about work." Elisha wanted her reaction.

She looked up at him. "What did he say?"

He told her what Mr. Weathers had said about the work and about them living in the house. "I think he likes having you and little Sam around." Elisha admitted to himself that he did. Watching Susana caring for their son was enough to make his heart break. She had a choice now that she didn't have when they first met. Now she could choose whether she'd rather live where life was easier and to no longer stay in their marriage. A giant fist threatened to squeeze the breath from his body. Was this something God could help him with now that he was a Christian?

Susana finished feeding the baby and put him into his cradle. "I'll miss being at the cabin in the summer, but for the winter, being here is much easier with the baby."

Her words told him more than he wanted to know. She'd prefer an easier life. He forced his thoughts to stay on course with their conversation. "I told Mr. Weathers about the land and building our own place. He encouraged it and even said that he and some of the hands could go up and help us build the house." Elisha watched her carefully. Was she eager for them to get the house built?

"You can get the house built a lot easier with some help." Susana slipped into her nightgown and climbed into the bed. She leaned over and kissed him, her hair falling around her face and brushing against his cheeks.

He wanted to pull her into his arms and love her, but instead he turned over and faced the wall. He couldn't risk another child, not if she might leave him. God, help me. I don't know how to handle this. Mr. Weathers was right. Becoming a Christian didn't solve all his problems.

~ ~ ~

After that first day back in the saddle, Elisha rode out every day. He still didn't have his full strength. By evening, he was usually exhausted. He read his Bible after he went to bed and it helped him fall asleep more easily.

Elisha rode Shadow in a trot around the south herd. The cattle were strung out along the area south of the creek. It had snowed about six inches during the night. He saw Josh approaching from the opposite direction and reined Shadow to a stop to wait on him.

"What did the herd look like from the south?" Elisha asked.

Josh pulled his horse alongside and crossed a leg over the saddle. "They're drifting some but not too bad. It's cold out here."

Elisha laughed. "You wouldn't have survived at the cabin. This is warm and mild in comparison."

Josh lifted his eyebrows. "So you're finding working down here easier?"

Elisha looked out over the large valley and the hills in the distance. "Yes, this is a lot easier. It's cold here at the ranch headquarters, but not the bitter cold of the higher range, and this lower part of the ranch gets about half the snowfall. Can't say I miss the severity of winter there."

Elisha and Josh both turned in their saddles as Mr. Weathers rode up. "Morning, boys. How's it going?"

Josh waved a salute. "Hey, boss. Elisha was just telling me how this area of the ranch is a lot easier work than winter at the cabin."

Mr. Weathers grunted. "Hmm. I can imagine. But to tell you the truth, Elisha I'm glad you're here as I have plenty of work for you. The area north of Pinto Creek will have to survive without you."

Elisha pushed his hat back. "It certainly is working out for Susana and me to be here."

"Well, boys. Let's ride back to the house. Dinner should be ready by the time we get there."

After they ate lunch, Susana stood and looked at Elisha and Josh. "Would you two do something for me before you ride back out?"

Elisha wrinkled his brow. "Sure, what do you need?"

She smiled. "Follow me."

They shuffled along behind her into the bedroom. "I want the bunk bed moved out and these bureaus moved over against that wall."

Elisha and Josh carried the bunk back to the bunkhouse. Elisha was relieved to get it out of their bedroom and out of his sight. It reminded him too much of pain and weakness. They then returned to place the other pieces of furniture were Susana directed them. Elisha saw that what she was doing would give them more space to maneuver.

Susana stood in the middle of the bedroom with her hands on her hips. "Put the cradle to the right of the bed, the two bureaus along that wall, and the rocker and small table in front of the window."

Elisha kept from laughing, as he didn't want her upset with him. But she reminded him of a drill sergeant ordering the troops.

"What's going on in here?" Mr. Weathers stood in the doorway.

Susana smiled. "We're arranging this room so it will be better."

"What about your sewing machine?" Mr. Weathers looked around. "You don't really have room for it in here. Why don't you put it into the front room?"

Susana placed her hand on his arm. "You wouldn't mind?"

He patted her hand. "Not at all, and it will also be warmer for you. Let's get it moved now."

Elisha picked up the sewing machine and carried it into the front room. Josh pushed a couch away from a wall and helped him place it in front of a window.

He looked around the front room with their son asleep in his cradle and the sewing machine now a part of the room, and then he walked into the bedroom that was completely taken over by their possessions. For the first time, he was at home at the ranch house.

Susana took his hand and looked around the bedroom. "This is all right."

Elisha squeezed back. "Yes, it is."

He rode out with Josh for an afternoon of work. Rubbing his clean-shaven jaw, he thought of the bucket of hot water that appeared outside their bedroom door each morning, meals cooked, and friends and family to sit with after supper each evening. Elisha had never known such comfortable living. Then why wasn't he content?

* * *

Susana noticed that Elisha was often silent and wasn't as cheerful as he'd been before the Utes's attack. She missed their long conversations when they had been at the cabin. Now she sat hoping that he would talk. She had hoped that after his baptism he would have a lighter heart, be more like his old self.

Elisha came in a little early from work and sat down in one of the chairs across from Susana. He stared into the fire.

"What's wrong, Elisha? Are you all right?" Susana sat in one of the overstuffed chairs holding little Samuel who was asleep after she had fed him.

"I'm all right." He looked over at her and the baby, and then turned back to the fire.

"Want to talk about anything?"

"No, don't worry, honey." He shook his head.

Susana wasn't satisfied with his short answers. But what could she do about it? She gazed at her thin, pale husband, whom she loved so much. She smiled every time she remembered that they were now both Christians.

"I hate to say it, but I'm worn out. I'm going to rest a while before supper." Elisha rose from the chair, shuffled to the bedroom, and closed the door.

Susana prayed that God would return her husband to health. She hadn't heard him laugh in weeks. She missed that so much. The tears came unbidden.

"Susana." Mr. Weathers entered the front room from the kitchen. "Look at the little fella." He beamed at the baby, and then he looked more closely at Susana who tried to stop the tears from running down her cheeks. "What's the matter, honey?" He handed her his handkerchief.

"Have you noticed how quiet Elisha has been? He's gone back to lie down, which is so unlike him. Is he going to get better? I know he's pushing himself to work all day. Maybe he's doing too much?" She couldn't hold back a little sob.

"Yes, I've noticed how quiet he is. He's not his usual self, that's for sure. But you got to remember he's been through an awful bad time. Sometimes, when a man has been as close to death as he was, it can knock a fellow down. And on top of that, to be unable to care for himself or you, makes it worse. You have to give him time to get back to his old self."

"I guess I'm too impatient. I want him to be all right. I love him so."

Mr. Weathers reached over and took the sleeping baby into his arms. "I know, but he's going to be all right. We need to be patient with him. This year has brought a lot of changes for both of you." He sat gently rocking the baby that was his namesake. "Why don't you go lie down with him? You look tired. I can take care of this little cowhand."

Susana leaned over and kissed Mr. Weathers on the cheek. "Thank you." She went into the bedroom and found Elisha asleep, lying on top of the covers. She quietly lay next to him. He roused a bit, and then put his arms around her. The warm feeling of being held by her husband comforted her. At least he was alive and with her. She lay there resting in his arms and prayed that God would grant her wisdom to be the wife Elisha needed.

~ ~ ~

Christmas brought a day off for the men. Nate even come up with a wild turkey to bake and made several pies. The men and Susana all made an effort to have small gifts for each other. Elisha and Susana were surprised that each man had a gift for the baby. Apparently, the cowhands had been getting things from town for several months. In the afternoon, Susana gathered all the men in the front room to play games and then to sing together.

Susana sat in the front room looking at the nine men of the ranch. Such a different Christmas day. She gazed at Elisha who sat holding his son. Exactly one year earlier, he had spent Christmas day digging a grave. How unsure she had felt and how scared of Elisha, but now she couldn't imagine why she had been so afraid. He had become her heart in the year that she had known him.

But she missed his laughter, and he didn't seem to have any joy at the birth of the baby. She wondered why. She wanted to give him joy. All she knew to do was keep loving him and give God time to work in his life.

* * *

Elisha was proud of the way Susana was able to make it a very special Christmas day for all the hands. She'd made it a special day for him too. His strength was slowly building, his baby son was healthy and growing, he had the love of a beautiful wife, and he was at peace with his God. He should be content, but instead, a constant ache centered in his chest every time he looked at his wife and son. He could feel them slipping away. What would he do without them?

Elisha was as considerate and attentive of Susana as he'd been at the cabin. But he held himself back from Susana physically.

He saw that she watched him with troubled eyes. He could feel her questions but he had no answers to give her.

He was enthralled with little Sam and had no regrets of having the baby. However, he hadn't made any move toward resuming their normal husband and wife relationship. Susana had let him know that she was ready after about six weeks, but he hadn't responded to her invitations. Elisha was determined not to be responsible for her going through another birth and such agony. He felt on edge and couldn't relax around his wife. And he couldn't shake the fear that she would leave him. Whom could he talk to about it? Not Susana or anyone else. He tried to pray and turn it over to God but it didn't seem to work. What was he doing wrong?

Elisha stood on the front porch and breathed in the crisp air of the early spring. He would take his coat but doubted he would wear it all day, it was that warm. He went back into the house and sat next to Susana at the breakfast table.

Mr. Weathers tapped the side of his cup with a knife. "All right. I want everyone to be hunting hard for cows that have calved. We found five yesterday and who knows how many calved overnight. Elisha, you take Abe and Josh and ride south. Red, you go with the rest of the men and go north. If you find any calves or cows in distress, try to get them back to the corral here. Let's try not to lose any."

Elisha walked with Susana back to the bedroom. He shrugged into his coat and put on his hat. He looked down at little Sam. The baby was kicking his legs and waving one of his arms. His thumb was in his mouth.

Susana stood next to the cradle. "He's getting so big."

"Why is he chewing on his thumb?"

Susana laughed. "His gums are sore because he has two teeth coming in."

Elisha lifted his eyebrows. "Already? I don't see any teeth. I didn't know babies got teeth this early."

"He's five and half months old. And the teeth aren't there yet, but feel right here on his bottom gum. Those two little bumps with be teeth soon."

Elisha gently ran his finger over little Sam's bottom gum and felt the two little bumps. "Well, I'll be. You're right." Little Sam gurgled and cooed at him. "I could stand here and watch him all day. But I better get to work." He leaned over and kissed his son.

Susana put her arms around his waist, stood on tiptoes to kiss him, and received one back. "Have a good day."

He strode out of the house and mounted the horse Josh saddled for him to begin his workday.

Elisha and the men rode back into the ranch yard at the end of the day.

"Elisha, could you help me in the barn?"

"Sure, Abe." He followed him into the barn and helped him move some hay bales in the barn loft, which Elisha thought was odd. It didn't take long. They were the last to wash up and then head to the kitchen for supper. When they entered the kitchen, Elisha saw that the men all stood and looked at him. Susana was dressed in her best dress, her hair loosely tied back with a ribbon.

"Here he is, the birthday boy!" Mr. Weathers said.

The men all congratulated him on his birthday.

Susana reached up and kissed him. "Happy birthday, my love."

"I forgot it's my birthday." Elisha looked at the men standing by around the table, grinning at him. He could feel his face flushing red, and yet he had a warm feeling about having people around who cared for him.

"Well, sit down and eat." Nate sat a pan of biscuits on the table. "Smithy and I made all your favorites."

"Thank you fellows. I appreciate it."

Josh slapped him on the back. "Susana told us of course. And we're glad you're having a birthday. Look at all we have for supper."

Nate and Smithy had killed a couple of chickens to give him his favorite, fried chicken. In addition, there were mashed potatoes, gravy, black-eyed peas, corn, and beets. At the end of the meal, they brought out a cake with a sugar icing. Elisha couldn't remember when anyone had ever made a cake with icing for him.

"Boy, you're getting old." Josh stuffed the last of cake onto his fork.

"Yeah. You're soon going to be as old as I am." Red grinned.

"You trying to say that you've quit getting any older?" Elisha raised his eyebrow.

"Me and Red here stopped having birthdays, and of course Nate and Smithy haven't had one in years." Mr. Weathers booming laugh filled the kitchen along with the other hands.

Elisha didn't mind the men poking fun at him because he was a year older. They wouldn't be joshing him if they didn't consider him their friend.

After supper, everyone gathered in the front room, talked about the day, and took turns telling stories. Little Sam sat on Mr. Weathers' lap, talking in his own way and smiling at anyone who would give him attention. With so much care, he was a happy laughing baby.

Elisha didn't mind sharing him. It gave him joy to sit across the room and watch the men fuss over his son. Even Josh demanded equal time to hold the baby.

At the end of the evening, the cowhands left for the bunkhouse.

Elisha and Susana took little Sam to their bedroom.

Susana changed the baby's diaper and put a sack dress on him to sleep in. Elisha held his son while she put on her nightgown and brushed her hair. Susana slipped into bed and sat with her back supported by the pillows.

Elisha handed the baby to her. He undressed and climbed into bed next to her.

"Thanks for remembering my birthday." He lay propped up on his elbow and watched her nurse the baby.

"Well, somebody had to remember. You forgot." She cocked her head and gave him her teasing smile.

"I feel so old this year." He couldn't imagine what it would feel like to be truly old. This was bad enough.

"You're not old, Elisha, you're only twenty-seven." She gave him a soft, gentle look. "Elisha, we need to talk about something."

"What do we need to talk about?" His chest tightened. He wasn't sure he wanted to hear what she had to say.

"Have I done something to offend you?" She put little Sam on her shoulder and patted him on the back.

"No. Never." His voice was low and fiercer sounding than he intended it to be. "You could never do anything to offend me. What makes you ask something like that?"

Little Sam gave a big burp and then smiled at his father. "Let me put him in his cradle and I'll try to explain." She put the baby to bed and readjusted her nightgown. Then she slipped underneath the covers until her face was even with Elisha's. "It's been five and a half months since little Sam was born, and I've tried to let you know in every way I could that I want you to love me again, but you won't, and I don't know why." Tears slipped down her face.

Elisha reached over and caught the tears with his fingers. "It's not because I don't love you, Susana. I'm scared." His voice was quieter now.

"What are you scared of?"

"I saw what it was like for you to give birth to little Sam. What right do I have to ask that of you when it wasn't even your idea to marry me?" His mouth went dry and swallowing was hard.

"What do you mean it wasn't my idea to marry you?" She raised her eyebrows.

"Well, it wasn't your idea. Your grandfather asked you and you went along to please him." He wanted to take her into his arms and love her. But fear held him back.

Susana sat up. "Yes, it was what my grandfather wanted, but Elisha Evans, I don't regret marrying you one bit."

"But you didn't even know me." He looked up at her stormy face. Why'd she get so angry so quick?

"And you knew me? Why did you marry me? Was it just to please my grandfather?"

"Susana, I can't say that when we married I loved you as I do now, but I already cared for you and was honored to marry you."

Her face softened and she lay back down. "Honored to marry me, that's a lovely thing to say. I must tell you, even though we had only spent a couple of days together when we got married I already cared for you, I just didn't know it." She placed her palm along his cheek. "I do love you, and that's why it hurts so much when you turn your back on me."

"I haven't turned my back on you. How can you say that?" Elisha hadn't wanted to.

"Every time I turn to you for some loving, you roll over and give me your back. What do you think that is?"

"Oh Susana, I never wanted to refuse you, but what if there's another baby? And what would I do if we had another baby, and then you left me." He wasn't sure his chest could hold the pounding of his heart.

She placed both of her palms on either side of his face and looked deep into his eyes. "Why would I ever leave you? You're my heart. And I want us to have more children."

"But with your grandfather's gold you can do anything you want. You don't have to live on a ranch, you can live in town with all the comforts. You don't have to stay with me if you don't want to." His muscles trembled. Could she hear the pounding of his heart? Even the Utes hadn't scared him as much as this conversation with his wife.

"Is that what you think I want to do? To leave you and move into town?"

"I've feared it. What do I have to offer you beyond years of hard work and loneliness? I can't hold you to a marriage if you don't want it. I just can't—no matter what I want." He spoke so quietly that he almost couldn't hear himself. It took everything he had to say the right thing, but it broke his heart to do it.

Susana gave a little sob, then reached out to him, and pulled him into her arms. "Oh Elisha, don't you know that I love living on the ranch with you? I don't want to go into town and live in comfort, especially if it means I'd not be with you. You're my comfort."

He raised his head from where he had it buried in her hair and looked her in the eyes. Did he dare believe her? Oh, how he wanted it to be true. "You mean that truly?"

"I mean that truly. That gold is a wonderful gift from my parents and grandfather because it came from their work. But it's only good if it provides us—you and me—our own place. A place for us to raise our son and all the other children we'll have. If that gold is a problem, then I give it to you. There, now it's your responsibility."

Did she think he wanted the gold? "I don't care about that gold. I care about my family. If I could believe that you're not sorry you had to marry me, it would mean so much to me. " He said it with all the longing of a lonely man.

"What would it take for you to believe me?" Susana frowned and paused a moment. "Should I swear to you on the Bible?"

"Of course not." It took his breath that she would suggest such a thing. It was almost as if she had accused him of calling God a liar. "I know your word is good." He remained silent for a moment, and then the frown disappeared. The fear that had been eating at him for weeks disappeared. "And that's the answer. You don't lie, and if you say that you love me, and want to stay with me, then I believe you." A brightness appeared in the dark corners of his mind. Joy.

"I don't lie to you, Elisha. I love you with all my heart, and I'm proud to be your wife. And unless you leave me, we're going to be together forever."

What had he done to be so blessed by such a beautiful wife? "I've asked so much of you and you're still so young. It's hard to remember that you just turned seventeen in October." He took her face in his hands and kissed her. It seemed so inadequate to what he felt for her at that moment.

"Elisha, you've been my strength. I thank God that he brought Grandfather and me to you. Who else would've been so strong and kind to us? Then you had the courage to marry me. God has so blessed me, and now with little Sam. I feel so safe with you and know that you would give your life for me and our son."

"It's been easy to be strong for you, Susana. With you beside me, I can do amazing things." He could achieve all his plans now that the dark fringe of fear was gone. "I didn't know much about God before you came into my life, but I'm getting to know how much He cares for us. I've never expressed my heart before, Susana. Only with you can I do that. I love you for that." He gently kissed her on her cheeks and then on the lips.

Susana responded to his kiss. "I love you. You're truly my heart. I want you to be content with me, and little Sam. We were happy at the cabin. Perhaps we need to go back there?"

"We don't need to go back to the cabin to be happy. We can go forward to whatever comes next in our lives." He could finally say it with surety. "And that is my loving you and being loved by you always." Elisha took her into his strong arms.

Made in the USA
San Bernardino, CA
26 April 2017